BETTER THAN THE MOVIES

BETTER THAN THE MOVIES

LYNN PAINTER

SIMON & SCHUSTER BFYR

NEW YORK AMSTERDAM/ANTWERP LONDON
TORONTO SYDNEY/MELBOURNE NEW DELHI

SIMON & SCHUSTER BFYR
An imprint of Simon & Schuster Children's Publishing Division
1230 Avenue of the Americas, New York, New York 10020

Also available in a SIMON & SCHUSTER BFYR hardcover edition
Interior design by Tom Daly
The text for this book was set in EB Garamond.
Manufactured in the United States of America
First SIMON & SCHUSTER BFYR paperback edition July 2022
24 26 28 30 29 27 25 23
The Library of Congress has cataloged the hardcover edition as follows:
Names: Painter, Lynn, author.
Title: Better than the movies / Lynn Painter.
Description: First edition. | New York : Simon & Schuster BFYR, [2021] | Summary: Michael, to whom Liz Buxbaum gave her heart long ago, has returned but to get his attention and, perhaps, a prom date she must scheme with her nemesis Wes, her next-door neighbor.
Identifiers: LCCN 2020042771 (print) | LCCN 2020042772 (ebook)
ISBN 9781534467620 (hardcover) | ISBN 9781534467637 (pbk) |
ISBN 9781534467644 (ebook)
Subjects: CYAC: Dating (Social customs)—Fiction. | High schools—Fiction. | Schools—Fiction. | Neighbors—Fiction.
Classification: LCC PZ7.1.P352 Bet 2021 (print) | LCC PZ7.1.P352 (ebook) | DDC [Fic]—dc23
LC record available at https://lccn.loc.gov/2020042771
LC ebook record available at https://lccn.loc.gov/2020042772

For my amazing mom, who's always been my biggest fan, harshest critic, and the woman single-handedly responsible for my distrust of those asshats in the shoe industry. Thank you for letting me read under the blankets when I should've been sleeping.

And for my beloved dad, who saw the cover but never got to read the book. He would've loved the Stella's scene and remembered the ketchup.
RIP, Jerry Painter (5/17/39–5/18/20)

—L. P.

BETTER THAN THE MOVIES

PROLOGUE

"I'm just a girl, standing in front of a boy, asking him to love her."

—*Notting Hill*

My mother taught me the golden rule of dating before I even hit the second grade.

At the ripe age of seven, I'd snuck into her room after having a nightmare. (A house-size cricket might not sound scary, but when it speaks in a robot voice and knows your middle name, it is terrifying.) *Bridget Jones's Diary* was playing on the boxy television on top of the dresser, and I'd watched a good portion of the movie before she even noticed me at the foot of her bed. At that point, it was too late to rescue me from the so-not-first-grade-friendly content, so she snuggled up beside me, and we watched the happy ending together.

But my first-grade brain just couldn't compute. Why would Bridget give up the cuter one—the charming one—for the person who was the equivalent of one ginormous yawn? How did that even make sense?

Yep—I'd missed the movie's point completely and had fallen madly in love with the playboy. And to this day, I can still hear my mom's voice and smell the vanilla of her perfume as she played with my hair and set me straight.

"Charm and intrigue can only get you so far, Libby Loo. Those things always disappear, which is why you never, ever choose the bad boy."

After that, we shared hundreds of similar moments, exploring life together through romantic movies. It was our *thing*. We'd snack-up, kick back on the pillows, and binge-watch from her collection of kiss-infused happy endings like other people binge-watched trashy reality TV.

Which, in hindsight, is probably why I've been waiting for the perfect romance since I was old enough to spell the word "love."

And when she died, my mother bequeathed to me her unwavering belief in happily ever after. My inheritance was the knowledge that love is always in the air, always a possibility, and always worth it.

Mr. Right—the nice-guy, dependable version—could be waiting around the very next corner.

Which was why I was always at the ready.

It was only a matter of time before *it* finally happened for me.

CHAPTER ONE

"Nobody finds their soul mate when they're ten. I mean, where's the fun in that, right?"

—*Sweet Home Alabama*

The day began like any typical day.

Mr. Fitzpervert left a hair ball in my slipper, I burned my earlobe with the straightener, and when I opened the door to leave for school, I caught my next-door nemesis suspiciously sprawled across the hood of my car.

"Hey!" I slid my sunglasses up my nose, pulled the front door shut behind me, and hightailed it in his direction, careful not to scuff my pretty new floral flats as I basically ran *at* him. "Get off of my car."

Wes jumped down and held up his hands in the universal *I'm innocent* pose, even though his smirk made him look anything but. Besides, I'd known him since kindergarten; the boy had never been innocent a day in his life.

"What's in your hand?"

"Nothing." He put the hand in question behind his back. Even though he'd gotten tall and mannish and a tiny bit hot since grade school, Wes was still the same immature boy who'd "accidentally" burned down my mom's rosebush with a firecracker.

"You're so paranoid," he said.

I stopped in front of him and squinted up at his face. Wes had one of those naughty-boy faces, the kind of face where his dark eyes—surrounded by mile-long thick lashes because life wasn't fair—spoke volumes, even when his mouth said nothing.

An eyebrow raise told me just how ridiculous he thought I was. From our many less-than-pleasant encounters, I knew the narrowing of his eyes meant he was sizing me up, and that we were about to throw down about the most recent annoyance he'd brought upon me. And when he was bright-eyed like he was right now, his brown eyes practically freaking twinkling with mischief, I knew I was screwed. Because mischievous Wes always won.

I poked him in the chest. "What did you do to my car?"

"I didn't do anything *to* your car, per se."

"Per se?"

"Whoa. Watch your filthy mouth, Buxbaum."

I rolled my eyes, which made *his* mouth slide into a wicked grin before he said, "This has been fun, and I love your granny shoes, by the way, but I've gotta run."

"Wes—"

He turned and walked away from me like I hadn't been speaking. Just . . . walked toward his house in that relaxed, overconfident way of his. When he got to the porch, he opened the screen door and yelled to me over his shoulder, "Have a good day, Liz!"

Well, that couldn't be good.

Because there was no way he legitimately wanted me to have a good day. I glanced down at my car, apprehensive about even opening the door.

See, Wes Bennett and I were enemies in a no-holds-barred, full-on war over the one available parking spot on our end of the street. He usually won, but only because he was a dirty cheater. He thought it was funny to reserve the Spot for himself by leaving things in the space that I wasn't strong enough to move. Iron picnic table, truck motor, monster truck wheels. You get it.

(Even though his antics caught the attention of the neighborhood Facebook page—my dad was a group member—and the old gossips frothed with rage at their keyboards over the blights on the neighborhood landscape, not a single person had ever said anything to him or made him stop. How was that even fair?)

But I was the one riding the victory wave for once, because yesterday I'd had the brilliant idea to call the city after he'd decided to leave his car in the Spot for three days in a row. Omaha had a twenty-four-hour ordinance, so good old Wesley had earned himself a nice little parking ticket.

Not going to lie, I did a little happy dance in my kitchen when I saw the deputy slide that ticket underneath Wes's windshield wiper.

I checked all four tires before climbing into my car and buckling my seat belt. I heard Wes laugh, and when I leaned down to glare at him out the passenger window, his front door slammed shut.

Then I saw what he'd found so funny.

The parking ticket was now on *my* car, stuck to the middle of the windshield with clear packing tape that was impossible to see through. Layers and layers of what appeared to be commercial-grade packing tape.

I got out of the car and tried to pry up a corner with my fingernail, but the edges had all been solidly flattened down.

What a tool.

When I finally made it to school after scraping my windshield with a razor blade and doing hard-core deep breathing to reclaim my zen, I entered the building with the *Bridget Jones's Diary* soundtrack playing through my headphones. I'd watched the movie the night before—for the thousandth time in my life—but this time the soundtrack had just spoken to me. Mark Darcy saying *Oh, yes, they fucking do* while kissing Bridget was, of course, as swoony as hell-fire, but it wouldn't have been so *oh-my-God*-worthy if not for Van Morrison's "Someone Like You" playing in the background.

Yeah—I have a nerd-level fascination with movie soundtracks.

That song came on as I went past the commons and made my way through the crowds of students clogging up the halls. My favorite thing about music—when you played it loud enough through good headphones (and I had the *best*)—was that it softened the edges of the world. Van Morrison's voice made swimming upstream in the busy hallway seem like it was a scene from a movie, as opposed to the royal pain that it actually was.

I headed toward the second-floor bathroom, where I met Jocelyn every morning. My best friend was a perpetual oversleeper, so there was rarely a day when she wasn't scrambling to put on her eyeliner before the bell rang.

"Liz, I *love* that dress." Joss threw me a side-glance between cleaning up each eye with a cotton swab as we walked into the bathroom. She pulled out a tube of mascara and began swiping the wand over her lashes. "The flowers are so you."

"Thanks!" I went over to the mirror and did a turn to make sure the vintage A-line dress wasn't stuck in my underwear or something equally embarrassing. Two cheerleaders surrounded by a puff of white cloud were vaping behind us, and I gave them a closed-mouth smile.

"Do you try to dress like the leads in your movies, or is it a coincidence?" Joss asked.

"Don't say 'your movies' like I'm addicted to porn or something."

"You know what I mean," Joss said as she separated her lashes with a safety pin.

I knew exactly what she meant. I watched my mom's beloved rom-coms practically every night, using her DVD collection I'd inherited when she died. I felt closer to my mother when I watched them; it felt like a tiny piece of her was there, watching beside me. Probably because we'd watched them together So. Many. Times.

But Jocelyn didn't know any of that. We'd grown up on the same street but hadn't become actual *good* friends until sophomore year, so even though she knew my mom had died when I was in fifth grade, we'd never really talked about it. She'd always assumed I was obsessed with love because I was hopelessly romantic. I never corrected her.

"Hey, did you ask your dad about the senior picnic?" Joss

looked at me in the mirror, and I knew she was going to be irritated. Honestly, I was surprised that wasn't the first thing she asked me when I walked in.

"He wasn't home last night until after I went to bed." It was the truth, but I could've asked Helena, if I'd really wanted to discuss it. "I'll talk to him today."

"Sure you will." She twisted the mascara closed and shoved it into her makeup bag.

"I will. I promise."

"Come on." Jocelyn stuck her makeup bag into her backpack and grabbed her coffee. "I can't be tardy to Lit again or I'll get detention, and I told Kate I'd drop gum by her locker on the way."

I adjusted the messenger bag on my shoulder and caught a glimpse of my face in the mirror. "Wait—I forgot lipstick."

"We don't have time for lipstick."

"There's always time for lipstick." I unzipped the side pouch and pulled out my new fave, Retrograde Red. On the off chance (so very off chance) my McDreamy was in the building, I wanted good mouth. "You go ahead."

She left and I rubbed the color over my lips. *Much better.* I tucked the lipstick back into my bag, replaced my headphones, and exited the restroom, hitting play and letting the rest of the *Bridget Jones* soundtrack wrap itself around my psyche.

When I got to English Lit, I walked to the back of the room and took a seat at the desk between Joss and Laney Morgan, sliding my headphones down to my neck.

"What did you put for number eight?" Jocelyn was writing fast while she talked to me, finishing her homework. "I forgot about the reading, so I have no idea why Gatsby's shirts made Daisy cry."

I pulled out my worksheet and let Joss copy my answer, but my eyes shifted over to Laney. If surveyed, everyone on the planet would unanimously agree that the girl was beautiful; it was an indisputable fact. She had one of those noses that was so adorable, its existence had surely created the need for the word "pert." Her eyes were huge like a Disney princess's, and her blond hair was always shiny and soft and looked like it belonged in a shampoo commercial. Too bad her soul was the exact opposite of her physical appearance.

I disliked her so very much.

On the first day of kindergarten, she'd yelled *Ewwww* when I'd gotten a bloody nose, pointing at my face until the entire class gawked at me in disgust. In third grade, she'd told Dave Addleman that my notebook was full of love notes about him. (She'd been right, but *that wasn't the point*.) Laney had blabbed to him, and instead of being sweet or charming like the movies had led me to believe he'd be, David had called me a weirdo. And in fifth grade, not long after my mom had died and I'd been forced to sit by Laney in the lunchroom due to assigned seating, every day as I picked at my barely edible hot lunch, she would unzip her pastel pink lunchbox and wow the entire table with the delights her mother had made just for her.

Sandwiches cut into adorable shapes, homemade cookies, brownies with sprinkles; it had been a treasure trove of kiddie culinary masterpieces, each one more lovingly prepared than the last.

But the notes were what had destroyed me.

There wasn't a single day that her lunch didn't include a handwritten note from her mom. They were funny little letters that Laney used to read out loud to her friends, with silly drawings in the margins, and if I allowed my snooping eyes to stray to the bottom, where it said "Love, Mom" in curly cursive with doodled hearts around it, I would get so sad that I couldn't even eat.

To this day, everyone thought Laney was great and pretty and smart, but I knew the truth. She might pretend to be nice, but for as long as I could remember, she'd given me crusty-weird looks. As in *every single time* the girl looked at me, it was like I had something on my face and she couldn't decide if she was grossed-out or amused. She was rotting under all that beauty, and someday the rest of the world would see what I saw.

"Gum?" Laney held out a pack of Doublemint with her perfectly arched eyebrows raised.

"No, thanks," I muttered, and turned my attention to the front of the room as Mrs. Adams came in and asked for homework. We passed our papers forward, and she started talking about literary things. Everyone began taking notes on their school-issued laptops, and Colton Sparks gave me a chin nod from his desk in the corner.

I smiled and looked down at my computer. Colton was nice. I'd talked to him for a solid two weeks at the beginning of the year, but that had turned out to be *meh*. Which kind of summed up the whole of my collective dating history, actually: *meh*.

Two weeks—that was the average length of my relationships, if you could even call them that.

Here's how it usually went: I would see a cute guy, daydream about him for weeks and totally build him up in my mind to be my one-and-only soul mate. The usual high school pre-relationship stuff always began with the greatest of hopes. But by the end of two weeks, before we even got close to official, I almost always got hit with *the Ick*. The death sentence to all blossoming relationships.

Definition of the Ick: A dating term that refers to a sudden cringe feeling one gets when they have romantic contact with someone and they become almost immediately put off by them.

Joss said I was always browsing but never buying. And she ended up being right. But my propensity for tiny little two-week relationships really messed with prom potential. I wanted to go with someone who made my breath catch and my heart flutter, but who was even left in the school that I hadn't already considered?

I mean, technically, I had a prom date; I was going with Joss. It's just . . . going to prom with my best friend felt like such a fail. I knew we'd have a good time—we were grabbing dinner beforehand with Kate and Cassidy, the funnest of our little friend group—but prom was supposed to be the pinnacle of high school romance. It was supposed to be poster-board promposals, matching corsages, speechless awe over the way you look in your dress, and sweet kisses under the cheesy disco ball.

Andrew McCarthy and Molly Ringwald *Pretty in Pink* sort of shit.

It wasn't about friends grabbing dinner at the Cheesecake Factory before heading up to the high school for awkward conversation while the coupled-off couples found their way to the infamous grinding wall.

I knew Jocelyn wouldn't get it. She thought prom was no big deal, just a high school dance that you dressed up for, and she would find me completely ridiculous if I admitted to being disappointed. She was already peeved by the fact that I kept blowing her off on dress shopping, but I never felt like going.

At all.

My phone buzzed.

Joss: I have BIG tea.

I looked over at her, but she appeared to be listening to Mrs. Adams. I glanced at the teacher before responding: Spill it.

Joss: FYI I got it via text from Kate.

Me: So it might not be true. Got it.

The bell rang, so I grabbed my stuff and shoved it into my bag. Jocelyn and I started walking toward our lockers, and she said, "Before I tell you, you have to promise you're not going to get all worked up before you hear everything."

"Oh my God." My stomach stress-dropped, and I asked, "What's going on?"

We turned down the west wing, and before I had a chance to even look at her, I saw *him* walking toward me.

Michael Young?

I came to a complete halt.

"Aaaand—there's my tea," Joss said, but I wasn't listening.

People bumped off me and went around me as I stood there and stared. He looked the same, only taller and broader and more attractive (if that was even a possibility). My childhood crush moved in slow motion, with tiny blue birds chirping and flitting their wings around his head as his golden hair blew in a sparkling breeze.

I think my heart might have stopped.

Michael had lived down the street when we were little, and he'd been everything to me. I'd loved him as far back as I could remember. He'd always been next-level amazing. Smart, sophisticated, and . . . I don't know . . . *dreamier* than any other boy. He'd run around with the neighborhood kids (me, Wes, the Potter boys on the corner, and Jocelyn), doing typical neighborhood things—playing hide-and-seek, tag, touch football, ding-dong-ditch, etc. But while Wes and the Potters had enjoyed things like flinging mud into my hair because it made me scream, Michael had been doing things like identifying leaves, reading thick books, and *not* joining in on their torture.

My brain cued up "Someone Like You," and the song started over from the beginning.

I've been searching a long time,
For someone exactly like you.

He was wearing khakis and a nice black shirt, the kind of outfit that showed he knew what looked good but also didn't spend too much time on fashion. His hair was thick and blond and styled the same as his clothes—intentionally casual. I wondered what it smelled like.

His hair, not his clothes.

He must've sensed a stalker in his midst, because the slo-mo stopped, the birds disappeared, and he looked right at me.

"Liz?"

I was so happy that I'd taken the time to apply Retrograde Red. Clearly the cosmos had known Michael would be appearing before me that day, so it had done everything in its power to make me presentable.

"Girl, chill," Joss said between her teeth, but I was helpless to stop the whole-face smile that broke free as I said, "Michael Young?"

I heard Joss mutter "Here we go," but I did not care.

Michael came over and wrapped me in a hug, and I let my hands slide around his shoulders. *Oh my God, oh my God!* My stomach went wild as I felt his fingers on my back, and I realized that we could very well be having our meet-cute.

Oh. My. God.

I was dressed for it; he was beautiful. Could this moment *be* more perfect? I made eye contact with Joss, who was slowly shaking her head, but it didn't matter.

Michael was back.

He smelled good—so, so good—and I wanted to catalogue every tiny detail of the moment. The soft, worn-in feel of his shirt under my palms, the breadth of his shoulders, the golden skin of his neck, scant centimeters away from my face as I hugged him back.

Was it wrong to close my eyes and take a deep brea—

"Oof." Someone bumped into us, hard, destroying the hug. I was shoved into and then away from Michael, and as I turned around, I saw who it was.

"Wes!" I said, irritated that he'd ruined our moment, but so unbelievably happy still that I beamed at him anyway. I was incapable of *not* smiling. "You should really watch where you're going."

His eyebrows crinkled together. "Yeah . . . ?"

He was watching me, probably wondering why I was smiling instead of going ballistic over the packing tape incident. He looked like someone waiting for the punch line, and his confusion kicked up my happiness to an even higher level. I giggled and said, "Yeah, you big doof. You could really hurt someone. Buddy."

He narrowed his eyes and talked slower. "Sorry—I was talking to Carson and doing the extremely difficult backward-walking thing. But enough about me. How was your drive to school?"

I knew he wanted to hear all the details, like how long it had taken me to remove the tape or the fact that I'd broken two freshly manicured nails, but I wasn't about to give that aggravator the satisfaction. "Really, really great—thanks for asking."

"Wesley." Michael did a bro handshake with Wes—when had they had time to choreograph that little touch of adorability?—and said, "You were right on about the biology teacher."

"It's because you sat by me. She haaaates me." Wes grinned and started talking, but I ignored that tool and watched Michael speak and laugh and be as sweetly charming as I'd remembered.

Only now he had a slightly Southern drawl.

Michael Young had a soft accent that made me want to personally handwrite a thank-you note to the great state of Texas for making him even more appealing than he'd already been. I crossed my arms and pretty much melted into a puddle as I enjoyed the view.

Jocelyn, who I might have forgotten existed in the presence of such lovely Michaelhood, nudged me with her elbow and whispered, "Settle down. You're drooling all over yourself."

I rolled my eyes and ignored her.

"Hey, listen." Wes hitched up his backpack and pointed at Michael. "Remember Ryan Clark?"

"Of course." Michael smiled and looked like a congressional intern. "First baseman, right?"

"Exactly." Wes lowered his voice. "Ryno's having a party tomorrow at his dad's—you should totally come."

I tried to keep my expression neutral as I listened to Wes ask *my* Michael to come to his party. I mean, Wes *did* hang out with the guys that Michael used to know, but still. They were best friends all of a sudden or something?

That wouldn't be good for me. Couldn't be.

Because Wes Bennett got off on messing with me—he always had. In grade school, Wes was the guy who'd put a frog in my Barbie DreamHouse and a decapitated lawn gnome's severed head in my homemade Little Free Library. In middle school, he was the guy who'd thought it was hilarious to pretend he didn't see me when I was lying out, and then water his mom's bushes, "accidentally" spraying the hose right over me until I screamed.

And now, in high school, he was the guy who'd made it his mission to harass me daily over The Spot. I'd grown a backbone since we were kids, so technically now I was the girl who yelled over the fence when his jock friends were over and they were so rowdy, I could hear them over my music. But still.

"Sounds good," Michael said with a nod, and I wondered what he'd look like in a cowboy hat and flannel shirt. Maybe a pair of shitkickers, even though I didn't technically know what differentiated a shitkicker from a regular cowboy boot.

I'd have to Google it later.

"I'll text you the details. I gotta go—If I'm late to my next class, I've got detention for sure." He turned and started jogging in the other direction with a yell of "Later, guys."

Michael watched Wes's disappearance before looking down at me and drawling, "He lit out of here so fast, I didn't get to ask. Is it casual dress?"

"What? Um, the party?" Like I had any idea what they wore to their jockstrap parties. "Probably?"

"I'll ask Wesley."

"Cool." I worked to give him my top-shelf smile, even though I was dying over the fact that Wes had screwed up my meet-cute.

"I've gotta run too," he said, but added, "I can't wait to catch up, though."

Then take me with you to the party! I yelled internally.

"Joss?" Michael looked past me, and his mouth dropped open. "Is that you?"

She rolled her eyes. "Took you long enough."

Jocelyn had always been closer to the neighborhood boys, playing football with Wes and Michael while I did awful cartwheels around the park and made up songs. Since then, she'd turned into this tall and freakishly good-looking human. Today her braids were all pulled back into a ponytail, but instead of looking messy like when I wore a ponytail, it showed off her cheekbones.

The warning bell rang, and he pointed up at the speaker. "That's me. See y'all later."

Y'all.

He went the other way, and Jocelyn and I started walking. I said, "I can't believe Wes didn't invite us to the party."

She gave me side-eye. "Do you even know who Ryno is?"

"No, but that's beside the point. He invited Michael right in front of us. It's common courtesy that he should invite us, too."

"But you hate Wes."

"So?"

"So why would you want him to invite you anywhere?"

I sighed. "His rudeness just pisses me off."

"Well I, for one, am glad he didn't, because I don't want to go to any party that those guys are having. I've been to Ryno's, and it's all about beer bongs, Fireball, and that never-have-I-ever kind of immature stuff."

Joss used to hang out with the popular kids before she quit volleyball, so she'd "partied" a little before we became friends. "But—"

"Listen." Jocelyn stopped walking and grabbed my arm to stop me from walking too. "That's what I was going to tell you. Kate said he lives next door to Laney and they've been talking for a couple weeks now."

"Laney? Laney *Morgan*?" Nooo. It couldn't be true. No-no-no-no, please, God, no. "But he just got here—"

"Apparently he moved back a month ago but was finishing classes online at his other school. Rumor has it that he and Laney are almost official."

Not Laney. My stomach clenched as I pictured her perfect little nose. I knew it was irrational, but the idea of Laney and Michael was almost too much for me to bear. That girl always got everything I wanted. She couldn't have him, dammit.

The thought of them, together, made my throat tight. It made my heart hurt.

It would crush me.

Because not only was he everything I daydreamed about, but he and I had history. The wonderful, important kind of history that involved drinking from garden hoses and catching lightning bugs. I thought back to the last time I'd seen Michael. It'd been at his house. His family had had a cookout to say goodbye to all the neighbors, and I'd walked over with my parents. My mom had made her famous cheesecake bars, and Michael had met us at the door and offered us drinks like he was a grown-up.

My mom had called it the most adorable thing she'd ever seen.

All the neighborhood kids played kickball in the street for hours that night, and the adults even joined us for a game. At one point, my mother was high-fiving Michael after stealing home base in her floral sundress and wedge sandals. That moment was pressed in my memories like a yellowed photograph in an antique album.

I don't think Michael ever had a clue as to how madly in love with him I'd been. They moved a month before my mom died, breaking the tip of my soon-to-be shattered heart.

Jocelyn looked at me like she knew exactly what I was thinking. "Michael Young is not your racing-to-the-train-station dude. Got it?"

But he could be. "Well, technically they aren't official yet, so . . ."

We started walking again, dodging bodies as we headed for her locker. We were probably going to be late because of our impromptu hallway meet-up with Michael, but it would totally be worth it.

"Seriously. Don't be that girl." She gave me her motherly scowl. "That there with Michael was not your meet-cute."

"But." I didn't even want to say it because I didn't want her to shoot it down. Still, I almost squealed when I said, "What if it was?"

"Oh my god. I knew, the second I heard he was back, that you were going to lose it." Her eyebrows went down, and so did the corners of her lips as she stopped in front of the locker and turned the lock. "You don't even know the guy anymore, Liz."

I could still hear his deep voice saying *y'all,* and my stomach dipped. "I know everything I need to know."

She sighed and pulled out her backpack. "Is there anything I can say to yank you back from this?"

I tilted my head. "Um . . . he hates cats, maybe?"

She held up a finger. "That's right—I forgot. He hates cats."

"He does not." I grinned and sighed, thinking back. "He used to have these two snarky cats that he *adored*. You should've seen the way he treated those babies."

"Ew."

"Whatever, hater of felines." I felt alive, buzzing with the thrill of romantic possibilities as I leaned against the closed locker next door. "Michael Young is fair game until I hear an official proclamation."

"I can't talk to you when you're like this."

"Happy? Excited? Hopeful?" I wanted to skip down the hall yell-singing "Paper Rings."

"Delusional." Jocelyn looked at her phone for a minute, then back at me. "Hey, my mom said she can take us dress shopping tomorrow night if you want."

My mind went blank. I had to say something. "I think I have to work."

She narrowed her eyes. "Every time I bring it up, you have to work. Don't you *want* to get a dress?"

"Sure. Yeah." I forced up the corners of my mouth. "Of course."

But the truth was that I *so* did not.

The thrill of the dress was its ability to inspire romance, to make one's date speechless. If that factor wasn't in play, the prom dress was just an overpriced waste of fabric.

Adding to that, there was the screaming fact that shopping with Jocelyn's mom for dresses was just a huge reminder that *my* mom wasn't there to join us, which made it a wildly unappealing outing. My mother wouldn't be there to take pictures and get teary as her baby attended the final dance of her childhood, and nothing made that hit home quite like seeing Joss's mom do those things for her.

To be honest, I hadn't been emotionally prepared for the emptiness that seemed to accompany my senior year, the many reminders of my mom's absence. Senior pictures, homecoming, college applications, prom, graduation; as everyone I knew got excited about those high school benchmarks, I got stress headaches because nothing felt the way I'd planned for it to feel.

Everything felt . . . lonely.

Because even though the senior activities were fun, without my mom they were void of sentimentality. My dad tried to be involved, he really did, but he wasn't an emotional guy, so it always just felt like he was the official photographer as I traversed the highlights alone.

Meanwhile, Joss didn't understand why I didn't want to make a big deal out of every single senior milestone like she did. She'd been pissed at me for three days when I'd blown off the spring break trip to the beach, but it had felt more like an exam I was dreading than an actual good time, and I just couldn't.

However. Finding a rom-com happy ending that my mother would have loved—that could change all the bad feels to good, couldn't it?

I smiled at Jocelyn. "I'll text you after I check my schedule."

CHAPTER TWO

"A woman friend. This is amazing.
You may be the first attractive woman I have not
wanted to sleep with in my entire life."

—*When Harry Met Sally*

Michael was back.

I propped my feet up on the kitchen table and dug my spoon into the container of Americone Dream, still beside myself with giddiness. In my wildest dreams, I wouldn't have imagined the return of Michael Young.

I didn't think I'd ever see him again.

After he moved, I daydreamed for years about him coming back. I used to imagine I was out taking a walk on one of those gloriously cold autumn days that whispered of winter, the air smelling like snow. I'd be wearing my favorite outfit—which changed with each imagining, of course, because this fantasy started back in grade school—and when I'd turn the corner at the end of the block, there he'd be, walking toward me. I think there was even romantic running involved. I mean, why wouldn't there be?

There were also no less than a hundred brokenhearted entries in my childhood diaries about his exit from my life. I'd found them a few years ago when we were cleaning out the garage, and the entries were surprisingly dark for a little kid.

Probably because his absence in my life was timed so closely with my mother's death.

Eventually I'd accepted that neither of them were coming back.

But now he'd returned.

And it felt like getting a little piece of happiness back.

I didn't have any classes with him, so fate couldn't intervene by throwing us together, which sucked *so* badly. I mean, what were the odds that we'd have zero occasions for forced interaction? Joss had a class with him, and clearly Wes did as well. Why not me? How was I supposed to show him we were meant to go to prom and fall in love and live happily ever after when I didn't ever see him? I hummed along to Anna of the North in my headphones—the sexy hot tub song from *To All the Boys I've Loved Before*—and stared out the window at the rain.

The one thing in my favor was that I was kind of a love expert.

I didn't have a degree and I hadn't taken any classes, but I'd watched thousands of hours of romantic comedies in my life. And I hadn't just watched. I'd analyzed them with the observational acuity of a clinical psychologist.

Not only that, but love was in my genes. My mother had been a screenwriter who'd churned out a *lot* of great small-screen romantic comedies. My dad was 100 percent certain that she would've been the next Nora Ephron if she'd just had a little more time.

So even though I had zero practical experience, between my inherited knowledge and my extensive research, I knew a lot about love. And everything I knew made me certain that in order for Michael and me to happen, I would need to be at Ryno's party.

Which wasn't going to be easy, because not only did I have no idea who Ryno even was but I had zero interest in attending a party filled with the jocks' sweaty armpits and the populars' stinky beer breath.

But I needed to get reacquainted with Michael before some awful blonde *who shall remain nameless* beat me to him, so I'd have to find a way to make it work.

Lightning shot across the sky and illuminated Wes's big car, all snuggled up against the curb in front of my house, rain bouncing hard off of its hood. That assbag had been right behind me all the way home from school, and when I'd pulled forward to *properly* parallel park, he'd slid right into The Spot.

What kind of monster parked nose-first in a street spot?

As I honked and yelled at him through the torrential downpour, he waved to me and ran inside his house. I ended up having to park around the corner, in front of Mrs. Scarapelli's duplex, and my hair and dress had been drenched by the time I burst through my front door.

Don't even ask about the new shoes.

I licked off the spoon and wished Michael lived next door instead of Wes.

Then it hit me.

"Holy God."

Wes was my in. Wes, who had invited Michael to the party in the first place, would obviously be attending. What if he could get me in?

Although . . . he didn't do things to help me. Like, ever. Wes's joy was derived from torture, not generosity. So how could I convince him? What could I give him? I needed to come up with something—some tangible thing—that would get him to help me out and keep his mouth shut at the same time.

I dug out another spoonful of ice cream and put it in my mouth. Stared out the window.

This was a no-brainer.

"Well, well." Wes stood inside his house, behind the screen door, looking out at me in the rain with a smirk on his face. "To what do I owe this honor?"

"Let me in. I need to talk."

"I don't know—are you going to hurt me if I let you in?"

"Come on," I said through gritted teeth as the driving rain pelted my head. "I'm getting drenched out here."

"I know—and I'm sorry—but I am seriously afraid you're going to junk-punch me for stealing the Spot if I let you come inside." He opened the door a crack, enough to show me how warm and dry he looked in jeans and a T-shirt, and said, "You're a little scary sometimes, Liz."

"Wes!" Wes's mom came up behind him and looked horrified as she saw me standing out in the rain. "For the love of God, open the door for the poor girl."

"But I think she's here to kill me." He said it like a scared little kid, and I could tell his mom was trying not to smile.

"Get inside, Liz." Wes's mom grabbed my arm and gently

pulled me across the threshold to where it was warm and smelled like dryer sheets. "My son is a nuisance and he's sorry."

"No, I'm not."

"Tell me what he did and I'll help you punish him."

I pushed the wet hair off my face, looked directly at him, and said to his mom, "He stole my spot when I was trying to parallel park."

"Oh my God, you told my mom on me?" Wes closed the front door and followed me and his mother inside. "Well, if we're randomly tattling, Mom, I should probably tell you that Liz was the one who called the cops on my car when I had pneumonia."

"Wait, what?" I stopped and turned around. "When were you sick?"

"Well, when did you call?" He put both hands on his heart, fake-coughed, and said, "I was too ill to even move my car."

"Stop." I didn't know if he was messing with me or not, but I suspected he wasn't, and I felt like a monster because as much as I loved besting him, I didn't like the thought of him being sick. "Were you seriously sick?"

His dark eyes swept over my face, and he said, "Would you seriously care?"

"Knock it off, you little brats." His mom gestured for us to follow her into the family room. "Sit on the couch, eat some cookies, and get over yourselves."

She plopped a plate of chocolate chip cookies down on the coffee table, fetched a gallon of milk and two glasses, tossed me a towel, reminded Wes that he had to pick up his sister at six thirty, and then she left us alone.

The woman was a force.

"Ohh." *Kate & Leopold* was playing on one of those retro TV channels that only old people watched, and I rubbed the towel over my hair as Meg Ryan's character tried evading the charm of a very British Hugh Jackman. "I love this movie."

"Of course you do." He gave me a grin that made me uncomfortable, like he knew things about me that I didn't know he knew, and he leaned down and grabbed a cookie. "So what do you want to talk to me about?"

My cheeks got warm, mainly because I was scared to death he was going to make fun of me—and tell Michael—when I told him what I wanted. I sat down on the sofa, set the towel beside me, and said, "Okay. Here's the thing. I kind of need your help."

He started smiling immediately. I held up a hand and said, "Nope. Listen. I know you're not one to help out of the goodness of your heart, so I've got a proposition for you."

"Ouch. Like I'm some kind of a mercenary or something. That hurts."

"No, it doesn't."

He conceded with a shrug. "No, it really doesn't."

"Okay." It took a lot of self-control not to roll my eyes at him. "But before I tell you *what* I want you to help with, I want to go over the terms of the deal."

He crossed his arms—when had his chest gotten so wide?—and tilted his head. "Go on."

"Okay." I took a deep breath and tucked my hair behind my ears. "First of all, you have to swear to secrecy. If you tell *anyone* about our deal, it is void and you don't get payment. Second, if you agree to the deal, you have to actually help me. You can't just do a little and then blow me off."

I paused, and he looked at me through narrowed eyes. "Well? What's the payment?"

"The payment will be uncontested, twenty-four/seven access to the parking spot for the duration of our deal."

"Whoa." He walked over and plopped down in the chair across from me. "You will give me THE parking spot?"

I *so* didn't want to, but I also knew how badly Wes wanted it. He and his dad were always tinkering with his old car, mostly because it never started, and their toolboxes looked wildly heavy whenever I got The Spot and they had to haul them all the way down to the end of the street to get it going. "That's correct."

His smile went big. "I'm in. I'm doing it. I'm your guy."

"You can't say that yet—you don't even know what the deal is."

"Doesn't matter. I'll do whatever it takes."

"What if I want you to run naked through the commons during lunch?"

"Done."

I grabbed the throw that was folded over the arm of the couch and wrapped it around my shoulders. "What if I want you to turn naked cartwheels through the commons during lunch while singing the entire *Hamilton* soundtrack?"

"You got it. I love 'My Shot.'"

"Seriously?" That made me smile, even though I wasn't used to smiling at Wes. "But can you even do a cartwheel?"

"Yup."

"Prove it."

"You're so high maintenance." Wes stood, shoved the coffee table out of the way with his foot, and did the most awful cartwheel I'd ever seen. His legs were bent and didn't turn over his head at all, but he stuck the landing with over-the-head gymnastics arms and a confident smile before plopping back into his chair. "Now tell me."

I coughed out the laugh I was trying to hold in and searched his face. I was looking for honesty, some kind of hint that I could trust him, but I got sidetracked by how dark his eyes were and the way he flexed his jaw. I thought of the time in seventh grade when he'd given me six dollars to get me to stop crying.

Helena and my dad had just gotten married, and they'd decided to remodel the main level of the house. In preparation, Helena had cleaned out the closets and drawers and donated all of the old stuff. Including my mother's DVD collection.

When I'd had an emotional meltdown and my dad had explained the situation to Helena, she'd felt awful. She'd apologized over and over again while I'd sobbed. But all I'd been able to focus on were her words to my dad: "I just didn't think anyone watched those cheesy movies."

I'd been a resourceful kid—still was resourceful, as proven by my being at Wes's house at that very moment—and it had only taken one phone call to find out where the movies had ended up. I'd snuck out, lying to my dad and saying I was going to Jocelyn's, and ridden my bike all the way to the thrift store. I had every penny of my babysitting money in my front pocket, but when I got there, it wasn't enough.

"We're going to sell this as a collection, kid—you can't buy them individually."

I stared at that price tag, and no matter how many times I counted, I was six dollars short. The jerk at the store was unyielding, and I cried all the way home on my hot-pink bike. It felt like I was losing my mom all over again.

When I was almost home, I saw Wes bouncing a basketball in his driveway. He looked at me with his usual face, half smiling like he knew some secret about me, but then he stopped dribbling.

"Hey." He tossed the ball onto the grass in his front yard and walked toward me. "What's wrong?"

I remember not wanting to tell him because I knew he'd think it was ridiculous, but there was something about his eyes that made me break down all over again. I bawled like a baby while I told him what happened, but instead of laughing at me, he listened. He stayed silent through my entire breakdown, and once I stopped talking and started hiccupping embarrassing little sobs, he leaned forward and wiped my tears with his thumbs.

"Don't cry, Liz." He looked sad when he said it, like he wanted to cry too. Then he said, "Wait here."

He gave me the *One sec* finger before turning and running into his house. I stood there, exhausted from the crying and shocked by his niceness, and when he came out his front door, he gave me a ten-dollar bill. I remember looking up at him and thinking he had the kindest brown eyes, but my thoughts must've shown on my face because he immediately gave me a scowl and said, "This is just to shut you up 'cause I can't stand to listen to you bawling for another minute. And I want my change."

My mind jerked me back to Wes's family room. Michael. The Spot. Needing Wes's help.

My eyes ran over his face. Yeah, his brown eyes still looked exactly the same.

"Okay." I picked up a cookie and took a bite. "But I swear on everything holy that I will hire a hit man if you blab about this."

"I very much believe you. Now spill it."

I had to look at something other than his face. I went with my lap, staring at the smooth texture of my leggings when I said, "Okay. Here's the thing. Michael is back in town, and I was kind of hoping to, y'know, *touch base with him.* We were close before he moved away, and I want to get that back again."

"And I can help with that how, exactly?"

I kept my eyes down, tracing the seam of my pants with my index finger. "Well, I don't have any classes with him, so there's no way for me to talk to him naturally. But you and Michael are already friends. You hang out. You invited him to a party." I dared to look at him when I said, "*You've* got the connection that I want."

He tossed the rest of his cookie into his mouth, chewed it up, and dusted his hands on the knees of his pants. "Let me get this straight. You are still starry-eyed over Young, and you want me to drag you along to Ryno's party so you can get him to like you."

I considered denying it, but instead said, "Basically."

His jaw flexed. "I heard he's kind of interested in Laney."

Ugh, no. My own personal investment in the situation aside, Laney Morgan was totally wrong for Michael. In fact, nudging him to fall in love with me would be doing him a favor simply by saving him from *that*. I said, "Don't you worry about that."

An eyebrow went up. "How positively scandalous of you, Elizabeth."

"Shut it."

He smiled. "You can't think that just showing up at a party is going to make him notice you. There's going to be a ton of people there."

"I only need a few minutes."

"Pretty confident, are we?"

"I am." I'd already written a script. "I have a plan."

"And it is . . . ?"

I tucked my legs underneath me. "Like I'm telling you."

"Nah." He got up, moved to the couch, and plopped down beside me. "Your plan sucks."

I wrapped the throw more tightly around my shoulders. "How could you possibly know that when you don't know my plan?"

"Because I've known you since you were five, Liz. I'm sure your plan involves a contrived meeting, an entire notebook's worth of silly ideas, and someone riding off into the sunset."

He was close, but I said, "You're way off base."

"Bet."

I sighed. "So . . . ?" All I needed was for The Spot to be a stronger draw than Wes's determination to antagonize me.

Wes crossed his arms and looked pleased with himself. "So . . . ?"

"Oh my God, you're torturing me on purpose. Are you going to help me or not?"

He scratched his chin. "I just don't know if The Spot is worth it."

"Worth what? Allowing me to be in your presence for a few hours?" I tucked a wet curl behind my ear. "You'll barely even know I'm there."

"What if *I'm* trying to hit it off with someone?" The look on his face was so creepy, I smiled in spite of myself. "Your presence might mess with my mojo."

"Trust me, you won't even notice me. I'll be too busy making Michael fall wildly in love with me to even touch your mojo."

"Ew. Stop talking about touching my mojo, you perv."

I rolled my eyes and turned toward him. "Are you going to say yes, or what?"

He smirked and kicked his feet up onto the coffee table. "I *do* love watching you take the walk of shame from Mrs. Scarapelli's. It's kind of my new favorite hobby. So I guess I'll drag you along to the party."

"Yes!" I stopped myself from doing a fist pump in victory.

"Settle your ass down." Wes leaned forward, grabbed the remote, and turned up the volume on the TV before looking at me as if I smelled bad. "Wait—this movie? You love *this* movie?"

"I know it's a weird premise, but I swear to you that it's great."

"I've seen it. This movie is trash, are you kidding me?"

"It is *not* trash. It's about finding someone so right for you that you'd be willing to drop everything and traverse *centuries* for them. She literally ditches her life and moves to 1876. I mean, that is a powerful love." I looked at the TV, and my brain started quoting along with the movie. "Are you sure you've seen *this* movie?"

"I'm positive." He shook his head and watched as Stuart begged the nurse to let him leave the hospital. "This movie is formulaic, aspartame-infused, tropey garbage."

"Of course." Why would I expect Wes to surprise me? "*Of course* Wes Bennett is a rom-com snob. I would expect no less."

"I'm not a *rom-com snob*, whatever that even is, but a discerning viewer who expects more than a predictable plot with fill-in-the-blank characters."

"Oh, please." I put my feet on the coffee table. "Exploding buildings and high-speed chases aren't predictable?"

"You're making the assumption that I like action movies."

"You don't?"

"Oh, I do." He tossed the remote onto the table and grabbed his glass. "But you shouldn't assume."

"But I was right."

"Whatever." He drank the last of his milk and set down his glass. "Bottom line—chick flicks are laughingly unrealistic. Like, 'Oh, these two are so different and hate each other so much, but—wait. Are they so different after all?'"

"Enemies-to-lovers. It's a classic trope."

"Oh, good God, you think it's awesome." He narrowed his eyes, leaned over, and patted me on the head. "You poor, confused little love lover. Tell me you don't think this movie is remotely connected to reality in any way."

I smacked his hand away from my head. "Yeah, because I believe in time travel."

"Not that." He gestured toward the TV. "Time travel is probably the most realistic part. I'm talking about rom-coms in general. Relationships never ever, ever work like that."

"Yes, they do."

His eyebrows went up. "They *do*? Correct me if I'm wrong, but it didn't seem like it worked that way with Jeremiah Green or Tad Miranda."

I was kind of taken aback by his awareness of my romantic history (or lack thereof), but I supposed it was inevitable when we were in the same grade at the same school.

"Well, they *can*." I pushed my still-damp hair out of my face and wasn't surprised that Wes thought the way he did. I'd never heard of him being serious with any girl—ever—so it was probably safe to assume he was your classic player-type jock. "It's out there, even if the jaded, cynical people like you are too, um . . . *cynical* to believe."

"You said 'cynical' twice."

Sigh.

He smiled at my irritation. "So you think that two enemies—in the real world—can magically get over their differences and fall madly in love?"

"I do."

"And you think that plotting and planning and trickery is

no big deal if it's done to spark some sort of true love?"

I chewed on my lip. Was that what I was doing? Trickery? The thought put a little twist in my stomach, but I ignored it. That wasn't what was happening here. I said, "You're making it sound ridiculous on purpose."

"Oh, no—it's just ridiculous."

"You're ridiculous." I realized I was gritting my teeth, and I relaxed my jaw. Who cared what Wes thought about love, anyway?

He got a little smirk going and said, "Have you thought about the fact that if your little love notions are valid, then Michael is actually *not* the guy for you?"

Nope; he *was* the guy for me. Had to be. Still, I asked, "What do you mean?"

"At this point, you and Michael aren't mad at each other, so it's doomed. Every rom-com has two people who can't stand each other in the beginning but eventually bang it out."

"Gross."

"Seriously. *You've Got Mail*. *The Ugly Truth*. Um . . . *When Harry Met Sally*, *10 Things I Hate About You*, *Sweet Home Alabam—*"

"First of all, *Sweet Home Alabama* is a second-chance-at-love trope, asshat."

"Ooh—my bad."

"Second of all, you're a little impressive with your rom-com knowledge, Bennett. Are you sure you aren't a closet watcher?"

He gave me a look. "Positive."

I really *was* a little impressed; I loved *The Ugly Truth*. "I won't tell anyone if you secretly fangirl over romance flicks."

"Shut it." He chuckled and gave his head a slow shake. "So what trope works for you and Michael, then? The followed-him-around-like-a-puppy-but-now-he-sees-the-puppy-as-a-potential-girlfriend-even-though-he-already-has-a-potential-girlfriend trope?"

"You are an obnoxious love *hater*." It was all I could think of to throw back at him, because—all of a sudden—Wes had the uncanny ability to make me laugh. Like, even as he made fun of me, I had to force myself to not give in to another giggle.

But we had a deal, so we exchanged numbers so he could text me after he talked to Michael, and we decided that he was going to pick me up for the party at seven o'clock the following day.

As I walked back to my house in the rain, I couldn't believe he'd agreed to it. I was a little unsure about going anywhere with Wes, but a girl did what she had to in the name of true love.

I wasn't a fan of running in the rain *or* in the dark, so doing both at the same time was a major suckfest. Helena had made spaghetti by the time I'd gotten home from Wes's, so I'd had to sit down for a full-scale family dinner—complete with *How was your day* conversation—before I could take off. My dad tried to convince me to hit the new treadmill he'd bought the day before, since it was pouring outside, but that was a non-option for me.

My daily run had nothing to do with exercise.

I tightened the string on my hood, put my head down, and hit the sidewalk, my worn-out Brooks splashing water up onto my leggings with every step. It was cold and miserable, and I picked up my pace when I turned the corner at the end of the street and could see the cemetery through the downpour.

I didn't slow until I went through the gates, up the familiar one-lane blacktop road, and just past the crooked elm; then I ran fifteen steps farther to the left.

"This weather sucks, Ma," I said as I stopped next to my mother's headstone, putting my hands on my hips and sucking air while trying to slow my pant. "Seriously."

I dropped to a squat beside her, running my hand over the slick marble. I usually sat down on the grass, but it was way too wet for that. The driving rain made it seem even darker than normal in the shaded cemetery, but I knew the place by heart, so it didn't bother me.

In a weird way, this was my happy place.

"So Michael is back—I'm sure you saw—and he seems just as perfect as ever. I'm going to see him again tomorrow." I pictured her face, like I always did when I was here, and said, "You'd be excited about this one." Even if I had to go to Wes for help. My mom had always thought Wes was sweet but that he played too rough.

"It just feels like it's a fate thing, the way he was kind of dropped into my lap right after I was listening to 'Someone Like You.' I mean, what's more fate-y than that? *Your* favorite song, from *our* favorite movie, and *our* favorite cute-ex-neighbor just happened to drop in? I feel like you're writing this Happily Ever After from your spot . . ."

I trailed off and gestured at the sky. "Up there somewhere."

Even the cold rain couldn't keep me from being excited as I described his Southern "y'all" accent for my mom. I squatted beside her chiseled name and rambled, like I did every day, until the alarm on my phone buzzed. This ritual had kind of become like an oral diary over the years, except I wasn't recording, and no one was listening. Well, except—I hoped my mom was.

It was time to head back.

I stood and patted her headstone. "See you tomorrow. Love you."

I took a deep breath before turning and jogging down the hill. The rain was still coming down hard, but muscle memory made it easy to stay on the path.

And as I ran past Wes's house and turned into my driveway, I realized I was more excited than I'd been in a really long time.

"Liz."

I glanced up from my Lit homework to see Joss climbing in my window, with Kate and Cassidy following behind her. We'd discovered years ago that if you climbed onto the roof of my old playhouse in the backyard, you were just high enough to slide open the bedroom window and step right in.

"Hey, guys." I cracked my back and turned around in my desk chair, surprised to see them. "What's up?"

"We just got done with a planning meeting for the senior prank, but we don't want to go home yet because my dad said

I could stay out until nine, and it's only eight forty." Cassidy—whose parents were wicked strict—plopped down on my bed, and Kate followed, while Joss sat her backside on my window seat and said, "So we're hiding here for twenty more minutes."

I readied myself for pressure from them about the senior prank.

"It was basically, like, thirty people jammed into Burger King, loudly shouting out ideas of things they think are funny." Joss giggled and said, "Tyler Beck thinks we should just let loose with, like, twenty thousand Super Balls in the hallways—and he knows a guy who can hook us up."

Kate laughed and said, "Swear to God he had the whole group convinced it was the money idea. Until he said he would need actual money."

"We seniors are funny, but cheap as hell." Cassidy lay back on my bed and said, "I personally liked Joey Lee's idea to just say screw it and do something horrible, like flipping over all the shelves in the library or flooding the school. He said it was 'ironically funny because it's so terribly *not* funny' and that it 'would never be forgotten.'"

"That's definitely true," I said, taking out my ponytail and digging my hands into my hair. I didn't want to look at Joss because I felt like she'd take one glance and know I'd been scheming with Wes, so I kept my eyes on Cass.

"You should've been there, Liz," Joss said, and I prepared myself for what came next. A lecture about how we were only seniors once, perhaps? She was really good at those. *Just do it, Liz. We're only high school seniors for a few more months.*

But when I looked at her, she grinned instead and said, "Everyone was talking about ideas, and then Conner Abel said, 'My house got forked once.'"

My mouth fell open. "Shut *up*!"

"Right?" Kate squealed.

Last year, when I was crushing hard on Conner, we thought it'd be funny to fork his front yard one Saturday night when there was nothing going on and we were all sleeping over at my house. Yes, it was silly, but we were juniors—we didn't know any better. But in the middle of the midnight forking, his dad came outside to let the dog do its business. We took off running into the neighbor's yard, but not before the dog managed to catch his teeth on Joss's pajama pants, exposing her underwear for all to see.

Joss cackled and said, "It was hilarious because, you know, he uttered the bizarro words 'My house got forked.'"

"I cannot believe he said that," I laughed.

She shook her head and added, "But it was also funny because someone asked him what the hell he was talking about, and listen to this. He said, and I quote, 'A bunch of girls stuck forks all over my front yard last year, and then one mooned us while running away. I shit you not, dudes.'"

"Shut *up*!" I died laughing then, leaning into the memory of those good times. They were pure, in a way, untouched by my stressful senior issues that had stained the memories we'd been making this year. "Did it kill you not to take credit for it?"

She nodded, stood, and went over to my closet. "Big time, but I knew we'd come out looking like obsessed stalkers if I confessed."

I watched as she flipped through my dresses, and then she asked, "Where's the red checked dress?"

"It's buffalo plaid, and it's on the other side." I pointed and said, "With the casual shirts."

"I knew the layout, but I would've pictured it with the dresses."

"Too casual."

"Of course." She looked through the other rack, found the dress, and then pulled it off the hanger and draped it over her arm. "So what'd you do tonight? Just homework?"

I blinked, caught in the headlights, but Cass and Kate weren't even paying attention, and Joss was looking at the dress. I cleared my throat and muttered a quick, "Pretty much. Hey—do you know how much of *Gatsby* we're supposed to read for tomorrow?"

Cass said, "Guys, we need to hit it" at the same time Joss said, "The rest of it."

"Thanks," I managed, while my friends made their way to the window and scrambled out the same way they'd come. Joss was about to swing her leg over when she said, "Your hair looks supercute like that, by the way. Did you curl it?"

I thought of Wes's living room and how drenched my hair had

been when I'd arrived. "No. I, um, I just got caught in the rain after school."

She smiled. "You should be so lucky every day, right?"

"Yeah." I pictured Wes's cartwheel and wanted to roll my eyes. "Right."

CHAPTER THREE

"You're late."
"You're stunning."
"You're forgiven."

—Pretty Woman

It was seven fifteen and Wes hadn't shown up yet.

"Maybe you should walk over there." My dad looked up from his book and stared directly at my tapping fingernails. "I mean, it *is* Wes."

"Translation," said Helena, giving me a smirk. "Your tapping is driving him to distraction and he thinks your date is capable of forgetting you entirely."

"This isn't a date."

My dad ignored my comment, set his book down on the table beside him, and gave Helena a grin. "Actually, her tapping is driving me to distraction and Wes Bennett is capable of anything."

My dad and Helena started doing their hilarious banter thing on the love seat, and I had to fight to hold in the eye roll. Helena was awesome—she reminded me of a blond Lorelai Gilmore—but she and my dad were sometimes a lot to take.

He'd met her in a stuck elevator—for real—exactly one year after my mother had died. They'd spent two hours in forced confinement between the eighth and ninth floors at the First National building downtown, and they'd been inseparable ever since.

It was the epitome of irony that they'd had the ultimate meet-cute and seemed *made* for each other, because she was the polar opposite of my mother. My mother had been sweet, patient, and adorable, like a modern version of Doris Day. She'd loved dresses, homemade bread, and fresh-cut flowers from her garden; that was all part of what my father had fallen madly in love with.

He'd said she was enchanting.

Helena, on the other hand, was sarcastic and beautiful. She was jeans and a T-shirt, let's-pick-up-takeout, I-don't-like-rom-coms, yet my dad was lost to her the minute that high-rise elevator malfunctioned.

In an instant, I'd lost my grieving buddy and gained a woman who was nothing like the mom I'd cried for every night.

That had been a lot for eleven-year-old Liz to handle.

I checked my phone—no message from Wes. He was fifteen—no, *seventeen*—minutes late, and he still hadn't sent a single *Sorry I'm running late* text.

Why had I even bothered being ready on time? He'd probably forgotten all about me and was already at the party with a beer in his hand. He'd texted me last night to say that Michael was happy to hear I'd be going to the party, and it'd killed me not to ask all the middle school questions.

Did he say anything about me?

Tell me his exact words.

Ultimately, I'd refrained because Wes would only use that against me.

My phone buzzed and I pulled it out of my pocket.

Jocelyn: What're you doing?

I put it back without responding as guilt twisted around in my belly. I usually told her everything, but I knew she wouldn't approve of me going to the party. *Do you even know who Ryno is? Michael Young is NOT your racing-to-the-train-station dude.* The minute she'd said that, I'd known she had no idea how much this mattered to me.

I was going to just go to the party, and I'd text her after I got home.

My dad asked, "You'll be home by midnight?"

"Yep."

"Not a second later, understand?" My dad looked more serious than usual and added, "Nothing good happens after midnight."

"I know, I know." He said those words every single time I went out. "I'll call if—"

"No, you won't." My always laid-back father gave a shake of his head and pointed at me. "You will just make it a priority to *not* be late. Understand?"

"Honey, relax—she gets it." Helena and I exchanged looks of understanding before she pointed out the window and started rambling to him about the grass. My dad was only ever tense when it came to curfew, and it was only because of my mother's death. His favorite thing to say if I ever dared to push back was *If your mom hadn't been out at midnight, that drunk driver couldn't have hit her.*

And he was right. And intense. So I pretty much always shut up about it.

I kept tapping my nails on the end table, shaking my crossed legs as nerves settled in. I wasn't nervous about Michael; I was excited about that part. What I was nervous about was going to a party with the populars. I didn't know any of them besides Wes, and my awkward self knew even less about how to act at a keg party.

Because I'd never been to a keg party.

I was more of a low-key girl. On a typical Friday night, Joss, Kate, Cassidy, and I went to a movie or hung out at the bookstore or maybe went to Applebee's for cheap appetizers. Occasionally we went shopping and ended up at Denny's or Scooter's Coffee.

And I liked my predictable life. I understood it, controlled it, and it made sense to me. In my head, my life was a rom-com and I was living it like a Meg Ryan–type character. Cute dresses, good friends, and the eventual appearance of a boy who would find me lovely. Keg parties played no part in that. They belonged in a *Superbad* kind of life, right?

"And the parents are home?"

I rolled my eyes and Mr. Fitzpervert jumped onto my lap. "Yes, Dad, the parents are home."

Spoiler: they were not home.

But my dad and Helena were super chill parents. They trusted me, mainly because I rarely went out and never got into trouble, so they didn't feel the need to call and check up on me when I was away from home. So yeah—I felt a little guilty about lying, but since I didn't plan to do anything they wouldn't approve of (except a best-case scenario that had me and Michael kissing on the back porch under a clear night sky with "ocean eyes" by Billie Eilish on a speaker in the background and his hands cradling my face as my right foot popped at just the right moment like in the movies), my guilt was but a fraction of what it could've been.

I scratched behind Fitzpervert's ear, which made him purr and bite my hand.

He was such a dick.

He was currently sporting the gingham bow tie that I'd purchased on DapperTabby.com, so he looked dashing in an I-want-to-murder-you-but-I-eat-too-much-to-actually-move kind of way. The tie *did* accentuate his recent weight gain, so I wasn't mad that he'd lashed out.

I got it.

I set him on the floor and walked over to the window, and there was Wes, as if my thoughts had summoned him. He hopped down his porch steps wearing jeans and a hoodie, and proceeded to walk across our front yard.

"He's here. Bye, guys." I grabbed my purse and reached for the door.

"Have a nice time, sweetie."

"Do you have money for a pay phone?" Helena asked.

I squinted at Helena, who shrugged and added, "I mean, you never know. You could get into a whole time machine, *Back to the Future* thing and need a pay phone to get home, and what would you do then?"

I did roll my eyes then. "Yes, um—I definitely have enough money to get back to this decade should we find a hole in the space-time continuum. Thank you."

She nodded and put her feet up on my dad's lap. "You're welcome. Now beat it, kid."

I opened the front door before Wes could knock, and closed it quickly behind me. Which resulted in us nearly running into each other. He stopped just in time, looking a little surprised.

"Hey," I said.

"Hey." He looked around me and said, "I don't have to come in for a parental lecture?"

I couldn't answer for a second because it was a bit jarring seeing Wes standing on my porch at dusk, smelling lightly of musky-manly cologne and looking freshly showered. He'd been next door my entire life, but it was surreal that our parallel lives were actually intersecting.

"Nah," I said as I dropped my keys into my purse and started walking toward his car, which was, of course, in The Spot. "They know this isn't a date."

It only took him two steps, and he caught up to me. "But what if I wanted to declare my intentions to your father?"

"Your intentions?" I stopped beside his car. "Do you mean how you intend to irritate me for multiple hours in a row tonight?"

He hit unlock and opened the door for me. "I was actually referring to the way I intend on blowing off the party entirely to use your body as a human shield at the paintball range."

"Don't even joke about getting neon paint on this dress."

He shut my door, went around the car, and got behind the wheel. "Yeah, what's with the dress? I kind of thought you'd wear something normal to a party."

"This *is* normal." I buckled my seat belt and pulled down the visor to check my makeup. As if Wes knew anything about fashion. I was in love with my mustard jumper dress and its flower buttons.

He started his car and put it in drive. "For you, maybe. I guarantee you'll be the only person at Ryno's wearing a dress."

"Which will make Michael notice me." I reached into my pocket—because of course my dress had pockets—and opened the tube of lipstick that was inside. My hands were shaking and I took a deep breath, trying to make myself chill. It was hard, though, when in mere minutes I'd be face-to-face with the boy I'd daydreamed about for more than half my life.

Deep breath.

"Yeah, that's definitely true." He pulled away from the curb and added in a cowboy voice, *"Howdy, partner. Who's the filly in the dress that's blocking my view of the hot girls?"*

"Oh, come on. Michael *does not* talk like that." I snort-laughed in spite of myself, which screwed up the lipstick application as I looked in the visor mirror. "He speaks like the intelligent, charismatic guy that he is."

"As if you even know." He turned right on Teal Street, and his foot was heavy on the gas pedal. "The last time we knew him, he was a fourth grader."

"Fifth." I put the cap back on the lipstick. "And I can just tell."

"Oh, you can tell." He made a little noise that was the

equivalent of him calling me a child. "For all you know, he's spent the past few years torturing baby squirrels."

"For all *you* know," I said, flipping the visor back up and reaching out to turn on his radio, "he's spent the last few years *bottle-feeding* orphaned baby squirrels."

"Well, if you ask me, that is no less alarming."

I rolled my eyes and turned the station, mildly irritated that he, too, thought I was ridiculous. They didn't understand how fated his reappearance was, so I was just going to ignore their negativity.

I loved Jay-Z, but I was feeling myself in my jumper dress so I scanned away from rap until I found a station playing a super old Selena Gomez song. That earned me another disapproving noise before Wes switched it back to "PSA."

"Hey—I liked that song."

"You like a song about Selena Gomez thirsting over Justin Bieber?"

I looked over at his smirking face. "You are seriously disgusting."

"You're the one who likes that seriously disgusting song."

If my mom had been right about the whole your-eyes-are-going-to-stay-that-way rule, spending time with Wes was going to leave me visually impaired for the rest of my life.

"You're not going to knock?"

Wes stopped with his hand on the front doorknob and looked at me like I was from another planet. "Why would I?"

"Because it isn't your house?"

"But it's Ryan's; I've been here a hundred times." He pushed open the front door. "And we're going to a party in the basement, not a wine tasting in the formal dining room. The butler doesn't need to announce our arrival *this* time."

"I know that, you jag."

He grinned and gestured for me to go ahead of him.

I stepped inside the fancy foyer, with marble on the floor and a glass chandelier overhead, and it was quiet. Too quiet. My stomach was full of butterflies, and I kind of wanted to go home, despite knowing that Michael was likely already here.

"Relax, Libby."

Wes was looking at me as if he knew how nervous I was, and the tone of his voice told me he was actually trying to make me feel better. That seemed like a stretch, though, when he was probably just thinking how hilarious it was that I was such a nerdy mouse.

"No one calls me 'Libby.'" My mom had, but since she wasn't there anymore, I couldn't count her, right?

"Aw—then I have a perfect pet name for you already."

"No. I hate it." I hadn't always, but I did now.

"Oh, you do not." He nudged my arm with his elbow. "And you can call me 'Wessy' if you want."

I couldn't *not* laugh at that; he was so ridiculous. "I will not want to do that, like, ever."

He walked over to a door and opened it, and noises came up from the bottom of the stairs. "Ready to party?"

Not at all. "Hey—don't ditch me until I find Michael, okay?"

"Call me 'Wessy,' and I totally won't."

I snorted. "Fine. If you ditch me, *Wessy*, I will stab you with the keg tap."

"My little Libby is such a savage."

"Where is he?"

Wes gave me a look as we stood near the keg. "We've only been here ten minutes—chill. He's here somewhere."

I held the red SOLO cup between my hands and looked around. "Up All Night" by Mac Miller would be the perfect choice if a camera were to pan out and capture the energy of the party. Because there were a *lot* of people in that unfinished basement, yelling and laughing and guzzling warmish beer. A small group sat around a table in the corner playing Presidents and Assholes, which appeared to be a game involving cards, drinking, and sporadically yelling, "Ooh-wee baby!"

But I didn't care about any of that. I only wanted to see Michael. I wanted my reunited-and-it-feels-so-good moment with him, our childhood-coming-full-circle moment, and everything else was just background noise.

"Maybe you should relax and try having fun." Wes pulled his phone out of his front pocket, checked messages, then put it back. "You do know how to do that, don't you?"

"Of course," I said, taking a sip of the beer and trying not to look like I found it as disgusting as I actually did. But I really had no idea how to have fun at a party like that; he was right.

Wes fit in, though.

Since the minute we'd walked downstairs, his name had been shouted no less than ten times. Our entire high school class seemed to adore my annoying neighbor. Weird, right? What was even weirder was that so far, he hadn't turned into the dude-bro I imagined him to be in a party situation.

He hadn't left me by myself, hadn't done a keg stand, and hadn't discussed breasts and/or butts with his friends in front of me. I mean, he'd passed on beer and was drinking water because he had to drive, for God's sake. Who *was* this guy? The guy I'd assumed him to be would've beer-bonged *while* driving.

Neighborhood friends were like that. You grew up with them, running over hot sidewalks and yelling to each other across fresh-cut lawns, but once you got older, you became acquaintances born of proximity with nothing but a surface level of basic knowledge. I knew he parked like an ass, played a ball sport—baseball maybe?—and was always laughing and loud when I saw him at school. I'm sure he knew even less about me.

"Wesley!" A pretty blond girl squealed and gave him a big hug. He looked at me over her shoulder as she very nearly jumped on him, and I rolled my eyes, which made him laugh. The blonde pulled back and said, "What took you so long? I've been looking for you everywhere."

"I had to pick up Liz." He gestured toward me, but she didn't even turn around. The girl was standing, like, an inch away from him as she said, "You look really hot tonight."

Was that how the upper echelon of my gender landed boyfriends at my school? If so, I'd never have a shot at Michael because I was a big fan of personal space. I actually felt a little sorry for Wes when he swallowed and took the tiniest step backward. He said, "Uh, thanks, Ash."

"I probably shouldn't tell you that." She was kind of yelling over the noise, but Wes still looked uncomfortable, like they were alone in a dark room and the door was locked. "But what the hell, right?"

She didn't move from deep within Wes's space, so I tapped her on the shoulder. He *was* a childhood pal, I supposed, so it was probably my neighborly duty to save him at least once.

She turned around and smiled. "Hey."

"Hey." I smiled and touched her arm. "Listen."

I leaned over and put my mouth closer to her ear, and I wanted to giggle when I saw Wes's eyebrow go up like a question mark. I said to her, "Don't tell anyone, but Wes and I are kind of . . . y'know . . ."

"Together?" Her eyes narrowed in confusion and then she smiled. Nodded slowly. "I had no ide—I'm so sorry!"

"Shh." The girl was loud. "No worries at all, we're just keeping it quiet."

"I mean, I was going after him hard-core." She gestured to herself with both of her pointer fingers and laughed. "I did *not* mean to make a move on your man!"

I shook my head and wanted that time machine Helena had mentioned, as everything clicked into place. She—*Ash*—was Ashley Sparks. Oh my God. Not only was she loud, but she was super popular and a terrible gossip. Every person in this building would think Wes and I were *together* in probably about ten minutes. I shushed her and said, "Shh . . . no biggie. He isn't my man yet, so—"

"He will be, girl." She nudged me with her shoulder and grinned at Wes. "You go get it."

"Oh my God." I muttered, "Shh. Um, okay."

She walked away and I squeezed my eyes shut, not wanting to look at him.

"Did you just tell her that—"

I opened my eyes. "Yep."

He bent his knees so his face was level with mine, and his eyes were squinty when he said, "Why would you do that?"

I swallowed and looked down at my beer. "Well, I was trying to save you, um, from her amorous clutches."

He started laughing. Hard. I raised my eyes to his face, and I couldn't stop myself from joining, because he had one of those laughs. Happy and mischievous and full-on little boy; it was contagious. And really, it *was* ridiculous that I'd tried to save six and a half feet of Wes from the hot girl that clearly wanted to get with him. I had tears in my eyes by the time we got ourselves under control.

"Hey, y'all." Michael came up beside Wes and said something about beer, but my heart started beating so fast that fainting became a distinct possibility and I didn't hear anything he said. The noise of the party dimmed to a buzzing murmur as I squeezed my fingers around my red SOLO cup and drank him in. He was everything I remembered, but better. His smile was the same powerful weapon that made me feel both queasy and like I might spontaneously combust, all at the same time.

Wes and Michael kept talking, but I heard none of their words as I raised my cup to my lips, wishing so badly that I had headphones with me. Because "How Would You Feel" by Ed Sheeran definitely should've been playing while my eyes strolled over his thick hair, his pretty eyes, and those perfect teeth that were bared as he smiled at Wes.

Note to self: *Create the Soundtrack of Michael and Liz after you get home.*

"How have you been, Liz?" He turned his attention to me, and my insides melted all together when he smiled. "You look exactly the same. I would've recognized you anywhere."

My voice wouldn't work for a second and my face was on fire, but then I managed to breathe the word, "Same."

"So where do you work?"

"What?"

He gestured to my dress. "Your uniform . . . ?"

"Oh." Oh no. He thought my adorable dress, the one that was supposed to make me stand out from the crowd *to him*, was a waitress uniform.

Kill me now.

I looked at Wes, and he gave me a *Let's-see-how-you're-going-to-get-out-of-this* look. I stammered, "My uniform. Yeah. Um, I, uh, pick up hours sometimes at the diner."

"What diner?"

"The, uh, *The* Diner."

Wes's face opened into a huge grin. "I love *The* Diner."

Sweat beads formed on the tip of my nose as I lied. "I barely ever work there."

Michael tilted his head just a little. "Where exactly—"

"I wish you'd moved back into your old house, Young," Wes interrupted. "Because we could totally re-up our last epic game of hide-and-seek."

I made a mental note to thank Wes later for the subject change.

Michael grinned and took a drink from his red cup. "Can you imagine?"

"I prefer not to." I smiled at him and ignored Wes's chuckle. "When our hide-and-seek games turned 'epic,' that usually meant that Wes and the twins were terrorizing me."

"How many times do you think I snuck over and warned you?" Michael's eyes ran over my face like he was reconciling the old and the new. "I saved you from so many bugs and frogs down your shirt."

Wes said, "The twins used to get so pissed when you helped her."

Michael shrugged and turned his attention back to Wes. "I just couldn't let you do that to Liz."

Ed Sheeran was back in my head as I watched Michael laugh with Wes. The three of us tripped back a few years to our firefly childhood, and it felt so good.

How would you feel,
If I told you I loved you?

"Every time I see a cheesy movie on TV, I think of Little Liz."

Only, when he said it, Michael managed to make the word "little" sound sexy. *Lil*, but he sounded like a sleepy rancher when he said it, as opposed to someone referencing the newest mumble rapper, *Lil* Liz.

He lifted his cup and finished the last of his beer. "Remember how she always watched *Bridget Jones's Diary* and got *so mad* if we made fun of it?" They'd never known it was because that movie had been my mother's favorite.

"Do we have to rehash the past?" I pushed my hair behind my ear and tried to direct them to a topic that would show Michael how interesting I was now. "I heard—"

"Can you get me a beer?" Ashley was back, holding her cup out to Michael and smiling at me like we were besties. "I'm bad with the keg and always end up with too much head."

Ugh—she said it in *that* way. You know the one.

Michael smiled but didn't sound flirty when he said, "Sure."

He turned his back to us and grabbed the tap while she turned her attention to Wes. "Are you going to prom, Bennett?"

Wes looked at me and raised an eyebrow, smirking. "I haven't decided yet."

"Dream on," I muttered, making him chuckle as Ashley continued, oblivious to our exchange.

"A whole bunch of us are going as a group." She was slurring pretty heavily now. I started to wonder if we should find her friends. "You two should come. We're getting a limo and everything."

I glanced at Michael, but he seemed to have missed the comment, thank God.

Wes leaned closer to her and said, "Ash, did we do a little pregaming before the party?"

Ash giggled and nodded. "At Benny's—his mom was gone."

"I see. How about some water?" Wes grabbed her a bottle from the cooler of ice by the keg and gave her a nice smile that I realized he'd never given to me. Not once. I only received mocking grins, sarcastic smirks, and eyebrow quirks from my neighbor. "Well, I do love me some limo, so I'll have to think about prom."

Michael turned around. "When *is* prom?"

Everything stopped for me as Wes took the beer Michael had poured for Ashley and set it aside. She didn't even notice. Wes said, "In two weeks."

It was total slo-mo. *Innnn. Twwooooo. Weeeeeeks.*

Michael said to Wes, "It's so bizarre, switching schools two months before graduation. Senior prom is supposed to be this really big deal, but I don't even know any girls here yet except for Laney."

You know me! Take me, my beautiful Michael, not the evil and vapid Laney! I'd have to explain the change in plans to Joss, but I could make her understand if my dream boy stepped up.

Michael gestured to Wes and me and asked, "Are y'all going?"

"Us?" My voice came out high-pitched, and I waved a hand wildly between me and Wes while making an exaggerated face, grateful Ashley had disappeared into the crowd. "Wes and I? Oh my God, no. Are you kidding me?"

"Yeah." Wes shook his head and did the slashing motion

with his hand. "We are *not* going anywhere together. Trust me. I wouldn't go to the gas station with this one."

"Well, I wouldn't invite you to the gas station, so you can just shut your big mouth," I said around a smile, following it up with a big old fake arm punch. "Believe me."

Michael looked at us like we were funny. "Oh. I thought I heard you were a thing."

"Yeah, well, you heard wrong," I said, horrified as I realized that I was the one who'd started the rumor. About myself.

God. And how freaking fast *was* gossipy Ash? Honestly, I'd have been impressed if I hadn't been so worried about her ruining everything.

"Way off base, dude." Wes tousled my hair and said, "No Little Liz for me."

I slapped his hand. "Nope."

"Oh." Michael did a slow nod of consideration and then looked at me. "Two weeks, huh?"

Twwooooo. Weeeeeeeeks. Huuuuuuuuh?

Goose bumps prickled up my arms as Sheeran floated back into my head.

"So tell me what's happened since I moved." Michael was apparently done thinking Wes and I were a thing and also finished making me light-headed by speaking the word "prom" in my presence. "Do y'all still hang out? How about the twins and Jocelyn?"

Wes and I looked at each other before I took over, mainly because I didn't want him to say something embarrassing or unpleasant about me. "Wes and I see each other long enough to fight over the parking spot in front of our houses, but that's pretty much it. And Joss is actually my best friend now, which even I find hard to believe."

He smiled at that, and he had the kind of smile that made you feel like you'd done something right. A million happy nerve endings were buzzing inside my body, and I wanted to bask in that smile and make it never go away.

Ashley reappeared and said something to Wes, making him turn his back to us to talk to her, which was fine with me, because it left Michael and me in one-on-one conversation. I said, "The twins, on the other hand, now attend Horizon High. They got sent to the alternative school after they landed in juvie for stealing a car."

"What?" Michael's mouth dropped open but his eyes were still smiling. "Their mom was super religious, wasn't she?"

"Yep." I took a sip of the warm beer and did my best not to gag. "She still teaches classes on Catholicism every Wednesday night at St. Patrick's, but she has to wear a scarlet letter on her denim jumper."

"Scandalous." He leaned his head closer. "This is wild—I still can't believe it's you. Little Liz, all grown-up."

"I know. And who would've thought Michael from down the block would return?" My cheeks were warm as I also leaned closer so he could hear me over the party noise. My heart was pounding as I went over the words—as I had been for the past few hours—over and over again in my head. The clock was ticking, so I needed to jump in with both feet. I said, "I don't know if you knew it, but when we were little, I had the biggest crush on you."

His lips slid into a dashing grin. "Well, I'll be honest. I kind of—"

I don't know if Michael finished his sentence or not, because just as I was having a tiny pleasure aneurysm at the next sentence's possibilities, I heard a noise. Like, the kind of gurgle a garden hose makes when you turn it on but the water hasn't quite made it out of the tube yet. I glanced in the direction of the sound, and Ashley opened her mouth wide and spewed chunky brown vomit all over my front, from my neck to my dress to my bare, exposed kneecaps.

Oh. My. God.

OhMyGod! I glanced down, seeing that I was *covered* in the liquified remains of Ashley's stomach. It was warm and thick and splattered across my outfit, making the top of my dress so drenched that it was sticking to my skin. In my peripheral vision I could see that there were wet chunks in the right side of my hair, over by my ear, but I couldn't focus on that because I could feel a trail of hot vomit running down my leg.

Running down my leg.

I'm not sure if I made a sound or if I just looked victimized as I stood there with my arms extended, but Wes quickly handed the vomitous blonde off to one of the girls standing nearby, and then he was at my side.

"I've got clean clothes in my trunk, Liz. Let's get you up to the bathroom, and you can clean up while I run to my car and grab them."

I couldn't even formulate words. I just nodded and let him grab my elbow and lead me through the gaping crowd—who seemed to think my situation was both disgusting *and* hilarious—and up the stairs. I was fighting back my gag reflex and trying not to inhale that god-awful smell as I died of mortification.

Not only was I a puked-on laughingstock, but Michael had witnessed the whole gruesome ordeal.

Talk about the opposite of a meet-cute.

I was seriously going to die of embarrassment. For sure. It was, in fact, a thing. My death was imminent.

When we got to the top of the stairs, Wes steered me to a bathroom that was right off the kitchen. He flipped on the light, led me inside, and bent his knees so he was at my level. He looked into my face so I could see nothing but him and said, "Get out of these clothes and clean up, and I'll be right back, okay?"

I still couldn't formulate words so I nodded.

Michael appeared at the top of the stairs, looking at me with his perfect nose crinkled up like *he* wanted to puke too, but in a sympathetic way. He said, "At least you were wearing your uniform and not your own clothes."

Now *I* wanted to puke—and disappear—so I just said, "Yeah."

"Is there anything I can do?" He looked queasy at the sight of me, but he still gave me a sweet smile and said in a Southern-comfort kind of way, "Need me to fetch you anything?"

Fetch. Aw.

I shook my head but felt—oh my God—something damp stick to my neck. I gritted my teeth and said, "No, but thank you."

I closed the door and turned the lock. Looked around and cursed whoever had built this house for not providing a shower in that particular guest bathroom. "You have got to be *kidding* me!"

I glanced at the sink. And apologized to Ryno—whoever he was—for what I was about to do to his bathroom.

First, I tore off every little piece of clothing I had on, including my underwear, letting them fall into a disgusting pile on the white marble floor. Next, I turned on the faucet and started shoving body parts under the hot running water. Left leg, right leg. Left arm, right arm. I had to do a near-backbend to rinse my neck and torso, spraying water all over the vanity and the floor, before jamming my head directly under the water.

Such a great idea, Liz, going to a beer *party with Wes.*

Terrible judgement.

I could see the chunks slowing the sink drain as I rubbed my hair with a bar of soap, so I had to be careful to keep my head raised just enough to avoid re-contaminating my hair with sink-yack.

I straightened and wetted down one of the guest towels and slathered it with another fancy bar of soap before giving myself a full-body sponge bath.

I caught a glimpse of myself in the water-splattered mirror, wildly scouring my nude self in a stranger's bathroom while humming tiny moans of disgust, and my brain added the next track to the album.

"Hello Operator" by the White Stripes.

The words weren't particularly befitting my uniquely horrible situation, but the guitar riffs while I manically and nakedly scrubbed would have been perfection.

"Liz?" Wes was at the bathroom door. "Do you want me to hand the bag through the door, or should I just leave it here on the floor and go back downstairs?"

"If you could leave it, that would be great." The fancy bathroom was like a fun house, with big mirrors all over the place, so there was no way I was opening the door with Wes out there. I would for sure end up showing him my bits. "Thank you."

"No problem." He cleared his throat. "Everyone is downstairs, so if you just reach your hand out the door and swipe the bag, no one will see anything."

"Okay."

"There's a Target bag in the side pocket that you can put your dirty clothes in. And I've got your purse downstairs—do you need it?"

"No." I'd totally forgotten I even had a purse. "Um—thanks. So much, Wes."

He was being very un-Wesley nice to me. Or at least what I'd *thought* was un-Wesley. I guess the reality was that maybe I didn't know who he was anymore. I mean, since we'd arrived at the party, he'd actually been . . . great.

"No problem. I'm going downstairs, then." I heard rustling outside the door, and then it went quiet. I covered my front with yet another guest towel—totally didn't cover enough, by the way—before I dropped to a squat, cracked the door, and stuck my hand through the opening.

I immediately made contact with the nylon string bag, thank God. I jerked it into the bathroom, then closed and locked the door. I needed to hurry and change if I was going to get another minute alone with Michael before Laney showed up and ruined everything. We'd been having a total movie moment before Blondie had rained her regurgitated foodstuffs upon me, and there was no way I was going to let that moment go.

I pulled the clothes out of the bag.

Aw, geez, Wes.

I don't know what I'd expected him to have in the trunk of his car, but I was going to look like a goofball in his sports clothes. I stepped into the gray sweatpants and pulled them up, but they were huge on me. I had to roll the waistband down two times in order not to trip over the bottoms, and I still suffered from a likely-to-be-pantsed fate, as one tiny tug would send those babies right to my ankles.

I pulled the EMERSON BASEBALL sweatshirt over my wet head—again, huge—but it smelled like fabric softener and felt like a blanket, so I kind of maybe liked it a little.

A horrified giggle escaped me when I saw my reflection—a gray marshmallow in the soft, puffy, oversize fleece ensemble. My buff-colored Mary Janes with the square heels were going to look amazing with the outfit, especially since they were also splattered with brown vomit.

I sighed and pulled my hair out of the sweatshirt hood. I was just going to have to text Wes that we needed to leave and I'd meet him in the car. I hated leaving Michael and our Big

Moment potential, but I looked too ridiculous to stay.

Only . . . where the? *Noooooo.*

My phone was in my purse. My phone was in my purse, which was downstairs with Wes and Michael, not to mention the rest of the partiers. I rolled my lips inward and breathed through my nose.

Was I on a hidden-camera show?

I took a deep breath and opened the door to the basement steps. I'd ditched Wes's hoodie, opting instead to knot the back of a ginormous T-shirt I'd found wrinkled up in the bottom of his bag. Since looking sophisticatedly adorable was no longer in the cards for me, I tried for the cool, casual, I-look-cute-in-my-boyfriend's-oversize-clothing vibe.

It probably looked more like the middle-schooler-in-her-brother's-hand-me-downs vibe, but since I was out of options, I preferred to be optimistic. I didn't have a lot of time before prom, so I was going to have to stick it out and make Michael fall for me, vomit be damned.

The stairs were cold and dusty under my bare feet, and as soon as I reached the crowded floor, I looked around for Wes, desperate to get out of there before anyone noticed me. Something by AC/DC was blaring, but not loud enough for the words to be heard over the party sounds.

"Vomit girl!" Some bear of a dude wearing a too-tight Lakers jersey grinned at me. "You came back!"

Why? Why in God's name would *I* be "vomit girl"? Ashley should have been "vomit girl," dammit.

I looked around the guy and spotted Wes. My handbag was dangling from his elbow as he talked to Michael next to the keg, and I forced myself to ignore all the looks I was getting as the newly crowned Vomit Girl and waved my hand in his direction.

Almost instantly, his gaze met mine. His eyes took a quick dip over my baggy sweats and T-shirt combo, and then his eyebrows went down before he walked toward me and pulled his keys out of his pocket.

"I'm assuming you want to go?"

"Yeah." I turned my gaze to Michael, who'd followed Wes over, and I nervously ran a hand through my damp hair. But his eyes were looking directly at my belly button, not my hair. *Oh God.* The huge sweatpants hung so low on my hips that I'd just exposed a *lot* of my stomach to the entire party. I yanked down the bottom of the shirt, but it was too late.

He gave me a smile that turned my insides to mush and said, "I really like your tattoo."

Oh God—he saw the tattoo.

At least he'd said it in a totally non-horny-bro way.

"Oh. Thanks." I resisted the urge to tug on my top again as I desperately hoped he wasn't being sarcastic.

Wes threw me a look of irritation, his jaw flexing. "Ready?"

Before I could respond, Wes took a handful of my waistband and wrapped it around his hand, pulling it higher so my belly was entirely covered. "Liz's clothes are falling off, so it's time for us to leave."

I froze when I felt Wes's hand on my skin. I looked at his face as he looked down at me, and I felt . . . off-kilter. I wasn't sure if it was in response to his touch or his sudden cavemannish protectiveness.

I also wasn't sure why it wasn't pissing me off.

I remained tethered to Wes's left hand as he and Michael shared a goodbye bro handshake, exchanging words I couldn't hear over the noise. Once they broke apart, Michael gave me a little SOLO cup raise and a sweet smile before he turned and walked away.

"Bye," I whispered under my breath, watching him disappear into the revelers.

"Come on, Buxbaum." Wes hitched my handbag over his shoulder, passed the handful of my pants to me, and led me up the stairs. "Let's get you home before you flash anyone else."

CHAPTER FOUR

"You're not as vile as I thought you were."

—10 Things I Hate About You

"So?" I looked out the windshield as he pulled away from the house, where cars lined both sides of the street. It occurred to me at that moment that Wes and his friends totally lived the *Superbad* life. "Did he say anything about me when I was changing?"

"He did, actually." He flipped on his blinker and turned the corner. "And it's probably going to piss you off."

"Oh God." I looked at Wes's profile and waited for the awful news. "What?"

He accelerated and switched lanes. "It's just very clear that he still thinks of you as Little Liz."

"What does *that* mean?"

His mouth curved a little, but he kept his eyes on the road. "Oh, come on."

"Seriously. What? Like he still thinks I'm in grade school?"

He smiled an I-shouldn't-be-smiling smile and said, "Like, he still thinks you're a nice little weirdo."

"Oh my God—are you kidding me?" I stared at his grin and

wanted to punch him. "Why would he think I'm a weirdo *now*? I was charming as hell until your girlfriend puked on me."

"It's not that." He reeled in his smile and shot me a quick glance. "It's just that he assumes you're the same person you used to be, because he's been gone."

"I wasn't a *nice little weirdo*."

His smile was back. "Oh, come on, Buxbaum."

I thought back to the old days in the neighborhood. "I wasn't."

"Yes, you were. You made up songs *constantly*, about everything. Terrible songs that didn't even rhyme."

"I was creative." True, I was less athletic and more dramatic than the rest of them, but I wasn't *weird*. "And that was my theme music."

"You lied about boyfriends all the time."

That was true. "You don't know they weren't real."

"Prince Harry?"

Oof—I had forgotten about that one. "He could've been my boyfriend; there was no way of knowing for sure."

He chuckled and pressed harder on the gas. "And the plays, Liz. Remember all the plays? You were a one-woman Broadway show every damn day of the week."

Wow—I'd totally forgotten about the plays, too. I used to *love* creating plays and getting the whole neighborhood to act them out. And yes, I might've been the instigator, but the rest of them had always played along, so they had to have enjoyed it too. "Theater is a noble calling, and if you guys were too uncultured to recognize that, then I feel sorry for you."

His chuckle turned into a laugh. "You begged Michael to be Romeo to your Juliet, and when he wouldn't, you climbed a tree and fake-cried for an hour."

"And you threw acorns at me, trying to knock me down!"

"I think the point here is that he sees you differently from other girls because of your history."

I looked at him and wondered—holy God—*had* I been a little weirdo? "So I'm a weirdo to him forever and there's nothing I can do about it?"

He cleared his throat. "Well, maybe not. But."

He looked guilty, and I said, "What did you do, Wes?"

"*I* didn't do anything, Buxbaum—you did." He pulled to a stop at a red light and gave me full-on eye contact. "Michael and I were saying how bad it sucked that you got puked on, and he made a comment about your ugly uniform."

My cheeks got hot as I remembered my beautiful outfit that was now ruined. "So?"

"So it was something about how it was classic Liz to wear a waitress uniform to a party and how you haven't changed a bit."

I sighed and looked out the window, suddenly feeling hopeless about ever getting a shot with Michael. "Awesome."

"I told him that you're completely different now."

I glanced across the darkened front seat. "You did?"

"Yep. I told him that you sing less now and that you're kind of considered a *hot girl* at school."

My weirdo heart felt warm. "I'm considered a hot girl?"

"Probably. I mean, you're not ugly, so it's possible. I don't know." Wes kept his eyes on the road and sounded irritated. "I don't make it a habit to discuss you unless it's in the context of 'Guess what my goofball neighbor did,' so I actually have no idea. I was just trying to change his impression of you."

I rolled my eyes and felt ridiculously bummed that he'd made that up.

"But here's your problem." He put on his blinker and slowed as we approached a yellow light. "As I was doing my best to convince him that you're no longer a little weirdy, he took it the wrong way and said, like, 'So you DO like Liz. I knew it.'"

"Oh no." Shit, shit, shit!

"Oh yes." He looked over at me after stopping for the red light. "He thinks we're into each other."

"*No!*" I dropped my head back onto the headrest and pictured Michael's face as he'd smiled and watched Wes and me. He thought I was into Wes, and it was entirely my fault. *I'd* started the rumor, for the love of God. "He'll never ask me to prom if he thinks you like me."

"Probably not."

"Ugh." I blinked fast, not wanting to get emotional, but I couldn't help it as I kept picturing his face. He was supposed to be my fate, dammit, and now Laney would have him in her clutches before I got my foot-popping kiss.

And I got vomited on for nothing.

"He did say something about you when we were leaving, if that makes you feel any better."

"What? When? What did he say?"

He accelerated around the corner and floored it. "All he said was 'I can't believe Little Liz has a tattoo' when I told him we were taking off."

I gasped. "Well, how did he say it?"

He glanced over at me. "Really?"

"I just mean did he say it like he was disgusted, or, like . . . like he thought it was maybe kind of cool?"

He kept his eyes on the road and said, "He definitely wasn't disgusted."

"Well, at least there's that." I stared out the window and watched as the lights of our neighborhood got closer. *What* am *I going to do?* If it were another guy, I might have just given up and called projectile vomiting a cosmic sign.

But this was Michael Young. I couldn't give up.

Honestly, the thought of it made my heart feel a little pinched.

There *had* to be a way.

I ran my teeth across my bottom lip and pondered. I mean, *technically*, regardless of the self-inflicted rumor about Wes and me, Michael *had* looked flirty when he'd looked at my tattoo. It wasn't much, but it was something, right? It proved that it *was* possible to change his "little weirdo" assumptions.

I just needed a chance to make him see *all* the things about me that had changed.

I felt hope bubbling back up. I mean, it wouldn't take long to open his eyes if I could just get some time with him, right? Time and perhaps some help.

Hmmm.

"You're so quiet, Buxbaum. Makes me a little terrified of what you're thinking."

"Wesley." I turned toward him in my seat. With my winningest grin, I said, "Buddy. I have the BEST idea."

"God help me." He pulled his car into The Spot, took the keys out of the ignition, and said through a half smile, "What is your terrible idea?"

"Well," I started, looking down at my hands and not moving to get out of the car. "Hear me out before you say no."

"Again with this? You're scaring me."

"Shh." I took a deep breath and said, "What if we let people think we're dating, but only for, like, a week?"

My cheeks were hot as I waited for him to make fun of me. His eyes narrowed and he looked at me for a long second before saying, "What exactly would that solve?"

"I'm still working this out, so bear with me. But if we pretended to kind of be into each other for a week, then that could help Michael see that I'm no longer Little Liz. He already thinks we're dating. Why not use that to show him I'm a perfectly viable romantic option?"

He drummed his long fingers on the steering wheel. "Why is this so important to you?"

I blinked and rubbed my eyebrow with my index finger. How was I supposed to answer that question? How could I tell him I was sure the universe had sent Michael back to me?

I hated that my voice was thick when I said, "I honestly have no idea, really. I just know that for some reason it really, really is. Does that sound silly?"

He stared out the windshield in front of him with an unusually serious look on his face. After a few seconds, I wondered if maybe he hadn't heard me, but then he said, "What's silly is that it doesn't."

"Really?"

"Really." He cleared his throat and turned to look at me, his Wes smirk back in place. "Now what's in it for me if I do this? Besides the joy of setting you up with the dude you want to bang, of course."

"Gross." I cleared my throat and was glad he was back to being the smart-ass I knew. Introspective, understanding Wes was kind of too much to take. I said, "You can have The Spot for another week."

"That hardly seems like enough. I mean, are you going to expect me to take you out again?"

"Well, that would help, yeah." I tucked my hair behind my ears and was hyperaware of how quiet it was in his car.

Wes crossed his arms as his mouth slid into a smug smile of satisfaction. "I've got it. I've got a brilliant plan."

"Doubtful."

"Shhh." He reached over and put his whole palm—which smelled like soap—over my face for a second before relaxing back into the driver's seat. "I will pretend like I'm trying to get something going with you, even though you're not that into me."

"Okay . . . ?"

"In addition to that, I will actively try to help you get Michael. Extol your many virtues to him."

Even though I knew there had to be a catch, it was fun seeing Wes get into the idea. I asked, "What's in it for you?"

"*If* you successfully get him to ask you to prom as a result of my assistance, I get The Spot forever."

I reached for the door handle. "*Forever?* Not a chance."

"You're not listening. I'm talking about me providing my expertise in getting him to prom you up. Our current arrangement was just for me to let you ride along to a party. What I'm talking about would be me giving you insider info, working on Michael for you, giving you helpful hints, fashion advice, etcetera."

"Fashion advice?" I snorted.

"That's right, fashion advice. Etcetera. For example, if you're going to a party and you want Michael to think you're hot, dress like it instead of a waitressed Doris Day."

"A waitressed Doris Day sounds like an excellent aesthetic, for your information, but honestly, I can't get over the fact that you know who Doris Day is."

"What? My grandma likes *Pillow Talk.*"

I loved that movie. Maybe there was hope for Wes yet.

"She also likes pickled pig's feet and attempting to escape her retirement home."

Ah. There it was.

He flipped his keys around his finger. "So . . . ? Are you in?"

I took a deep breath. If he could help me with Michael, I'd give him The Spot, along with the moon and the stars and possibly a kidney. I inhaled and said, "I'm in."

"Good girl." He got out of the car, slammed the door, and

came around to my side just as I was closing mine. He leaned down a little and murmured, "I'm going to love my Forever Spot, by the way."

I rolled my eyes. Incorrigible boy. "You don't have to walk me to the door, Wes."

He took the bag from my hand anyway. "Come on—it's not every day that a guy has the chance to carry a girl's sack full of vomity clothes to the door for her."

"True." That made me smile to the point of a laugh. "Although, I sure hope I can manage to hold up my own pants without your help."

"I doubt you can—I literally saved your ass at the party."

He walked beside me up to my house, and I could smell his cologne. It smelled good and fresh, and an ad exec would probably say it had "notes of pine," but I nearly stumbled as I realized that I recognized it as his. That was Wes's scent, plain and simple. So . . . when had *that* knowledge occurred? I must've subconsciously noticed it during our parking dustups, or perhaps he'd been wearing it since puberty.

But when we got to the porch and he handed me the bag, I looked up at his face and was overcome by the feeling that I was waking from a dream or something. Because how else did it make sense that I'd just left a beer party at the mansion of one of the populars and now Wes Bennett was on my porch—and we weren't arguing?

But the most surreal part of it—by far—was that it didn't necessarily feel wrong. It kind of felt like the start of something.

I said, "Thanks for the clothes and . . . well, everything. You were way cooler than I expected."

"Of course I was." He gave me a smile then, a smile that was different from all the others he'd ever given me. It was a nice smile, genuine like the one he'd used with his friends at the party. I didn't mind being looked at like that by him. He said, "Don't forget to wash your dirty uniform before your next shift. I imagine *The* Diner probably takes great pride in their employees' appearances."

I smiled back at him. "I'll kill you if you ever tell."

"My lips are sealed, Libby."

The next morning at work, I was feeling positive about the whole outing as I replayed it in my mind. I mean, yes—I got vomited on, Mr. Right thought my adorable dress was a job uniform, and oh, yeah, he also thought I was still a "weirdy" (I hoped that was Wes's personal term and not one that had ever left Michael's lips in reference to me)—but those were the only negatives.

Yes, I had an outrageously unrealistic optimistic nature.

Michael had also seemed fairly interested in attending prom, so I still had a chance. Especially with Wes helping to illuminate the non-weird, once-was-a-caterpillar-but-is-now-a-beautiful-butterfly Liz.

"Jeff?" I said the name loudly, and a silver-haired customer in red suspenders and matching red sneakers walked in my direction with two books in his hand.

He stopped at the counter and held out his claim ticket. I

grabbed it and said, "We can give you twenty-four dollars for your records."

His furry eyebrows squinched together like two caterpillars, and his lips flattened. "Twenty-four dollars? I know for a fact that the Humperdinck album is worth at least that much by itself."

"You're probably right," I started, desperately wanting to roll my eyes. Old record dudes were the worst. They always knew what their LPs were worth to other old record dudes, and consistently argued with me when I offered them half of what we could actually sell them for. "But at this store, we'll only be able to get a fraction of that for it. You're certainly welcome to hold on to it, if you think you can sell it online for more."

He glared at me without saying a word. Just stood there and eyeballed me, as if his powerful stare were going to make me shrink and start throwing money at him. I'd been working at Dick's Used Books for three years, and I could pretty much look at a person entering the store and know if they were going to try to haggle or not.

I stared back, with a smile, of course, and waited for him to grow tired of his Big Man games. A solid twenty seconds went by before he finally said, "I don't need two copies. I guess I'll take your offer."

Yes, I knew that you would.

I was ringing up his credit when the bell on the front door tinkled.

"Good morning," I said, not looking up from the cash register.

"Can you tell me where your fart books are?"

I looked up, and there was Wes, looking as serious as a heart attack, and Jeff the Old swung his gaze in Wes's direction.

"Excuse me?" I had to distort my face to keep from laughing. I wasn't going to smile at his childishness. Not in front of a customer, at least.

Wes was wearing basketball shorts and a SURELY NOT EVERYBODY WAS KUNG FU FIGHTING hoodie, his dark hair sticking up in the front like he'd showered and rubbed his hand over it instead of using a brush. I wasn't sure when he'd gotten so long and lean and ropy, but honestly, it was a good look.

If you were into guys like Wes.

"Your *fart* books. Hello?" He said it with great impatience, like I was the one acting strangely for just staring at him. "I need some relief, ma'am. Where are the books on gastrointestinal emergencies?"

I handed Old Jeff his money and receipt. "Thank you very much—have a great day."

He muttered and put the money in his wallet before leaving the store. I glanced at Wes and shook my head. "What is wrong with you?"

He shrugged. "I'm funny?"

"No, I don't think that's it. Why are you here?"

"Because I like books and . . ." He turned around and looked at the store behind him. "Records."

"Is that so? What's your favorite record?"

He pointed at the album I'd just bought from Old Jeff. "That one. Engelbert Humperdinck."

"Really."

"Yep. No one raps quite like the Dink. I could listen to that Engelbert—or, as I like to call him, Big E—spit rhymes all day long."

"Seriously, why are you here?"

He stepped closer to the counter. "I needed to talk to you, and your stepmom said you were here."

Stepmom. It'd be normal for me to think of Helena like that, and to call her that, but for some reason, I never could. It was either "my dad and Helena," or "my dad's wife." I'd lived with her for years now, but she was still just Helena to me.

"What's up?"

"Michael texted me this morning."

"He did?" My mouth dropped wide open, and I let out a squeal that should've embarrassed me but didn't because it was just Wes. I tiny-clapped and said, "What did he say? Did he mention me? What'd he say?"

He grinned and shook his head at me like I was an over-sugared toddler. "So a bunch of us are going to the game tonight."

"Would this be a *ball* game?" I turned the pricing gun to three dollars and started labeling the clearance books. I had told Joss I'd go dress shopping that night, mainly because I needed to create an opening to mention the party before she heard about the barf incident at school on Monday. If I could appease her on the dress, she might not give me too much grief about the party.

"Basketball, dipshit."

"How would I know that?"

"Because it's basketball season and we're in the playoffs . . . ?"

I just gave him a shrug and kept labeling, which made him smile. "*Any*way, me and Michael and some of the guys are going, and I thought it might be a casual way for you to hang without other girls stealing your thunder."

I stopped tagging. "Did you seriously just imply that I'm invisible if other girls are in the equation?"

"No. God, you're uptight. I—"

"No, I'm not."

"You're not?"

I set down the gun and put my hands on my hips. "No, I most definitely am not."

One side of his mouth slid up. "You're wearing a dress at a thrift store for books, your planner is scarily organized, and every one of your price tags is perfectly straight. Up. Tight."

I squinted at him while closing my elaborately color-coded and stickered planner. "This is a skirt and sweater, not a dress."

I freaking *adored* my plaid kilt, ruffled cardigan, and nearly new, never-been-vomited-on patent leather Mary Janes.

"Same difference. When everyone else is in jeans, you're skirted up."

I rolled my eyes. "Just because I like dresses and I'm organized doesn't mean I'm uptight."

"Sure it doesn't."

I picked up the gun and started labeling faster, irritated that he seemed to disdain everything that I was. "So finish telling me about basketball before I hurt you."

"That's pretty much it. If you ride with us, you'll have time to show how cool you are on the way to the game."

I stopped with the tags again and imagined Michael and me, lost in smiles and in-depth conversation in the back of an intimate car. "A little one-on-one sesh of Liz coolness, huh?"

"God help us all."

I ran a finger over the top of the gun and asked him, "That wouldn't be weird, you bringing me?"

He did a no-biggie shrug. "Nah. It's super chill."

"Then, um, yeah." I straightened and set down the gun yet again, excited about this unexpected opportunity. "Totally. Count me in."

"Here's the thing, though, Liz." He pulled a set of keys from his pocket and flipped them around his finger. "Don't get all pissy with me for saying this, but I'd like to help you with your outfit."

"Excuse me?" I tilted my head and couldn't quite believe *he* had said that to *me.* "I think I've got it, but thank you."

"Seriously, you need to listen to me."

"If it's about fashion, I seriously don't. No offense."

"Some taken, but this isn't about that. This is about the fact that no one is going to buy into the idea of you just casually watching some hoops if you're wearing a ruffly dress and shoes with flowers on them."

I blew the bangs out of my eyes. "Bennett—I do own a pair of jeans, you know."

"Color me surprised." He put his palms on the desk and leaned on his arms. His face was closer, and I got distracted by the super-light freckles I'd never noticed and the way his eyelashes weren't just long, but also perfectly curled. "But I bet they aren't even normal. Like . . . um, they're probably those weird-waisted trendy jeans, right? Or jeans with creases ironed into them and cuffs on the bottom?"

"Nope."

"Well," he said, sighing like this was important, "I think if you're serious about the whole Michael thing, you need to expand your closet."

"Are you kidding me with this, kung fu hoodie?"

He grinned like I'd just complimented his outfit, and rubbed a hand over the lettering on his shirt. "Hear me out. I know what girls at our school wear. Girls like Laney Morgan—yeah, remember her?"

As if I could forget her. Good skin, good Instagram following, good dating history, and a doting mother. Enviable and unforgettable.

"Are you gritting your teeth, Liz?"

I released the clench and said, "No. Continue with your rambling."

"If you want to land your man, you need to quit being stubborn and let me help you."

"I just don't think you're capable."

"Of coaching you to the win or picking out your clothes?"

"For sure the clothes." I reached down and grabbed a stack of books off the bottom shelf of the cart. Doubt crept in as he spoke like we were officially *planning* something. What was I even doing—trying to live-action my own personal version of *She's All That*?

To be honest, though, the part of me that loved makeover rom-coms was a tiny bit intrigued.

But I liked myself. I liked my clothes.

I wasn't a little weirdo, and I didn't need Wes's fashion assistance.

"Listen." He grabbed a piece of paper off the counter and said, "What if we just stroll through the mall and I point out things that look cool? You'll be with me, so you don't have to get anything you don't like. But it wouldn't hurt you to look like an actual high schooler when you're trying to charm your long-lost love, right? Nothing wild or trashy, just something that doesn't make you look like a librarian."

I was clearly losing my mind, because all of a sudden it seemed like maybe it wasn't a bad idea to go with Wes and see what he thought I should be wearing. I wasn't about to change my looks for a boy—screw that thought forever—but if he could point me to an outfit that I liked *and* he thought made me look less uptight, that wouldn't be a bad thing, would it?

"I'm pretty broke right now, so I can't afford to go for *rich* hot girl. Is there a way to do a girl-on-a-budget, moderately-attractive look?"

He gave me a full-throttle grin then, the grin of someone who'd just beat someone else. "Trust me, Buxbaum—I got you."

As soon as he left, I texted Joss.

Ugh—looks like I have to work a double. Can we dress shop tomorrow? SO SORRY.

I felt like a garbage friend. I knew I needed to stop putting her off and just do the dang dress thing already, but I was really having a hard time forcing myself to step up.

Perhaps tomorrow.

CHAPTER FIVE

"Just because she likes the same bizarro crap
you do doesn't mean she's your soul mate."

—500 Days of Summer

"Seriously, Wes?" I looked around the store and couldn't shake the guilt. It was one thing to blow off shopping with your best friend to do another activity, but blowing off shopping with your best friend to shop with someone else? It felt like crossing a big old line. "You are ridiculous."

He grabbed a red tunic from a display rack and threw it into the cart. "Ridiculously smart. Now you only have to go into the fitting room once."

I looked at the heaping cart and wondered if he knew that you could only take in six items at a time. I didn't say anything, though, because the man was on a mission. He'd picked me up from the bookstore when my shift was over, sped the two blocks to the mall, and nearly pulled my arm out of its socket every time I failed to keep up with his brisk pace.

Apparently Wes hated shopping.

We were in Devlish, the high-school-trendy-worldwide-franchise store that I usually avoided. I was all about buying vintage clothes online or hunting through thrift stores for the perfect throwback pieces; Devlish wasn't my game. Wes had asked me my size when we'd entered the three-level store, and since then he'd been hurling items into the cart like he was on some kind of speed-shopping game show.

We had finally taken a pause in the middle of an aisle, between the sequined and revealing formal dresses and the faux-business attire. Wes looked through the contents of our cart, holding up a few items to reconsider them, either nodding or shaking his head thoughtfully. Finally he said, "I think we probably have enough."

I tried not to sound sarcastic when I said, "Probably."

He pointed a finger at me and said, "But I know you well enough to know this is my only shot."

"True." He'd tossed in jeans, T-shirts, some supercute tops, some not-so-cute tops; the boy was definitely covering all of his bases. "But why so much white?"

He pushed the cart toward a huge rack of folded shirts and said, "People with red hair look good in white. Shouldn't you know that?"

I just followed, trying not to smile at his confidence in his own fashion beliefs. "I missed that memo."

He grabbed a handful of shirts and added them to our pile. "White and green, dude. Those are your go-to colors."

I couldn't stop the laugh. *Dude.* "Noted."

He stopped manic-shopping for a second and smiled down at me, his eyes warm as they traveled over my face. It reminded me of the look Rhett gave Scarlett in *Gone with the Wind* when he attempted to tie her new bonnet for her. It was a look that admitted he knew nothing about what he was doing, and that he knew he looked foolish.

But he didn't care because he was enjoying himself.

It was weird, but part of me thought that might be the case with Wes. Not that he like-liked me, but I felt like he enjoyed our verbal sparring. Honestly, I did too, when he wasn't saying things that made me want to choke him out.

He reached out and grabbed a plaid flannel shirt from a rack. That wasn't going to work for spring, but I didn't say anything. I just tucked my hair behind my ears and let him finish. It didn't escape my notice that our makeover-ish shopping trip was *exactly* like I'd imagined, but it was more *The Ugly Truth* than *She's All That*. It was so reminiscent of Mike taking Abby shopping that it was almost funny, only Wes wasn't the leading man and I wasn't falling for him.

"Think we should head to the fitting room?" he asked.

"Oh, praise the Lord, you're finally done. Yes."

He charged toward the fitting room, leaning his big body on the cart, and I was a little impressed by his focus. He hadn't checked out anyone since we'd arrived at the store, and there were a *lot* of girls in that place. Trendy girls that were just his type.

But he was all about the shopping.

"Liz?"

I glanced up and—holy shit—there was Joss, exiting a room. JOSS? *Crap, crap, crap*—what were the odds? What were the freaking odds? There was nowhere to hide, nowhere to hide

Wes, as she looked at me with confusion on her face.

"I thought you were working." She walked over and glanced at Wes before saying, "A double, right?"

Shit. I felt like I'd been caught cheating, and I wanted to disappear.

But at the same time, I looked at her and realized I'd much rather be nonsense-shopping with Wes than dress shopping with her.

Because there were no ties with Wes, no connections to anything painful. Prom dress shopping, on the other hand, was layered in melancholic bindings that made me feel a world of things I didn't want to feel.

First—there was the fact that by watching Joss and her mom shop for dresses together, I got to hyperfocus on the fact that my mom wasn't there to shop with me. Next, the event we were buying them *for* made me dwell on the reality that my mother wouldn't be there on prom night to help me get ready or take too many pictures.

And then, of course, there was the dress itself. My mother had been smitten with formalwear, and trying on dresses with her would've been a fashion show of epic proportions, complete with homemade lookbooks and jewelry pairings.

"I got off early." I was a horrible person. I saw her glance into the heaping cart and I said, "And when I got home, Wes's car was dead, so he asked if I could give him a ride to the mall. He's buying a present for his mom."

What was happening? It was alarming the way the lies were just pouring out of my mouth.

"I know how to speak, Buxbaum. Christ." He gave me a look and then shook his head at Joss while my heart raced. He asked her, "You got any ideas on what to get my mom for her birthday? Liz has pulled a cart full of clothes, and I'm not convinced."

"I'd trust her if I were you." Joss draped the shirt she was holding over her arm and told him, "No one is as good at gifting as Liz."

"Are you sure?" He gave me side-eye. "Because she's wearing a kilt, Joss."

She started laughing, and I felt like it might be okay. She said to Wes, "She's got her interesting style thing, but it's by choice. You're good."

"If you say so."

She adjusted the shirt that was hanging over her arm and said, "Call me later, Liz. I want to do the dress thing tomorrow, and I swear to God I'm going to get for-real pissed if you ghost me again."

"I won't."

"Promise?"

I felt grateful enough that she wasn't pissed about my Wes shopping trip that I genuinely meant it. "Promise."

She said goodbye and headed for the register, and the second she was out of earshot, Wes said, "Your pants are *so* on fire."

"Shut it."

"I thought you guys were besties."

"We are." I rolled my eyes and gestured for him to push the cart toward the dressing rooms. "It's complicated."

He stood still and said, "How?"

"What?" I wanted to push him and physically get that big body going, as he still wasn't moving.

"How is it complicated?" He looked genuinely interested. Could it actually be that Wes cared?

I sighed and groaned a little, running a hand through my hair. Part of me wanted to tell him about all of it, but Wes wouldn't understand my grief any more than Joss would. "I don't know. Sometimes I keep things to myself and it causes tension."

Wes tilted his head. "Is everything okay? I mean, you're okay . . . ?"

His face was—I don't know—sweetly concerned? It was a little unnerving, how sincere he looked, and something deep inside me didn't hate it. I waved a hand and said, "It'll be fine. And thanks for going along with it."

"I got you, Buxbaum." He watched me for a minute, like he was waiting for more, but then he winked and leaned on the cart. "You're on my team now."

"God help me."

He *finally* wheeled the cart into the fitting room area and proceeded to drop into one of the waiting chairs, stretch his legs out in front of him, and cross his arms.

"What are you doing?"

His eyes narrowed a fraction. "Sitting."

"But why? I'm not trying these on for you."

"Oh, come on, Liz. If I'm responsible for making you over, I need—"

"Oh my God, you are *not* making me over. Are you serious with that?" Sometimes he was beyond infuriating. "I'm taking your opinion into consideration, but I'm not pathetic and I don't need Wes *Broseph* Bennett to make me over."

He looked up at me with laughing eyes. "I think Michael was right about you being high-strung."

"You're impossible. Please go somewhere else."

"How're you going to know how they look if I'm not here?"

"I have eyes."

"Eyes that okayed a waitress uniform for a party, remember?"

"That was an adorable dress."

"Debatable. And does the use of the past tense mean it wasn't salvageable?"

"No, there was vomit in the pockets. I said my goodbyes last night."

He smirked at that and his dark eyes crinkled at the corners. "Well, I'm sorry. It was an ugly dress, but it didn't deserve to die."

I rolled my eyes, and the fitting room attendant walked out from the back. "How many?"

"A few," Wes muttered at the same time I said, "How many can I take in at a time?"

"Eight."

"Only eight?" Wes's voice was loud in the tiny dressing room area. "Come on, that's going to take forever."

I ignored him and took eight items to a fitting room. The third top I tried on, a slouchy white fleece thing that fell off one shoulder in a way that would look adorable with a tank underneath, was actually cute. I paired it with faded jeans that had shreds all over them, and I was glad Wes had suggested this.

He'd managed to find me something trendy that I liked; I couldn't believe it.

Just as I was switching into an emerald-green sweater, I heard him say, "Can you possibly change a little faster? I'm falling asleep out here."

"Don't you have some shopping to do while you wait for me? I think I saw a sale on obnoxious jock costumes in the back."

"Ouch." He whistled. "You're so mean."

"Give me two minutes and I'm done."

"Seriously?" He sounded shocked.

"Seriously."

"But you're only on the first eight."

I pulled off the sweater and put my shirt back on, sliding my feet into my shoes while straightening my hair in the mirror. "I got what I needed, so there's no reason to keep going."

He seemed doubtful when I came out, like he didn't trust my answer, but when we got to the register, he looked like he approved of the items I'd selected.

"I still can't believe I'm taking fashion advice from you. I feel like this is some kind of rock bottom." I handed my debit card to the cashier and looked at the small stack of clothing on the counter.

I pointed at the shoebox sitting right beside my clothes. "Those aren't mine."

"I have great taste. I'm like your own personal fairy godfather." Wes gestured to the shoes. "And those are my contribution."

"What?"

He leaned an arm on the counter and gave the cashier a smile that said, *See what I'm dealing with*? "I know you don't have any Chucks, Libby, and you definitely need some."

"You bought me shoes."

"Not shoes. Chuck Taylors."

I looked at his funny smirk and had no idea how to react so I reached out and opened the box.

Wes Bennett had bought me shoes.

No boy had ever bought anything for me, yet here was Wes, the antagonistic neighbor boy, spending his own money because he thought I needed Chucks. I touched the white canvas. "When did you even have time to do that?"

"When you were in the dressing room." He looked sweet as he smiled down at me and said, "I asked Claire to take care of it."

"Who is Claire?"

"The dressing room attendant. Pay attention."

The cashier handed me the receipt and my bag, and I was still fumbling around with how to react. It was sweet and thoughtful and *so* un-Wes. "Um, thank you for the shoes. I—"

"Quit gushing, Buxbaum." He smiled big enough that his eyes squinted. "It's embarrassing."

We left the store, and before we hit the mall exit, I made him go into Ava Sun with me, my favorite store. It was like Kate Spade style on a T.J. Maxx budget, mostly dresses and skirts and delicate accessories.

"Holy balls, it's like a giant version of your closet."

I knew he meant it as a dig, but as I headed toward the sale racks in the back, I said, "Thanks."

"I meant that this feels like a nightmare."

I ignored him and started flipping through the racks.

"Like an actual nightmare. Monsters and goblins and god-awful flower dresses."

"Shhh. I'm trying to shop."

I found a sale shelf and started digging while he leaned against the wall and looked at his phone. Part of me wondered if his incessant teasing was his way of flirting. I mean, from another guy it so would be, but this was Wes. He'd always teased and tormented me, so why would I take it any differently than I had in the past?

It was his way.

"Wow. That dress is so Liz Buxbaum."

"Hmmm?" I glanced up, and he was pointing at a mannequin.

"That dress. It is so you."

I followed his point to the mannequin and was totally taken aback. Because to clarify, he wasn't pointing at just any mannequin. He was pointing at *my* mannequin, the one who was wearing *my* houndstooth sheath, the dress I'd fallen instantly in love with when it had arrived two weeks before.

The one I'd looked at online no less that twenty times since then.

It was pricey, so I was forcing myself to wait until I could ask my dad to buy it for my birthday, but there was something about the fact that Wes looked at it and thought it was "me" that was . . . something. It made me happy.

"I actually love that dress."

"See? I'm incredibly intuitive for a fairy godfather."

I readjusted the shoulder strap of my bag and said, "Let's go before I throw up on *your* uniform."

As soon as I got into his car, my phone buzzed. It was a notification that Insipid Creation's new album had just dropped. I must've made a little sound of excitement, because Wes said, "What?"

"Nothing. I just saw that the album I preordered is shipping today."

"Shipping, grandma?" He put his key in the ignition and said, "You don't stream music like the youths?"

I slammed my door. "Of course I do, but some things are meant to be played on vinyl."

He glanced over as he started the car, and I buckled my seat belt. "Have you always been so into music? I mean, I think I see you with headphones on more often than not."

"Pretty much." I shoved my phone into my purse and looked out the window. "My mom put me in piano lessons when I was four, and I fell in love with it, and then she used to play this game with me where we created soundtracks for everything."

"Seriously?" Wes looked over his shoulder before backing out of the parking spot.

"Yep. We would spend hours and hours selecting the perfect songs to go along with whatever event we were soundtracking."

I realized as I said it out loud to the interior of his car that I'd never told that to anyone before. It was a memory that'd solely belonged to her and me, and I'd always found it to be terribly sad that I was the only one on the planet who knew about it.

Until now, I guess.

I smiled but sounded like a frog when I said, "I made one for summer camp, for Christmas vacation, for the six-week swimming course that I hated and never passed; anything and everything was worthy of a soundtrack."

Wes looked away from the road long enough to glance at me, and then it was like he sensed I didn't want to talk about my mom anymore.

"So that's what it was!" His mouth slid up into a grin. "You made a soundtrack for you and Michael."

"What?" I turned a little in my seat and knew my cheeks were insta-red. "What are you talking about?"

How in God's name did he know about that?

"Relax, Miss Love—your secret is safe with me."

"I have no idea what you—"

"I saw the paper." Wes looked like he was trying not to laugh as his entire face smiled. "I saw the paper, so it's pointless to deny it. It was sitting on your planner this morning and it said 'The Soundtrack of M&L.' Oh my God, Buxbaum, that is freaking adorable."

I laughed even though I was mortified. "Shut up, Wes."

"What songs are on it?"

"Seriously."

"Seriously, I want to know. Is it all boot-knocking songs, like Ginuwine and Nine Inch Nails, or is it cheesy romance? Was Taylor Swift on the list?"

"Since when is Nine Inch Nails boot-knocking music?"

"I'm the one asking questions here."

I just sighed and looked out the window.

"Well, can *we* make a soundtrack?"

"I hate you."

He said, "Oh, come on."

"Don't you have better things to do than *this*?" I gestured between the two of us, teasing but also kind of interested in his answer. Was it all about the Spot, or was it maybe a little about me? "Seriously?"

"Of course, but I'd sell my own grandmother for The Spot. *This,*" he said, mimicking my gesture, "is all about moving Wessy's car closer to Wessy."

And there was my answer.

"*Such* a disgusting nickname." I kept my gaze fixed on the windshield but I could hear the grin in his voice when he said, "So back to the soundtrack of W&L. What should we put on it?"

"You're an ass."

"I'm not familiar with that little ditty, but you're the audiophile here, not me. I was actually thinking of something more like the love theme from *Titanic.*"

"*If* we were making a soundtrack," I said, pointing at his face, "and we're not, it would be all about the parking war."

"Ah, yes, the parking war." He put on his blinker and came to a stop at the red light. "What song would accompany that glorious battle?"

"Not *Titanic.*"

"Okay, so then . . . ?"

"Hmm." I closed my eyes and thought, not caring that he was being sarcastic. This was my favorite thing in the entire world to do. "First we need to decide if we want the song to be an accompaniment to the scene, or if we want it to be a juxtaposition."

He didn't answer, and when I opened my eyes, he was watching me. He swallowed and said, "Juxtaposition for sure."

"Okay." I ignored that and kept going. "So if we're thinking about the day that you taped my windshield like a total miscreant, I would select something that celebrated you. You know, because you were remarkably unworthy of celebration."

"'Isn't She Lovely' by Stevie Wonder?" he suggested.

"Ooh—I like that." I hummed the first bar before saying, "Or. The Rose Pigeons have a song called 'He's So Pretty, It Hurts My Eyes' and it catalogues how sweet and amazing some dude is. So that's totally the juxtaposition of you in the parking war, right?"

"I did what I had to. All is fair in love and parking."

When he pulled up in front of the bookstore so I could get my car, I thanked him and grabbed my bags. He said he was going to text Michael and mention I was coming, and he also said he would throw in some good words about me. I wanted to help him craft the perfect adjectives, but I bit my tongue. I stepped out of his car, and just when I was about to slam the door, he said, "You should maybe straighten your hair for tonight."

"I'm sorry—it sounded like you just told me how I should wear my hair." I knew that he was trying to help me win Michael, but did he realize that it made me feel like total shit when he acted like my style was a joke? I was 100 percent good with my fashion choices—I dressed for me and me only—but it still didn't feel good to know that he didn't like the way I looked.

My hair was in a braid at that moment, and though it wasn't particularly cool, it also wasn't like I had hair down to my ankles that had never seen a brush, either. "Since that can't be right, what did you actually say?"

He held up a hand. "That came out wrong. All I meant was that instead of just changing up your clothes, you should give Michael the full-on hot-girl treatment. He still thinks of you as Little Liz, but if you show up looking like the kind of girl he's dated since moving away, it might be a good start."

I still didn't like it, but he had a point. "So what's the plan for later?"

"I'll pick you up at fiveish."

"Okay."

"Wear the Chucks."

"You're not the boss of me." I said it with a teasing childish pout, but I was still confused as to why he'd bought me the shoes. Everything else that he'd hand-selected for my "new Liz" wardrobe, I'd paid for. So why had he gone to the trouble of paying for them while I'd been changing? Why had he paid for them at all?

He put his big hands together as if praying. "Can you *pretty please* wear the Chucks?"

"We'll see."

CHAPTER SIX

"When I'm around you, I kind of feel like I'm on drugs. Not that I do drugs. Unless you do drugs, in which case, I do them all the time. All of them."

—Scott Pilgrim vs. the World

At four forty-five, I tied my Chucks—which, I had to admit, looked pretty cute with my whole sporty ensemble—and went downstairs. They were comfortable, and something about them made me kind of soft, but I wasn't going to waste a minute trying to figure that out.

My dad had taken my grandpa to the driving range, so it was quiet in the house. Helena was around somewhere, but I wasn't sure where.

The doorbell rang, and I couldn't believe it. Wes was early?

I walked over to the door, but when I pulled it open, it was Jocelyn, not Wes.

"Oh. Hey." I'm sure my face totally showed my shock at seeing her instead of Wes, and I tried hard not to look shook. "What're you doing here?"

Her mouth dropped open for a sec, and she looked me up and down. "Oh my God, who did this to you?"

I glanced down at my clothes. "Um—"

"I want to tongue-kiss them—you look incredible!"

She walked through the front door, and my mind was racing as I shut the door behind her. I still hadn't told her about the party, or the game, or Michael or Wes or any of the questionable things I was doing with my personal life. And Wes was going to be there any minute now.

Shit.

"Did you buy this when you were with Wes?" She was still smiling, so she wasn't pissed at me.

Yet.

"Yeah—that jag actually found a couple of nice things." My cheeks were hot and I felt like the guilt was all over my face. I was a garbage friend. "Go figure."

"Oh, hey, Joss." Helena came out of the kitchen looking way cooler than me in jeans and a hockey jersey. "I thought I heard the door. Do you want a pop or something?"

God, Wes would be there any second with his big mouth. *No pop!*

"No, thanks—I only have a second. I'm on my way to get my little sister from soccer, but Liz won't respond to my texts, so I had to stop by."

Crap.

Helena smiled and said, "She's the worst, right?"

Jocelyn smiled at Helena but also leveled me with a look. "Right."

"I, um, I'm about to leave too." I swallowed and hoped I could get her out of there quickly. "In five minutes."

"Where are you going?"

Helena had asked the question, but they both stood there, staring at me as I tried to come up with something.

"Um, Wes from next door is going to the basketball game and he, um, asked if I want to go. I mean, it's a casual, no-big-deal thing—I was just bored and it sounded less boring, y'know? I totally don't want to go but I said I would. So."

Jocelyn's eyebrows shot up. "*You* are going to a basketball game." She said it like I'd just professed myself a triceratops. "With Wes. Bennett."

Helena crossed her arms over her chest. "Didn't you call the parking police on him a few days ago?"

"No, I, um, I said I *almost* did." I spit out an awful fake laugh and shrugged. "Yeah, honestly, I have no idea why I said I'd go with him."

I knew exactly why.

"Did Bennett make you buy those Chucks, too?" Jocelyn was staring at my shoes. "Because you *hate* those shoes."

It was true. I'd always thought Converse high-tops were ugly and utterly lacking in arch support. Now I had a weird affinity for them that made me question my own mental fortitude.

"They were on clearance, so I said, 'What the hell.'" Again with the terrible laugh. "Why not buy some Chucks, right?"

Jocelyn did a little head shake, like she had no idea what she was witnessing.

Same, girl. Same.

"Well, person I used to know, I only swung by because my mom needs to know which day we're going dress shopping next week."

Ironically, after I'd finally agreed earlier to go shopping with her, her mom had had to reschedule for a different day. Initially I was relieved to put it off longer, but now it felt like the universe just wanted to torture me. At this point, I kind of just hoped for a dress to be stuffed into my closet so I could stop hearing the phrase "dress shopping."

"Ooh—I love dress shopping." Helena tilted her head and added, "I rarely wear them because sitting like a lady sucks, but every spring I want racks and racks of floral dresses."

"This is prom dress shopping." Jocelyn was still looking at my clothes as she said, "Liz and I are going together, and my mom said she can take us dress hunting."

"Oh." Helena blinked and glanced at me for a second, and I felt like a monster. She'd mentioned multiple times that she thought I should go to prom because I'd regret it if I didn't, and she'd also mentioned multiple times that she could take me dress shopping and we could "make a whole day of it."

She'd thought it would be *so* fun.

But that had been, like, a month ago, and I'd kind of forgotten.

Kind of.

My feelings about Helena doing the things my mom should've been there to do with me were tricky, and most of the time I just avoided them until they went away.

Or until this happened.

"Well, I'm sure that will be a blast." Her eyes were sad, but she said, "Just don't get anything too revealing, okay, guys?"

Jocelyn grinned. "We'll do our best, but no promises."

The doorbell rang—it had to be Wes this time, right?—and I felt nauseous as both of their eyes landed on me.

I squeezed in between them and stepped toward the door. "That's probably Wes."

I wrapped my fingers around the doorknob and braced myself. What were the odds that Wes would keep his mouth shut and not sic Jocelyn and Helena on me with talk of our collusion?

I pulled the door open. And tried to communicate the situation with only my eyes. I hoped they were saying *Don't make this worse*, but it's likely that I just looked twitchy. "Hey," I said.

Wes was smiling, but as he looked at me, his smile changed into a weird thing, like the smile of someone who'd just discovered something. It slid up into a wide grin, and he said, "You're a good listener."

I slammed the door.

"Um?" Joss pursed her lips and Helena furrowed her brows. "What's the plan here?"

Sighing, I opened the door again and held up a hand. "Don't talk. Seriously. Can you just not say a word until we're in your car? Or maybe, like, ever?"

"Hi, Wes." Helena gave him a little wave. "I take it you found Liz this morning?"

He gave me a look that was the equivalent of a tongue stick-out and beamed at Helena. "I did—thank you. I don't think Liz appreciated my presence at her workplace, but I got there just the same."

Jocelyn tilted her head. "So you went to her work to ask her to go with you to the game tonight?"

"I did."

A casual observation: Wes had grown into a pretty attractive guy. I mean, I wasn't personally attracted to him, but the faded T-shirt he was wearing showcased some well-defined biceps. Combine the muscles with his mischievous smile and heavy-lidded dark eyes, and he was pretty fine.

Just not my type at all.

"Liz?" Joss gave me a loaded look. "Can I see you in the bathroom for a minute?"

Not a chance. "We really have to go, actually, but I'm sure—"

"I'll wait." Wes came fully inside the foyer and swung his keys around his finger. "Take your time."

Jocelyn grabbed my elbow and pulled me all the way to the tiny bathroom that sat just past the kitchen. As soon as the door closed behind us, she said, "I thought Wes's car was dead this morning."

"What?"

She sighed. "You told me that he needed a ride to the mall because his car was dead. But Helena just said that he drove to Dick's to find you."

Holy crap—Helena said that? Was I so distracted by Wes that I'd totally tuned them out? *Craaaaap.* I cleared my throat and said, "No, his car died *at* Dick's."

"That's not what you told me at the mall."

How was I supposed to remember what I told anyone anymore? Not only was lying an uncool thing to do, but it was also hard to keep on top of. "Yes, it is."

She sighed. "Whatever. The bottom line is that you are about to go on a date with Wes Bennett, girl."

"It's really more—"

"Nope." She shook her head. "For someone super into love and shit, you're kind of clueless. Now listen to me. Wes came to your house this morning, and when you weren't here, he drove all the way to your work to ask you to go to the game with him when he knows you are clueless about sports."

Oh no—*no, no, no*. She was getting the wrong idea, and if she heard the rumor that *I* actually, you know, started at the party and hadn't had the guts to tell her about yet, I was screwed. "Hey—"

"You know it's the truth. And then he pretended to need your shopping help. This is a *date*, Liz. A date."

I wanted to tell her what was really going on, but I was a coward. I knew she'd act like I was Michael's obsessed stalker, and I just couldn't hear it. I liked Wes's description better, anyway; Michael was my long-lost love. I said, "It isn't a date, but I agree that it has date potential."

Finally, something that wasn't a lie. It *did* have date potential. Just not regarding Wes.

"So do you want that?"

If I'd referenced a certain boy in a way that was easily misconstrued, well, that wasn't *my* fault, was it? I gave a shrug and said, "I don't know. I mean, he's gorgeous and fun sometimes, y'know?"

"Well, yeah, of course I know—everyone loves Wes. I just thought *you* hated him."

Was that a thing? Did everyone love Wes? I mean, it'd seemed like the attendees of the keg party adored him, but it hadn't occurred to me that it went beyond his social circle. I lived next door to him and we went to the same school. Was it possible he was loved universally without my ever knowing?

I said, "Oh, I do. But hating him is fun sometimes. So."

That made her laugh and open the door. "I don't get it, and we're going to have to talk tomorrow about this new look of yours, but I just wanted to make sure you weren't misleading our boy Wesley."

When we got back to the front door, Helena was making Wes laugh as she shared her take on the dating reality show that had had its finale the night before.

"I mean, the woman actually said the words 'I want a man who will put flower petals on my bed every single night if he thinks it makes me happy.' If that isn't a red flag, I don't know what is."

"Because who would ever want that, right?" Wes gave Helena one of his best smiles. "Someone has to clean that stuff up."

"Thank you, Wes." Helena threw up her arm in appreciation of his commiseration. "And wouldn't you have to dust the petals off the bed before boarding, anyway? I mean, nobody needs flower petals sticking to their parts, am I right?"

Wes said, "I know I don't."

Joss lost it, and Wes was laughing; I mean, it *was* pretty funny. But Helena was purposely missing the point of the romantic statement. Yeah, it maybe was a little cheesy, but there was something to be said for making the grand gesture.

My mom would have understood.

"You ready to go, Buxbaum?" Wes turned his attention to me, and my face grew hot as his eyes did a trail over my hair and outfit. I *hated* the way my complexion always showed the world what I was feeling, and I desperately wished there was a way to turn down the heat on my cheeks.

Alas, no such luck.

"You definitely *look* ready for some hoops," he said with an eyebrow raised, "but I'm still not sure you can pull it off."

"My vote is no." Jocelyn leaned in and lowered her voice. "Care to make a wager, Bennett?"

"You guys are hilarious. Ha, ha, ha—Liz knows nothing about sports." I opened the front door. "Now, I'm going to go watch the team sprain some ankles. You coming or not, Wes?"

"It's *break* some ankles." He gave Jocelyn and Helena a skeptical look that made them both chuckle as he said, "And I'm right behind you."

Helena said, "Don't forget that your dad and I are going to the movies tonight and won't be back until late."

"Okay." I pulled the door closed behind us, stressing about whatever the hell Joss was thinking now, and said to Wes, "God, you need to chill with the charm, okay?"

His eyebrows went up. "Excuse me?"

"I had to let Joss think I might like you, so cool it. Those two are your target audience; they totally go for your boy-of-mischief vibe." I gave him knock-it-off eyes and pointed at him as we approached his car. "So for the love of God turn it down, or they are going to be all over me to *actually* date you."

He opened the door for me and leaned his arms on the top of the window while I got in. "That would be the worst, right?"

"The absolute worst." He slammed the door, and I buckled my seat belt as he walked around the car. He got in and started the engine, and I couldn't help but notice that he smelled really, really good. I couldn't stop inhaling.

"Is that soap or deodorant?"

His big hand landed on the shifter, and his eyebrows crinkled when he looked over at me. "Pardon?"

"You smell really good, but it isn't your usual scent."

He didn't put the car in drive but instead just looked at me. "My usual scent?"

"Don't act like I'm weird. Your normal cologne is kind of, like, piney, but tonight you smell more . . . I don't know . . . spicy." The image of him shirtless and putting on deodorant popped into my head, and I cleared my throat, sending it away.

His voice was deep and kind of rumbly as he gave a throaty chuckle. "Holy shit, Liz Buxbaum knows my scent."

"Y'know what? Forget it." I was glad he'd just put the car in gear and was pulling away from the curb, because if he looked at me, I was certain my cheeks were crimson. "You smell like ass."

That made him slide into a full-on laugh. "Spicy, piney ass, you mean."

"Hilarious." I turned on his radio in hopes of a subject change.

It seemed to work because he said, "I can't believe you're actually wearing the clothes." He turned on his blinker and slowed for the corner. "I fully expected to see you in a grandma dress when I showed up."

"I spent money on them—of course I'm going to wear them."

He glanced over and looked directly at my outfit before returning his gaze to the road.

What the hell? I toyed with one of the threads on my shredded jeans and wondered what he thought. Not that I was thirsty for a compliment from Wes Bennett—because I so wasn't—but you couldn't look directly at someone's outfit and not comment on said outfit, right?

It was totally disconcerting. Did it not look good?

I scratched at the crisscrossing shreds and said, "I suppose I owe you a thank-you. Not for trying to *make me over*, you asswad, but—"

"Still not over that, I see."

"Because I like this outfit. I never would've noticed it on the rack, but I like it."

"See? I'm good—"

"Nope." I leaned forward and started scanning radio stations. "That's all the props you're getting from me today. Unless you want me to spew like your blond friend."

"No, thanks."

I glanced into his empty back seat. "Where are 'the guys'?"

"They're at Adam's house. We're all going to load into his minivan, and he's driving."

Just like that, my stomach was a ball of nerves. I didn't know his friends, so that was stressful enough, but the thought of sitting in the back of a minivan with Michael brought out all the worries.

Because I wanted—so badly—for him to see I wasn't Little Liz anymore.

"Everyone is super chill, so don't worry." It was like he read my mind, but before I could give it too much thought, he said, "Ooh—I like that song."

"I do too." I stopped scanning, surprised that Wes and I agreed on anything. It was "Paradise" by Bazzi, which was pretty old and pretty poppy. But it was one of those songs that just had a feel to it, like along with the notes, you also received a healthy dose of summery sunshine that kissed your shoulders as you walked downtown at dusk.

His phone buzzed at that moment, and we both glanced down at where it sat in the cupholder. The top of the little notification box said "Michael Young."

"Looks like your boy is texting."

"Oh my God!" I pictured Michael's face, and my heart speed picked up.

"You look. I don't text and drive."

"How very responsible of you," I said as I grabbed his iPhone. Holding it felt oddly personal, like I was holding the book of his social life in my hands. I wondered who was saved in his favorites, who he texted on a regular basis, and—God help me—what images lived on his camera roll.

"Not really. I just hate death and prison."

"Understandable, although I must tell you, I'm utterly fascinated by someone so casual about having their phone in someone else's hands."

"I have no secrets," he said, and I wondered if that were true.

"Passcode, please." His lock-screen picture was a shot of his dog, Otis, which was pretty dang adorable. He'd had that old golden retriever for as long as I could remember.

"Zero-five-zero-four-two-one."

"Thank you." I opened his messages and looked at what Michael had sent.

Michael: So did you talk Liz into coming?

"Holy crap—he asked if I'm coming!" I turned down the volume on the radio and said to Wes, "Does that mean he's hoping yes?"

"Since he's texting *me*," he muttered, giving me side-eye and a jaw flex, "I'm going to go with no."

"He might." I didn't like that answer. "You don't know."

"Sounds like he's just taking a head count, Liz." He looked over at me and pointed to his phone. "Want to answer him?"

"Seriously?"

He gave a shrug. "Why not?"

I inhaled. "Um, okay. Uh . . ."

"You're pathetic." Wes turned down a wooded street. "I think a solid answer would be 'Yep,' don't you?"

I said the words out loud as I texted. "Yep. We are almost there."

Send.

I was about to set the phone in Wes's cupholder when it buzzed in my hands.

Michael: Sweet. I'll put in a good word for you.

Wes (me): Awesome, dude. I glanced over at Wes, then

added: Btw, I love your hair. You have to tell me what product you use in it.

I bit my lip to hold in the smile.

Michael: You're joking, right?

I glanced at Wes again before quickly adding: Dead serious. You're my hair hero. See you in a few.

I put the phone in the cupholder and gave Wes a full smile when he pulled in front of a house and looked my way.

"This is it," he said as he put it in park, his eyes going up to my hair before returning to my face. "Ready?"

"As a heart attack."

"You know that's not right, right?"

"Yeah." Sometimes I forgot that not everyone was in my head. "I like mixed metaphors."

The side of his mouth hitched up. "How very rebellious of you, Elizabeth."

I just rolled my eyes and got out of his car.

We didn't even go up to the front door. I followed Wes as he walked around the house and opened the fence gate.

But he stopped short of going into the yard, causing me to run into his back.

"God, Wes." I felt ridiculously awkward as I rammed my breasts into his back. "What're you doing?"

He turned around and looked down at me, the tiniest hint of a smile on his lips. There was something about his smile, the way it not only showed off perfect teeth but also made his dark eyes fun and twinkly, that made it impossible not to smile back. "I just want to remind you that Michael thinks I'm trying to make ground with you. So if he doesn't seem into you, don't take it personally. He's a good guy, so he's probably going to keep his distance until he knows we're not a thing. Cool?"

I didn't know if it was the slight breeze that was doing it or the fact that he was so close, but his masculine cologne (or deodorant—he'd never answered my question) kept finding my nose and making it really happy. I inhaled again and tucked my hair behind my ears. "Are you trying to reassure me?"

His eyes squinted like he wanted to grin, but he gave his head a shake instead. "God, no. You're on your own, emotionally speaking. I'm just in this for the Forever Spot."

The smile took over my lips, whether I wanted it to or not. "Okay, good."

He tousled my hair like I was a little kid—the jag—and then started walking toward the unattached garage in the back. His sudden physicality had been jarring—familiar and strange all at once—and it took me a minute to fully recover. I could see three people standing next to the first door, and I quickly finger-combed my hair as I followed, my pulse quickening as I-don't-know-these-people nerves slithered through me.

I took a deep breath and there was Michael, talking and leaning against a rusted silver van in jeans and a black fleece jacket that made his baby-blue eyes pop. *So, so pretty.*

"Don't be nervous." Wes said it out of the side of his mouth and nudged me with his shoulder before immediately launching into introductions. "This is Noah, Adam, and you know Michael."

"Hey," I said, my face burning as they all looked at me. I was terrible with names, but nicknames would help. I committed Smirky Face (Noah), Hawaiian Shirt (Adam), and Mr. Right with the Perfect Butt (Michael, of course) to memory. Everyone was friendly enough. Hawaiian Shirt said he remembered me from middle school because we'd had the same homeroom teacher, and then he and Noah started discussing how cool Ms. Brand had been in seventh-grade reading.

It was all very bland and uninteresting, so I tuned them out and tried to look everywhere but at Michael. Tried and failed. No matter what I told my brain, my eyeballs continually searched him out and took a stroll all over his handsome face.

Wes was totally onto me, and when he made eye contact, he shook his head.

Which made me stick out my tongue.

Smirky Face tilted his head—totally saw the tongue—but Wes saved me by saying, "Are we going or what?"

We all loaded into the minivan, and just as I was about to grab a seat in the middle row, Wes pushed me toward the back and muttered, "Trust me."

He pushed around me and plopped into the left window spot, which left me the open seat right between him and Michael. I looked at Wes as I sat down, and he gave me a *Go for it* eyebrow raise that made my nose get warm as Adam started the van and pulled out of the alley.

Wes started talking to the guys in front, leaning forward to talk over the second row, *kind of* giving me and Michael a tiny bit of privacy. I cleared my throat and was hyperaware of how close his leg was to my leg. *What to say?* My mind was a complete and total blank, sending a solidly flat EKG line as my mouth ceased to function.

Time of death: 5:05.

In all the times I'd imagined our magical first moments, I'd never once considered that I would be awkwardly staring at my knees, totally mute, hoping whatever smelled mildewy in the car wasn't somehow me, while a terrible song by Florida Georgia Line twanged in the speakers behind our heads.

Michael was looking down at his phone, and I knew I was running out of time. *Say something clever, Liz.* I opened my mouth and almost said something about the party, but I closed it again when I realized that reminding him of the vomit incident—and conjuring the image of hurled-upon me for him—was a terrible idea.

Oh my God—say anything, you loser!

Then—"Liz."

My eyes jumped up to his face, but looking at him made my stomach do wild things, and I lowered my eyes to his jacket zipper to steady my nerves. Even though my face was on fire and I was pretty sure there were tiny beads of sweat on the tip of my nose, I tried to act breezy and teasing by saying, "Michael."

He smiled. "Can I tell you something?"

Oh God.

What was he going to say? What could he possibly say when he'd only been back for mere days? I braced myself for his confession that my perfume made him nauseous or that I had something disgusting sticking out of my nose. "Of course."

His eyes went up to my hair for a tiny second before they landed back on my eyes and he said, "You really look a lot like your mom now."

Was it possible to feel your own heart stop? Probably not, but there was a catch in my chest as I pictured my mother's face and had the realization that Michael still remembered her face too. He could still picture her. I had to blink fast to keep it together, because in the whole of my entire life, that was the most important compliment I'd ever received. My voice was froggy and pinched as I said, "You think so?"

"I really do." He smiled at me but looked a little unsure, doubtful in the way people always looked when they wondered if they'd made a mistake by mentioning my mom's existence. "I'm sorry about the, um, the—"

"Thank you, Michael." I crossed my legs, shifting so I was facing him a little more. The truth was, I liked talking about my mom. Bringing her up in casual conversation—putting words about her out into the universe—felt like keeping a piece of her here with me, even though she had been gone so long already. "She always liked you. I mean, it was probably because you were the only person who didn't hide under her birdbath and trample her daisies during hide-and-seek, but it counts."

His blue eyes sucked me in as he smiled and gave an incredibly pleasing deep chuckle. "I'll take it. Is that what your tattoo is about? Your mom's daisies?"

My heart for sure stopped then, and all I could do was nod in response as happy tears sprung up in the corners of my eyes.

I turned my head away from him, blinking quickly a few times. He'd seen my tattoo, and without any explanation, he'd *gotten* it. He might not have known that my mother had loved the line in *You've Got Mail* about daisies being the friendliest flower, but the flowers had made him think of her. Wes looked over at me, and his eyebrows pulled together as he went to speak, but I just shook my head. For some reason, the van began slowing even though we'd only been on the road for a few minutes.

"Why are we stopping?" Wes called up to Adam.

"This is Laney's house."

My head whipped to the left, and just past Wes's face I could see Laney through the window, exiting a big, white colonial-style home. She skipped down the steps in her dance outfit, a sparkly black leotard that would have illuminated my flaws but was coming up empty on hers, and I felt queasy as I watched her pull open the van's sliding door.

So that's why there was an open seat.

My moment with Michael and the happy memories of my mom disappeared as Laney stepped into the van and pulled the door shut behind her. Had Michael invited her? Did he want me to move so she could sit in my spot? Was she, like, his date? And I was Wes's?

"Thank you so much for coming back for me." She sat down in the seat in front of Michael, and her subtle perfume wafted back to where I was sitting, an olfactory reminder that she was amazing down to the smallest detail. She glanced back at us and said to me, "Oh, hey, Liz—I didn't know you were coming. I would've assumed you didn't like sports."

I forced a smile, but it didn't feel like my lips were fully extended as I seethed inside. Of course she was right, but why would she assume that about me? Because I didn't wear a silly letter jacket? And I was pretty sure it was no accident that she was pointing it out in front of Michael. I tried to sound breezy for the second time that night when I said, "Yet here I am."

And *dammit*—she'd made me forget to look and see what Michael's house looked like.

She faced forward and said to the guys in front, "Well, there was no way I was going to be ready by the time Michael left, but in my defense, he didn't have to put on stage makeup and squeeze into a costume either."

Everyone laughed—of course—as Laney launched into a cute diatribe about what it took to get *dance-ready.*

"I had no idea she was coming," Wes said, surprising me. His mouth was so close to my ear that I literally shivered. "I swear."

Whatever Wes said about the Forever Spot, in that moment I couldn't help but think that he was also helping me out because he was genuinely nice. Joss's words echoed in my head. *Everyone loves Wes.*

I was starting to see why.

I leaned closer to him so he could hear me when I murmured, "You were right about the whole thunder-stealing thing, though. I am actually invisible now."

He gave me a *No-you're-not* look, but I wasn't even going to try to convince myself otherwise. Laney had turned around in her seat and was giving the play-by-play directly to Michael, and a lightly sick feeling settled in my stomach. How was this fair? The girl was wearing heavy makeup, a bedazzled catsuit, and a ridiculously huge bow smack-dab on the top of her head. She should've looked like Queen of the Clowns.

But she looked *cute*.

And the worst part was that she was unbelievably charming. She somehow managed to bury her rancid soul and totally pull off that she was a genuinely delightful human being.

It was witchcraft, that.

There was no way to compete with a one-woman perfection show, so I gave up and got out my phone to read. I'd started a really good book that morning, so I picked up where I'd left off and tried getting lost in the joy of Helen Hoang.

Joss texted me a minute later.

Joss: Hey. Did you go to Ryno's party?

Shit. My stomach sank as I typed: Wes invited me at the last minute, and it was a total nightmare. I was going to tell you about it earlier but Helena interrupted.

Joss: WTH? I always invite you to my stuff.

Me: I thought about it, but you said Ryno's parties were immature bullshit, so I knew you wouldn't want to go.

Joss: I just think it's weird that you wouldn't tell me you were going. You're sketch all of a sudden.

I glanced up from my phone, searching for excuses, but all I got was the impression that Laney was brainwashing all of the boys into joining her cult of adorability. Nothing to save me from the fact that I was being a crappy friend.

Me: I was just trying to rescue you from a wholly terrible time.

Joss: Whatever. I gotta go to work now.

I sighed, telling myself I'd make it up to her somehow, and went back to reading. But I'd only read about three paragraphs when Wes said, "Mind if I read over your shoulder? I'm bored."

I gave him side-eye. "You wouldn't like this. Trust me."

"Will you shut up so I can read?"

My mouth wanted to smile but I cleared my throat and said, "Sorry."

I tried getting back into the book, but now I was hyperaware that he was reading every paragraph of the flirty, sexy-sweet book as well. I kept scrolling, but the words were different now, cartwheeling over each other with new tumbling context as the main characters started having a mildly sexual conversation.

I turned off my phone when they went into a bedroom together.

"Your cheeks are so red," he said quietly, his deep voice rich with restrained laughter. "Why'd you stop reading?"

I coughed out a laugh and faced him, his dark eyes mischievous as he gave me a knowing smirk. I said, "It's just too bumpy to read in here."

"Ah, yes." He gave me a slow nod as his lips slid into a full smile. "It's the bumpiness that made you stop reading."

"I might get carsick and vomit on you if you aren't careful."

"Oh, Liz." Laney leaned through the space between the two seats and said, "I heard about that—about Ash getting sick on you. That is so terrible. She feels *soooo* bad."

My smile went away as she put a hand over her heart and gave me an empathetic pout. Was she bringing it up on purpose to make me look bad? I shrugged and said, "What's a party if you don't get puked on?"

I heard Michael chuckle beside me and felt like I'd won that point. Laney jumped right back into her nonstop chatter, so I put in my earbuds to let the sounds of Wicked Faces drown out her nonsense. Before I hit play, I paused to offer Wes an end. He took it, and we listened in silence until we made the turn into the school parking lot.

As Adam put the car in park, Laney finally said something that made me happy. She pulled open the sliding van door and said, "Thanks again for the ride, Adam. I've got to go find the team. And don't forget—I'm riding the bus back."

That meant I would have all of the basketball game to talk to Michael—without the distraction of dreading the ride home. No one actually watched the game at sports functions, right?

Wes handed me back my earbud, but when I tried to catch his eye to silently communicate how thrilled I was at the good news, he was too busy texting someone to notice.

As it turns out, high school basketball games are incredibly loud.

I sat between Michael and Wes, and the others sat in the row in front of us. The pep band was to our left, and they seemed to be all hopped-up on deafening enthusiasm. They blasted out a constant stream of tunes that made it impossible to converse. It looked like the hope of making Michael see the real me was going to have to wait until after the game.

I was kind of okay with that, though, because I liked the vibe of the gym. The place was teeming with energy, like every single person in that gym was about to explode with their uncontrollable excitement. The team was warming up, and it felt like something big was about to happen.

Balls bounced, students climbed the steps of the bleachers looking for their friends, minutes ticked down on the giant scoreboard, and cheerleaders danced in time with the band. I looked at Laney and watched for mistakes, but of course there were none to be seen. She did every choreographed move like she'd created it, her smile never wavering as she kicked, spun, and cheered in perfect unison with the other girls.

Disappointing.

I glanced at Michael, but thankfully he was talking to the guy next to him.

Wes nudged me with his shoulder. "Having fun?" He kind of yelled it into my ear. "At all?"

I laughed into his ear. "The band is on their third performance of 'Uptown Funk,' so I really feel like it's gearing up to be a special evening."

That made him smile. He leaned in closer, but his face remained fixed on the basketball court. "All right, Buxbaum—let's make this interesting. If that guy right there," he said, pointing to number 51 on our team, "outscores number twenty-three on the other team, you win fifty bucks."

"What? Why?"

"No questions. Do you want a fitty or not?"

"Er, of course." I was fifty dollars short on THE dress, after all. "But what if he doesn't?"

"Then you wash my car."

I pictured his car. "Your car seemed pretty clean earlier. What's the catch?"

"No catch." He gave a tiny shrug, crossed his long arms, and said, "I mean, I may or may not be off-roading in Springfield tomorrow, but I wouldn't call that a catch."

"You're such a cheater." I looked at his teasing face as the band started playing "Hit Me with Your Best Shot," and I said, "But you're on. What's fifty-one's name?"

"Matt Kirk."

I watched number 51 hit a shot from behind the white line, and I turned to smile at Wes. But he wasn't watching the court. He was looking at me—smirking, actually, in a way that made my stomach do a little stutter thing. I blinked, turning back to the court, hoping he didn't notice whatever little blip that was. Then the buzzer went off, and thankfully jolted me back from whatever weird place that moment was all about.

"I had no idea y'all were so into basketball." Michael looked a little impressed by my fanhood as we walked past the concession stand and down the hallway, following Wes, Noah, and Adam.

I owed Wes a huge thanks for the fifty-buck bet, because not only had it caused me to get into the basketball game to the point that I forgot about Laney and everything else in the world, but apparently it had raised my value in Michael's eyes.

"Well, um, it's the playoffs." I knew Wes would smile if he heard me using his words. It was halftime, and we were about to sneak into Lincoln's practice gym so we could shoot around until the game restarted. By "we" I meant everyone but me.

"I take it you're pretty good friends with Matt?"

"Who?"

He looked confused, even though he was still smiling. "Number fifty-one? You were all over his game."

Duh. "Oh, yeah. Matt. We're . . . buds."

Buds? Really? Say something cool for once in your life! Something that elevates you beyond Little Liz. I cleared my throat and added, "We dated for a while, but ultimately decided that we're better as friends."

Yeah, lying definitely makes it better.

I didn't know what I was doing anymore with all the lying, to be honest. I'd always considered myself a pretty truthful person, but now I'd lied to Joss, to Helena, and to Michael. When was it going to stop?

Wes was the only one I hadn't lied to lately, and that was because I wasn't trying to please him or impress him. He *knew* the mess that I was, so there was really no point.

"Yeah, I get that." Michael's shoulder bumped mine in a casual yet—I was 99 percent sure—purposeful way. I was pretty sure my unnecessary lie had just scored me a point. He said, "I've had girlfriends like that."

"Come on." Noah was holding open a door and gesturing for us to hurry. "Get in before someone sees us."

We followed him through the door and into the practice gym. Adam found a ball over by the corner drinking fountain while the other guys decided teams.

"You playing, Buxbaum?" Wes gave me a look like I should say yes, but I knew my skill level would do nothing to help me.

"I'll watch, but thanks." I pulled the earbuds out of my front pocket—I always had at least three pairs on my person at any given time—before clicking on my music. I dropped to the floor and sat crisscross applesauce as I popped the earbuds in and watched the boys play.

And just like that, they were all-in on their halftime game. Wes and Noah were one team; Michael and Adam were the other. Noah talked nonstop shit, and his verbal sparring with Michael and Adam made me laugh because it was brutal and cocky and hilarious.

Michael made some shots, but he was overshadowed by Wes, who seemed really, really good at basketball.

This was going to be fun.

I'd never created a soundtrack for a sporty event—and my running playlists didn't count—but I always thought there was a specific magic to them. I mean, the soundtrack to *Remember the Titans*? Stone-cold ridiculous. The curator had managed a masterpiece that left the songs forever changed for every person who'd seen the film.

Who could hear "Ain't No Mountain High Enough" without picturing Blue singing in the locker room after that nightmarish practice at training camp? And James Taylor's "Fire and Rain" was completely reincarnated by that movie. I couldn't remember what I'd imagined when listening to that song before I'd seen the movie, but for the rest of my life I was always going to picture the car accident that left Bertier paralyzed.

I watched Noah dribble down the court. He bounced the ball with the confidence of one who knew the ball wouldn't be stolen from him. Inspired, I scrolled for something loud, because the game I was watching was all about noise. It was a cacophony of voices, grunts, sneaker squeaks, and bounces.

I cranked "Sabotage" by the Beastie Boys. It wasn't original, but it was perfection. I kept raising the volume as Ad Rock set the perfect backdrop for this sweaty matchup. Noah smirked as he juked around Adam, and right after the first set of record scratches, he stepped back and let go of a shot that arced high into the air before swishing into the basket. Nothing but net.

So-so-so-so listen up 'cause you can't say nothin'

Michael passed the ball to Adam, who was fast and sprinted down to the corner, but Wes was already there with his hands up. Adam bounced it over to Michael, who dribbled underneath the basket and just put it in, like it was easy.

Listen all y'all it's a sabotage . . .

Adam passed the ball right at the song's middle scream, and I was buzzing, alive in the way that I only felt when I got the matchup *exactly* right. If life was a movie, this song was meant for this moment.

Music made everything better.

When Noah popped a three-pointer to win the game, I totally sat up and yelled. Only, I was cheering my own little victory, not theirs.

Everyone instantly relaxed once the game was over, talking and casually taking shots at the basket. I scrolled to Joe Cocker's "Feelin' Alright" as I watched the sportsmanship in front of me. Noah was arguing—loudly—with Adam as they both laughed, and Wes was doing some terrible dance move beside them, also laughing.

There was something sweet in the way they moved from foes to friends, from athletic rivals to simple teenage boys, the minute that the metaphorical whistle blew the game over.

"Whatcha smilin' at?"

I jumped and my hand flew up to my heart before yanking the buds from my ears.

I turned my head at an awkward angle to see Michael standing beside me and looking down at my face.

"You scared me!"

"Sorry." He gave me a little smile, and my stomach flipped all the way upside down. His blond hair was sweaty on the outer fringes, but it was like the sweat worked as a gel and held all the spiky parts in place. His eyes were warm as he said, "You looked so happy, just sitting there with your earbuds in. I shouldn't have disturbed you."

"Oh, that's okay." I tucked my hair behind my ears and said, "I, um, I just love . . ."

Lord knows I didn't love sports, so I waved my hands, gesturing around the gym, hoping that would suffice and save me from another fib.

"Wanna shoot around?" He was smiling down at me, and I

noticed that he really *did* have great hair. He actually could be a hair hero if that were a real thing.

"I'm terribly uncoordinated," I said, and I caught a glimpse of Wes in my peripheral vision. I made the mistake of turning my head in his direction, and he gave me a double thumbs-up with a cheesy smile and eyebrow waggle.

Oh, for the love.

Michael dribbled and said, "You can't be that bad."

I returned my attention to him and said, "I *so* can."

"Come on." He stopped dribbling and held out a hand to pull me up. "I'll help your shot."

I grabbed his hand, and warmth shot through my every molecule as he pulled me to my feet. I followed him as he dribbled toward the open hoop, and as soon as we got close, he let a shot fly and it went in. I got the rebound and he said, "Let's see your shot."

It hit me at that second that we could be about to have a movie moment. I gave him a smile and said, "Here goes nothing."

Of its own accord, "Paradise" by Bazzi started in my head.

This shit feel like Friday nights
This shit make me feel alive—

I released, and watched my hard-core airball fail majorly. As in, the ball flew many, MANY feet short and to the side of the basket. When I started to laugh, Michael just smiled at me, and the look on his face was so charming, it made me want to write a poem.

Instead I said, "Are you biting the inside of your cheek so you don't laugh?"

He narrowed his eyes. "You can see that?"

"I see all, young Michael."

He gave me an adorably playful look and said, "It's actually 'Michael Young.'"

"Oh, yes," I said, "That's right."

"Well." He retrieved the ball and bounced it through his legs, giving me a half smile that made me a bit light-headed. "If you can see all, you can probably see that Wesley kind of has a thing for you."

The song stopped with a record scratch.

"Pft—whaaat? No," I stalled. Even though I knew this was the angle we were playing, I pictured Wes on the day when he'd dragged a rusted old truck bumper into The Spot just so I couldn't park there. If Michael only knew the half of it.

"I'm telling you, Liz." He passed me the ball, and I actually caught it. "The boy told me."

Oof. Suddenly the lie wasn't as easy to manage as I'd thought it would be. Wes had already talked to him? What was I supposed to say again? I bounced the ball, focusing on not letting it get out of control. "Oh. Um. I *like* Wes, but only as a friend."

"You should reconsider—he's a really good guy."

I smiled at him, trying not to beam like a lovesick fool as he stood there looking like the poster boy for everything I'd ever wanted. "Wes is *not* a 'really good guy,' Michael—come on. He's . . ." I stopped dribbling. "Wes is fun and unpredictable and the life of the party. He's got good qualities, but he is not good."

But as I said it, I didn't quite *feel* it anymore. That was how I'd always thought of him, but it was becoming clear to me that either he'd changed or I'd been wrong all along.

Michael gave a small nod as if recognizing my point. "Still."

I raised the ball to shoot, but Michael came behind me and moved my hands so I was holding the ball a different way. It felt like his fingertips burned their every groove into my skin, and I had a hard time remembering how to even use my appendages. His tanned hands were spread around my pale fingers and chipped turquoise polish, and in spite of that somehow-romantic image, I still managed to release the ball and actually send it through the hoop.

"Did you teach her that, Young?" I turned away from the basket, and there was Wes, walking up beside Michael. "Because she damn sure didn't know how to do that before."

I picked up the ball. "How would you know?"

"I know all, Buxbaum."

I rolled my eyes and dribbled in the other direction.

"I may have given some pointers, but that shot was all Little Liz," I heard Michael say. I cringed. "And by the way, about my hair."

I stopped dribbling and glanced over my shoulder. Wes's eyebrows were quirked like he was both confused and interested to hear what was about to follow. Michael touched the front of his hair and said, "I use Ieate styling pomade on the front, to get it to hold but not look rigid, and then I just put a little gel on the sides."

"I see." The corners of Wes's mouth looked like they wanted to smile, but I could tell he wasn't sure if Michael was seriously talking about his hair or being a smart-ass.

"Your hair would probably do the same thing, honestly, if you grew it out and got a good cut."

I almost laughed when I saw the change on Wes's face as he realized that Michael was dead serious. "You really think so?" Wes said.

"For sure." Michael gave Wes a pat on the shoulder, flashed an adorable grin, and said, "You can be your own hair hero."

Uh-oh.

"Um, Michael?" I had to step in and shut it down.

"Yeah?"

Shoot—I had to say something. "Erm—have you given any more thought to prom? If you're going to go with someone? Maybe a friend or whatever." Oh, for the love of Nora Ephron, that seemed way too forward. I cleared my throat and added, "What about you, Wes—are you going? It just seems like a lot of people are skipping this year. I heard."

Michael's eyes were on me, like he'd considered me for the position, and I felt electric. He said, "I'm still—"

At that same second, I heard Noah yell, "Heads up!"

Which was a half second before a hurtling basketball slammed into my face and knocked me flat on my ass.

"I am *so* sorry."

I tried to look at Noah but couldn't see him through the wadded shirt over my nose and because of the way my head was tilted all the way back. The only things I could see were shirt and ceiling. "Stop apologizing. It's fine."

It wasn't fine. I mean, it *was* in that I wasn't mad at Noah. Apparently he'd been goofing around and had tried to violently chest-pass the ball to Adam, who hadn't known and had moved out of the way at the *most* inopportune time.

Things had been going so well with Michael just before that ball had pounded into my nose. One minute we'd been having a potential movie moment, and the next there was blood gushing from my face.

And it couldn't have just been a tiny bloody nose. Nope. Not for me, not in front of Michael Young. The moment the ball hit, it was like a faucet had been turned on. Wes pulled off his shirt, shoved it against my nose, and helped me sit up while Michael squatted beside me, asking if I was okay, with concerned eyes.

My new white shirt was *covered* in blood, and my jeans were pretty splattered too. I was glad I didn't have a mirror; I was sure I'd die of embarrassment if I could see myself. No one in the world had ever looked attractive with blood pouring from an orifice.

No one.

And as I sat there bleeding, I couldn't help but wonder if the universe was sending me a message. I mean, I was more optimistic than most and I wholeheartedly believed in destiny, but I'd be lying if I said red flags weren't poised to raise.

Because both the vomit and the blood had happened right when I'd been having moments with Michael. Both times, it'd felt like we were connecting, and then *BOOM*. Bodily fluids.

"Still okay, Buxbaum?"

I couldn't see Wes's face, but his deep voice made me relax. Probably because I knew him better than the rest of them. He'd dropped to the ground beside me after shoving his shirt against my face, and the smell of him, combined with his unexpected nurturing side, kept me calm.

"Noah, you broke the girl's face."

"If you would've actually caught the pass, you bum, poor Liz wouldn't be on the transplant list."

I was starting to sightlessly recognize their voices because they never stopped jawing.

Adam said, "How can I catch something I didn't know was coming?"

"How can you not?" Noah said it around a snort. "It's called instinct."

"*Is* there such a thing as a nose transplant?" That sounded like Adam again. "Just curious."

"Listen to you with the good questions." Michael sounded like he was laughing and bouncing the basketball. "Because that's certainly relevant to this situation."

Not going to lie, it was kind of alarming how Michael was so loose and relaxed while I was practically bleeding out.

Adam said, "I can't help it if I'm a curious boy."

"You're such a nerd." Noah sounded like he was kind of laughing too.

"I still need an answer," Adam said.

"I think yes." My voice sounded weird and muffled behind the shirt. "There was a lady who got her whole face ripped off by a monkey, and she had a face transplant."

"For real?" Adam sounded fascinated. "Her whole face?"

"I'm pretty sure." The small talk was a nice distraction from my anxiety over potential nasal damage. I mean, didn't people who got their noses broken end up with massive bumps on them? Was my nose broken?

I tried squinching it up, and it freaking killed. *Shit.*

Wes's face popped into my line of sight, something to look at besides the gym ceiling. "You okay?"

He looked really concerned, and for some reason I felt compelled to reassure him. I blindly reached for his hand and gave it a squeeze. "I think it's fine. As soon as the bleeding stops, we'll probably be good."

"She's so much tougher than you, Bennett," Adam said.

"No shit." Wes adjusted one side of the shirt so I could see a little better, and I felt his big, warm hand squeeze around mine. "I'd be bawling."

Michael added, "Same."

"Oh my God, what happened?" An adult appeared in my line of sight, a blond woman with a severe bob, looking worriedly down into my face. "Are you okay, sweetie?"

I repeated what I'd said to Wes, and she suggested I try removing the shirt. She said in a knowing voice, "I bet most of the bleeding is done."

As she took a second to lecture the boys on how they shouldn't be in the practice gym, I steeled myself for moving the shirt. Even though I knew it was really immature, part of me didn't want to, because surely there were blood smears on my face. And ewwww, right? I didn't want Michael—or anyone—to see me like that.

But I took a breath and lowered Wes's shirt, glancing up at everyone.

And . . . The expressions on the boys' faces were *not* good.

Michael coughed a little and said, "Well, it doesn't seem to be bleeding anymore."

I looked at Wes. He was perpetually tactless, and I knew he'd be honest with me. "What's wrong?"

I stared at him, waiting. He was shirtless, having donated his shirt to my bloody nose, and I got momentarily distracted by the sight of his chest. I mean, I wasn't usually one to ogle anyone's physique, but my neighbor was wicked defined.

"Don't take this the wrong way," Adam said, answering before Wes and yanking me out of my pectoral revelry, "but your nose looks kind of like . . . Mrs. Potato Head's nose."

"Holy shit, that's it!" Noah nodded emphatically. "Not the rest, but for sure the nose."

Michael didn't even hide his laugh, but it was at least a warm, friendly laugh. "It *does* resemble a potato nose. And it's bleeding again."

He was right—I felt a warm trickle on my upper lip. "Oh my God!" I re-covered my nose.

"No, it doesn't; don't listen to them." Wes lifted my chin in his thumb and forefinger, and his eyes dropped down to my covered nose. "Your nose is just a tiny bit swollen."

Noah muttered, "Tiny bit?" at the same time the lady said, "You should probably go to the ER, dear. Just to make sure it isn't broken."

The ER, really? What about my Laney-free ride home with Michael? I said, "Um—"

But Wes interrupted with, "Nope, no objections. I'm taking

you to the ER, and you can call your parents on the way. Cool?"

Adam said, "Dude, you didn't drive. And quit being so bossy to the missus."

My nose was throbbing but I couldn't stop the smile. Wes's friends were ridiculous. "I don't need you to take me to the hospital. I'll call my dad."

"But Helena said she and your dad would be at the movies." Wes looked worried, which made me feel a little warm and fuzzy. *Which meant I probably had a concussion.* He looked up something on his phone and said, "The hospital is literally right down the street."

"Oh yeah." He was right about my dad and Helena, and probably about the hospital, too.

"I'm sure they can meet us there if you call them." Wes gave me his hand to help me up. "Think you can stand?"

"Of course." I let him pull me to my feet.

"You better shirt up, man." Adam made a face. "You look like a perv in just jeans, like an underage stripper."

I pressed the shirt tighter against my face as Wes grabbed his jacket from the floor and put it on over his bare chest. My cheeks were on fire—I felt like I was watching something dirty—and I shakily managed to say, "Let's go, you pervert."

But as we exited the gym, it occurred to me that Wes had donated his clothes to me twice now. Either I was on a hidden-camera show and Wes was pranking me, or he was seriously the nicest guy.

"Hair hero. Oh my God, I don't even have words." Wes's face was serious as he walked with me down the steps on the side of the school, but there was that mischievous twinkle in his eye, the one that never went away. "You think you're pretty funny, don't you?"

"I mean, yeah, I think I'm a fairly amusing person." I grabbed the metal railing and wondered how I'd ended up alone with Wes at the end of this night, instead of making magic with Michael. I was a little surprised that I didn't feel more disappointed, but perhaps that was just my body's defense mechanism to keep me from dying of embarrassment.

"What if Michael tells everyone that he's my hair hero?"

It hurt to smile but I did it anyway. Wes was acting like my nose hadn't just exploded in front of my forever crush, and I loved him for it. He was picking up right where our convo would've headed if not for my accident. "He won't."

"Because I could do so much better." He started naming people as we walked down the dark sidewalk. "Like, Todd Simon—that guy's got some good hair. And Barton Brown—you could get lost in Barton's shiny mane. Those guys are worthy of hair heroism. Those guys are worthy of follicle adoration. But Michael Young? Puh-leeze."

"You could never get Barton Brown; be realistic."

"I *so* could get Barton. He'd probably lose it if I asked him to be my hair hero."

"You would never ask him, Wes, and you know it. He's in another hair league."

"Why are you hurting me like this?"

"Sorry." I tried not to stare as we walked under a streetlight, but I realized as I looked at him that his face was always fun. He almost never looked pissed or like an asshole, and I couldn't imagine him being legitimately angry. "I guess I'm projecting."

He glanced over at me and gave me a closed-mouth pity-frown. "How *is* the honker feeling?"

"It doesn't really hurt now. Except when I touch it."

"So don't touch it."

"Really?"

He shrugged and put his hands in his jacket pockets. "Seems logical."

I was getting sick of holding that shirt over my nose. I pulled out my phone and flipped the camera to make a mirror, then stopped walking and slowly removed the shirt from my face. "Oh my God, I *am* Mrs. Potato Head."

The bridge of my nose was so swollen that the entire thing looked wide. It was like my nose blended in with the rest of my face.

The good news: when I tilted my head back, it didn't look like any more blood was waiting to fall.

This whole thing was just gross.

"I've broken my nose twice, and it'll heal fast." He put his finger on my phone screen and unflipped the camera so I could no longer see myself. "You might look like a child's toy for a day, but after that you'll barely be able to tell."

I glanced at his profile in the dark and didn't see any bumps or knots in his nose. But I said, "Define 'barely.'"

He ignored me and said, "Call your dad."

"Oh yeah." I exited the camera and went into the actual phone. "Thanks."

I called my father as Wes stood beside me on the sidewalk, scrolling on his phone, and after I told my dad what'd happened and then retold Helena, they said they were headed toward the hospital and they'd find us when they got there.

"By the way, thanks a lot." I put my phone into my pocket and looped the disgusting shirt over the strap of my bag, and we started walking again. With every step I tried to figure out what was up with Wes's sudden-onset niceness. The guy was apparently all-in on getting that parking spot. "You didn't have to escort me."

He nudged my shoulder with his and teased, "My luck, you'd bleed to death and then my guilt wouldn't allow me to enjoy the Forever Spot."

"Wait—you'd still take it, even after having a hand in my untimely demise?"

I attempted to give him a playful punch, but he caught my fist in his huge hand. He grinned at the little noise I made and let go.

"Well, it's *right there,* Buxbaum—how could I not?"

We stopped at a red light when we reached the corner, and he turned and looked at me. We were quiet for a moment, our smiles slowly simmering, and then he asked in his deep-and-gravelly voice, "So were you making any headway with Young before you got bashed?"

I don't know why, but I was hesitant to tell him for a second. We'd been having fun and I didn't want to get serious. But then I reminded myself that it was my let's-get-Michael teammate, Wes. Why *wouldn't* I tell him? "You know, I think I was. He was being a little flirty before you walked over to the small court, and he *physically* moved my arm to help me shoot better."

"Sweet Lord, he touched you?" His eyes widened like this was a really big deal.

"He did." I proudly raised my chin.

"Like, *how* did he do it? Was it coachy and clinical, or . . . ?"

"It was like this." I reached over and moved his elbows from their position at his sides to a few inches higher in the air. "Only maybe lighter and more fingertippy."

"Holy shit, Liz." He gave his head a little shake and his mouth was wide open. "That's huge."

My lips slid all the way up into the beamingest geek smile ever, even though it sent a jolt of pain through my nose. "It *is*?"

"Oh my God, no. It isn't." Wes put his hands in his pockets and gestured for me to walk, as the light had turned green. "That was sarcasm. I thought you knew that until you said 'fingertippy.'"

"Oh." I cleared my throat and said, "Well, it *felt* like something."

"Like something *fingertippy*?"

As he mocked my words and my Michael obsession, it hit me that everything was all wrong. Wes was the one walking me to the hospital, and it was Wes's shirt that'd staunched the flow of blood from my face.

Wasn't it supposed to be Michael?

He glanced over again, his expression unreadable as we walked up to the entrance of the ER. Just before the doors opened, he said, "You don't seriously think his fingertippiness was a thing, do you?"

"How should I know?" I shivered in the cold and wondered why Wes all of a sudden seemed a little cynical. "It could've been."

He let out a noise that was a cross between an exhalation and a groan. "How are you so bad at reading signals?"

"Wha—"

"Liz." My dad stepped out through the hospital doors and rushed at me, his face harsh with worry. "We were literally at the theater across the street. How's the nose?"

We went through the doors, and Helena, waiting beside the check-in desk, glanced at Wes and gave me a funny smile. Which immediately stressed me out on top of everything. The last thing I wanted was my dad to be looped into the false narrative of me and Wes being a thing.

Wes was nice to them and did the small-talk thing for a few, but he didn't really even look at me the rest of the time. When he left, he said, "Later, Buxbaum," and just kind of threw his arm up in a wave before disappearing.

I wasn't sure what to think. He couldn't be *mad* at me, could he? Why the weirdness? Was it all in my head?

I texted Joss about my nose (leaving out any Michael references, of course) while we waited for the doctor, because I knew she'd appreciate the ridiculous story. Her response:

Joss: Wes Bennett took you to the hospital??

Me: Yeah, but he was my ride so it was no big deal.

It felt good to text her about my nose, probably because it was safe territory. It had nothing to do with senior year—her obsession—and nothing to do with my Michael scheme.

Joss: SO?? OMG! Methinks Mr. Bennett has a crush . . .

So much for safe. I knew it was weird, but as I sat there on the paper-covered exam table, I missed my best friend pre–senior year. I missed being silly and obnoxious and 100 percent myself without having to dodge unwelcome emotional conversations.

Me: Shut up—I have to go.

Joss: Will Monday work for dress shopping since there's no school?

See? I missed being able to text more than one sentence before stress and conflict came into our conversations. I felt like the total worst, but it didn't stop me from texting:

Me: I think I have to work—SERIOUSLY—don't be mad.

Joss: Shut up—I have to go, loser.

Ugh. I really needed to do the shopping thing before her feelings got hurt. Joss was a strong person with a lot of opinions, but underneath her stubbornness she was sweet and extremely sentimental.

Which was why we *usually* got along so well—we both were.

The doctor finally came in, and after poking and prodding my tender beak, she determined it wasn't broken. She said it would look normal in a day or two, so I only had to Potato-Head it for a couple days. By the time we got home, it was eleven and I was exhausted. I showered and crawled under my covers, and was almost asleep when my phone buzzed.

I rolled over and looked at the screen. It was a text from a number I didn't know.

Unknown: Hey, Liz—it's Michael. Just wanted to check on you.

"Oh my God." I fumbled for my glasses and turned on my lamp. *Oh my God!* I stared at the phone. Michael Young was texting to see if I was okay. Holy shit. I took a shaky breath and tried to think of a response that didn't make me sound like a dweeb.

Me: Well, my Mrs. Potato Head nose isn't broken so it's all good. 🙂

Him: Haha glad to hear it. Wes told me you refused all pain meds at the hospital because you're a badass, so I figured that was the case.

Note to self: thank Wes for that one. I smiled and rolled over onto my stomach. It was like I could hear his rich, drawling voice speaking his texts aloud. It made me feel like rolling on the bed and kicking my feet like when Julia Roberts freaked over three thousand dollars in *Pretty Woman*.

Me: He's right about my badassery, by the way.

Him: Um, I seem to remember a girl who cried when she got wet.

I rolled my eyes and wished he could forget that little girl.

Me: That girl was left behind a LONG time ago. Trust me when I tell you that you don't want to mess with the new Liz. 😉

Him: Is that so?

Oh God—was he flirting? Was Michael Young actually flirting with me? I was beaming like the nerd I'd always been, as I typed, That is most definitely so.

Him: Well, I guess I might just have to get to know this new Liz.

I died. I don't know how I managed to text from beyond the grave, but I was cool.

Me: I guess you might have to. If you think you've got the coconuts for it.

Him: What?

Aw, geez. What was he whatting? The coconuts? I was such an awkward texter.

Me: I meant that you might have to, if you think you're up for it.

Him: Got it.

I didn't want to ruin the chance to have a text conversation with Michael, but once again I was drawing a total blank on what to talk about. School, basketball, nose . . . hmm.

Me: So what are you doing right now?

Him: Texting you.

Well, that wasn't much of a help.

Me: Sounds exciting.

Him: What does?

Was this for real? Was I really this awful at textual chitter-chatter? Shit.

Me: Nothing. On a random side note, I'm starving. Send food. SOS.

Him: I have to go get my pizza out of the oven because the smoke alarm is about to go off and wake my parents, but put me in your contacts. I'll text you sometime.

I was going to pass out.

Me: You got it.

Him: Night, Liz.

I slowly set down the phone on my nightstand. Um . . . I was pretty sure I was excited. But what did it mean? Was I back in the game? I wasn't sure, but he'd cared enough to get my number—I was guessing from Wes—and to personally text and see how I was feeling.

So even though it'd been awkward, it was still a good sign, right?

The love theme I'd written when I was seven suddenly came back to me full blast. *Liz and Mike, love and like, together forever in all kinds of weather.*

After I came down from my emotional roller-coastering, I got tired again and my nose started throbbing.

And I started worrying.

Because I had no idea what'd happened with Wes at the hospital. One minute we'd been walking there, doing our usual schtick, and the next it had seemed like he was mad.

And I hated the thought of him being mad at me, especially after he'd been so nice since the moment he'd picked me up that night.

I grabbed my phone from the nightstand and dialed his number, unaccountably nervous as I heard it ring. I thought it was going to voicemail when he picked up on the fifth ring.

"Hey, Libby Loo." Wes sounded tired, or like he hadn't used his voice in a while. It had that gravelly thing going on. "What's up?"

I pulled my covers up under my armpits and ran my finger over the stitching on my comforter. "Did I do something to piss you off at the hospital?"

"What?" I heard him clear his throat before he said, "No."

"Because you seemed . . . um, terse . . . ? When you left?" I sounded like a nervous middle schooler, and I rolled over onto my side. "I'm just sorry if I said something to upset you."

"Wow." I could hear the smile in his voice. "I had no idea you cared so much about making me happy."

"Okay, stop *that*." I laughed—which hurt my nose—and I said, "I just wanted to make sure we're cool."

"We're cool, Lib." His voice was deep as he said, "I promise."

I rolled over onto my other side, trying to get comfortable. "Did you give Michael my number, by the way?"

"Yeah, I did. He wanted to check on you."

"And he did!" I was smiling again and squealing a little. "He texted me to see how I was doing."

"And? How's the honker?"

"It's okay." I rolled onto my back and looked up at my ceiling fan. "Sore, but I'll live. I still look like a freak, but the doctor said the swelling will go down soon."

"That's good." Wes cleared his throat and said, "If I tell you something, you have to promise not to ask me more than three questions."

Oh God. What could he possibly want to say that I wasn't allowed to give him the third degree about? "What are you talking about?"

He sighed, and I could hear a TV in the background. "Just promise, Buxbaum, and I swear you'll fall asleep smiling."

I didn't know why, but something about Wes saying those words made my stomach dip. I swallowed. "Okay, I promise."

"Okay. So when we were playing basketball earlier, Michael mentioned your look."

"What did he say?" I kind of shouted it as I sat straight up in bed. "What did he say?"

"I don't remember his exact words—"

"Come on, Wes, you've got one job and it's—"

"—but he essentially said that he could see why you're so popular."

Oh my God. I glanced at Fitz, who was curled up in the corner on top of a crumpled Barnes and Noble shopping bag, and I hoped it wasn't *all* about my look. "What did he say, exactly?"

"I already told you that I don't remember his exact words, goofball. But the general sentiment was that he gets it. You're no longer Little Liz."

"Oh." I flopped back down onto my back, conflicted. A tiny part of me was uncomfortable with that. Like, before I straightened my hair and put on a cookie-cutter outfit, he couldn't understand how Wes could be interested in me? When I looked the way *I* liked looking, it was inconceivable to him that Wes would find me attractive? That kind of stung.

I pictured Michael and told myself not to get hung up on it. The bottom line was that he had noticed me. "Did he say it cute, like, 'Ooh, dude, I totally get it now,' or was it more matter-of-fact?"

"We were playing basketball. He was panting and grunting."

"You're terrible at this."

"No, you're just a weirdo."

"Why didn't you tell me about this earlier?" I glanced toward my window, where all I could see in the darkness was the side of his house. It was a little surreal that I was talking to Wes like he was a friend, when he'd always been my neighborhood nemesis. "There was plenty of time when you were walking with me to the hospital."

"I was distracted by your Potato Head face and the concern that you were going to pass out from lack of blood." He cleared his throat. "As soon as the image of your ginormo-nose left my mind, I remembered to tell you."

I tried to picture him on the other end of the phone. Was he still fully dressed, or was he wearing adorable pajamas and snuggling with his dog? "Where's your room?"

"What?"

I sat up in bed and crossed my legs. "Total random curiosity. Your house is outside my window, and I just realized that I've never been upstairs, so I have no idea what side your room is on."

"Put the binoculars away because my room faces the back. You've got no shot of a peep show."

"Yeah, because that was what I wanted." My mind instantly conjured the image of his half-naked body in the practice gym. When he'd taken off his shirt and I'd nearly swallowed my tongue. You know, while also bleeding out.

"And I'm not in my room. I'm in the living room, watching TV."

I got up and walked over to my window. My bedroom was the only one with a window on the side of the house, and when I looked down, I could see the light glowing out their living room window.

"I can see your light."

"*Such* a creeper."

That made me smile. "What're you watching?"

"I think the proper line is 'What are you wearing?'"

I couldn't stop smiling—that was so incredibly Wes. It was weird how talking to him was so easy—way easier than texting with Michael. I wasn't sure if it was because I knew Wes better, or perhaps it was because Wes knew *me* better. He knew I wasn't cool—he'd always known that—so maybe that was why it felt so relaxed.

I didn't have to try.

I said, "Maybe if I cared it would be, but I'm actually curious about what you're watching."

"Guess."

I crossed my arms and leaned against the wall, looking out at the side of his house where there were flowering bushes moving in the breeze under his lit living room window. "Probably a game of some sort. Basketball?"

"Wrong."

"Okay. Is it a movie or a TV show?"

"Movie."

"Hmm." I grabbed my beanbag and slid it in front of the window. I felt like I needed to be looking at his house. I plopped down and asked, "So, I need to know. Did you select it, or did you just happen to stop by when remote-flipping?"

"Remote stop-by."

"Hm. That complicates things." Mr. Fitzpervert jumped onto my lap and put his front paws on my chest so I would scratch his head. I approved of the paisley bow tie that Helena must have selected for him, since I'd left him tieless when I was in a hurry that morning. "Um . . . *Gone Girl*?"

"Nope. But decent guess. I thought Emily Ratajkowski was brilliant in that flick. Her scene with Affleck is still embedded in my brain."

"You're disgusting."

There was laughter in his voice as he said, "I'm just messing because I *knew* you'd know what I meant. My little Libby is just so easy to get riled up."

I ignored his comment, the incorrigible boy. "Well, the book was amazing, even without Miss Ratajkowski's assets."

"Agreed."

"Okay." I tried thinking about what would make Wes stop and watch. "Um, maybe *The Hangover*?"

"Nope."

"*American Pie*?"

"Not even close."

"In what era," I started, wondering if maybe I had him pegged totally wrong, "did this cinematic masterpiece come out?"

"I feel like you're assuming that I only like boob movies."

"Um." His assumption about my assumption was correct, but now I was having doubts. The more I knew about Wes, the more he proved my preconceived notions wrong. "Yeah, that's pretty much it."

"I'm watching *Miss Congeniality.*"

"What?" I almost dropped the phone. "But, Bennett. That's a rom-com."

"Yup."

"So . . . ?"

"So, I stopped because it looked funny."

"And . . . ?"

"And it is."

"I love that movie. What channel?"

"Thirty-three. Wait—your parents still have cable too?"

"Yes. My dad is afraid to cut the cord because he isn't sure if he'll get all the good boxing matches if we switch to streaming." I flipped on my TV and turned it to the movie. It was the beginning, where Sandra Bullock's character was eating steak with Michael Caine at a restaurant. "The thought of losing them terrifies the man."

"It's soccer for my dad. He's convinced that all you can watch on Hulu are movies and NBC shows."

That made me smile. Wes's dad was a super-nerdy college professor who I never would've pegged as a fan of anything athletic. "Do you think we'll be technology-challenged when we're old too?"

"Oh, for sure. You'll probably be one of those old people who doesn't even have a TV. Every day will be the same. You'll play the piano, drink tea, and listen to records for hours, then take the bus to the movie theater."

"You make aging sound incredible. I want that life now."

"So do you sing when you play?"

"What?"

"I've always wondered. When you play the piano, do you sing?"

He'd "always" wondered? Did that mean he'd thought of it often? When we were kids and I practiced with the windows open, he used to howl like he was a dog and it was hurting his ears. I guess I hadn't realized he knew I still played.

I hadn't heard him howl in a lot of years.

"It depends what I'm playing." It seemed incredibly personal, sharing this with him, but it also didn't feel wrong. Probably because I'd known him so long. I glanced over at the piano book sitting on my desk. "I don't really sing when I'm doing scales or warm-ups, and I definitely don't sing if I'm playing something super challenging. But when I play for fun, look out."

He said around a laugh, "Gimme a song that makes you belt."

"Umm . . ." I giggled. I couldn't help it. Sharing private things about myself while sitting in the dark made me feel . . . *something*. Some kind of way.

Maybe I was just feeling introspective, because—out of nowhere—I realized that my life for the past few days had felt different. I was suddenly living this stereotype of a high school life. I'd gone to a *booze* party, and the following night I'd loaded into a car with a bunch of people to watch a high school sports game.

And my love interest had texted me.

Not only that, but I was talking on the phone to the boy next door as if it was a thing.

Those things were normal, but not for me.

And it was fun. All of it. Even with the vomit and the bloody nose. And it kind of made me wonder if I'd been missing out. Most of the time, I preferred staying home and watching movies. That was my happy place. Joss had her softball friends that she went out with, and even though she always invited me, I always chose to stay home with my rom-coms.

But now I was questioning that decision.

Wes jerked me back out of my head. "'Umm' is not an answer, dipshit."

"I know, I know, I know." I laughed and admitted, "I actually pretty much turn into Adele when I play 'Someone Like You.'"

"You do *not.*" He was full-on laughing now. "For real? That's a big-voice song."

"Don't I know it." I pulled the blanket from my bed, lifted Fitz from my lap, and wrapped us both up in it. "But when no one's home, it feels amazing to totally shatter glass with my pipes."

"I would pay money to hear that."

Fitz gave me a deep-throated growling meow and ran up my body, jumped off my shoulder, and escaped from my room. I said, "You'll never have enough."

He made a comment, but I didn't hear what it was because I got distracted by the fact that his living room light went out. Was he still in that room? Was he getting comfy on the couch? He didn't sound like he was walking. "How come you turned off the light?"

My hand went to my mouth out of habit—that was a nosy question to be embarrassed about—but then I remembered it was just Wes. I could say these unfiltered things to him because he didn't care. Wes Bennett knew what a mess I was underneath it all, and there was a little bit of joy in knowing he saw the real me.

Freedom.

I would *never* ask Michael why he'd turned off his light (if he lived next door). That would be a total creeper move.

"I *knew* you were staring in my windows, Buxbaum." Wes did a deep chuckle thing that made me laugh too. "I never would've guessed someone so uptight would be such a pervert."

I stared out at his dark window. "I'm not that uptight, for the record."

"I will say that you've been pretty cool about the disasters that have befallen you since you started hunting Michael."

"Um . . . thanks? And I'm not 'hunting' him. I'm just trying to . . ."

I blinked—what exactly *was* I trying to do? Michael was it—the guy. Just like in the book we were reading in Lit—*The Great Gatsby*—he was the green light across the bay, the symbol of the dream, the cohesive-thread-come-full-circle love interest that my mom had written into all of her scripts. I guess I was trying to put the happy ending on my script, so to speak. I said, "I just need to know that happily ever after really exists."

He was quiet for a minute, and then he said, "I think your cat is out in my yard."

I was grateful for the change of subject. "It isn't Fitz. He never goes outside."

"Smart cat—my dog would probably use him as a chew toy."

"As if Fitzpervert would let him." I looked back out the window and tried to see a cat, but all I could see was a dark yard and the white flowers on my mother's bushes. "So where are you? Did you go to bed, or are you sitting in the dark like a complete Patrick Bateman?"

"Oh my God, you're so obsess—"

"Will you just shut up and tell me?" I was laughing—hard—and it made my nose throb a little. "I need to go to bed."

"And you can't sleep until you know where I am. I see you."

"So delusional. Just forget it."

My face literally hurt from smiling, and out of nowhere I wondered what things were going to be like with me and Wes when our deal was over. Would he go back to only thinking of me as his weird neighbor, only noticing me when he felt like messing with me? Would we return to just being classmates who didn't particularly like each other?

The thought of that made my stomach get a little heavy.

I didn't like it.

He laughed and the lights flashed in his living room. On-off, on-off. "I'm still here, Liz. Just messing with you."

"Okay, well, good ni—"

"Your turn."

"Huh?"

"Flash your lights. It's my turn to know where you are."

Fair was fair. I leaned over and flicked on my desk lamp, wondering if he was going to walk over to the window in order to be able to see up to my room.

"So that's your room, huh?"

Apparently yes. "It is."

Could he see me? I didn't think so—my beanbag was pretty low—but I still felt exposed.

"Wow." He let out a low whistle. "Not gonna lie, there's

something about knowing that that is where Mrs. Potato Head sleeps. I mean, damn, you know?"

I leaned forward and waved into the darkness. "Damn, indeed. Good night, dipshit."

He gave me a deep, rumbly chuckle but didn't say anything about the wave. "Good night, Elizabeth."

Instead of going back to bed, I went over to my dresser and grabbed the pink photo album. Talking about happy endings and staring out at my mom's favorite bushes had given me the mom-feels.

Although, lately *everything* had been giving me those.

I spent the next hour looking at pictures of my mother; her wedding photos, shots of her holding me when I was a baby, and the funny surprise takes my dad liked to snap when she hadn't been expecting them.

When I got to the photos from one of the neighborhood picnics, I squinted and smiled at the group shot. My mom had been dressed in a paisley sundress and pearls, while everyone else looked like shoeless summer slobs. So on-brand for her, right?

My eyes scanned to the front row, where we kiddos—probably age seven at the time—looked eerily similar to our current selves. Not in appearance, but in expression. The twins were looking away from the camera with their mouths wide open, clearly up to something. Michael was smiling like a perfect little model, and I was beaming at him instead of looking at the photographer. Joss was making an adorable little smirk, and Wes—of course—had his tongue all the way out.

Something about that photo album made me feel good about the present, but I was getting too tired to analyze it. Also my Potato Head nose was aching. I put away the pictures, shut off the light, plugged my phone in, and went back to bed. But just before I fell asleep, I got one more message.

Wes: Make sure you add "Someone Like You" to the Wes and Liz playlist.

CHAPTER SEVEN

"I'd rather fight with you than make love with anyone else."

—*The Wedding Date*

"Good morning, sunshine."

I grunted and went straight for the Keurig. I adored my father, but the sight of his bright-eyed, smiling face peeking out from behind the newspaper at the breakfast table was just a little too much. My eyes didn't want to be open, and I definitely didn't want to engage in chipper morning conversation after being up all night with a throbbing nose.

"How's the honker?"

I smiled—that's what Wes had called it—and hit the button that made the water warm. "Sore, but I'll survive."

"You work today?"

"Yup—I'm the lucky opener."

He closed the paper and started folding it. "Did you fill out the dorm paperwork I sent to your email?"

Crap. "I forgot. I'll do it today."

"You have to stop putting it off. If you're old enough to go to college on the other side of the country, you're old enough to fill out a few forms."

I sighed. "Got it."

File that under Another Thing Liz Was Avoiding. I was dying to go away to school and get started at UCLA. I was even looking forward to the actual studies. Classes on music curation wouldn't seem like work, would they? But every time I thought of *living* there, I got this huge ball of dread in my stomach that had nothing to do with California and everything to do with leaving the only place I'd ever lived with my mother.

And the few times I'd allowed myself to consider the reality that I would no longer be able to just toss on my running shoes and see her at the cemetery, my vision instantly blurred with tears and my throat felt like it was closing.

So, yeah. I had some issues to resolve there.

He gave me a dad look. "Quit procrastinating. The early bird gets the better dorm room, Little Liz."

"Hey. Speaking of that." I put the pod into the machine and closed the top. "Was I a nice little weirdo when I was a kid?"

He cocked an eyebrow. "Come again?"

I hit the button, and the Keurig started whirring. "Wes said that back in the day, I was a *nice little weirdo*, and I just don't remember it that way. Is he right?"

My dad's face split into a wide smile. "You don't remember it that way?"

"Not at all." I stared at the coffee as it spat into my cup. "I mean, I maybe wasn't supercool, but—"

"You were definitely a strange little kid."

"What?" I looked at his grin and was torn between laughing and being annoyed. "I was not."

"You made our deck into a wedding chapel when you were seven—remember that? You spent *days* setting it up with stolen flowers from your mom's garden and white sheets. You tied a string of empty corn cans to Fitz's collar."

"So? That's some impressive creativity right there."

He gave a little laugh as I joined him at the table. "That's right—that part was cute. The part that was weird was when you talked that kid who used to live on the corner—Conner something—into pretending to marry you. He let you boss him around until you told him that it was legal and he was married to you forever. Then he tried going home, but you tackled him to the ground and said he couldn't leave until he carried you over the 'tressel.'"

"A reasonable expectation from a bride."

"He cried until we finally heard his wails through the screen door, Liz."

I blew on my coffee. "I'm still waiting for the weird part."

"You broke your black oval glasses in the scuffle and you still wouldn't let him up."

"He should've stayed put like a good husband."

He started laughing and so did I. So maybe I *had* been a little weird.

• • •

"Excuse me—do you work here?"

I rolled my eyes as I tried to finish shifting the bottom row of middle-grade fiction to the next shelf over. I'd made it through a full morning of *What happened to your nose?* at the cash register, so I'd switched to stocking new releases in hopes of avoiding further human contact.

I stood from my squat and turned around.

And almost swallowed my tongue when I saw Michael. "Oh my God—hey."

"Hey, Liz." His face jumped into a big grin. "I didn't know you worked here."

"Yeah." I *so* wanted to cover my hideous nose and maybe disappear. He'd been the instigator of our text conversation last night, but I felt weird about how awkward it'd been.

"I'm impressed." His hands slid into his pockets and he said, "Two jobs *and* school?"

"What?"

"I can't believe you wait tables *and* work here, when I don't even have *one* job at the moment."

Ugh—"The" Diner. My lies were really becoming difficult to manage. "What can I say? I like money."

I felt my breath hitch as I looked at him. He was wearing a button-down plaid shirt—not casual plaid flannel, mind you, but, like, a *nice* shirt. And it was paired with perfect pants and leather shoes that looked like they belonged on a fancy boat. He looked beautiful and classy, like someone who could successfully win an argument without raising his voice.

I bit down on my lower lip and tried not to stare at his perfect face. "Is there something I can help you find?"

His smile turned into a self-deprecating, embarrassed smirk. "I'm looking for a book. It showed up as available online, but it isn't in the section."

"What book?"

He looked like he didn't want to tell me. He put his hands in his pockets and said, "Okay, don't laugh. I'm looking for *The Other Miss Bridgerton* by Julia Quinn."

I rolled my lips inward and tilted my head, trying to figure out what the story was. I'd read that book—I mean, I'd read all of the Bridgerton novels—but historical romances were typically read by women. "Why would I laugh? That's a great book."

His eyes narrowed. "Are you being sarcastic?"

"Not at all. I love everything Quinn has ever written."

His mouth loosened a little in relief. "You're judging me for reading them because I'm a guy, though, aren't you?"

Hmmm . . . let's see. A guy who reads romance—really, really good romance? Someone who doesn't care about labels and loses himself in books about clever, funny heroines and the men who appreciate their individuality?

No judgment here. A little light-headed smittenness, perhaps, but no judgment.

I casually rested my hand over my horrible nose and said, "Absolutely not. I'm kind of curious how you picked them up, but I sincerely think they're of Jane Austen quality."

That made his mouth curl in a tease. "You don't think that's maybe a stretch?"

"Trust me, Michael, you don't want to debate this with me. I've got a four-hour shift in front of me and an obsessive love of romance books. You can't win this one."

He gave a chuckle that reached his eyes, squinting them in the warmest way. "Noted. And for the record, it all started with a bet."

"As all good things do." Before the last word left my lips, an image of Wes's face popped into my head. All day long I'd been replaying our phone call, the gravelly sleepiness of his voice as we'd watched *Miss Congeniality* together from two separate houses.

Michael laughed again, and just like that I was back in the present and we were both smiling all over each other next to the secondhand Judy Blume section. He crossed his arms in front of his chest and said, "A friend of mine challenged me to read *The Duke and I* a few years ago. She put money on the idea that if I actually read it, I would like it."

I loved that book. "And that was it?"

"That was it." He gave me a sheepish smile and said, "Besides, what's more fun than a story that starts with a fake relationship?"

Every fiber of my being wanted to laugh maniacally at the words he'd just spoken, but I nodded and said, "I wholeheartedly agree."

"You *do* know that your hand isn't doing anything to cover your nose, right? I can still see it."

I rolled my eyes, which made him grin. I dropped my hand

and said, "It's just so atrocious that I can't help but try to cover it, y'know?"

"I get it, but it doesn't look bad at all compared to last night. Maybe a little swollen, but that's it."

"Thanks. You know, for lying to me." I owned a mirror, so his words only served to confirm that he was as nice as he'd ever been. And that accent? Oh, baby. I gestured for him to follow me. I knew exactly where to find the book he was looking for, and it was on the other side of the store. "I do think it *is* shrinking, even though it's still Potato Head-y."

"Agreed."

"So how are your parents?" I glanced over my shoulder. "Catch me up."

"Well, the folks are good," he started, and I wondered if his parents were still super serious. I had blurry memories of thick glasses and frowning mouths.

"Do you still have cats?" I'd *loved* that he liked cats better than dogs. It had been another reason why he always seemed smarter than the rest of the neighborhood kids. "Purrkins and Mr. Squishy?"

"I can't believe you remember their names." He was grinning again, looking the kind of happy that made me want to eat his face off. "Squish lives with my grandma now, but Purrkins still resides with us, tormenting us on the daily with his shitty cat attitude."

"His cattitude." I stopped in front of the large-print section. "Good boy."

My mind went to Wes then, because when we'd talked on the phone the night before, he'd asked if my cat was outside. It'd taken forever for me to fall asleep once I got into bed, mostly on account of the incessant smiling that I was doing as I recalled our conversation.

The growly sound of his voice when he teased, *And you can't sleep until you know where I am. I see you.*

Michael said, "Speaking of Wes—"

"What—I wasn't," I blurted, blinking fast while trying to figure out what the hell I'd missed, and what words he'd been saying as I'd zoned out.

Michael frowned as he looked at me strangely and said, "I really think you should give him a shot."

Wait, what?

Michael had already done his wingman duty by mentioning it to me at the basketball court, right? Sure, they were friends, but if he had any thoughts about me that went beyond friendship, it seemed like he wouldn't be pushing so hard.

But *he* had texted me, and *he* had been the playful one. So what did it all mean? I needed a bulletin board and some string at this point. As we got to the Quinn section, I said, "A *shot*. What constitutes a *shot*, exactly?"

He reached up and pulled the book from the shelf. "Just get to know him."

"I already know him."

"The *now* him, not the *hide-and-seek* him." He opened the book and flipped through the pages. "Wow—those are some large words."

"Sorry, we only have the large-print edition in stock."

"Anyway," he continued, giving me enough eye contact to make me fidget. "He likes you, Liz. Honestly, I've only been here for a few days, and I can't get him to shut up about you."

What exactly was Wes saying when I wasn't around? Was he playing it up too much? Because if he did, the plan might totally backfire. I said, "He doesn't even really know me—he knows the *hide-and-seek* me."

"Just *try*—that's all I'm asking. Go out with him and try."

I looked at him and gnawed on the corner of my lip. "Are you asking me out *for* him?" *How in the flipping flip were Wes and I going to get out of this?*

That made him smile again. "Not at all. But I'm having people over Wednesday night to watch movies since seniors have late-start Thursday, and y'all should come."

I swallowed and teased, "You mean together, right?"

That made him smile. "Just carpool with Wes. Please?"

God, this whole thing was starting to spin out of control. Now Michael was having people over so Wes could make a move. But Wes was only pretending to think I was amazing to show Michael how amazing I was. I was getting whiplash, and this was my own plan. I needed to end it soon. I asked, "What if, after that, I still only like him as a friend? What then?"

"No harm, no foul." His eyes moved over my face, and it felt like a moment. It felt like he was really seeing me, or considering something about me, and I wondered just how bad my nose looked.

"Fine," I said. Maybe he was giving his friend one last shot before he moved in. I said, "I'll give him a *shot*."

"Yes." He beamed down at me and did a little fist pump thing. "Now if you'll excuse me, I'm going to take my romance novel home and read it in a steamy bubble bath."

I laughed. "Go treat yourself, honey."

"It was just straight-up adorable, Ma." I leaned back against the headstone and crossed my ankles, inhaling the smell of fresh-cut grass. Sometimes April was slow to hit in Nebraska, with the occasional late snowstorm blowing in to destroy the promise of spring, but not this year.

Birds were chirping in the budding leaves of the cemetery's tall trees, the evening sun was warm(ish), and that springtime feeling of anticipation floated through the air, along with the smell of the blossoming chokecherries.

"Not only was he buying a romantic book that no typical insecure male would ever admit to reading, but he was funny and charming and, between you and me, flirty with his eyes. Flirty with his eyes, and he'd been for *sure* flirty with his text last night. I think he thinks . . . I don't know, I don't want to say he thinks I'm cool, but maybe funny . . . ? Yeah, I'm pretty sure he thinks I'm funny."

I pictured his laughing face again—for, like, the twentieth time since he'd left the bookstore—and I wanted to squeal. "I swear to God you would love him so much."

She *so* would. He was mature and polite and charming and smart, totally the kind of guy she made the hero of every single one of her screenplays. Every script she'd written had the solid, dependable cutie landing their love.

Which was why I just wanted him to ask me to prom so badly. Somehow, going to prom with someone she'd known—who'd known *her* well enough to know about and remember her daisies—seemed vitally important. Like it might make it feel like she was somehow involved in my senior year.

Ridiculous, right?

But I just wanted the hole of emptiness in my life to shrink just a tiny bit. Was that so much to ask? I kept waiting for the "closure" I was supposed to feel, but I was starting to think it would never come.

The chokecherry tree I'd been looking at got blurry, and I swallowed down the pinch in my throat. "Dad and Helena keep asking me about prom—if I'm going, if I need a dress—and the thing is, I don't want their help with anything. It's selfish and they don't deserve it, but if I can't have *you* doing those things with me, I don't want anyone else."

"Are you talking to yourself?"

I jumped, knocking my head against Mom's headstone, before turning around to see Wes. He was standing there in sporty clothes with a sweaty running brow, and I put my hand over my racing heart and said, "Oh my God—what are you doing here?"

His mouth went down and his eyebrows squinched together like he was confused. "Whoa—sorry. I didn't mean to startle you."

For some reason, I was pissed by his appearance. I knew I should feel embarrassed that he'd caught me talking to a piece of marble, or worried about what exactly he'd heard, but all I could think about was the fact that he was in this space. It was *my* space—my mom's and mine—and he shouldn't be there.

I scrambled to my feet. "Wes, did you follow me here? What is your problem?"

"Oh." His smirk disappeared and he glanced at my mother's grave—now that I'd moved, he could see her name—before saying, "Shit. I was already running when I saw you turn in here. I thought you were just cutting through."

"Yeah, well, I wasn't, okay?" I blinked fast, trying to stop my emotions from speeding down whatever chute they were headed for. "It's probably best if you just don't run after people without them knowing. That'd probably be your best bet."

He swallowed. "I didn't know, Liz."

I rolled my eyes and pulled my earbuds from my pocket. "Yeah, well, now you *do* know. You know that weird Little Liz is the freak who can't get over her dead mom. Awesome."

"No. Listen." He stepped closer and wrapped his hands around my upper arms, gently squeezing as his intense brown eyes moved all over my face like he was desperate to convince me. "I'm gonna go now, and you stay. Forget you ever saw me."

"Too late." I breathed in through my nose and gritted my teeth, stepping back from him and his hands. "Stay if you want, I don't care."

I jammed my earbuds into my ears and started the music. I cranked Foo Fighters so loud that I couldn't hear whatever Wes was saying to me, and I turned away from him and started running down the road, even though I knew he was yelling my name.

I ran home at a record pace, trying to think about mundane things like homework in a weak attempt to shut down my emotions. I needed to write a paper on patriarchy in literature, and

I couldn't decide if I should use "The Yellow Wallpaper" or "The Story of an Hour." I liked the second one better, but the first had more material.

I slammed through the front door and had almost made it to the safety of my room when my dad yelled for me.

"Yeah?"

"Come in here for a sec."

I went down the hall to his room and pushed open his bedroom door, still breathing hard from the exercise. "Yeah?"

He was sitting up in bed, reading a book, with an episode of *Friends* on TV in the background. He didn't even tear his eyes from the paperback when he asked, "Hey, did you go prom dress shopping with Jocelyn yet?"

"Not yet—her mom got tied up and I didn't really feel like it because of my nose."

"Oh, yeah. How's that feeling, by the way?"

I shrugged and thought about how much I loved hearing *Friends* reruns in my dad's room. He and my mother had watched that show in bed so many times that it'd become like a lullaby to me, a sound that conjured the sights and smells of my early childhood. "Better, I guess."

"Glad to hear it." He turned the volume on the television down to zero and finally looked at me. "Listen, since you haven't gone yet, maybe you could see if Helena wants to go with you guys. I know she'd love to do this, and I'm pretty sure she'll pay for your overpriced dress too."

Oh, the timing. I didn't want her to come, and I definitely

didn't want her to pay for my dress. I felt an anxious skip in my heartbeat and tried, "I think she's probably too—"

"Come on, Libby Loo." My dad took off his reading glasses. "She really wants to do this with you. Why is it such a big ask?"

I swallowed. "It's not."

"Really? Because I've heard her mention two or three times that she'd be happy to take you shopping, yet you made plans with someone else."

"I'll take care of it." Why couldn't he—and Helena—let it go? Why did they have to pile on to the prom pressure? It felt like everyone wanted me to do something—multiple somethings—that I didn't want to do.

He cocked an eyebrow. "You'll invite her? And not say something like it was my idea?"

My throat was tight, but I said, "Sure."

He moved on to talking about something else, but I didn't hear any of it. Why should I have to go dress shopping with Helena? For the rest of our chat and the entire duration of my shower afterward, my brain shouted arguments to the great unknown. I felt suffocated by the thought of Helena taking my mom's place, the kind of helpless desperation that caused your fingernails to leave tiny crescent grooves on your palms. *I don't want her there, so why is it getting forced down my throat? Why do her wishes count more than mine?* The arguments boiled through me as I brushed my teeth and laid out my clothes, and by the time I shut off the light and climbed into bed, I was exhausted.

And totally racked with guilt about what a bitch I'd been to Wes at the cemetery. He'd done nothing wrong, but the sight of him in that weirdly sacred place had set me off. I guess it was because that was the only place where I *felt* her anymore. The rest of the world—and my life—had moved on, but in that one spot, nothing had changed since she'd died.

I was pathetic.

I flipped on my TV and loaded the *Two Weeks Notice* DVD. It was another movie where Hugh Grant was playing a sketchball, but the banter between him and Sandra Bullock more than made up for that fact and actually made him forgivable. I pulled the blankets up to my chin as Sandra Bullock's character ordered too much Chinese food. When I reached for my phone to plug it in, I noticed I'd missed a text.

From Wes.

Wes: I'm sorry. I didn't know that your mom was there or I never would've followed you inside. I know you think I'm a dick but I promise you—I would never intrude on that.

I sighed and sat up. I was so embarrassed. How could I even explain it? No one normal would ever understand.

And wait—he thought that I thought he was a dick?

Me: Forget it. I'm the one who should be apologizing because you didn't do anything wrong. You caught me at a bad moment and I freaked out—not your fault.

Wes: No, I get it. It wasn't a parent so I know it's not the same, but I was close to my grandma. Every time we go to MN, the first thing I do is go to the cemetery to talk to her.

I looked up from my phone and blinked. Then I texted: Really?

Wes: Really.

I nodded in the darkness and blinked fast while my thumbs flew over the keys.

Me: I started "running" as a way to go talk to her without having to explain.

Wes: No shit—that's why you started running?

I could hear Fitz meowing at my door, so I got up and went to open it.

Me: Not past tense—that is why I run.

Wes: Wait a second—are you telling me that every day when I see you take off and I assume that you're training in order to make it to the Olympic trials, you're actually just running to Oak Lawn to talk to your mother? ☺

Mr. Fitzpervert looked up at me, meowed, and walked away. Now *there* was a dick. I shut my door.

Me: Bingo. But I swear to God I will gut you with a vegetable peeler if you tell anyone.

Wes: Your secret is safe with me, Buxbaum.

I walked over to the window. Your house looks dark—are you up in your room?

Wes: Are you ever not creeping on me, creeper? And before you ask, I'm wearing a kicky pair of trousers, a pirate blouse, and a black beret.

I laughed in the quiet of my room.

Me: I wasn't going to ask, but that sounds hot.

Wes: It is. I've got heatstroke up in here.

I looked down at their front yard, where someone had left a football next to the hydrangea bushes.

Wes: And the answer to your question is that I'm out back, in the Secret Area.

The Secret Area. I hadn't thought of it in years. Wes's house had a bit of land behind their fence that had never been developed. So while the rest of the houses on this street backed up to other backyards, Wes's had a tiny little forest behind it.

In grade school, during peak hide-and-seek days, we'd dubbed it the "Secret Area." It was where we'd explored, pretended, started unapproved campfires . . . It had been incredible. I hadn't been back there since the summer before middle school.

Me: Why?

Wes: Come see why.

Did he really want me to come hang out? Hanging out by ourselves, in a way that had nothing to do with Michael? My mom had cautioned against dating flighty boys, but it was okay to be friends with them, right? I texted: My dad and Helena are already asleep.

Wes: So sneak out.

I rolled my eyes—so typical. Unlike you, I've never snuck out. It seems ill-advised.

I couldn't, but part of me felt like I could hear him laugh at my response. After about a minute, my phone buzzed.

Wes: "Ill-advised." Buxbaum, you never fail to make me laugh.

Me: Thank you.

Wes: Not a compliment. BUT. You're looking at this the wrong way.

Me: Oh? And what is the right way?

Wes: You—a very well-behaved teenager—simply want to get some fresh spring air and look at the stars for a couple minutes. Instead of waking up your parents, you decide to quietly slip out for a few minutes.

Me: You're a sociopath.

Wes: Dare you.

I glanced in the direction of the hall as those words—"dare you"—brought back so many memories of Wes goading me to do things I shouldn't, like climbing onto Brenda Buckholtz's roof and ding-dong-ditching Mr. Levine's house.

Before I could respond, he texted: I'm shutting off my phone so I won't get your excuses. See you in five minutes.

CHAPTER EIGHT

"I like you very much. Just as you are."

—Bridget Jones's Diary

I couldn't believe I was doing it. I stepped over the creaky floorboard in the hallway and quietly crept toward the sliding glass door in the dining room. It was risky, but for some reason I needed to do this.

I *wanted* to hang out with Wes.

It was probably just that his understanding of my grief made me feel a camaraderie with him. I'd always felt like my visits with my mom were freakish, but I'd also felt like something inside me would break if I had to stop.

That theory would be tested in the fall, though, wouldn't it?

Regardless, finally sharing it with someone felt almost like a release. It didn't make sense that he was the one—of all people—for me to share it with, but I was starting to move beyond questioning it.

It also felt nice to not be fighting with Wes for once. Which was weird, because that was our thing; he messed with me and I got pissed. Rinse and repeat, for our whole lives. But now I was discovering that he was hilarious and nice and seemed like more fun than pretty much everyone else I knew.

I slowly pulled open the door, listening for any sounds coming from the other end of the house as Mr. Fitzpervert snaked in between my stockinged feet.

I stepped out onto the deck and slid the door closed behind me. It was a chilly night, with a clear sky and a bright, high moon that lit up the town. I could see moon shadows everywhere, which were beautiful and eerie at the same time.

I crept down the stairs, and once I hit the cold grass, I jogged across the backyard and over to the chain-link fence that separated our yards. It suddenly felt like it had been mere days—not years—since I'd climbed that fence as a kid, and I was over it and in his yard in seconds.

The shadows were creepy, so I kept jogging to the back gate, forgetting any semblance of coolness or composure. I pulled up the arm, opened the gate, and whisper-yelled, "Wes?"

"Over here."

I could barely see because the thick trees blocked out the moon, but I walked in the direction of his voice. I went around a flowering bush and a wide fir tree, and then there he was.

"Oh my God, Wes." I looked around, amazed.

There were hundreds of tiny twinkling lights strung in a grouping of trees that circled four wooden Adirondack chairs, one of which Wes was sitting in. A firepit roaring with flames was at the center of everything, and a rock waterfall ran behind him. The space was so thick with foliage that it felt like a wild, hidden spot instead of a suburban backyard. "This is incredible. Did your mom do all of this?"

"Nah." He shrugged and looked uncomfortable. Wes Bennett looked awkward—for perhaps the first time ever—and he sat there with his long legs stretched out in front of him and looked up at the sky. "This is my favorite spot, so I actually did it."

"Nope." I sat down in the chair across from him. "You didn't do this. No way."

"Yes way." He kept his eyes up and said, "I worked for a landscaping company three summers ago, and everything we charged clients a fortune for, I would just do myself back here. Retaining walls, waterfalls, pond; it's all simple and cheap to make if you know what you're doing."

Who was this guy?

Tucking my legs underneath me, I pulled my sleeves over my fingers and looked up at the sky. It was clear and there were stars everywhere. "Bella Luna"—a very old Jason Mraz song—was the choicest of all musical numbers to set the background for this surprise moonlit oasis.

Bella luna, my beautiful, beautiful moon
How you swoon me like no other—

I stopped the music in my head and said, "Hey, I saw Michael today."

"I know."

I squinted, trying to better see his face in the darkness, searching for some giveaway. He just kept looking at the sky, though. "He told you?"

"He did." I looked at Wes's profile. His lips barely moved as he quietly said, "He texted me. Said he'd run into you and, Liz—he said you were funny."

"He did?" I wanted to howl. I knew it. "What *exactly* did he say?"

"He said, 'She's pretty funny.' And then he mentioned the get-together at his house."

"Yep. I said I'd give you a shot." I looked into the fire. Funny—he'd said I was funny. That was good, right? I guess that meant my awkward *coconuts* text hadn't kicked me off the island. "But part of me worries that I'm screwing up my chances with our little version of fake-dating."

That brought his eyes right back to my face. "You want to quit?"

I shrugged and wondered what he was thinking. Because as fun as this actually was, and in spite of the fact that it was kind of working, I was done with all the lying. I said, "I always think I know what I'm doing, but what if you're right about my terrible grand plans? What if I'm just ruining both of our dating lives?"

And jeopardizing my friendship with Joss and also sinking into a life of habitual dishonesty.

"Then I'll have to kill you. Dating is my everything."

"Smart-ass." I rolled my eyes because, for a popular guy, I'd only ever heard of him being in a few relationships, none of which had turned into anything serious.

I ran my teeth over my bottom lip and said, "Maybe you should take me to Michael's, and then we should decide we aren't a match. And, I don't know, send out a group text?"

I blinked fast and tried to figure out why the thought of being done with our plan made my heart beat in my neck.

He looked at me then, and I was surprised by how soft his smile was. He looked almost sweet as he said, "I can't believe your ridiculous plan is working."

"Right?"

He kind of laughed and so did I, and then he said, "I really am sorry about earlier, by the way."

I waved a hand. "No biggie."

"I made you cry." He looked away, but I caught a glimpse of his clenched jaw. It was almost like it mattered to him that he'd upset me. And, in the moonlight, I felt something that I had never felt about Wes before. I wanted to move closer to him.

I swallowed and checked myself. What was this influx of Wes-fondness? I was probably just aware of how much fun I'd had with him during our deal, and now it was almost over.

That was it.

So instead of following through on the absurd instinct to move closer, I just said, "God, you're so arrogant, Bennett. I was already crying when you showed up. Everything isn't about you, you know."

But it was actually that moment, that crying moment, that'd forged some sort of connection between me and Wes.

And it was a good connection.

I saw his Adam's apple bob around a swallow as I stared at his silhouette. He lifted his eyes to me and said, "Promise?"

"Ugh. Yes." Good Lord, he was killing me with his concern. I cleared my throat and looked back at the sky. "I'm good now, so forget you ever saw it."

"Done."

We sat quietly for a few minutes, both of us lost in the starry sky, but it wasn't awkward. For once in my life, I didn't feel compelled to fill the empty space with constant chatter.

"I can still picture her perfectly, you know," he said.

"Hm?" I said. I was confused, and must've looked it, because he added, "Your mom."

"Really?" I curled tighter into the chair, wrapping my arms around my legs and picturing her face. Even I wasn't sure I could remember her exact features anymore. It broke my heart a little.

"For sure." His voice was warm, like it was holding a smile, and he cracked his knuckles when he said, "She was so . . . Hmm . . . What's the word? Charming, maybe?"

I smiled. "Enchanting."

"That's perfect." He gave me a little-boy grin and said, "There was this one day, I was running in front of your house and totally wiped out. Absolutely *shredded* my knee on the sidewalk. Your mom was out there, trimming her roses, so I tried jumping up and being cool. Y'know, because I was, like, eight and your mom was hella pretty."

I smiled and remembered how much she'd loved tending her garden.

"Instead of treating me like a little kid, she cut one of her roses and pretended to hurt her finger. She did a whole 'ouch' thing before saying, 'Wesley, would you mind helping me for a minute?'"

"Now, mind you, I just wanted to crawl off into a corner and die from my horrific battle wounds. But if Mrs. Buxbaum needed me, I was damn well going to help."

Wes was grinning, and I was helpless to do anything other than the same. I hadn't heard a new story about my mother in such a long time that his words were oxygen and I was breathing them in with a life-and-death desperation.

"So I limped on over and followed her inside your house, which, by the way, always smelled like vanilla."

It was vanilla candles—I still bought the same scent.

"Anyway, she had me help her get a Band-Aid on her finger like she couldn't do it herself or something. I felt like the hero when she kept thanking me and telling me how grown-up I was getting."

Now I was beaming like a dork.

"Then she 'noticed' my bloody knee and said I must've been so concerned about helping her that I hadn't even realized I was bleeding. She cleaned me up, put on a Band-Aid, and gave me a Fudgesicle. Made me feel like a damned hero for face-planting on the sidewalk."

I laughed and looked up at the sky, my heart full. "That story is so on-brand for my mom."

"Every time I see a cardinal in your yard, I think it's her."

I looked at his shadowed face and almost wanted to laugh, because I never would've imagined Wes having such a fantastical thought. "You do?"

"I mean, there's the whole thing about cardinals being—"

"Dead people?"

He scrunched his eyebrows at me, cringing a little. "I was trying for verbiage a tad more delicate than that, but yes."

"I don't know if I buy the whole dead-people-come-back-as-birds thing, but it's a nice thought." It was. The nicest. But I'd always felt like if I allowed myself to believe in those notions, I'd never get past her death because I'd surely spent every second of my life tearfully bird-watching.

"Do you miss her a lot?" He cleared his throat and made a little sound like he was embarrassed by his own question. "I mean, of course you do. But . . . is it at least a little easier now than it used to be?"

I leaned forward and held my hands in front of the fire. "I miss her a lot. Like, all the time. But lately it feels different. I don't know. . . ."

I trailed off and stared at the flames. Was it easier, he wondered? I felt like I couldn't answer that question because I refused to let it get easier. I thought about her a lot—every single day—and if I started doing that less, surely it'd get easier.

But the easier it got, the more she'd disappear, right?

He scratched his cheek and asked, "Different how?"

"Worse maybe?" I shrugged and watched the bottom of the log as it heated to almost a shade of white. I wasn't sure how to explain it, when I didn't even get it myself. "I don't know. It's really weird, actually. I just . . . I guess it kind of feels like I'm really losing her this year. All of these milestones are happening, like prom and college applications, and she isn't here for them. So my life is changing and moving forward, and she's being left behind with my childhood. Does that make sense?"

"Holy shit, Liz." Wes sat up a little straighter and ran his hands over the top of his hair, messing it up as his serious eyes met mine in the firelight. "That makes total sense and it also sucks."

"Are you lying?" I squinted in the darkness, but the fire's flicker made it tough to read his expression. "Because I know I'm weird about my mom."

"How is that weird?" The breeze lifted his dark hair and tousled it just a little. "It makes perfect sense."

I didn't know if it did or not, but a wave of emotion crashed over me and I had to roll my lips in and blink fast to hold it back. There was something about his casual confirmation of my sanity, my *normalcy*, that healed a tiny little piece of me.

Probably the piece that had never discussed my mother with anyone other than my dad.

"Well, thanks, Bennett." I smiled and put my feet up on the edge of the firepit. "The other thing that's messing with me is that Helena and my dad keep trying to insert Helena into every one of these things where my mom is supposed to be. I feel like the bad guy because I don't want Helena there. I don't need a fill-in."

"That's tough."

"Right?"

"But at least Helena is supercool. I mean, it'd be worse if your stepmom was a total nightmare, wouldn't it?"

I wondered that all the time. "Maybe. But sometimes I think her coolness makes it harder. No one would understand why I feel this way when someone so cool is right here."

"Well, can't you include her and just *not* replace your mom? It seems to me that you can still hold on to your memories, even if Helena is with you. Right?"

"It's not that easy." I wished it was, but I didn't think there was room for both of them. If Helena went dress shopping with me and we had a great time, that memory would be stamped forever, and my mother would have no part in it.

"Do you want a cigar?"

That stopped my train of thought. "What?"

I saw the upward movement of his lips in the dark before he said, "I was about to enjoy a Swisher Sweet out here before you showed up."

That made me laugh, immature Wes enjoying a gas-station variety of cigar in his backyard like some kind of grown-ass man. "Ooh—classy."

"I'm nothing if not sophisticated. In fact, it's cherry-flavored."

"Oh, well, if it's cherry, I'm totally in."

"Really?"

"No, not really." I rolled my eyes at his total Wes-ness. "I just don't think I'd appreciate the cherry-flavored death stick, but thanks for the offer."

"I knew that would be your answer."

"No, you did not."

"I thought you'd say 'cancer stick,' but the rest I got right."

I tilted my head. "I'm that predictable?"

He just cocked an eyebrow.

"Fine." I held out my palm. "Hand over one of your elegant,

cherry-flavored sticks of disgustingness so I can set it on fire and suck its death smoke into my lungs."

He raised his eyebrows in surprise. "Seriously?"

I shrugged. "Why not?"

"You should write ad copy for the Swisher people, by the way."

"How do you know I don't?"

"Well, if you did, you would know that you don't inhale cigars."

"You don't?"

"Nope."

"So . . . you just take a pull and hold it in your cheeks like a bloated chipmunk?"

"You definitely do not. You just inhale less than a cigarette."

"Are you like a hard-core smoker or something?"

"No."

"Well, it seems to me like if you're lighting up out here all by yourself after a long, hard day, you maybe have a problem."

"C'mere." He patted the chair beside him.

"Eww, no." I said it teasingly, feeling somehow busted since I'd thought about moving closer to him earlier.

"Relax—I was just going to light your flaming nasty stick for you."

"Oh." I stood and moved to the chair beside him. "My bad."

"That's the first time you've ever said that, isn't it?"

"I think so."

He chuckled and opened the package. I wasn't sure why I was doing this, especially with Wes Bennett, but I knew I wasn't ready to go inside. I was kind of having fun.

"Have you ever smoked?"

"Yes."

"Seriously?" Wes put one of the cigars in his mouth and flicked the lighter.

"I smoked with Joss at a party last summer."

He grinned and puffed as the Swisher lit. "I would've loved to witness that. Little Libby Loo, coughing her lungs out while Jocelyn probably laughed and blew perfect smoke rings."

"You're not that far off." Jocelyn was nauseatingly good at everything. I'd never seen her fail at anything. Not back in the day, and definitely not since we'd become friends. If I were honest—and I'd never say it out loud—it bugged the shit out of me.

Not that she was good at things. I could handle that. It was more that she was good at things without really trying or caring about them. She breezed through life, never seeming to stumble like I did on an hourly basis.

"Here." He handed me the cigar and lit the other one. I took it and leaned back in my chair, casually stretching out my legs and looking up at the stars. It felt important to lean into the cigar attitude.

I took a drag. The cherry was nice, and the thing wasn't quite as nasty as a cigarette, but it still tasted like butt.

Wes was watching me with a half grin on his face, which made me say, as smoke poured out of my mouth, "It sure feels good to be back in flavor country."

He started cackling.

I added, "Love me a good stogie."

That sent him over. It was impossible not to join him as he

laughed with his head all the way back. When he finally stopped, he took a puff and said, "You can put it out, Buxbaum."

"Oh, thank God." I put out the cigar, carefully stubbing it out against the edge of the firepit. "That was a super relaxing ten seconds, though. Really helped me wind down."

"Uh-huh."

"By the way, I heard that Alex Benedetti has a crush on you." I'd overheard that in chemistry, and my initial response had been that they could be a good match. They were both attractive athletes. So surely they were meant to be, right?

I pictured Alex hanging out here with Wes instead of me, and I didn't like it. I'd started looking forward to our weird camaraderie, and even though I was struggling to accept it, I kind of thought he was a nice person.

He puffed on his cigar, his face unchanged. "I heard that too."

And . . . ? "She's cute."

He dipped his head. "Yeah, I suppose. She's just not really my type."

"What? Why not?" Alex was a stunning cheerleader with a thousand friends, the kind of girl I assumed guys like him tended to drool over. In addition to that, she was genuinely nice and really smart. Like, I-heard-she-wanted-to-be-a-dentist level of smart.

"I don't know. Alex is great but . . ." He looked at me and shrugged like that explained everything.

I grabbed the hair tie from my wrist and pulled back my hair. I felt like I owed Wes since he'd spent so much time helping me with

Michael. Yes, there was still a shot of him winning The Spot, but something about the night air in the Secret Area made me want to do something nice for him. "I know chemistry plays a big part in attraction, but she is gorgeous. I can't believe you aren't jumping at that chance."

"She *is* gorgeous." He flicked ash off the end of his cigar and gave me the kind of eye contact that forced you to listen. "But, like, what does that mean, really? Unless my goal is just to sit and stare at her like someone would stare at an ocean or a mountain range, pretty is just a visual."

I widened my eyes and covered my mouth with both hands. "Oh, dear Lord, tell me more, Wesley."

"Shut it." He flipped me off with his free hand and said, "I'm just saying that I like a girl who can make me laugh, that's all. Someone I have fun with no matter what we're doing."

I sat back in my chair and crossed my arms over my chest. Tilted my head, furrowed my eyebrows, and said, "Don't take this the wrong way, but you're different than I always thought you were."

His eyes were twinkly-warm as he said, "You're shocked I grew out of the gnome-decapitation phase, aren't you?"

"Kind of." I giggled and shook my head. "But I also thought that you would jump at the chance to, um, to 'hit it.'"

That made him smirk and look at me with one of his dark eyebrows raised. "That is disgusting, Buxbaum."

"Right?"

"Is that the first time you've ever said those words?"

I just laughed and nodded, which made him big laugh.

We sat out there after that, just talking about nothing, until he finished his Swisher.

"Are you going to have another one?" I asked.

He tossed the butt into the fire and stood, grabbing a big stick and messing with the wood. "Why—you want one?"

"God, no." I lifted my hair to my nose and said, "Those things make my hair smell like a dumpster."

He propped the stick next to the firepit and picked up the bucket sitting behind his chair. "I actually have early lifting tomorrow, so I should probably shut this down if you're ready to go in."

There was something about how soft his face was at that moment—calm and happy and licked by fireglow—that made me feel lucky I'd discovered who he'd grown into. "Yeah, I'm ready."

He dipped the bucket into the pond and poured it on the fire, sending up a cloud of smoke. As we walked out of the Secret Area and into his backyard, he said he'd text me when Michael told him what time the movie night was happening.

I went to bed feeling happy, even though I wasn't entirely sure about what. Or, rather, *who*. I lay there, kind of thrummingly relaxed, until the smell of smoke in my hair drove me so crazy, I had to take a midnight shower and change my pillowcase.

Then I went to bed happy.

CHAPTER NINE

"Love is patient, love is kind, love means slowly losing your mind."

—27 Dresses

"Hey, kiddo." Helena looked over at me from the doorway that led to the kitchen as I practiced piano in the living room. I liked playing in the morning, and I liked playing in my fancy flowered pajamas with the matching silk slippers. It made practicing feel like an elegant pastime, like I was an erstwhile Austen character honing one of the skills that would make me *a fearsome thing to behold.*

"You hungry? Want me to toast you a Pop-Tart or something?"

"No, thanks." I tried to keep playing while I talked to her, but I'd never been able to pull off that particular skill. If I practiced for more than an hour or two a week—like my mother used to—it probably wouldn't seem so difficult. She'd played every single day, and it had showed. "I had a banana already."

"Got it."

She turned to walk back into the kitchen, and I forced myself to do it. I said, "Helena. Wait."

She tilted her head. "Yeah?"

"I know it's last minute," I blurted out, steeling myself against the feelings as I extended the invitation, "but, um, Jocelyn just texted me and said her mom can take us prom dress shopping later this morning, since it's a teacher in-service day. Do you want to come?"

Helena lifted her chin and lowered her brows, tucking her hair behind her ears. "That depends. How come you're asking?"

"Um, because I thought you might want to come . . . ?"

Her look told me that she knew better. "Your dad didn't tell you to do this?"

Part of me felt like being honest, but instead I said, "No, was he supposed to or something?"

She blinked and looked at me for another second, and then her face transformed into happiness. "I would *love* to come, honey. Oh my God. I think we should hit Starbucks first, where we can guess people's coffee orders by their outfits. Then we can do the dress thing, and maybe land at Eastman's for some lunch that includes that hot lava dessert which is supposedly to die for. Although, I seriously doubt any food is *to die for*. I mean, I'm obsessed with Caramello bars, but I would certainly never give my life for one."

She was being her usual rambling, sarcastic self, but I felt like I'd made her really, really happy.

"What about ice cream?" I reached over with my right hand and tinkled out an ice-cream-truck-ish tune, glad I'd asked her. Perhaps this would be good for us. "That could be considered to die for."

"It's not even a solid. If I'm going down for a food, it's not going to be a food that's hovering somewhere between two chemical states."

"Good point." I stopped playing. "Do we even discuss your beloved banana bread?"

"It's worthy of felonious thievery, maybe, but not death. I would steal it from the president himself, but I wouldn't just lay down my life for its delicious moistness, either."

"But wouldn't stealing from the president get you killed by the Secret Service, and therefore be the same thing?"

"Well, I'm not going to get caught, of course."

"Of course, indeed."

I went upstairs and got ready, and by the time I was done, Helena was waiting for me in the living room. She was wearing a boss bitch leather jacket that looked perfect with her jeans, and I once again marveled at the fact that she was my dad's age.

"You ready to do this? I'm thinking we buy a joke dress just to freak your dad out. Like, we get you a stunning gown, but we also get a trashy little number that gives him a coronary."

"Do you really want to have to nurse him back to health after his triple bypass?"

"Good point. He's a total baby when he doesn't feel good." She grabbed her keys and tucked her phone into her pocket. "I'll just text him a pic to give him a tiny scare."

I followed Helena out to the garage and got into her car. She had a matte black Challenger, which was a brute of a car that rumbled so loud, you couldn't hear the radio unless it was cranked. A guy at the auto-parts store asked her about it once, about why she wanted to drive a car that was clearly meant for a man and probably too much horsepower for her to handle, and I'll never forget her answer.

"It was true love, Ted. I looked over, saw this guy, and I totally lost my mind. I know he's loud and in-your-face, but whenever I look at him, I feel a little weak-kneed. And when I drive him—forget about it. He's fast and wild and a little unruly, and I can feel his throaty rumbles all through my body when I bury that gas pedal. That beast has forever ruined me for all other vehicles."

Ted at NAPA lost the ability to speak, while Helena beamed at him like she had no idea what she'd done. She'd wielded her power like a goddess, and regardless of my complicated feelings about her and her place in my life, I had mad respect for that.

"Pumpkin spice latte."

"Seriously? That's your guess?" I rolled my eyes and took a sip of my Frappucino. "It's like you aren't even trying. *Think,* Helena—it's April. Starbucks doesn't even offer that drink in April."

"You think I don't know that?" Her lips barely moved as she watched the girl step up to the register. The orderer in question was young—probably a freshman—and she was dressed like a Gap model. "She's a baby, so she doesn't know the rules. She only knows that her older sister let her try one once, and it was ah-may-zing."

I giggled.

The girl opened her mouth and said, "Could I please get a gingerbread latte?"

To which the barista responded with, "I'm sorry, but that's a seasonal drink."

I looked at Helena with a wide-open *O* mouth. "You were so close!"

"Not my first rodeo, kid." She shrugged and took a sip of her espresso. "You've got Messenger Bag over there—don't disappoint me."

I looked at the guy with the messenger bag who was staring down at his phone. His bag was total butter, rich leather worn to perfection in the way that only expensive bags could be worn. His tortoiseshell glasses made him look smart but also stylish, and his watchband was perfectly coordinated with his belt and shoes.

"Venti iced Americano with soy milk." I leaned back on my stool and crossed my arms. "He's embracing spring by selecting a cold beverage, but he can't let go of the strong seriousness of the Americano's bite."

"That is excellent, my pupil."

Messenger Bag looked at the barista and said, "Yeah, I just need an iced dark roast."

"Ooh, so close," I muttered, pulling my phone out of my dress pocket and checking for messages. There was no reason to think Wes would text me, but after hanging out last night and having such a good time, it felt like a possibility.

"And can I get a splash of soy, please?"

"Boom." Helena slapped the table. "That's pretty freaking close, Liz."

"We're on fire today."

She nodded and said, "Speaking of fire, what's up with Wes?"

"What does he have to do with fire?"

She shrugged. "Nothing. I'm too impatient to wait for a good segue."

"Oh." I cleared my throat and watched as Messenger Bag took his coffee and joined a table of three other Messenger Bags. "Um. Nothing is really 'up' with Wes."

"Are you sure? Because you spent at least an hour outside with him last night."

My eyes shot to hers, but instead of looking pissed, she gave me a *Gotcha* smile. "Don't worry—it was purely by accident that I know. I happened to be looking out the window at the exact moment that you shot across the backyard like your butt was on fire and climbed his fence."

"Does my dad know?"

"Why would I wake him up when you were just going outside to look at the stars?"

I shrugged and bit down on my smile. As much as I didn't want to fall under the she's-so-cool spell that everyone who met Helena seemed to fall under, sometimes she really *could* be unbelievably cool. "I don't know. Thanks for not telling him. It was nothing, but I feel like it'd be a big deal to him."

"Oh, it definitely would be." She lifted her cup and toyed with the lid. "He trusts you, though. We both do."

"I know." I crossed my legs and traced one of the grooves on my tights with my finger. "And Wes and I are just friends, for the record. He's kind of helping me with something."

"What?" She swung her leg back and forth over the side of her stool. "Last I heard, you two were battling over that parking spot. Now, all of a sudden, you're friends and he's providing helpful assistance? How in the frack did that happen?"

"It's kind of complicated."

"I'd expect nothing less." She looked through the opening in her lid before swirling her cup around. "But you *have* to be a little attracted to Wes. I mean, not only is the guy pretty and muscular, but he's also hilarious. Like, if I was a teenager, I would totally go for that one."

Before I had a chance to utter a sound, she interrupted herself with, "Oh, good God, please scratch that from the record. I sound like one of those teachers who sends pictures of her bits to her students. You *do* know I didn't mean it like that, right?"

That made me smile. "Of course."

"I find Wes adorable in the way that one finds a puppy with huge paws adorable."

"Settle down. I know."

"Oh, thank God."

"And I agree. Until recently, I hadn't really noticed Wes. But now that I've spent time with him, I can totally see why a girl might be into him."

"His shoulders, right? They're wildly broad."

I squinted. "They are?"

"You hadn't noticed?"

"Not really. But that's not the point. What *I* was going to say was that I can see how a girl would get into him because he's kind of thoughtful for a . . ." How would I even categorize Wes anymore? My previous labels didn't seem to fit. "For Wes."

I pictured him at Ryno's party, saving me from certain humiliation by holding up the pants he'd loaned me. Holy God, Wes

Bennett was kind of a catch, wasn't he? He listened well, made late-night phone calls, built beautiful firepits that belonged in lifestyle magazines. Wes was a little bit dreamy.

"But not for you?"

"No." No matter what I was learning about Wes, any real relationship with him would end in sure disaster. And—as if I needed to convince myself—just like that, I wanted to tell her. Everything. "So here's what's happening. But this is top secret, okay? Like, even Jocelyn doesn't know."

"Oh my God, I love being the one in the know." She beamed and leaned a little closer. "Tell me everything, you sneaky little tart."

And I did. I told her about Michael, and she made a heart-fluttering gesture when I described him and his unexpected re-emergence in my life. (Though I left off the connection to my mom.) I told her about Wes's and my plan, and she laughed and called me an evil genius.

She cried actual tears when I described getting vomited on, and she snorted *while* crying when I added the details of the nose-meets-basketball accident to the story. She was wiping at her eyes when she said, "Oh my God, it's like fate is trying its hardest to keep you away from him."

What? It wasn't like that, was it? Those were just unfortunate coincidences.

"Every time you get close to having a moment with Michael, it sounds like the universe breaks it up with a ball to the face or a puke to the outfit. I think the universe likes Wes better."

I'm pretty sure I looked at her as if she had a snake crawling out of her mouth. "No, it doesn't. Those things were freak accidents. If anything, I'd say bad luck just follows in Wes's wake. Me being near him was probably what fate was pissed about."

Her eyebrows went up. "Oh-kay, Liz. Whatever you say."

The universe likes Wes better.

My brain was fried by that single, solitary sentence as we went out to her car and drove to the shopping center. Did the universe like Wes better?

"I'm going to be sick." I shook my head and stared as Jocelyn looked at her reflection in the mirror. She was wearing an orange floor-length gown, and she looked more like someone on the red carpet at the Oscars than a high school student trying on a prom dress. "Does anything look bad on you?"

Joss's mom barked, "It's too grown-up. Take it off."

Her mother was one of those nice-but-intimidating parents. She'd always been supersweet to me, but when she was mad at Joss, it made *me* nervous. She was tiny—barely over five feet, but every inch of her was in charge.

She was an attorney, and I'd always assumed she was amazing at her job because I'd yet to see Joss ever win an argument with her.

Jocelyn rolled her eyes and muttered something about shaking her mom until the woman's hair fell out of its bun, which made me giggle but also think about the way Wes was always messing up my hair. It was super annoying, but something about it made me smile every time.

I cleared my throat and frowned, just to make sure I wasn't creepily grinning into space.

That could ruin everything.

Because so far, Joss and I were having fun like a normal shopping trip. Her irritation with my reticence on senior activities and my irritation with her badgering had yet to rear their ugly heads.

It was great and I didn't want my boy-drama lies to mess it up.

We were at our third store, and it was going the same way that it'd gone at every stop. I tried on a handful of dresses that were so-so, and every dress that Jocelyn slid into looked amazing. She was having a hard time narrowing it down to one, and I was having a hard time finding even one.

"It's not that I look good; it's that I'm trying on great dresses." Jocelyn looked at me in the mirror. "You, on the other hand, keep trying on retro floral things that don't even look like prom dresses. I know you've got your whole romantic-vibe thing, but try on a damn floor-length gown that is considered a prom dress, for the love of God."

"She's right, Liz." Helena was eating a corn dog she'd bought in the mall while she sat on a chair and watched us try on dresses. "Just grab a stack and get rolling."

"Step outside of your comfort zone," Jocelyn's mother said, giving me a maternal smile and a reassuring nod. Then she barked at Joss, "That one is too tight and the cleavage is too much. On to the next."

I glanced at the racks and didn't feel like any more searching. "Ugh."

"Here. Wait." Jocelyn held up a finger. "Go to the dressing room and wait for me. I'm going to bring ten dresses for you to try on. Just trust me."

"But you don't—"

"Trust me."

I sighed and strolled back to the fitting rooms, already so done with the dress shopping. I plopped down on the bench and felt my phone buzz when I sat. I pulled it out and saw a message from Wes.

Wes: What happened to your car?

The minute I saw that the text was from Wes, I felt . . . something. Something good and equally confusing that I chalked up to being related to Michael. He could have been texting about Michael—that had to be the reason for my reaction.

His question cracked me up, because of course Wes would notice. My dad, the man whose name was on the title, hadn't noticed the damage I'd done when I'd scraped the car against the side of the drive-thru post the day before, but Wes Bennett had.

Me: Keep your mouth shut if you know what's good for you.

Wes: Are you threatening me?

Me: Only if you broach the topic of my car again.

Wes: So . . . um . . . nice weather out today, eh? Whatcha doin?

Me: Prom dress shopping. It's awful.

Wes: Worse than shopping with me?

I thought about that for a second. Actually, yes. At least you were in a hurry. These ladies are all about stretching it out, and I kind of want to make a run for it. I think I could belly-crawl out of this dressing room undetected. . . .

Wes: Who are you going to prom with? I thought the goal was Michael.

My brain produced an image of Wes in a tuxedo, and I quickly cleared it. *Michael* was the goal.

"Okay." Jocelyn appeared in the doorway with an armful of dresses. "Promise me you will try on all of these. Even if they don't look like something you'd normally go for, just humor me and try them on for us. Deal?"

I set my phone on the bench. "Deal."

She furrowed her eyebrows together. "Who were you texting?"

I furrowed my eyebrows right back at her. "Why?"

"Seriously?"

I shrugged and felt like I'd been busted looking at dirty pictures. "Wes, okay? He texted me about the paint on the side of my car."

Jocelyn knew about the paint because I'd texted her when I hit the pole, so she wasn't fazed by that revelation. But her face lit up and she said, "You and Wes text each other now?"

"Not really." I cleared my throat and tried to remember what I'd told her before the basketball outing. "It's just been a couple times and it's totally casual."

"Yeah, right. You aren't fooling me, by the way." She hung the dresses on a hook and put her hands on her hips. "Even though you're acting all cool, you like-like Wes Bennett."

"I do not." I didn't! My emotional responses to Wes were all about his connection to my mother and the fact that we were partners in crime.

That was it.

"Oh, yes, you do. You've been daydreaming all day long, every time you've tried on a dress." Her eyes narrowed and she said, "Oh my god—you better not ditch me for Wes."

"Shut up." My stomach got tight when she gave me that little preview of just how unhappy she'd be if Michael asked me to prom. "I'm not ditching you for Wes."

But I might do it for Michael. God, I was a garbage friend.

"Well, you have some boy on the mind, and if it isn't dear Wesley, then who is it?"

Part of me wanted to come clean and just tell her. Who cared if she thought my plan was a bad idea? Perhaps it was time.

But just as that thought was firing up, I heard Helena and Joss's mother laughing out by the big mirror. They sounded like two moms, happily waiting on their daughters, and that brought all of my screwed-up emotions rushing back.

Nope. I just couldn't find the fortitude for a disagreement, not there in the fitting room at Ralph's Department Store. It wouldn't be so bad to double down on the Wes thing, would it? I mean, technically he *was* the one who'd been on my mind all day. It was totally within the realm of believability that I had a tiny crush on Wes that would ultimately not pan out, right?

I dragged a hand through my hair. "I'm still trying to figure it out, okay? I totally have fun when I'm with Wes, but he's also not my type and—"

"What do you mean, not your type? Because he's not some character who writes poetry and knows what your favorite flower is?"

I hated when she did that. When she reduced me to a lovesick, airheaded child. I said, "It doesn't even matter because we're just talking, okay?"

"Okay." She gave me a funny grin, and the emotional roller coaster I'd just enjoyed a three-minute ride on went undetected. "My money's on Bennett, though. If anyone can slip in and shake up your romantic notions, it's Wes."

I rolled my eyes and remembered what Helena had said earlier. "I think you're making this *way* more of a thing than it is."

"We'll see. Now try on the dresses."

She slammed the door behind her, and I pushed the lock over. Before I started in on the dresses, I grabbed my phone and replied to the previous text, knowing my response was a lie.

Me: Jocelyn and I had planned on going together, but I'm sure she'll understand if I get asked by someone I care about.

Just putting it into the universe could make it true, right?

I pulled on the first dress, a long red sparkly thing that could probably be seen from space, and giggled at my reflection. I looked like a pageant contestant who'd lost her makeup bag and hair supplies. From the shoulders down—good. From the shoulders up—not so much.

My red hair totally clashed with the dress.

I went out to the three-way mirror anyway and spun for my fans, who agreed.

"But the style is *so* much better than the ones you tried earlier." Helena put her hands together like she was praying. "Praise Jesus, I feel like we're getting close."

When I got back to the fitting room, I glanced at my phone before changing.

Wes: Why don't you like dress shopping? That seems like your jam.

I unzipped the dress and shimmied out of it while texting.

Me: My preferences don't exactly match up with prom trends, and the people I'm with don't care.

Wes: Ah. You want flowers, pockets, and old lady ruffles, and they want you to wear something hot.

Why did his take on most things—even when he was mocking me—make me laugh? I smiled and reached for the black gown. It was short in the front and long in the back, with a top that tied behind the neck. I was about to step into it when my phone buzzed.

Wes: Don't forget that white is your color, gurl.

Okay—that made me laugh out loud. I glanced at the dresses, and there *was* a white one in there. I dropped the black one and reached for it. And wow.

It was actually . . . wonderful.

It was strapless, with a simple silk bodice that tapered into a white beaded belt and a long, full floor-length skirt. It was stunning in that 75 percent of the dress was simple and understated, and then along the bottom there was a burst of colorful wildflowers.

I pulled it on, sucking everything in as I slid the side zipper into place. And when I looked at my reflection—

I grabbed my phone. You might be right, Bennett. The only dress I've liked so far is white. WTF is with you nailing my fashion?

I lifted my hair and turned sideways to see the back. It was really a glorious dress. And when I ran my hands down the sides, I found pockets.

Wes: Why do you ever doubt me?

Me: Good judgment. Experience.

Wes: Pic, please.

"*What?*" I said it to myself, and a nervous snort came out of me even as I thought about the best angle. God, why was I thinking *that* when it was Wes asking? I muttered a stream of obscenities—*shit, shit, shit*—under my breath before finally responding with Um, that's a big no.

Wes: Okay, then send me a pic of something else just so I feel included.

I looked around the fitting room for something funny to send him, and then I thought—what the hell? I took a picture of the gown in the mirror and texted it to him.

Had I really just done that? Had I really just sent Wes Bennett a motherloving *prom dress* selfie? Holy shiiii—

"Liz! Do you have a dress on?" Jocelyn was yelling from her spot in the gallery. "You need to let us see, because even though they're not your style, one of those *will* work, dang it."

I dropped my phone and went out to the big mirror. Like it was *Say Yes to the Dress* or something, Jocelyn and Helena both gasped and covered their mouths with their hands when I stepped in front of them. Jocelyn's mom just smiled.

"That dress was made for you." Jocelyn crossed her arms. "Please don't tell me that you hate it. You can't."

"You look incredible." Helena was on her feet, smiling like she was about to get teary-eyed. "Do you like it?"

I shrugged. "It has pockets. And flowers. I pretty much *have* to get it, right?"

I looked at my reflection in the mirror and knew—I just knew—that my mother would've loved that dress. She would've picked out that dress for me. Heck, she would've worn that dress herself if she'd had reason to go formal. Maybe she couldn't be there, shopping with me, but finding that dress was something, right?

"Oh, Libby, I can't wait for your dad to see you in this." Helena's head was tilted to the side and she was smiling, but her words were like a bucket of cold water, jolting me back to the momless present. Because what Helena had just said was exactly what my mother would've said if she'd been there. In fact, I could perfectly hear her lilting voice saying those words.

But Helena wasn't my mom, even if she was suddenly calling me *Libby* like she was.

I crossed my arms over my chest and needed to be out of that dress STAT. "I'm going to go change."

"Aren't you excited?" She gave me a smart-ass excited look and a fake fist pump that probably would've cracked me up an hour ago. "You found your dress."

"Sure." I watched her smile falter, but I couldn't stop myself. Some part of me believed that if I didn't push back, she was going to erase the fact that my mother had ever existed. I thought about the whole day Helena had planned. I just wanted to be alone. "I'm not hungry, by the way, so can we just go home after this?"

Helena glanced at Jocelyn and her mom, who were thankfully talking to each other and not paying attention to us, before she said, “Sure. If that’s what you want.”

After I changed, instead of joining the others by the big mirror, I took the dress to the counter and paid before Helena had the chance. When I joined the group with my dress already bagged up and hanging over my arm, they all looked confused.

“You already bought it?” Jocelyn’s eyes were big as she put the strap of her cross-body bag over her shoulder and muttered sarcastically, “Yeah, that’s not a weird thing to do at all.”

I held up the dress and pretended everything was fine. I even smiled. “Since we have to go back to the last store and get yours, I thought I’d speed things up.”

She gave me a look that told me she knew what I was up to. “Good thinking, Liz.”

An awkward vibe hung over the four of us as we fake-happy conversed and walked toward the exit. Jocelyn and her mother knew what was up, Helena knew what was up and also knew that the others knew what was up, so we all just did our best to pretend I hadn’t screwed up the entire day.

After buckling into the car, I put in my earbuds and quickly queued up a song before Helena could bring up what’d happened.

Then I noticed the message on my phone.

Wes: Buy that dress. I’m begging you.

My stomach flipped. I could hear those words being spoken in his deep voice. Still, it was Wes. Surely he didn’t mean it the way it seemed.

I faltered over my response, staring down at the phone in my hand as visions of Wes Bennett danced in my head. I started writing more than one "cool" response, but then I just gave in to my pathetic needs.

Me: You like it?

The bubbles appeared like he was typing, but after a few minutes they disappeared. I waited, and they finally appeared again.

Wes: Michael will love it. Trust me.

I started to respond, like, five different times over the course of the day, but in the end, I said nothing. Because what was there to say? I'd been getting a little sucked into Wes's performance, stumbling over his charm, but his response had reminded me of my endgame.

Me. Michael.

Prom.

Boom.

CHAPTER TEN

"But mostly I hate the way I don't hate you. Not even close, not even a little bit, not even at all."

—10 Things I Hate About You

Wes: Movie at Michael's tomorrow. Are you still in?

I looked up from my phone to make sure the teacher was still lecturing and not looking at me as I broke the rules. My foot accidentally kicked Joss's chair in front of me as I held my phone down by my lap and texted: Definitely.

Wes: I'll pick you up at 6 so we can grab food on the way.

I glanced up for a second. I'd been going over my recent interactions with Wes in my head, and I needed to shore up our boundaries. All of our nice moments as of late were muddying the waters, and I needed to keep it together and focus on my goal.

The last thing I wanted was to mess everything up by having a silly flirtation misconstrued. It's not a date, right?

Wes: Ewww, Liz.

Me: Just checking. Can't have you getting attached.

Wes: As hard as this might be to believe, I'm having no trouble fighting the feels, you nice little weirdo.

That made me snort out a little laugh.

"Oh my God."

I glanced up, and Jocelyn was turned all the way around in her chair, looking at me with a huge grin on her face. She whispered, "You're texting him, aren't you?"

I cleared my throat. "Who?"

"You know who." She glanced over at the teacher before turning back and saying, "Bennett."

I inhaled through my nose before saying, "Yes, but we're just flipping each other shit. Totally platonic stuff."

"When are you going to admit that you like him? I'm not saying it's love or whatever you write about in your secret diary, but you genuinely enjoy the boy."

"Enjoy the Boy. Band name—called it."

"Damn you." She giggled and turned back around. Another point for me in the game we'd been playing for over a year.

I looked at the back of her head as the now-familiar feeling of guilt filled my stomach. I mean, technically she wasn't wrong; I *was* enjoying Wes. In a friend way, he was quickly becoming one of my favorite people.

But it was kind of bothering me, not knowing what was going to happen after tomorrow night. Would we still be friends once this all came to an end? Did he have any interest in that at all?

My phone buzzed at that very second. As if he knew I was thinking about him.

Wes: Meteor shower tonight, if you're interested. I've got Swishers, fyi.

I squeezed my lips together in an attempt not to smile, but it was no use.

Me: Who cares about meteor showers? If you bring the cherry ciggies, I'm so there.

Wes: You're such a shit. See you there.

"I was merely hiding it amongst your nerd books so I didn't get caught. I wasn't terrorizing you."

"Not buying it." I turned my stick so the marshmallows rotated in the fire. "First of all, you didn't have to decapitate the little cherub thingy at all. Second, you put red paint around the mouth and eyes and set the head up so it was staring out at anyone—namely me—who dared to access that little free library."

"I forgot about the paint." He smiled and put his big feet up on the side of the firepit. "Maybe there was a *little* terroristic intention."

"You think?" I removed the mallows from the fire and blew on them before pulling one off the stick. "Time has softened your memory of your old self. You believe—unless you're straight-up faking—that you were simply a rambunctious boy with no ill will toward me at all. And that is categorically untrue."

His eyes followed the squishy mallow that I shoved into my mouth. As I chewed, I realized that I was completely un-self-conscious around him. Instead of worrying that I looked like a pig, I said through a mouthful of marshmallow, "Admit it."

He looked at me filling my mouth for another few seconds. Then he said, "I will do no such thing. I will, however, admit that you were a lot of fun to mess with. And still are."

"Well, I didn't enjoy it back then, but now—now I can take you so it's cool."

"Please stop with the big talk." He grabbed the bag of snack-size Hershey bars, unwrapped one, and tossed it my way. "You cannot—and will not ever—*take* me. At least not when it comes to messing."

I caught the chocolate and sandwiched it with the other marshmallow between two grahams. I was holding the world's most perfect s'more. "You sure you don't want me to make one for you?"

"No, thanks, but your form is impressive."

"Not my first time, sunshine." I smiled and took a big bite. "Mmm—so good."

Wes chuckled his deep chuckle and looked up at the stars. He hadn't pulled out any cigars since I'd gotten there, so I wasn't sure if he was no longer in the mood or if he was holding off out of courtesy for me. He'd made fun of my armful of s'more supplies when I'd showed up, but he'd also eaten about ten of my tiny Hershey bars so far.

I heard the first few notes of "Forrest Gump" by Frank Ocean come out of Wes's Bluetooth speaker, and I smiled. Such a great sit-under-the-stars song. I hummed along with the intro and felt spring-giddy as the lyrics dripped over me like starlight.

My fingertips and my lips
They burn from the cigarettes

"What are your plans next year, Buxbaum?" He was still looking up at the sky, and my eyes lingered on his profile. Even though he wasn't my type, that strong jaw, prominent Adam's apple, and thick hair made a pretty, pretty picture.

I ignored the knot in my stomach at the mention of next year. "UCLA. You?"

That made him look over at me like I was crazy. "Seriously?"

"Um . . . *yeah* . . . ?"

"Why UCLA?"

I tilted my head. "Do you have a problem with UCLA?"

He had a weird look on his face. "No. Not at all. That was just . . . really unexpected."

I squinted at him in the darkness. "You're acting really weird about this."

"Sorry." His lips slid up into a half smile. "UCLA is a great school. What do you want to study—unrealistic romantic films?"

I rolled my eyes as he grinned a self-satisfied smile. "You think you're funnier than you actually are."

"I don't think so." He gestured with his hands for me to go. "Plan of study, please."

I cleared my throat. I hated ruining the night's vibes with talk of college. Talk of next year always left me feeling devastated because I knew firsthand how fast everything changed. Life pressed forward with a burning velocity that left all of the beautifully-pressed details quickly forgotten.

Once I went away, nothing would ever be the same again. My dad, the house, *her* rosebushes, our daily talks; those things would all be different when I returned. They'd fade into the past before I even had a chance to notice, and there would be no getting them back.

Even Wes. He'd been there since the beginning, living his life parallel to mine, but next year it would be different.

For the first time, he wouldn't be next door to me.

I cleared my throat and said, "Musicology."

"Sounds made up."

"Right?" I felt like I had UCLA's catalogue verbiage memorized after reading it so many times. "But it's legit and a really, really good program. I can minor in Music Industry and get a certification in Music Supervision."

"What job do you get with *that* after college?"

"I want to be a music supervisor." Usually when I said that, I was met with a screwed-up face and the one-syllable *Huh?* But Wes just sat there, listening. "It basically means I want to curate music for soundtracks."

"Whoa." He gave his head a little shake. "First of all, I had no idea that was a thing. But second—that is the perfect job for you. Holy shit, you already do that all the time."

"Yep." I took another bite of my s'more and licked off the marshmallow dripping onto my fingers. "And you have no idea; I have shelves *full* of soundtrack notebooks. I cannot wait to get started."

"Damn." He gave me a serious look that I felt in my belly. His voice was so deep in the dark of the Secret Area that anything other than silliness felt intimate. "You've always kind of done your own thing, Liz, and it's cool as shit."

Was it weird that his compliment sent warmth from the tips of my toes all the way to the squint of my eyes? All of the stresses were pushed away with that one *cool as shit* comment. "Thanks, Wes."

"That's Wessy to you."

"Yeah, no."

The moment was broken, but the warmth under my sternum remained, rendering me relaxed and blissfully content to thoughtlessly ramble. "What about you? Where's everybody's all-American going to college?"

"No idea." He leaned forward and moved the fire around with the s'more stick. "Baseball is just getting started, so it's still up in the air."

"Oh—so you want to play in college?"

"Yes, ma'am."

"And you're good enough . . . ?"

"Yes, I'm good enough, Liz." He coughed out a laugh. "Well, I hope."

"I don't mean that as a slam, by the way. I've just never gone to a game. What are you, like a hitter or something?"

"Okay—we are not talking baseball until you've actually watched a game. That was pathetic."

"I know." I brought my legs up to the chair and wrapped my arms around them. "So, do you think you'll go away to school or stay local?"

"Away." He looked into the fire, and the shadows from the flames danced on his face. "I've already had offers from schools in Florida, Texas, Cali, and South Carolina, so why would I want to stay in Nebraska?"

"Wow." How good *was* he? And even though *I* was planning on going away, why did the thought of Wes not being here—

forever in the house next door—cause a tiny little heart pain? I studied the fire and asked him, "Doesn't UNL have a really good baseball team?"

"They do—I can't believe you know that, by the way." He smiled but it didn't reach his eyes and he didn't look away from the fire. "I'm just ready to leave Nebraska behind. There's really nothing here for me, y'know?"

"No, I don't know." I unwrapped my arms from my legs and put my feet back down on the ground, bothered by what he'd just said. "I *hate* leaving it behind, but my dreams are all in California or New York."

He looked at me through narrowed eyes. "Are you mad?"

"No." Maybe? I rolled my eyes. "I mean, you do you. I just don't understand—"

"Libby?" My head whipped around at the sound of my dad's voice. There he was, standing in the clearing in his pajama pants and DINKER'S HAMBURGERS T-shirt, looking at me as if I were break-dancing naked on top of the fire. "What in God's name are you doing out here at eleven thirty on a school night?"

I thought back to Wes's original sneaking-out text. "I came out to see the meteor shower, and then Wes yelled over the fence for me to come over."

"Ooh—I forgot about the meteor shower." He came over and sat on the empty chair between Wes and me, plopping down on the cushion before casually rubbing the top of his curly hair. "How is it?"

Wes and I looked at each other then, because neither of us had really remembered the shower once we'd gotten out there. I said, "It's just great."

"Hand me a mallow, will you, sweetie? I haven't had a s'more in years."

Wednesday dragged by, mostly because I spent all day obsessed with two things. First, I was still bothered by Wes's comment the night before. *There's really nothing here for me.* Why would he say that? Did he really feel that way? I still didn't know that *much* about his whole, big life, but for some reason that hurt my feelings.

Maybe it was because I'd been having fun getting to know him, and I'd thought he felt the same way.

But when I forced myself to stop dwelling on that, I got super excited about the night to come. As I listened to Mr. Cooney drone on in trig, I decided I was going to wear the green top I'd bought with Wes and straighten my hair. I'd actually told Joss about it—yay, tricky honesty—so I was able to get her opinion on my outfit.

While Mrs. Adams encouraged the class to explore our inner writers in Lit, I popped in my earbuds and explored my inner daydream. I put "Electric" by Alina Baraz and Khalid on repeat, the perfect song to accompany my imaginings of the evening.

Darker than the ocean, deeper than the sea
You got everything, you got what I need

Only, the song kept making me think of Wes instead of Michael, which frustrated the crap out of me. No matter how many times I started thinking about what the night would bring, my brain flipped it and I was thinking about dinner with Wes.

Because I'd never eaten an actual meal with him. Well, not since our moms had given us both ham sandwiches at the Parkview Heights annual neighborhood picnic, but that didn't count, just like our s'mores last night didn't count either.

Did he eat a lot? Did he go all datey and pull out chairs for his female dinner partners?

It didn't help that Joss thought I was excited about going out with Wes. All through lunch, I babbled about how I was going to do my makeup, and her collusion made it kind of *feel* like I was excited about going out with Wes.

My lack of sleep the night before was clearly making me confused.

As soon as the final bell rang, I nearly ran to the car. My phone buzzed as I walked across the parking lot.

Wes: Okay—weird question.

Me: All questions from you are weird.

Wes: Ignoring that. Actually I have two questions. First—did I piss you off last night?

Kind of, but I didn't want it to spoil the impending evening so I responded with: Nope.

Wes: Liar. Tell me.

Like he really wanted to know. He just wanted to leave it all behind because there was nothing here for him. I rolled my eyes and texted: Get on with your question, Bennett.

Wes: Fine. Do you like dive bars with good food? I kinda feel like you're too ruffly for greasy burgers on napkins.

I unlocked my car and opened the door. Thank you for calling me ruffly, but I'm actually a shameless carnivore who'd sell her soul for a good burger.

Wes: Thank God. I'm jonesing for Stella's and I thought you might not be down for it.

He'd just bumped the already-appealing night up to wonderfully mouthwatering. I freaking LOVE Stella's!

Wes: I'll pick you up at 6. And FYI—"ruffly" wasn't a compliment.

I smiled and got into my car. Sure it wasn't.

When I got home, I ditched my school outfit—a supercute dress that was covered in bright red poppies—and took a second shower. After shooing Fitz off my clothes, I blow-dried and spent an eternity straightening the hair that wasn't meant to be anything other than kinky-curly. I even took extra time getting my eyeliner tails on point.

By the time Wes texted that he was about to ring my doorbell, I felt like I looked pretty good in an I-look-like-everyone-else kind of way. I quickly texted him: Don't ring. I'll be out in one minute.

Wes: I feel like you're ashamed of me.

Me: I so am.

Wes: Well if you aren't out in thirty seconds, I'm going to start honking the horn.

I threw open my bedroom door and ran down the hallway, zipping my cross-body bag as I flew down the stairs.

"Ooh—someone's in a hurry."

I stopped at the bottom of the steps and looked over at Helena, who was reading a book on the living room sofa and smiling at me as if I were entertaining. Things had been super awkward since dress shopping, but then yesterday it was like she'd decided to forget it. She'd picked up pizza for dinner and acted like my assholery had never happened. Thank God, because I really felt bad but wasn't sure how to apologize without eliciting further discussion.

I said, "I already told Dad that I'm going to Michael's with Wes. For movies. You weren't home yet when we talked about it."

She turned the book over and set it on the end table. "He told me. So . . . Wes is still helping you land the Michael, then?"

I could totally read on her face that she thought there was something going on— emotionally—with Wes. "Yep."

She looked at her watch. "It's awfully early for movie night, isn't it?"

"Wes and I are going to Stella's before we go over there." I didn't smile, but I felt like she could see the changing truth in my eyes. I waited for a comment.

"Well, isn't that just tasty?" She grinned, and we kind of had a whole conversation with our faces before I said—

"Whatever, dork." I ran a hand over my smooth hair and said, "You're just jealous that I'm going to Stella's and you aren't."

"God, I would lick the floor for one of those burgers right now."

I laughed. "I get that."

"Seriously. If someone said I could have a Stella burger this very minute if I licked the kitchen floor, I totally would."

That made me snort and I asked, "Do you want me to bring one back for you?"

"Oh my God, yes, please!" She leapt up and ran to her purse on the counter. "Are you serious?"

"Yes—" I started to answer when I heard the first honk. Oh, good Lord, Wes was honking. "I'm serious. But it'll be pretty cold by the time we're home."

It felt good to do something for her after the weirdness on Monday, but I kind of wished she'd come right out and asked me to get her one. Did she feel like she couldn't? I felt bad if that was the case, and there was a very large part of me that wished we were closer.

I was such a conflicted mess.

She pulled out a twenty and shoved it in my direction. "Don't care. Get me a double hamburger with everything on it."

"No way can you eat all of that."

"Bet."

I shook my head as I took her money. "I'll be home by eleven thirty or twelve, 'kay?"

"Be good, kid."

Wes laid on the horn then, and Helena said, "He's doing that on purpose, isn't he?"

I glanced at her over my shoulder, picturing Wes pushing me into the seat that ensured I was sitting next to Michael in the minivan. "I'm pretty sure he does *everything* on purpose."

I ran out the door and got into Wes's car. "I can't believe you honked."

"You can't?" He smiled over at me and waited while I buckled my seat belt. "It's like you've never met me. Nice shirt, by the way."

"Thanks." I buckled and tucked my hair behind my ears. "Someone told me that green is my second-best color."

"That makes sense, with your red hair and all."

I rolled my eyes again. "That isn't a thing."

"How can you not know the rules? I mean, Style 101."

"And you would know this how, Mr. Jockshop?"

"Because I'm smart." His mouth slid into a smirk as he put the car in reverse and backed out of the driveway. "Obviously."

"And you do this *why*?" Wes asked.

I smiled as I wrote my initials with ketchup on the napkin, encircling them with a big heart. "Tradition. Growing up, whenever we came here, I always wrote things with ketchup on the napkins while I waited for our food."

"That's weird."

"No, it isn't." I surrounded the big heart with smaller hearts. "You have to try it and see. There's something about the squirty ketchup tip that makes it great."

"Um, I'm good, but thanks."

"Oh my God, you're too cool to write with ketchup?"

"Well, yeah—for sure I am." He reached across the table and took the condiment from my hand. "But for the sake of being a good dinner partner, I will try your childish pastime."

"Good." I pulled some napkins out of the dispenser and laid them on the table in front of him. "And it isn't wasting, because you can dip your fries in it."

"I don't like ketchup on my fries."

"I don't even understand you, Wes."

He started making something on the napkin, and I noticed that *Wheel of Fortune* was on the TV behind the bar as Tom Jones's cover of "Kiss" wafted out from the antiquated jukebox. Stella's was a greasy bar that had formerly been a house, and even though they served the hamburgers on napkins and the place was entirely lacking in atmosphere, you considered yourself lucky if you were able to get a table during the lunch rush.

My city appreciated a good burger and hand-cut fries.

I looked back at his napkin, and he'd totally drawn a cartoony dude. It was a face in ketchup, way better than the childish letters I'd made. "So how was baseball today?"

He kept working with the ketchup. "Why are you asking me that?"

I watched his face as he concentrated. The length of his dark lashes was totally unfair. "Because now I know it's important. Like, not just a hobby. So . . . did you hit a homer? Or bunt a dinger?"

His lips turned up. "Stop it."

"Or are you a pitcher? Did you slide a curve ball?"

"You have to stop, Buxbaum." He gave me a good smile, and I curled my toes in my funky brown booties. "Either learn about the game, or never speak of it again."

The waitress appeared with our food (and Helena's in a to-go box), and we were alike in that our whole focus turned to the greasy offerings. No more small talk, no more banter. Our eyes were for food only.

"OhmyGodthisissogood." I swallowed my first bite of burger

and reached for my soda. "God bless you for bringing me here."

"I selfishly wanted it. You're just collateral damage."

"Don't even care." I dipped two fries and shoved them into my mouth. "All that matters is that my mouth has these delights inside it."

"Eww."

That made me snort. "Right?"

"Don't be snorting while you eat. If you aspirate food, you could get a lung infection and die."

I swallowed. "I have no idea how to respond to that statement."

He said, "'Thank you so much, Wessy, for looking out for me.' *That* is a perfect response."

I grabbed another fry. "Thank you so much, Wessy, for entertaining me with your inane conversation while we eat. This is definitely not boring."

"Well, that's good."

"Isn't it, though?"

We got quiet while we ate, but it was a comfortable quiet. I was lost in the food until he said, "Don't take this the wrong way, but you eat like a man."

"Sexist much?"

"Let me rephrase." He cleared his throat, wiped his hands on his napkin, held up a finger, and continued with, "Society—wrongly—expects a pretty girl to eat a salad and pick at her food, but you wolf down a burger like a person who's been starved for weeks. And probably raised by wolves."

It was ridiculous that his usage of the word "pretty" set my nerves on edge. He thought I was pretty? "I like food. Sue me."

He sat back a little in his chair and cracked the knuckles on his left hand. "So what's your plan tonight? How are you going to win over Mikey if I get you a one-on-one?"

Record scratch—Wes was a knuckle-cracker, wasn't he?

Knuckle-cracking was one of those things that I wouldn't call a pet peeve of mine, but whenever I heard that sound, I immediately jolted into a doglike sense of alert, looking around to see where the sound was coming from. It *usually* set me on edge.

"Well," I said, wiping my mouth with a napkin before reaching for another French fry. "I'm going to give him the one-two punch. First, I'll start by hitting him in the sentimentals, bringing back the cicada songs of his childhood with my soul-stroking reminiscing."

"Not bad," he said, and cracked the knuckles on his right hand. "Stroking is always a winner."

I looked at his half smile and wondered why his knuckle-cracking seemed *right.* Like, it somehow went with his face or something. "You know, I think I'll keep the rest to myself."

"Oh, come on." He reached out a hand and tugged at the tendril of hair by my face that stubbornly refused to straighten. "I'll be good."

Why did his physical nature and the way he had no problem with close contact—the hair tousles, the tugs, the nudges—always make my stomach go wild? I smacked his hand and grabbed one of his fries, saying a very calm "No, thank you."

But inside, I was freaking the freak out. What in God's name was happening? Knuckle-cracking was proven to bring on that icky this-one-is-not-right-for-me feeling; it *always* did. It was a straight-up eject button from any potential romantic relationship. But there I was, scant feet away from Wes and his knuckles, and I almost found his habit to be . . . endearing? Like, he kind of looked adorable when he smiled and cracked?

This was very, very wrong.

Because (A) Wes was the wrong guy, (B) my mother had warned me about falling for guys like him, and (C) he had no interest in me at all, hence the *There's really nothing here for me* comment the night before. What on earth was I doing with my emotions?

"Oh my God, you beat me."

"What?" I looked around, unsure of what he was talking about.

He swallowed and grabbed a napkin. "You finished your food already."

He was right. I looked from my plate—completely clean save for some small grease puddles, ketchup smears, and tiny grains of salt—to his, which still held three bites of burger and a small grouping of fries. "So?"

"So holy shit, you eat fast."

"Or holy shit, *you* eat like an octogenarian."

That made his eyes squint. "Want the rest of my fries?"

I looked at the greasy, hand-cut fries. "You're not going to eat them?"

He shoved the plastic bowl of fries toward me. "This little old man is full."

I grabbed four fries and dunked them into his ketchup. "Well, then, thank you, grandpa."

As I wolfed down those fries, it was impossible for me to ignore the fact that I was in no hurry for dinner to end. I'd been having fun with Wes. I'd been smiling the entire time (when I wasn't rolling my eyes)—and even knowing Michael was waiting, I wasn't ready to go.

But it was just because things were so easy between us—*that* was what had confused me. Our friendship was so comfortable that it muddied the waters.

Boom.

It made me think of *When Harry Met Sally*. Minus the ending-up-together part.

"Do you think men and women can be friends, Bennett?"

He picked up his water. "Sure. I mean, *we* are, aren't we?"

"I guess we kind of are." I was playing it cool—he had no idea what his friendship over the past week meant to me. I hadn't realized it either, to be honest, but the fact that we'd had some seriously incredible conversations that centered on my mother made it different from every other relationship in my life.

"Weird, right?" He took a drink, his eyes never leaving me as he swallowed. "You never thought that shit would happen, did you?"

"For sure no." I swallowed the bite of fries and reached for more. "But a lot of people say it doesn't work. That—"

"Is this the Harry-Sally thing?"

"How do *you* know about that?"

"My mom loves that movie. I've seen it a few times."

"A *few* times? See? I *knew* you liked rom-coms!"

"Oh, for the love of God, no." He shook his head like I was

ridiculous. "I just like Billy Crystal. If he can be Mike Wazowski, he can be anybody. It's a funny movie and that is all."

"And you don't think he's right? The fact that they get together in the end pretty much proves his theory, yeah?"

"Maybe. I don't know." He did a little shrug thing that made me notice his shoulders. *Damn you, Helena.* He said, "I think he has some valid points, but it's irrelevant for us."

"It is?"

"Sure." He scratched his cheek and said super matter-of-factly, "We're the exception because I'm not your friend—I'm your little love fairy godfather."

"That sounds gross." I made the joke, but I didn't like that he'd said he wasn't my friend.

He ignored the joke and said, "It's true, though. We're *like* friends, for now, but the fairy godfather is all about helping you get what you want. Once the magic starts happening, he doesn't stick around for the fairy-tale ending. I mean, how creepy would *that* be?"

"*Really* creepy?" I fake-laughed, like we were on the same page. But was he saying that if I ended up with Michael, then we wouldn't be friends anymore? That we really weren't friends at all now, but merely role-players making my wish happen?

It made sense after what he'd said last night.

"That's right, Buxbaum." He reached across the table and touched the tip of my nose—a boop—with his finger. "Creepy as hell."

I was struggling to keep up, to process what he was saying and what it meant for us, while also overanalyzing the fact that even a finger-boop made my stomach go wild, when his mouth turned into a smirk and he said, "Now finish those fries so we can get you to your Michael."

"Done." I shoved the last fry into my mouth and pushed back my chair, needing to get out into some fresh air before my brain exploded. "Let's go, fairy godfather."

CHAPTER ELEVEN

"If you look for it, I've got a sneaky feeling you'll find that love actually is all around."

—Love Actually

"Hey, it's Mrs. Potato Head!"

I followed Wes through the kitchen door and smiled when I saw Adam standing at the center island, loading up a plate full of Pizza Rolls. I gave him a chin-nod and said, "It's me."

"Your face looks way better, by the way. You're very un-potatoey now."

"Gee, thanks."

"Noah felt like shit about breaking your face, so make sure you make him feel extra bad." He picked up his plate and grabbed a can of Coke. "He deserves it."

Wes and I went into the living room behind him, and it was clear we were the last ones there. The room was filled with mostly the same people from the basketball game, plus three others. Ashley, the girl who'd puked on me; Laney (ugh); and Alex, the one who liked Wes.

Talk about a nightmarish trifecta of people, right?

"Liz, I am so sorry about your nose." Noah was sitting on the sofa between Alex and Ashley, and he pointed at my face. "It looks good now, though."

That made me smile. "Thanks. And don't worry about it."

Adam said, "Come on, Potato Head—you had one job."

"I know, and I'm sorry."

"Oh, hey, Liz!" Laney, who was stretched out in the recliner, smiled over at us. "I didn't know you guys were coming."

My brain mocked her in a high-pitched, Muppet Babies kind of voice before I just said, "Yeah."

"Hey, guys. Snacks are in the kitchen and the movie's about to start." Michael popped up from where he was lying on the floor and gave us a small wave.

"That's good," Wes said from behind me. "Because I think Liz's probably getting hungry."

"Haha." I turned around, and his face did that thing to my stomach again, which pissed me off because he didn't even think of me as his friend. "I eat a lot; you're hilarious."

"I know."

There wasn't a way for me to remove myself from Wes without causing weirdness, so we sat together on the floor, and everyone got quiet as the movie started. It was this really intense thriller, and everyone was silent so they wouldn't miss out on anything important. But I couldn't concentrate on the movie because I was trying to figure out why Wes was making me irrationally emotional.

I also couldn't concentrate because my thigh was touching Wes's thigh.

We both had our legs stretched out in front of us as we leaned back on our palms; nothing was intimate about our position. But it's like the spot where my right outer thigh touched his left outer thigh was inflamed and I couldn't ignore it. Every tiny molecule of my existence was focused on that one solitary spot.

Was it warm in that house?

My eyes watched as a man on the television was murdered by a serial killer who jammed the man's head into the propeller of a boat motor, but my mind was on Wes. Wes and the fact that if he and I were reclined a little more, like, resting back on our elbows, all he'd have to do was lean his body a little in my direction, so he was hovering over me, and we'd be perfectly aligned for him to kiss me.

He'd look down at my lips with those dark eyes and he would visibly swallow with that prominent Adam's apple that for some reason always distracted me, and then—

"Buxbaum."

"Huh?" I turned my head to the right and looked at him, a tiny bit gaspy and feeling like I'd been woken from a dream. What the hell was I doing?

My face was hot as he leaned a little closer, to where his shoulder nudged mine. He gave me a squinty-eyed smirk and whispered, "I'm a little uncomfortable with the level of attention you just gave to that slashing. I don't think you blinked."

I blinked then, my cheeks getting even hotter—if that was possible—as he whispered to me in the dark. My mouth curled up into a smile that I had no control over, and I whispered back, "Quit watching me, creeper."

And then the moment just stopped.

Paused.

Held.

His smirk disappeared and his face turned intense. His jaw flexed and I could hardly breathe as I looked back at him, my heart pounding as I let myself be obvious and look at his mouth for the quickest of seconds.

His mouth that was just so incredibly close to mine.

When I brought my eyes back to his, I knew without a doubt that if we were anywhere else—alone—he would kiss me. He swallowed, and my eyes tracked down to his throat before slowly climbing back up by way of his strong chin, nose, and dark-as-night brown eyes.

He raised one eyebrow, an unspoken question, and I realized at that moment that I wanted it. I wanted Wes. Michael had been my endgame, but I couldn't bring myself to care about that anymore.

I wouldn't run through a train station for Michael. But I would do it for Wes.

Holy shit.

I raised my right shoulder in a shrug that nudged his shoulder, a touch of my cotton against his fleece.

"Scoot over." Noah plopped down beside me and said, "I'm going deaf sitting between those screamers."

Nooo!

I sat up and moved a hair closer toward Wes, careful not to look at him as I shifted over. The moment had been broken, and part of me was disappointed that we'd been interrupted, while the other part was embarrassed and utterly clueless about whether what I thought had just happened had actually happened at all.

I stared blankly at the TV for what seemed like an eternity before I heard Wes whisper, "I'm going to get a drink. You want one?"

I took a deep breath—*please don't be mocking*—and turned to face him. But instead of the smart-ass expression that was Wes's default, he gave me a devastatingly hopeful smile as he waited for my response.

I swallowed and felt trembly as I smiled back at him. "That'd be great. Thanks."

"Diet Coke, right?"

I nodded and had to concentrate on not sweating after he got up and left the room.

What in the actual the hell?

When I came back from the restroom, Wes still hadn't returned to his spot on the floor. I glanced around the dark living room before noticing that he was out on the deck. At first, I couldn't tell who he was talking to, but then I saw it was Alex.

Talk about a glass of cold water to the face.

He was out there with the pretty girl that he knew liked him, while I was feeling near-vomitous over the confusing things I was thinking about my next-door neighbor. Talk about a yawning chasm.

I gnawed on my lip and squinted, trying to see them better. He'd said he wasn't interested in her, and I believed he'd meant it, but that didn't mean it couldn't change, right? And what if I'd been misreading every little thing between Wes and me to begin with?

My little fairy godfather might only be interested in finding love *for* me, not with me, right?

Had I completely imagined the moment on the floor?

I took my spot and watched the rest of the movie, but my attention was now on the two people I could see in my periphery. What were they talking about? Why were they out there? I totally lost focus and was happy when the movie ended and they came inside.

I needed to get my head straight.

The people around me started talking to each other, and I felt awkward and out of place. And I missed Jocelyn. We texted every day, like always, but I hadn't spent any quality time with her lately. Being with all these people who were close friends with each other made me homesick for her; I needed to go over there after I got home.

In fact, it was probably time for me to come clean to her about the whole thing.

"Did you know that Michael's father has a grand piano?" Wes looked down at me from where he'd perched his big self on the back of the sofa and held out a hand to help me up. "It's upstairs in an acoustically designed room."

I grabbed his hand and climbed to my feet, and oh sweet Lord, it felt like a Mr.-Darcy-hand-flex-from-the-best-version-of-*Pride-&-Prejudice* moment. The world stopped spinning for just a second when his big hand wrapped around mine.

But then, just as fast, the spinning returned, and I was face-to-face with Wes and all of my confusion. I looked at his face—and then at Michael, who I hadn't even noticed until then—and realized they were waiting for a response from me.

To what, again? What was words? How was talk?

"Wow." *Dad. Piano. Room. Got it.* "For real?"

"I think he's convinced he could've been a classical pianist if he'd had that room at a younger age." Michael crossed his arms and said, "He's obsessed with it."

"Our Little Liz plays piano." Wes gave me a look and said to Michael, "She's really good."

I said, "No, I'm not—"

Just as Michael said to me, "Do you want to see it?"

I blinked. "I would *love* to."

"Well, then, follow me, Miz Liz."

Michael walked over to the stairs and I followed, but I almost tripped when I glanced behind me and saw that Wes wasn't coming with us. He was laughing at something Adam was saying, so I took a deep breath and proceeded upstairs, overwhelmed by my thoughts as I climbed the steps.

Was this some sort of a signal? By literally handing me off to Michael, was that his figurative way of handing me off and walking away?

Gosh, it probably would've been funny if it were happening to someone else. Here was my beautiful Michael, inviting me—and not Laney—to see a dream-come-true music room, and I just wanted him to go away so I could be with Wes.

Was that okay? I was having trouble keeping up with myself.

How would my mother have written this part? Would she have seen the good in the "bad boy" and twisted the plot?

Dammit.

Stop thinking, Liz.

"Where are your parents?" I cleared my throat and shut down my inner thoughts. "I haven't seen them in, like, a million years."

"They went to a movie," Michael said as he took the stairs two at a time. "But my mom would love to see you."

When we reached the top of the stairs, he led me to a closed door that looked like it belonged to just another bedroom. He pushed it open, and . . .

"Oh my God."

The room had a shiny wood floor, and a thick rug sat underneath the baby grand piano that was turned diagonally on one side of the space. He started telling me about reflection, diffusion, and absorption, about how the decorations in the room were strategically placed for better-quality sound, but I couldn't listen to him.

That piano was so beautiful. I walked over and sat down on the bench. I wanted to play it—badly—but clearly this was a big deal to his dad, and I was a chump player. Wes liked to act like I was good because I was the only person our age who still took lessons once a week, but I was decent at best.

I loved the piano, though. I loved it so much. I was sure my mom's obsession with the instrument had something to do with it, but there was also nothing quite like closing my eyes and just losing myself in a song I'd played a hundred times before, tweaking the tempo and passion and listening to see if I could hear the minute differences I'd attempted to create.

"You can play it, Liz," Michael said, walking over to the door and closing it. "My dad had the room insulated so no one downstairs can hear you playing if the door's closed."

"It's too nice—I can't." The black piano didn't have a speck of dust on it. How was that possible? "And it's your dad's instrument—no one else should touch it."

"He's been fixing to play it but hasn't since we moved here—go ahead."

I pushed back the keyboard cover, cleared my throat, and said, "Prepare to be underwhelmed."

Michael grinned. "Consider me prepared."

I smiled and started playing the beginning of Adele's "Someone Like You," remembering Wes telling me to add it to our soundtrack after our phone conversation on the night when my nose got smashed.

Michael's mouth turned up into a grin. "You have it memorized?"

"It's really easy, actually." I felt awkward as my fingers ran over the keys. "It's mostly a four-chord loop. Anyone could play it."

"Pretty sure I couldn't."

My eyes went up to his as he leaned against the piano, looking down at me. He was so handsome, with the same smile he'd first charmed me with in grade school, but I couldn't stop wondering what Wes was doing downstairs. I was barely into the song when the door flew open and there was everyone . . . except Wes and Alex.

My hands jumped into my lap, and I felt like the world's biggest dork. Wes's friends looked at me, and I'm sure they thought I was a weirdo for playing piano when everyone else was hanging out.

And it was obvious they all hung out a lot, because the entire group just picked up where they'd left off downstairs, talking and laughing like they were best friends.

Laney came over and stood beside the piano, saying to me, "I can't believe you can play like that."

"I thought the room was soundproof."

"It's insulated." Michael said it to both me and Laney. "You can't hear it downstairs, but you can from the hallway."

"Ah." I felt silly, seated at that piano.

"Your Adele was awesome."

"It's a super easy song." *Like I need your compliments, Laney.* "But thanks."

"It was still great and I'm jealous." Her eyes moved to Michael where he stood on my right, and her face kind of got prettier as she smiled at him. Maybe it was because my night had gone completely off course, but her expression made me feel a little bad for her. That look on her face, what it said? I could relate.

I told her, "I seriously could teach it to you in an hour. It's so nothing."

"Seriously?" She crossed her arms and gave me wide eyes. "You could?"

Wes finally appeared in the doorway, with Alex trailing right behind him, and he said, "We should order a pizza."

"Ooh—I'm in," Alex said, and I felt a tightness in my sternum as she smiled at Wes. He looked down at her and smiled right back. He was giving her his best smile, the one that was fun but also warm and happy, and I gritted my teeth as she flipped her hair and asked, "But from where?"

And then—Wes looked at me.

It was fleeting, barely even a glance, but his gaze met mine for a brief second and I felt it in my every nerve ending. What was he doing? Was he still trying to wingman me, after everything?

"Zio's," Noah said, and he and the others started following Wes and Alex out of the room and down the stairs. I stared at the empty doorway, unable to think about anything other than Wes and that scorching look and the unfortunate proximity of Alex.

You just ate, Wes—what are you even doing?

Alex was lovely, and I'd *thought* they'd be a good match when I'd initially heard of her feelings, but now I thought that she was a little too serious for him. I mean sure, she seemed fun enough, but compared to Wes's total disregard for anything mature, she was a bit stoic.

Besides, Wes and I had had a moment downstairs, dammit.

Right? Or had I imagined it?

"You say the word 'pizza' and the room clears."

I jumped when Michael spoke. I hadn't even realized he was still there.

I smiled and casually stood. "Who doesn't love pizza, right?"

He gestured to the hallway. "Do you want to go get in on that?"

"Um, no, thanks." I shook my head, not wanting to follow Wes, especially if he was canoodling with Alex. "Wes and I went to Stella's before we got here and I'm still full."

"That's right—he told me you were getting dinner before you came."

"Yeah."

"He also told me that things were more friend-y with you two and he's thinking about asking Alex out."

I tried to look like I didn't care. I smiled over the heavy feeling in my stomach and said, "Yeah, he's right. He totally should—she seems great."

"Yeah. Apparently he's sick of being stuck in your friend zone so he's moving on."

"Finally." I rubbed my lips together and focused on Michael's blue eyes. *This is what you wanted. Starting anything with Wes would be bad, bad news. Eyes on the prize, girl.* "I didn't want things to get weird, so this is really good."

"Probably."

"Um, when did he tell you that?" *Days ago, please.* "About Alex?"

"When we were in the kitchen."

"Ah." I looked at the piano keys and swallowed, and it felt like there was something stuck in my throat. I mean, it was exactly what we'd planned for Wes to say, so there was no reason for me to feel unsettled by this, right?

Michael's phone made a noise, bringing me out of my daze. He looked down at the message, sighed, and then put his phone back in his pants pocket.

"Um—are you okay?" I asked, because his anxious face looked the same as it had back in grade school when he'd dropped his favorite Boggle game on the sidewalk and all the little letter pieces had bounced into the bushes. He'd always been the kind of person to stress about every little thing.

Except—dear Lord—I knew nothing about Michael *now*. At all. I knew he spoke with a Southern drawl and had good hair—that's all. Sure, the Michael I knew in elementary school liked bugs and books and being kind, but what did I know about him today? I knew Wes a thousand times better than Michael, and I was kind of starting to adore that next-door neighbor of mine.

Shit.

What was I even doing in this room with Michael?

He fingered the sharp keys, staring at the piano. He pressed his index finger down on the middle C and said, "It's this whole thing with Laney and prom."

My body's innate response to the name "Laney" was to jump for joy when it was said in a less-than-positive tone. But now I couldn't muster up the emotion. I asked, "Are you guys going? I didn't know. I mean, I heard you were talking. But, y'know . . ."

I trailed off, not wanting to seem like I knew all the gossip.

"Well, no. I mean, no, we're not going yet." He sighed yet again. "See, we *have* been talking, and Laney's wonderful. But on the day I met her, her boyfriend had just broken up with her. Literally. I met her because she was outside crying."

"Oh." I had no idea who she'd dated, but it was kind of hard to believe that Laney Morgan got dumped.

"So I have no idea what's going on in her head. I don't want to move too fast if she isn't ready, and I especially don't want to start something if she's still hung up on her ex."

I felt a little bad for him because I could totally empathize. Wanting something but being unsure if you're able to have it?

Or if it's safe to have? Yeah, I got that. And now that I knew how I actually felt, the new, enlightened, emotionally honest Liz wanted to help Michael with Laney, give him some kind of advice.

But at the same time, I wanted to leave this conversation and bolt downstairs to find Wes before Alex started wearing him like a shirt. I said, "Can't you ask her to prom as a friend and see where it goes?"

"I could." He played with the keys a little more. "But prom should *mean* something. Maybe it's the Texas bigness I'm used to, but to me, it's about the promposal and dinner and flowers and *more*. Is that silly?"

I snorted a laugh. "Oh my God, no—think about who you're talking to here."

He looked up and grinned.

"That's right. Little Liz," I said, and pointed to myself and rolled my eyes. "I feel the exact same way. I'm supposed to go with Joss, and I'm sure it'll be fun, but I'm with you. That's not how I've always daydreamed senior prom would be."

I pictured Wes's face, and my hands felt hot. I shook them out and said, "The more I think about it, the more I don't want to settle. I want the possibility of more, even if it doesn't work out. I want to take the chance for a magical night, because even if it flops, I can at least have a date with possibility instead of a friend."

He tilted his head a little and smiled at me. "You might have a point, Liz."

"I know I do." I was getting worked up at the thought of going to prom with Wes. Someone needed to douse me with cold water, fast. Because suddenly it felt like it was all I'd ever wanted. "Trust me when I tell you that sometimes the person with the most 'magical night possibility' is the last person you'd expect. Sometimes there can be someone you've known forever, yet never really noticed."

God, I wished I'd noticed sooner. My brain was spewing out little montages of Wes and me—in the Secret Area, at Stella's, on the way home from the party . . .

How had I not noticed sooner?

"I think I know what you mean," Michael said, staring at me intensely, and alarm bells started going off in my head. I wasn't sure why he was looking at me like that, but now definitely wasn't the time.

Adam popped his head in the doorway and said, "We need you guys. We're doing team Cards Against Humanity."

"Yes!" I shouted my response, thrilled to be interrupted.

Adam tilted his head and gave me a *What's-the-matter-with-you* grin, and Michael was still eyeballing me. I cleared my throat and tried to recover, saying with a casual look, "I mean, count me in."

"I've never played that on teams," Michael said, giving me a weird look.

"Me either," I agreed, anxious to find Wes.

"We're only playing teams because Alex wants to pair up with Wes." Adam gave me a look of commiseration, like we were of the same opinion, and I wasn't quite sure what to do with it. "She says it's more fun that way, but I'm pretty sure she just wants to share a chair with him."

"Well, let's do it." Michael gave me a nice smile, but it did nothing for me. At all. It just reminded me that I needed to get down to that card game before Alex ended up with my happy ending.

CHAPTER TWELVE

"He had kissed her long and good. We got banned from the pool forever that day, but every time we walked by after that, the lifeguard looked down from her tower, right over at Squints, and smiled."

—*The Sandlot*

"Thank God we parked close." Wes started the car and turned on the windshield wipers as the rain pounded down. "We would've been drenched if we'd been a second later."

My heart was beating in my neck. The inside of the dark car felt intimate against the roaring storm, and I was wholly unsettled. Since the moment I'd realized the way I truly felt about Wes, I'd been overwhelmed with a sort of panicked need to tell him. To make sure he knew before Alex got comfortable on him. "For sure."

"Sorry about my sketchy friends."

"Nah—it's cool." He was referring to the fact that his friends had played Cards Against Humanity for about five minutes before deciding they *all* wanted to go along when Noah got the pizza. I'm fairly certain I was smiling maniacally when Alex climbed into the minivan. "I was supposed to go home as soon as the movie ended, anyway."

"Yeah, what's with that? You're months away from leaving for college, but your dad's still all over your business. Is he a smidge overprotective, maybe?"

He looked over his shoulder before putting the car in drive and pulling onto the street, and the new song from Daphne Steinbeck—"Dark Love"—was starting on the radio. It was slow and heavy on the sexy building beat, and I considered switching the station because it felt like too much.

It was too perfect.

I said, "Big-time. Even though he's moved on with his life, he never forgets about my mother's accident and the fact that sometimes the things that seem unlikely to happen in life *do* actually happen."

"Wow." He glanced over at me. "Pretty tough to argue over that one, eh?"

"I don't even bother."

The rain intensified, and Wes switched the windshield wipers to full speed. He pulled out slowly onto Harbor Drive, the busy street that ran parallel to Michael's neighborhood, and the bright, multicolored lights from the businesses lining the road were completely blurred by the downfall. I leaned forward, cranked the defroster, and said as casually as I could, "So Alex, huh? You're going to ask her out?"

"Did Michael say that?" He craned his neck closer to the windshield, taking his time as we neared an intersection. The stoplight switched to green, and he accelerated when the cars at the cross street all came to a stop. All clear, we got back up to speed, but in the distance I saw a Jetta zip out of a gas station and onto the road in front of the Suburban we were following entirely too closely and—

"Car!" I braced myself for impact as the brake lights in front of us glowed bright red through the drenched and foggy window. Wes's tires tried to stop on the wet pavement, but the brakes locked, and we were going to slam into that Suburban.

Wes steered the car to the right, throwing us up and over what might've been a curb, and then we were headed for something very green. It looked like a forest.

"Shitshitshitshit," he chanted as he attempted to control the car. His foot mashed on the brake, but as the headlights lit up the steep, muddy slope in front of us, we just kept moving down that hill and toward the trees. We were going to hit a tree—there was no way we weren't—and I said a prayer as fast as I could while my heart pounded.

He jerked the wheel again, and as soon as he did, I felt a huge bump, like we'd hit something, and I worried the car was going to flip over.

But it lurched to a stop instead.

I looked over at Wes, and his face was flushed like he'd just come back from a run. We were both breathing hard as thunder continued to pound, the rain slapped on the roof of the truck, and the radio still played "Dark Love." "Did that just happen?"

"Are you okay?" His hands were still tightly wrapped around

the wheel, and he blinked at me, frozen, before he unclenched his fingers and put the car in park. "Holy shit, Liz."

"I'm fine." I tried to look out the windshield but still couldn't see anything. "Oh my God, we're fine . . . ?"

"Oh my God." He laid his back on his seat and let out his breath. "That was wild."

Wild. From the time he'd slammed on the brakes until now had probably been a minute—tops. But that minute had been like an hour. In the span of that minute I'd worried that we were going to die. I'd worried about how my dad would survive if something happened to me, I'd worried about Joss, I'd worried about Wes's mom, and I'd mourned the fact that I'd never get the chance to see things through with Wes.

Bizarre, right?

"I can't believe we're okay," I said, remembering the way Wes had jerked the wheel. I said, "You were incredible."

He unbuckled his seat belt and didn't look at me. "Incredibly reckless for driving in this weather, you mean."

"No, I mean not only did your driving keep us from slamming into that car, but then it kept us from slamming into a tree." I unbuckled my seat belt too, and added, "Thank you."

"Don't thank me yet. I might've gotten us stuck." He reached in front of me and opened the glove box, rummaged until he came up with a flashlight. "Wait here—I'm going to check it out."

He opened his door and got out. I tried peering through the windshield, to see for myself, but the windows were so fogged,

I saw nothing. I opened my door and stepped out, immediately getting pummeled by the hard pounding rain as my foot squished down into the wet mud.

"Shit!" I lowered my head and ran around the front of the car to where I could sort of see Wes kneeling next to the tire. I stopped beside him and squatted. Yelled, "Seriously? A rock?"

It looked like our tire had slammed into a huge boulder and then gotten hung up on it. Wes's front tire was literally off the ground. He squinted, rain sluicing over his face as he looked surprised to see me. "I thought I told you to wait in the car."

"You're not the boss of me," I hollered through the rain, and his face went from rock-hard seriousness to amused softness in a second. I said, "Besides, if you die, I'm stuck out here all alone."

"True," he bellowed, grabbing my wet hand with his and pulling me up. "I'm getting back in the car—would the lady care to join me?"

"She would, actually."

Instead of coming around to my side, he opened his door and gently pushed me inside. I giggled and climbed in, scooting over to the middle of the bench seat, and when his big body got in and the door slammed shut, the inside of his car seemed incredibly insulated.

For a few seconds we were quiet, each of us wiping water from our faces and pushing drenched hair from our eyes. Then he pulled out his phone and dialed a number.

"I'm calling my dad," he said as he raised the phone to his ear, looking at the steering wheel. "He can get here fast, and his buddy has a tow truck."

"Cool." I looked down and whispered, "Oh no—my Chucks."

They were covered in wet, sticky mud, and that made me more upset than it should've. They were just sneakers, after all, and it was just mud. But . . . I'd wanted them to stay as perfect as they'd been when Wes had walked them over to the counter at Devlish and paid for them.

Maybe I could wash them in bleach when I got home.

I pulled down the visor and looked in the mirror as he told his dad what had happened and where we were. I wiped under my eyes in an attempt to eradicate raccoon-eye, but my trembling fingers were no good.

I flipped the visor back up and took a deep breath. I was shaken by the accident, but this weird surge of adrenaline I was feeling was something more.

Because it occurred to me, as Wes's car sat there with one tire in the air, that life was unpredictable. No matter how much planning you did, and no matter how safe you played it, something intangible was always going to rear its head and shake things up.

Which made me wonder.

If my mom had still been alive, would she have changed her tune by now on the whole bad-boy thing? It seemed to me that *because* of things like car accidents and lost loves, life and death and broken hearts, we should grab every moment and absolutely devour the good parts. Wouldn't she want that? For me to ad-lib my life instead of living by some typed-in-twelve-point-Courier-New script?

"He'll be here in ten minutes." Wes dropped his phone into the cupholder and turned his eyes on me. "I am so sorry, Lib."

I suppressed a shiver and wondered if he'd meant to call me that. He usually only said it when he was teasing, but this time it'd been personal. Intimate. Almost as if we really were a thing. My voice didn't sound right as I said, "No worries—you didn't drive me headfirst into a tree, so we're good."

That made his face soften. "Good."

I rolled in my lips and felt nervous, mostly because I really, really, really wanted to tell him how I felt and what I wanted. I took a deep breath and said, "Wes."

"Hey. Your curls are back." His brown eyes narrowed a little and his lips turned up. "I think I've missed them."

He started to lift his hand, like he was going to touch my wet hair, but then he didn't.

Disappointment shot through me as I breathed around a laugh. "Weren't you the one who demanded I straighten my hair?"

"I was." His skin was wet from the rain too—obviously—and a drop was poised to tumble off the tip of his nose. Those brown eyes traveled all over my face, dipping over my eyes and cheeks and mouth before he said in a hoarse, deep voice, "And I think I regret all of it. I miss your clothes and curly hair. You look best when you're you."

You look best when you're you. Oh, God.

We were so close, lips mere inches away as we sat face-to-face on his front seat. I felt like there was no one else in the world, nothing but me and Wes in the steamy-windowed cab of his car as the rain cocooned us in showers. I wanted him to lean in and kiss me—I wanted it so badly—but I knew he wouldn't.

How did I know?

Because I'd spent my entire life making sure Wes Bennett knew just how much I would never-ever-ever want him to kiss me. I said on a breath, "Gee, thanks, Bennett."

His voice was quiet when he said, "I mean it."

And then I kissed him.

Going for it, I slid my arms around his neck and pressed my lips against his, turning my head just a little and scooting my hips over on the bench seat. The smell of his cologne mixed with the smell of the rain, and he was all around me.

Wes was frozen for a second, unmoving as my mouth rested against his mouth. The thought that he might not want to kiss me crossed my mind too late. Could I retreat and play this off? Do a whole *Oops, I was unbalanced from the accident and fell on your mouth with my mouth* bit?

And then, as if struck by lightning, Wes inhaled and his hands tightened on the sides of my face. He was kissing me back. I was kissing Wes Bennett, and he was kissing me.

It went from breathily timid to scalding hot in an instant.

He angled his head and kissed me the way Wes was supposed to kiss, wild and sweet and entirely overconfident all at the same time. He knew exactly what he was doing as his big hands slid into my hair, but it was the shudder in his breath and the slight tremor in his touch that I drew on. The fact that he felt as out of control as I felt.

Wes slid me even closer to him on the seat, so we were pressed chest-to-chest. For the first time in my life, I understood how people could just forget where they were and have wild, indiscriminate sex in the front seat of a car. I wanted to wrap my legs around his waist, climb all over him, and explore everything that had ever been done with two bodies. And I was still (sort of) a virgin.

I couldn't stop my hands from going everywhere as I got lost in the all-encompassing everything of our moment. I slid them under his hoodie as his teeth nipped at my bottom lip, and then they were on his face, feeling the rigid solidity of his jawline while he kissed me like it was his job and he wanted a raise. He made a sound when I dug my hands into his hair—like he liked it—and I wanted it to rain like that forever and never stop.

It wasn't until he said my name—whispered it into my mouth—three times that I came back to reality.

"Liz."

"Hmmm?" I opened my eyes but my vision was kind of unfocused. I smiled when I saw his pretty face so close to mine. "What?"

His dark eyes were heavy-lidded as he said, "I think my dad's here."

"What?" I felt totally out of it as I blinked up at him and his hand moved slowly back and forth on my lower back. I don't think I would've heard or noticed if a pack of wild dogs had run by.

Then I saw the headlights next to his car.

"Oh." I took a deep breath and ran a hand over my hair, squinting as the too-bright light illuminated everything. I whispered, "Shit."

"I should probably go talk to him before he opens your door." His lips were *almost* touching my ear as he quietly spoke to me. "Okay?"

My eyes were barely open as I felt his hot mouth whisper over my earlobe.

"Libby?"

I shook my head. "Nuh-uh."

That earned me a deep, dirty chuckle that curled my toes inside my shoes. His breath tickled my nerve endings as he said, "I'm good with staying if you don't mind my dad seeing us like this."

"Fine, go," I muttered, and pushed on his chest, feeling somehow possessive of Wes Bennett as I reveled in the feel of his chest under my palms. His eyes went down to my hands for the quickest of seconds and his forehead creased, but just like that it was normal again.

I gave him a look and said, "I was done with you anyway."

"Whatever, Miss *Nuh-Uh.*" His smile told me he knew exactly how much he'd affected me. He opened his door and said, "Be right back, Elizabeth."

"I'll be here, Wessy," I said, which received more dirty chuckling before he got out and slammed the door behind him.

I adjusted my wet clothing and attempted to straighten my hair. *Oh my God, oh my God, did that really just happen?* I felt like Wes's dad would be able to tell just by looking at me that I'd been making out with his son, but there probably wasn't a lot I could do about that.

"Hey." The passenger door opened and Wes leaned in. "He's going to need Webb's truck to get my car out so he's just going to take us home and come back."

I blinked and wondered why I hadn't spent my entire life being awestruck by the sight of his face. I let my eyes stumble all over it. "Okay."

His lips turned up into a sexy grin, and I swear to God, he knew what I was thinking. He put his mouth next to my ear and said, "I was *not* ready for him to be here yet."

I felt warm all over when he lifted his head and we smiled at each other. "I wasn't either," I admitted.

"Come on, kids—I'm gettin' soaked out here," Mr. Bennett yelled from somewhere behind Wes before he got into his car and closed the door.

Wes held out his hand, and when I grabbed it and climbed out of the car, he didn't let go. Instead he laced his long fingers between mine, without looking at me, and led me over to his dad's car in the pouring rain.

Wes Bennett was holding my hand.

He opened the back door . . . and a big box was on the seat.

"Other side," his dad said, and Wes let go of my hand and

opened the front passenger door for me instead. I got in, and he gave me a wink before closing my door.

I was in deep trouble because that wink straight-up made me light-headed.

"Thanks," I said as he shut my door, ran around to the other side, and got in the back. Not only was it awkward, sitting in the front with his dad, but I desperately wanted to sit by Wes.

"Thanks for coming to get us, Mr. Bennett."

"No problem, sweetie." He buckled his seat belt and put the car in drive. "Last time I gave you a ride somewhere, you were pretty tiny."

I smiled and remembered the time he'd driven all of us kids to Dairy Queen when there was a massive power outage. "Dairy Queen, right? That had to be ten years ago."

He nodded. "That's right."

As he turned out onto Harbor Drive, I wished I could see Wes's face and know what he was thinking. Was he freaking out like me—in the good way? Did he want to find a way to get together later and make out a little more?

Was he interested in me—like, *really* interested?

Because I was beside myself with excitement, bursting with the utter *ahhhhh!* that could only follow our little game of five minutes in the steamy car.

His dad started talking about the car situation, and he and Wes got lost in automobile talk all the way home as I stared out the window and replayed the kiss in my head. When Mr. Bennett pulled into my driveway, I grabbed Helena's to-go bag and my purse. I had no idea what to say, so I blurted out, "Thanks for the ride."

"Of course. Nice seeing you, honey."

I got out, slammed the door, and ran through the rain until I reached our covered porch. Only . . . I couldn't not say anything else to Wes, right? I couldn't let the night's last words be from Stuart Bennett.

I watched as their car left my driveway and pulled into theirs next door, and as soon as I saw Wes get out in the garage, I set down the stuff in my hand and charged out into the rain. Once I got to the corner of his yard, I stopped and yelled, "Wes!"

The rain pounded down on me, but I yelled his name again as I tried to get his attention.

He looked over, but it was raining too hard for me to see his face. The rain flattened my soaking hair against my face, but I shouted, "Thanks for everything!"

I ran back to the porch, pushed back my dripping hair, and got out my key.

"Libby!"

I smiled and turned around, and there was Wes, standing in the pouring rain in my front yard. I tilted my head and said, "What?"

"You said 'everything'!" His clothes were drenched as he shouted, "Does that mean you're thanking me for the kiss, too?"

I laughed and picked up Helena's food. "I should've known you'd ruin it!"

"Nuh-uh, Buxbaum." He dug his hands into his wet hair and made it all stand straight up as he grinned at me through the storm. "That was too perfect for anything to ruin. G'night."

Nuh-uh. I sighed and felt warm inside, even as my wet body shivered. "G'night, Bennett."

"Oh my God, oh my God, oh my God." I closed the door behind me and rested my dripping forehead on the cool of the white wood. What was that and what did it mean? "Holy *crap.*"

"That good, huh?"

I turned around, and Helena was sitting on the chair beside the fireplace with Mr. Fitzpervert asleep on her lap, a book still in her hand and a smirk on her face. I wanted to be mad or embarrassed, but I couldn't stop smiling. I pushed at my wet hair and said, "You have no idea."

"Come in the kitchen before we wake up your dad." She got up, making Fitz grunt out a cranky *mrrf* as he jumped down to the floor. Helena dropped the book and gestured to me while walking toward the kitchen. Once we got there, she grabbed her food before whipping a towel at me and saying, "Now start talking."

I giggled—I couldn't help it—and rubbed the towel over my head. "I, um, I had a really great time with Wes tonight."

"Yeah . . . ?" She opened the to-go container and stuck it in the microwave. "And . . . ?"

"And." I kept rubbing my hair, replaying his mouth on mine. The sound of his breathing, the smell of his cologne, the feel of his hands holding my face—

"Hey. Excuse me. Can you focus for a minute?"

That made me laugh again. "I can't, okay? I'm sorry, but I can't focus on anything because I had an incredible night with Wes Bennett, of all people. An incredible night that ended with him kissing me like a world-champion kisser. I am shook, Helena."

"I'm not sure how. I mean yes, you've hated him forever, but I still feel like you guys have been leading up to this."

"Really?" I set the towel down on the counter. "Have we? God, I've been so oblivious." Somehow, for so long, I'd managed to be fully unaware that Wes was attractive, funny, and smart, as well as the one person I was totally able to be myself around. I'd been so blinded by the idea of Michael that I hadn't even realized what was happening between us.

"But it's good, yes?" Helena leaned on the counter and beamed at me. "It seems to me that it's really, really good."

I opened the fridge—still smiling—and said, "I'm scared to say it, but I think it could be."

Although . . . I was still concerned about Alex. I knew what he'd said about her, but sometimes feelings changed. Just because she wasn't his "type" the other day didn't mean that with more time together and more time to gaze upon her beauty, he wouldn't change his mind.

She clapped her hands together. "What if he asks you to prom?"

I almost dropped the orange juice when she said that. I straightened a little and pictured his face as I stared into the fridge, the way his dark eyes had looked almost black after we'd stopped kissing. It was Wes Bennett we were talking about, and yet it wasn't. It was Wes 5.0, the grown-ass man version, and I felt like I was in over my head because I had no idea where things stood with us. He'd kissed my face off. That was the only thing I knew to be true. Did he still think he was helping me with Michael? He couldn't, right?

And I didn't know if he wanted to pursue anything with *me*, but I was desperately hopeful that the fervor of the kiss meant that he did.

The whole Michael thing felt silly now. I wished I could go back in time and play Michael and Laney's personal cupid instead of pulling all the stunts I did. I hoped that my heart-to-heart with Michael by the piano had given him what he needed to ask Laney out.

"I'm sure he won't." I closed the fridge and was realistic about prom, even though my *poor, confused little love-lover* side was squealing at the thought. Regardless of my pinings, I'd told Joss I'd go with her, and I needed to stick to that. So far I'd lucked out and my shittiness as a friend hadn't cost me anything with her, so I needed to step up and keep that going. "Plus, I've got a date."

"Would Joss care if you went with him?"

"Oh, yeah—but maybe we could all go together . . . ?" Dressing up with two of my favorite people? It sounded so much more amazing than what I had previously envisioned as the perfect prom.

"Well, whatever happens," Helena said, "I'll be happy to underwrite a pre-prom salon and spa day."

I unscrewed the juice lid and said, "That sounds really fun. But you have to come along." And I meant it. I wanted her there with me.

She raised an eyebrow. "Really?"

I shrugged and said, "I mean, if you piss me off, I'll just tell your stylist that you secretly want mini-bangs."

"Can you even imagine how they would look on this runway of a forehead?"

"They look terrible on everyone—period."

After that, I went up to my room and sent Jocelyn a text about Wes, which led to us going back and forth for, like, an hour.

Me: I think I might like-like him.

Her: OBVIOUSLY.

Me: I think HE might like-like me.

Her: Tell me every little thing that happened.

I didn't mention that we'd kissed, which was weird because I usually told her everything. Well, except for lately. But it had been so perfect—both the kiss and his sweet comment about my style—that I didn't want Joss's opinion to mar the evening's flawlessness.

I stayed up way too late making a Wes and Liz playlist and went to sleep thinking of his face after he'd kissed me. Because the way he'd looked at me—like he couldn't believe it had happened and also like he wanted to do it again—weakened my knees with its mere recollection.

His eyes had been soft and hot all at the same time, intense and sweet, and I wished there was a way to archive the memory so it could never be lost.

How was I ever going to sleep?

CHAPTER THIRTEEN

"Nice boys don't kiss like that."

"Oh, yes, they fucking do."

—*Bridget Jones's Diary*

"Oh, bless you." Jocelyn took the coffee from my hand and raised it to her mouth. "And why are you wearing *that*?"

I looked down at my adorable owl dress before unlocking my locker. "Why wouldn't I? I love it."

She made a face as she sipped from her cup and leaned against the locker beside mine. "I was hoping you were going to stick with the new look."

You look best when you're you. My face got hot as I remembered Wes and the rain and his hands in my hair. I'd been on high alert since arriving at school that morning, looking for him around every corner and in every hallway, my stomach wild at the thought of laying eyes on him.

Of him laying eyes on me right back.

Lord.

He hadn't texted since the kiss, but it'd been late when he'd dropped me off, and he'd still had to go back for his car. I grabbed my history book from the top shelf and said, "I still like my dresses. Sue me."

"Don't get me wrong," she said, swirling the coffee around in her cup. "You're adorable no matter what you wear, but you were just ultra-adorable in modern casual."

"Thanks, although that outfit is totally ruined now from my bloody nose."

Jocelyn's mouth twitched as she stared into the hole in her lid. "I still cannot believe that happened."

"Right?" I slammed my locker, and Jocelyn and I went to first block. I was so disappointed not to run into Wes, especially since his radio silence led me to obsess all morning and become paranoid that the kiss was nothing to him and absolutely nothing had changed between us.

I nearly squealed when my phone buzzed at lunch. I'd just sat down with my strawberry salad and lemonade when I saw it was a text from Wes.

Wes: I like your bird dress.

I looked around but didn't see him at any of the busy cafeteria tables.

Me: They're owls. Where are you?

Wes: In the library—saw you walk by a few minutes ago. Owls are birds, btw.

Me: Yep.

Wes: Stop yelling at me about birds, Buxbaum. I just said you look cute in your dress—that's all.

I smiled and then immediately looked around to make sure he

wasn't lurking nearby, watching my pathetic reaction.

Me: You didn't actually say that.

Wes: Sure I did.

Me: Um . . .

Wes: Gotta run. Talk later?

I set my phone on the table like it was burning my hands. *Talk later?* That was never good, right? What kind of ominous sentiment was that? I opened the packet of vinaigrette on my tray and drizzled it over the salad before picking the phone back up and texting:

Me: Yup.

If I'd been obsessing in the morning, I was ridiculous in the afternoon. Because I needed to know *more,* more than the fact that we'd shared a good kiss. Did he like me? Did he want to hold hands and maybe kiss more? Was he maybe going to be my boyfriend in the near future, or was the kiss just part of our fun hangouts and didn't really mean anything to him at all?

And it occurred to me, as I walked down the hall with Joss after school, that I hadn't had a chance to tell Wes that I was no longer interested in Michael. He knew that, right? I mean, the kiss had to have expressed that sentiment.

"Do you think Wes is going to ask you on a date-date?"

My stomach flipped over as a flash of the kiss hit me. "I hope so."

"Who would've thought?" Joss pushed the exit door, and I followed her out into the sunshine as she said, "The boy who tortured you in grade school is now your romantic dreamboat. Weird."

"What's happening over there?" I said, distracted. There was kind of a crowd over by the main driveway. "I bet it's a fight."

Joss said, "Probably Matt Bond and Jake Headley."

Matt and Jake were two of *those* guys at our school. When word got out that they had beef with each other, the entire student body lost their shit over the possibility of something going down.

We weaved through the crowd, mostly because my car was in the lot that they were all blocking. I said, "I *did* hear that they were going to throw hands."

"You did not just say that, Owl Dress."

"Well, that's *literally* what I heard. Word for word." I moved past a couple people and said, "Excuse me."

"Oh. My. God."

My head whipped around to look at Jocelyn. "What?"

She was staring over my shoulder. Without looking at me, she covered her mouth with one hand and pointed with the other.

I turned my head and followed her finger to a car that was parked in the center of the concourse. It was a black Grand Cherokee, and the fact that it was parked there was unusual, but that wasn't what made it a focal point.

No, what made it unusual was that the entire driver's side of the car was covered with white boxes, boxes that each had a black letter on them, and there was a big, orange square framing them all.

The side of the car was a huge Boggle board.

A Boggle board that had diagonal letters in red spelling out the question "Prom?"

"Holy crap, Liz—get up there!" Bailey Wetzel was standing in the crowd, and she grinned at me and held out an arm. "Go!"

I was slow to absorb what was happening until I saw Michael. He was standing next to the car, smiling at me and holding a poster that said WANNA PLAY BOGGLE WITH ME, LIZ?

It was a promposal.

Michael was asking me to prom.

I felt confused and disjointed as I smiled and everyone standing around started clapping. Michael was asking me to prom—in a romantic, thoughtful way—but I was in shock. It was totally what I'd wanted a week ago, but not anymore.

I slowly walked toward him, my legs rubbery as I approached.

I heard Joss say, "Let him down easy, Liz."

I looked at Michael's smiling face. *What the hell?* I couldn't think of any way to make this make sense. Every single encounter I'd had with Michael had basically ended in disaster—vomit, bloody nose, Laney talk—so why was this even happening?

The irony, right?

Having so many people watching me made me feel hot and itchy. Uncomfortable. When I reached his side, I had no idea what to say. He looked handsome and warm and like everything I'd daydreamed about since kindergarten.

And nothing like Wes.

I could finally see him—us—clearly, and now that I could, I didn't want "the one" to be Michael anymore.

"This is incredible," I said, looking at the Boggle car. He'd covered shoeboxes with white paper and affixed them to the side to make the board, which was a task that would've taken a ton of time. "I can't believe you did this."

"I've known you long enough, Liz, to know that you'd need a big gesture pr—"

"What about Laney?" I interrupted. I was whispering so no one else could hear me, hoping I could save both of us some public humiliation.

He did a little shrug thing and said around a smile, "I really took to heart what you said in the music room. Just like you, I want the possibility of something more. So . . . why not you? Why not us?"

I felt my mouth drop open, and I quickly slammed it shut. But come *on*—seriously? Someone actually listened to my terrible ideas for once? I could just kick myself for rambling about Wes without actually naming a name.

It's like I'd never seen a rom-com before or something. Talk about your comedy of errors.

I glanced into the crowd and—oh no—there was Wes. We locked eyes as he stood next to the building, watching me with an unreadable expression. I swallowed and stared intently at his face, the face that had been kissing mine the last time I'd seen him.

I silently begged those brown eyes to give me an answer.

Or for him to give me a smile.

Give me something, Bennett. Please.

But he turned his head and looked away from me.

Before that punch to the gut could even register, I watched

Alex sidle up beside him. She smiled and grabbed his arm, pulling him down closer so she could talk into his ear.

I could barely breathe as I stared at them while everyone in the courtyard looked at me. My silence was getting awkward, and I was very aware of it. Slowly people began cheering and clapping, but I could only hear my heart beating in my ears. Amidst everything, I kept my eyes on Wes. He lifted his hands, put two fingers in his mouth, and whistled loudly. And then he dropped his right arm across Alex's shoulders and gave me a thumbs-up.

Rejection, bitter and hot, washed over me. The other night—the kiss, everything—was a blip. Wes didn't feel about me the way I felt about him. This was how it was supposed to end.

"This is getting embarrassing, and I have to take off in, like, two minutes. Do you maybe want to answer?" Michael looked uncomfortable as he waited.

I took a deep breath and simply accepted the flowers he was holding—I couldn't manage words when Wes was snuggling with Alex and whistling for me to say yes. Then Michael flipped the poster over, revealing a back side that said SHE SAID YES in the same Boggle format.

The people standing around clapped and—thank God—started dispersing, while I stood there feeling shell-shocked. Michael squeezed my hand and said, "I really do have to go now, but this felt right after our talk in my dad's room last night. We can work out the details tomorrow, okay?"

"Um, sounds good."

"Your 'talk' last night?" Jocelyn stepped in front of me as soon as

Michael turned away, her eyes narrowed. "You were with Michael Young?"

I felt the blood drain from my face as my lies caught up to me. I fumbled for words and said, "I told you we were watching movies—"

"You said you were hanging out with Wes." She shook her head as she said in a low voice, "What is wrong with you? You're so screwed up about romantic bullshit that you lie to your best friend—and for what? To go out with a guy who's already talking to someone else?"

I swallowed, feeling the urge to defend myself, even though I knew I was in the wrong. "Maybe if you weren't so judgmental, I could've been honest with you. But you make it *so* hard sometimes."

Joss looked at me like I was disgusting. And she was right. "Are you saying it's my fault you're a liar?"

"Of course not. God, I'm so sorry. I just—"

Her eyebrows went down as she squinted at me and said, "So what's the deal with Wes, then? Do you even like him?"

I sighed. Was there any reason *not* to spill it all to Joss now? "Well, that part is true—I like him a lot."

She folded her arms over her chest. "So what were you doing at Michael's house if you like Wes?"

I adjusted my messenger bag and glanced at Kate and Cassidy, who I hadn't even noticed were behind her until then. "I went there with Wes, actually."

"You went there with Wes and ended up with Michael in his dad's bedroom? You're kidding, right?"

"Um, it was actually a music room."

She opened her mouth, but before she could speak I said, "But I know that's not the point. Wes was fine with the whole thing—he wanted me to go talk to Michael."

"He did." She gave me a stare that made her look like her mother, like a lawyer who had a lying criminal on the stand and she was about to make him cry.

"Yes." I cleared my throat and decided to come clean. I said, "See, he'd been helping me—"

"Oh my God, you schemed with him to get Michael, didn't you?" Her eyes squinted in revulsion. "I knew you'd lose your shit when he showed up again. What is wrong with you?"

"Nothing." I blinked and tried to justify it. "He and Laney weren't official so—"

"That explains the clothes and the straightened hair, doesn't it? Were you lying to me when you guys were shopping too?"

I just looked at her. I mean, what could I even say?

"And you liking him was total bullshit too?"

"Only at first—"

"Screw you, Liz." She pulled her bag higher on her shoulder and turned away from me. Kate gave me a closed-mouth half smile, like she felt bad for me, but she was still going to go with Joss, and Cassidy looked at me like I was kind of awful.

There was a time when those two wouldn't have taken sides, but since I'd blown them off one too many times on senior events, they were Team Joss all the way.

"Wait." My throat was pinched and my vision blurred as I

watched her walk back toward the school. "Joss, wait! I'm sorry, okay? Don't you need a ride home?"

"Not from you." She just threw an arm up in the air and yelled, "I'd rather walk."

"Hey, you." Helena was sitting on a stool in the kitchen when I got home, working on her laptop in paint-splattered pajama pants and a hoodie. "How was your day?"

"Meh." I dropped my backpack on the floor, drained from crying all the way home, and went to the fridge to scope for something good.

"Oh my God, I forgot—did you see Wes?" She looked up from her screen, nearly squealing those words, and I had to remember not to roll my eyes. It wasn't her fault that the story line had changed.

"Um, yeah." We were out of chocolate pudding, and that made me want to cry. Again.

"What is that face?"

I shrugged and shut the door. "Michael asked me to prom."

"*What?*" Helena's mouth dropped wide open. "You are *kidding* me."

"Nope." I went to the pantry and looked for cookies, wondering if the feeling in my stomach that wouldn't go away was an ulcer.

I didn't even really know what an ulcer was.

"Did you turn him down?"

"No." I gritted my teeth. "Actually, I said yes."

"You said *yes*?" She said it like I'd just said yes to selling my organs on the black market or something. "Why would you do that? Oh my God, does Wes know? Oh, poor Wes."

I slammed the pantry door and grabbed my backpack. *Poor Wes?* Poor Wes had no real interest in Little Liz, but I didn't have the energy to tell her that. Or to think about it for another second. Because in addition to how soul-crushingly rejected I felt by his apparent lack of feelings for me, I felt duped.

Betrayed by my own heart.

Because I had known better than to get drawn in by him; I'd *always* known better. Yet it had happened. I'd fallen for basketball shorts and gross cigars and rain-soaked kisses. How could this have happened?

Beyond that, I'd schemed and lied and screwed up my very best friendship in the world. And—oh, yeah—I'd also gotten in the way of Laney and Michael, two people who actually seemed to be made for each other.

I said, "Yes, he knows, and trust me, he's fine. I need to go study."

"Liz?"

I stood still but didn't turn her way. "What?"

"I know you thought you wanted Michael, but do you really want to stick with over-romanticized ideas when you can have an awesome *real* thing?"

Over-romanticized ideas. As close as she got sometimes, Helena didn't get it. My mother would've understood. My mother would've been cheering the entire time for me to go for the mark.

I'd ignored her golden rule and was suffering the consequences.

"Liz?"

"I have to go study."

"Wait—are you mad at me?"

I hoisted my backpack and let out my breath. "Nope. Not at all."

"Do you want—"

"No. God." I said it through gritted teeth and it came out way harsher than I'd intended, but I couldn't do this. Not with her. "I just want to be left alone, okay?"

CHAPTER FOURTEEN

"I am not running away."

"Bullshit."

—*How to Lose a Guy in 10 Days*

"I'm going for a run," I called as I jogged down the stairs. I rounded the corner to the living room and found my dad on the couch with his feet propped up on the coffee table, watching the news. I was all tied up in knots and didn't know what to think about anything, so instead of torturing myself, I was going to visit the cemetery.

No less torturous, right?

I looked toward the kitchen, but the only movement I saw in there was Mr. Fitzpervert, rolling on the rug under the table and kicking his catnip mouse with his back paws. "Where's Helena?"

"The second I walked in, she said she had to go. Had an errand or something like that. Are you okay?"

I had no interest in a heart-to-heart, so I said, "Yep—just tired. Think I might be coming down with a cold."

He nodded, looked at me like he knew something, and said, "Helena said the same thing."

"Oh yeah?" I put on my headphones. "Bummer."

He sighed. "Be careful."

"Will do."

After turning on my Garmin, I took off down the street, intentionally avoiding laying eyes on *his* car. I mean, what was with that, anyway? Why did I feel something like nostalgia when I laid eyes upon Wes's beat-up old car that seemed to have survived our accident without any visible damage?

Nostalgia that made me want to take a bat to his car à la Beyoncé in the *Lemonade* video and *cause* some visible damage. I'd been replaying everything in my mind, every awful second of what'd happened, and Wes's rejection was starting to piss me off.

Because it wasn't just that he'd rejected me. No, it was the fact that he'd known my end goal was Michael, yet he'd still pushed hard on the charm with his dinner date and his Secret Area teasing and his straight-from-*The-Notebook* kiss in the rain.

He *knew* I was susceptible to romance, and he'd used it against me.

And for what?

He was moving on to Alex, so what'd even been the point?

As if that wasn't bad enough, every time I thought of Jocelyn, my stomach hurt so intensely that I wanted to puke. How was I ever going to earn her forgiveness? I'd been a lying weasel lately, and no matter how much I justified it, I couldn't find a defense to make it okay.

I turned into the cemetery and was glad it was getting dark, because I didn't feel like being polite or talking to anyone who might be nearby. Sometimes there were other people there, doing the same thing as me, and sometimes they liked to small-talk. I just wanted to sit by my mother, spill the details of my latest debacle, and then bask in the imaginary feeling that I wasn't alone.

But when I got closer, I could see a figure standing right where I wanted to be. And just like the time when Wes showed up there, I was instantly—and illogically—irate. Who was in my spot?

The person turned around as I approached, and I saw that it was Helena. Her face was serious, and she was still wearing those paint-stained pants.

"Liz. What are you doing here?" she said.

I raised my hand toward my mom's grave marker. "No offense, but what are *you* doing here?"

She looked startled by my appearance, almost like I'd interrupted something. She dragged a hand through her hair and said, "I guess you could say I needed a word with your mother."

"Why?"

"What?"

I inhaled through my nose and tried to stop this unexpected rage from escaping. "You didn't know my mother, so I don't understand why you would need *a word* with her. You never spoke to her or heard her voice or even watched a *silly* romantic comedy with her, so call me irrational, but it just seems really weird that you're camped out where she's buried."

"I was hoping she might know how I can get through to you." She blinked fast and pressed her lips together, crossing her arms over her chest. "Listen, Libby, I know—"

"Don't call me that."

"What?"

"Libby. It's what she called me, but that doesn't mean that you need to, okay?"

"What is this?" She said it in a tired voice that had a bit of an edge to it. "I feel like you're *trying* to fight with me."

I blinked fast. "No, I'm not." I totally was. Nobody who I wanted to fight with was speaking to me. So why not Helena?

"Really?"

"Yes, really."

"Because you just got mad that I called you by the nickname that I've heard your dad and the next-door neighbor call you. I don't see you having a problem with *anyone but me* saying it."

"Well, *they* actually knew her."

She looked at me, exuding disappointment at the brat I knew I was being. "I can't help that I didn't."

"I know." It wasn't about whether or not she knew my mom; it was about the infringement of my mother's memories. Her legacies. I mean, it wasn't irrational to try to keep those pure, was it?

She sighed and dropped her arms to her sides. "You *do* know, Liz, that your mother's memory won't disappear if you get closer to me."

"*Excuse* me?" The words felt like a physical slap because—God—she'd just lent voice to my biggest fear. How would it *not* disappear if Helena got closer? Because no matter what he said, it'd disappeared for my father. When he talked about my mom now, it was like he was referencing some historical figure that he was incredibly fond of.

Her place in his heart was gone, and she only lived in his head now.

Helena tilted her head and said, "It won't. You'll still remember her exactly as you do right now, even if you let me in a little."

"How do you know that?" I blinked back tears and said, "What if it *does* disappear? I know that you're great for my dad and super-cool, and I know that you're here to stay. I *know* all of that, but it doesn't change the fact that you're here and she isn't and that feels sort of shitty."

Her mouth snapped shut. "Of course it does. I would've been lost without my mom. I totally get that it feels awful. But pushing me away is not going to bring her back, Liz."

I sniffled and wiped at the tears on my cheeks. "Yeah, I think I know that, Helena."

"Maybe if we—"

"No." I gritted my teeth and wished she would disappear so I could cry and lie on the soft grass. But if she wasn't leaving, I'd have to. I put in my earbuds, scrolled to "Enter Sandman" by Metallica, and said, "Maybe if you just leave me alone and let me live my life without trying to fill her shoes every time I turn around, we'll all be happier."

I didn't wait for her to respond. I started running the way I'd come, only I pushed my legs to sprint as fast as I possibly could. I swiped at my cheeks and tried outrunning the sadness, but it stayed with me all the way home.

I was almost to my house when I saw Wes getting out of his car.

He slammed the door and started walking across the street, to where I was, before he noticed me. He gave me a chin-nod and said, "Hey."

Hey. Like we hadn't kissed, or texted, or talked on the phone, or eaten hamburgers together. Just *hey.* Wow—he really *was* a jerk, wasn't he? I stopped running and yanked out one of my earbuds. "Hey. By the way, thanks for helping me get Michael." The words spilled out. I was aware of my own horribleness as I racked my brain for something to say that would make him hurt as badly as I did, and I couldn't seem to stop myself.

His eyes moved over my face before he said, "Sure, although he does still have that pesky Laney around. I think you'll have to deal with that before you officially 'get' him."

"Nah." I waved a hand and swallowed down my emotions with a smile. "He told me that he's not going to make a move."

"He did?" He rubbed his eyebrow and looked past me for a minute before his gaze returned to my face. My breath caught as I looked at the same eyes that had been hot and wild for me in the front seat of his car, and he said, "Well, you're just about to get everything you've ever wanted, then, aren't you? Why didn't you tell me that before?"

Um, it was hard to talk when we were driving off a cliff and then you were eating my face. I inhaled through my nose. I was so pissed at him—at myself—so damned disappointed, and I wanted to make him feel some of that. "Like I'm really going to share all my secrets with the person who was just doing me a solid and filling in for Mr. Right."

He swallowed and crossed his arms over his chest. "Good thinking."

"Right?" I expelled a fake laugh and said, "I mean, no offense, but you guys couldn't be more different. He's like a gourmet restaurant, and you're a super-fun sports bar. He's a limo, and you're a Jeep Wrangler. He's an Oscar-winning film, and you're . . . a car-racing movie. Both good, but good for different people."

Those dark eyes narrowed marginally. "Is there a point to this, Buxbaum?"

"Nah." I reached up, pulled out my ponytail, and dug my fingers into my hair. It felt like a victory, the way he was visibly irritated. "Just grateful to you for everything you did for me."

"Really."

"Yep." I did my best to force my mouth into a giant happy smile. "You should ask Alex to prom, by the way."

"Yeah, I was already planning on it."

I felt that one in my heart. Picturing him smiling at Alex made the backs of my eyelids burn. I said through that fake smile, "We should all go as a group—that'd be fun."

He looked pissed when he said, "Don't you think it's a bad idea to mix 'gourmet restaurants' with 'super-fun sports bars'?"

I shrugged. "Alex is like a very nice restaurant, so I'm sure if you two stick together, you'll level-up to, like, a trendy sushi place."

He looked at me like I was scum, and he was right. He flipped his keys around his fingers and said, "Even so, I'd rather go solo with Alex."

Then his eyes moved down to my T-shirt and running shorts, and his face got a pitying, I-know-all look to it. "Oh. You just saw your mom."

I blinked. "What does that have to do with anything?"

He gave me a look like I should know what he meant.

"What?"

"Come on, are you that lacking in self-awareness? You hold on to this notion of your angelic mother and the romantic comedy like her greatest wish in life was for her daughter to be swept off her feet *in fucking high school*. Just because she liked those movies doesn't mean that if you live your life like an actual teenager, you're disappointing her."

"What are you even talking about? Just because—"

"Come on, Liz—at least be honest with yourself here. You dress like her, you watch the shows she watched, and you do everything in your power to behave as if she's writing the screenplay of your life and you're her character."

My throat ached and I blinked fast as his words came at me like blows.

"But news flash: you're not a character in a movie. You can wear jeans sometimes and straighten your hair if you feel like it and curse like a sailor and honestly do whatever you want, and she'd still think you're amazing because you *are*. I guarantee she would've found you charming as fuck when you were smoking a Swisher in the Secret Area—I know I did. And when you attacked me in my car. Talk about out of character. It was—"

"Oh my God, I did *not* attack you. Are you kidding me with that?" It was official—I was dying of mortification. Because while I'd been humming along to love songs since the make out session in his car, he'd been considering it terribly "out of character" for me.

He ignored me and said, "But you're so caught up in this idea of who you think your mom wants you to be, or Michael, or even me. Forget me! Be who you want to be. Just do it, and quit playing games, because you're hurting people."

"Shut up, Wes." I was crying again, and I hated him at that moment. For not understanding, but also for being right. I'd thought, regardless of the prom situation, that he was the one person who had understood about my mom. I wiped my cheeks with the backs of my knuckles. "You don't know shit about my mom, okay?"

"God, don't cry, Liz." He swallowed and looked panicked. "I just don't want you to miss out on the good stuff."

"Like what—you?" I gritted my teeth. I wanted to howl and kick things over. Instead I said, "Are you the good stuff, Wes?"

His voice was quiet when he said, "You never know."

"Yes, I do know. You're *not*—you're the opposite of everything I want. You're the same person you were when you ruined my Little Free Library, and you're the same person my mom thought was too wild for me to play with." I took in a shaky breath and said, "You can have the Forever Spot and let's just forget this whole thing ever happened."

I turned and walked away from him, and I was just opening the front door when I heard him say, "Fine by me."

I fell asleep before eight that night, listening to "Death with Dignity" by Sufjan Stevens on repeat. I slept the entire night with my Beats on, and that soft song haunted my ears until morning.

Mother, I can hear you
And I long to be near you

I dreamed of her. I rarely did anymore, but that night, I chased my mother in my dreams.

She was trimming roses in the front yard and I could hear her laughing, but I couldn't see her face. She was too far away. All I could make out were her gardening gloves and her fancy black dress with the ruffled collar. And no matter how much I walked, or how fast I ran, I wasn't close enough to see her unblurred face.

I ran and ran, but she never got any closer.

I didn't wake up with a gasp like in the movies, though that might've made me feel better. Instead I woke up with a sad resignation as the song continued its soft, solemn loop.

CHAPTER FIFTEEN

"I love you. I've loved you for nine years; I've just been too arrogant and scared to realize it, and . . . well, now I'm just scared. So, I realize this comes at a very inopportune time, but I really have this gigantic favor to ask of you. Choose me. Marry me. Let me make you happy. Oh, that sounds like three favors, doesn't it?"

—*My Best Friend's Wedding*

The days leading up to prom crept by, mostly because I was the world's biggest loner. Jocelyn wasn't talking to me, Wes was just a neighbor now, and Helena was completely avoiding me.

I worked every night and picked up extra hours, so at least I was making bank in my solitary, pathetic life. And I watched my favorite movies when I wasn't working, so I had my emotional-support DVDs to keep me from thinking about all the things I didn't want to think about.

Michael met me at my locker the day after the promposal, and he was as thorough and efficient as he'd always been. We discussed what time he'd pick me up, what colors we'd be wearing, and where we were eating.

He was perfect.

Which was why, as I did my hair on the day of prom, I tried to convince myself that maybe everything had happened for a reason. I mean, the Joss thing was still a big nightmare that I *had* to fix, and it felt oddly empty that Helena was out for the day when I was getting ready for prom, but maybe I'd been *meant* to momentarily go over to the dark side with Wes in order for me to really appreciate the incredible lightness of Michael.

A cautionary tale, perhaps? I turned on the Michael playlist as I straightened my hair and tried getting excited for the night. The bottom line was that I was going to prom with Michael Young, the boy I'd loved for as long as I'd been old enough to create memories.

It was actually happening.

The problem with the playlist was that all the songs now had Wes memories attached to them.

The Van Morrison song from my original meet-cute with Michael now made me think of Wes bumping into us in the hallway and then giving me a smart-ass look about my taped windshield. And the Ed Sheeran song from the party now reminded me of Wes giving me his pants—and holding them up for me—after I got vomited on.

"Dammit, Bennett, get out of my head." I finished my hair and moved on to makeup, applying casual glam so I looked better than usual but not too made-up. When I was finally finished, I checked my phone and, of course, there were no messages.

I put on my dress—it was so pretty, I wanted to be buried in it, by the way—but it felt slightly wrong. Jocelyn should have been there, putting on her dress too, and Helena should have been hanging around, making jokes and taking pictures.

I shushed the voice that added Laney to that list, including her as someone who should have been getting ready to have her dream prom with Michael but couldn't because I'd decided to take her out of the equation.

Just when I was about to go downstairs, I heard a door slam and looked out my window. Wes walked out his front door in a black tuxedo, and he was carrying a corsage box. He hopped down the steps with his usual relaxed gait, and his dark sunglasses made him look rebellious in addition to handsome.

Kind of perfect, and it hurt my eyes to look at him.

I pressed a hand to my stomach as he walked to his car, which was parked in the driveway for once. It looked like he'd washed it, because all the mud that had been splattered on the side for as long as I could remember was finally gone. He climbed inside, started it up, and I felt something pinch in my center when he drove away.

I went downstairs and was putting on my shoes when the doorbell rang. While I felt a couple of half-hearted butterflies in my stomach, the anticipation was minimal.

But—and I was hopeful with this but—if I really pushed myself, perhaps there was still the possibility of an enjoyable night with a sweet date. I stood and ran my hands over the front of my dress, walked over to the front door, and pulled it open.

Wow.

Michael was on my doorstep, his tuxedo perfectly accentuating his blond hair and tan skin. He looked like Hollywood, like one born to wear tuxedos. He smiled at me and it was all warmth and good feelings as he said, "Wow. You look great, Liz."

"Thanks."

"Stop!" My dad strode into the room with a half smile on his face, cargo shorts, and a GOT MILK? shirt. "I need to get pictures, you two. Helena had stuff to do," he said, his eyes landing on me. "But she'd kill me if I didn't get photos."

I bit the inside of my cheek as the guilt curdled in my stomach. Because even though I'd meant what I'd said to Helena, I felt like trash for making her feel bad.

"Of course." Michael gave my dad a charming smile and said, "Nice to see you again, Mr. Buxbaum."

"You too, Michael. How are your folks?" As he said this, my dad gestured for us to go stand in front of the piano. "I heard your dad is a colonel now."

"He is." We walked to the piano and faced the camera. "He got the official title change last year."

"Do we have to use a title for you now?" My father thought he was funny. "Like Junior Colonel Michael?"

"Come on, Dad, he's not the son of the chicken guy." I rolled my eyes, and Michael laughed. "Just take the picture."

My dad directed us to stand in a super-awkward pose, with Michael's arm around my waist, and I just shut my mouth and smiled to get it over with. Thankfully he was quick, and after about four shots he let us leave.

"Have fun, kids."

"Sorry about him," I muttered to Michael as we walked to his car. "He's just as dorky as he always was."

"Your dad was always great," he said, smiling as he opened the passenger door for me.

"Yeah—I s'pose." I grabbed a handful of long dress and got in, and looked out the window after he shut the door and walked around to the other side. I looked at my dad on the porch, smiling and waving all by himself, and it occurred to me that he could've been like that all along if he'd never met Helena.

Alone.

It was wrong that she wasn't there.

"So you're good with Sebastian's?" He pulled out of the driveway, and I noticed his car was immaculate. Clean, vacuumed, not a speck of vent dust—the interior was perfect. From somewhere in the center of my brain, I wondered if the inside of Wes's car looked like that too. I mean, he'd clearly washed the outside of the Bronco. Was it to impress Alex?

"Liz?"

"What? Hm?" I blinked and came back from the delay. "Yes. Sebastian's sounds great."

When we got to the restaurant, the hostess led us to a stunning table with white linens, a vase full of lilies, and white candles, already lit. I sat in one of the chairs and said, "Wow."

Michael sat across from me and immediately put his napkin on his lap. "I assumed that romantic Little Liz would want flowers before her senior prom."

"Wait, what? You got those for me?"

He smiled and sighed. "It was the least I could do. I kind of caught you off guard, last minute, with the whole thing."

I lifted off my seat just enough to lean forward and smell the gorgeous flowers. How could he be that thoughtful? It was such a *perfect* gesture. "Yeah, not gonna lie, I was shocked when you asked."

"After what you said in the music room, I decided what the hell."

What exactly had I said? I racked my brain but I was clueless. I'd been so focused on Wes and Alex that I really hadn't paid attention to Michael at all. *Bad move, Liz.*

"What about Laney?"

A shadow passed over his face before quickly disappearing. He said, "She's going to prom with her friends."

"Oh. And you're good with that?"

"Here's the thing. I have no idea what she wants, and I don't want to waste senior prom trying to figure it out. I'd rather—"

The waiter showed up, interrupting him with menus, specials, and drink offerings, and I could tell Michael was relieved. It was clear to me that he wanted Laney but was too afraid to put himself out there. He'd rather pretend I was his magical date, safe Little Liz but maybe something more, than risk going for it and getting denied.

That should've made me feel like garbage, but I didn't really feel *anything* about it. In fact, I felt the same about his non-burning-love for me as I would about his opinion on the whole ketchup vs. mustard condiment war.

Utterly unaffected.

Holy crap—I did not care.

I felt more relaxed just by admitting it to myself. Because really—why was I forcing it? Michael wasn't the one—no big, right? And maybe I wasn't going to find the one. That was okay too, right? Why was I wasting my life trying to live up to the ridiculous expectations that I was setting for myself?

I changed the subject by pointing out a twenties art deco print on the wall, and by the time the food came, we were in the thick of a conversation about *The Great Gatsby*.

"I hear what you're saying, Liz—I do. But Daisy's sole purpose in the story is to be Gatsby's unattainable dream. She *is* the green light. So she can't be a monstrous antagonist."

I rolled my eyes and put a piece of steak in my mouth. "Wrong. His memory of her is the green light. Remember—'His count of enchanted objects had diminished by one.' Once he reconnects with her in the flesh, she's no longer the green light."

He nodded and spread butter on his roll. "That *is* true."

I said, "Daisy in the flesh *is* a monstrous antagonist. She toys with his affection, cheats on her husband, and lets Jay cover for her when she drives over her husband's mistress. Then, when he's murdered and left to be a pool bobber, she leaves town without ever looking back."

"Well," he said, reaching out and grabbing his water glass, "those are all valid points. I still don't think she's the villain here, but you've succeeded in knocking her down a notch for me."

"Aha—victory is mine." I dipped my fork into the creamy baked potato and scooped out a bite. "At this rate, before I die I'll be responsible for turning hundreds of readers against Daisy Buchanan."

"A life well lived, I suppose."

We'd just finished with dinner when dessert showed up—he'd taken the liberty of ordering cheesecake for me ahead of time—and I very nearly fainted with gratitude.

I stuck my fork into the cheesecake and asked, "How did you know I love cheesecake?"

He leaned his face forward and said, "I didn't—I just wanted it."

I smiled and felt the cheesecake slide against the roof of my mouth. "Well, it was still thoughtful."

"Hey, you guys," came a voice from behind me.

I picked up my water and took a sip.

Michael said, "Hey, Lane."

The water went down the wrong tube and I started coughing. A tiny squirt shot out of my mouth, but I quickly recovered, catching the spray with my napkin, though it took me a solid ten seconds to stop coughing. I could feel the eyes of everyone in the restaurant on me as Michael asked, "You okay?"

I blinked away tears and nodded, a couple more cough-spurts forcing their way out before I was able to say, "I'm f-fine."

Another cough.

I tried for a calm smile as I took a deep breath and attempted to regain my composure.

"I hate when that happens." Michael tried making me feel less embarrassed by grinning and saying, "I swear it happens to me, like, once a month."

"Same," Laney said, walking around the table as if to make sure

I could see just how pretty she looked while I tried being a human fountain. "Drinking is hard, right?"

Michael laughed and she smiled at him, and I kind of felt like spitting water at the two of them. Not because I cared that they seemed adorably perfect, but because it made me miss Wes. Laney must've realized she was just standing and staring at my date because she blinked and said, "Oh. Well, I should go back to my table. Have fun tonight, guys."

"You, too, *Lane*," I muttered, and did a little wave with my fork. Yeah, some attitudes were hard to change.

Michael looked a little lost for a second after she walked away, but he recovered and took a bite of his cheesecake. "Wow—this is really good."

I nodded and stabbed my cheesecake with my fork, scraping the filling all over the fancy plate. "Yeah."

I don't know what I was thinking, but I asked, "Did you know her when you lived here the first time? Laney, that is."

His mouth turned up a little and he grinned. "Oh, yeah. She was a total brat back then and used to tell on me *all the time* at recess when I didn't let her play kickball with us. I hated that little snot."

Okay, that made me smile. "I hated her too."

"Honestly, I expected her to grow into a total witch."

Hadn't she?

"But somehow she didn't. Did you know that she volunteers every weekend at the animal shelter?"

"Wow." Seriously? Even though I was suddenly empathetic to Michael and Laney's star-crossed-lovers plight, that didn't mean

I wanted firsthand knowledge that Laney Morgan was a better human than me. "Um, no, I did *not* know that."

"And she's saving up so she can go on a mission trip this summer."

I wanted to flip the table and yell something along the lines of "Are you fucking kidding me?"

Instead I nodded and said, "I had no idea."

"But let's talk about you, Liz." He set his chin on his hand. "Wes told me that you're 'literally' the coolest person he's ever met, so you've changed a lot too. I mean, the last time I saw you before we moved, you wore a kimono and bright red lipstick to a neighborhood cookout. You ate your hot dog with silverware."

I laughed in spite of myself as he said, "That's one hell of a level-up."

I cleared my throat and said, "Wes was exaggerating. I may not eat hot dogs with a knife and fork anymore, but I haven't changed that much."

"Don't be modest." He pulled out his phone and started scrolling, clearly looking for something. After around thirty seconds, he muttered, "Boom" and held out his phone for me to look. "See?"

I took his phone and looked at the screen. It was a message thread between Michael and Wes, dated right around the time Wes agreed to help me.

Wes: She's definitely cute, but she's also cool AF.

Michael: She is? Thought she was always kind of high-strung.

Wes: Liz is . . . different. She's the kind of girl who

wears a dress when everyone else wears jeans. She listens to music instead of watching TV. She drinks black coffee, has a secret tattoo, runs three miles every day rain or shine, and still practices the piano.

Michael: You sound cuffed already lol.

Wes: Whatever. What time are you going to be there?

My eyes were scratchy as my heart stuttered in my chest. I gave an exaggerated eye roll and handed back his phone. "That isn't real."

"What?"

I sighed, and it occurred to me that it was a good time to fess up. Maybe if I confessed my sins, he could follow his heart and find happiness with Laney. Because why should they suffer just because I was a shitshow? I looked at him and said, "He was trying to help me. I asked Wes to talk me up to you, so that's why he said all that. He was doing me a favor."

His eyebrows crinkled. "Are you serious?"

I didn't want to make things weird with him and Wes, so I just glossed over how planny it all had been and pretty much just said that Wes did me that tiny favor.

He gave a little chuckle. "You really haven't changed that much, then, have you?"

That made me laugh. "Sadly not."

I went on to tell him about how my waitress uniform had actually been my favorite dress and how I'd totally made up *The* Diner, and we both laughed until we had tears in our eyes.

I excused myself and went to the restroom while he settled the bill, and once the door closed behind me, it was a struggle to keep the tears at bay.

Because—Wes's text. God. Yes, he'd sent it to help me, but all those things he'd said? I wanted him to see me that way so badly. He'd gone above and beyond what I'd asked him to do when he'd sent that text, and now I would never be the same.

"Oh. Hey, Liz." Laney came out of a bathroom stall and began to wash her hands.

"Hey, Laney." I turned on the faucet even though I hadn't even used the bathroom, and started washing my hands.

"I love your dress—it's gorgeous." She smiled at me in the mirror.

"Thanks. Same, only more," I muttered, and gestured toward the long pink gown.

"Are you okay?"

I gave her side-eye in the mirror. "Yeah, why?"

She shrugged and looked down at her hands. "You're here with Michael Young, and he got you flowers and cheesecake and can't stop looking at you, but you look sad."

Butt out, Lanesville.

"Is it because of your mom?"

"What?" I was so shocked by her words that I stopped lathering my hands. The only sound in the bathroom was the faucet continuing to run.

"Oh, I'm so sorry." Laney's smile dropped. "I'm tactless. I'm so sorry for saying anything. I just think all the time—when I see you—about how hard it would be not to have your mom around, especially during your senior year when everyone is sharing all these milestones with their parents. I'm so, so sorry for bringing it up."

I stared at my foamy hands and didn't have words. Laney Morgan had seen something that no one else had, and it felt totally foreign to be understood by her. "No, it's fine. I didn't know what you meant."

She turned off her faucet and reached for a hand towel. "Still. Sometimes I can't help sticking my foot in my mouth. I'm really sorry."

I raised my eyes to the mirror as I rinsed off the soap. "You're right, though. It sucks. That's not what my problem is at the moment, but that is always there."

"I can't imagine. My mom still talks about you all the time."

"What?" I shut off the faucet and straightened. "Your mom remembers me?"

Laney nodded. "She used to come up to school for lunch—remember how parents did that sometimes in elementary school?"

I nodded and grabbed a towel, remembering how smiley her mom had been when she'd joined the class.

"It was the year your mom died, and she said you had the biggest, saddest eyes she'd ever seen and she wanted to take you home with her. She always used to get an extra order of fries in case you wanted some, but you always just shook your head *no*."

I blinked hard then, but couldn't stop one tear from escaping. "I don't remember that, but I do remember how perfect your mom seemed."

"Oh no, Liz, I didn't mean to make you cry." Laney grabbed a tissue and handed it to me. "Your makeup is perfect, so knock it off."

That made me smile, and I wiped at my eyes. "Sorry."

She leaned toward the mirror and checked her teeth before straightening. "I should probably go back. And Michael's probably wondering where his date went."

She had the same slow-blink, slo-mo disappointment that Michael had when she said that. I breathed in through my nose before saying, "You know Michael only asked me as a friend, right?" It was practically true, so I didn't add this to my tally of fibs that had been piling up lately.

I swear to God, Laney Morgan looked nervous and awkward. She said, "No way! I saw the promposal. That can't be true."

"It is. And Michael told me that you guys have been talking, but he also thought maybe you weren't over your ex. Which is probably why he asked me to prom instead of you to begin with."

She looked like she didn't know how to respond, but something that looked a little bit like hope sparked in her eyes.

I glanced in the mirror and ran a hand over my hair. "If you have feelings for him, you're going to have to tell him. He seems to be shy about putting himself out there, which is why he could never be the lead in a rom-com, by the way, so if you like Mike, you're going to have to be brave."

Her closed mouth turned up into a little smile and the girl's princess eyes were sparkling. "Y'know, you're kind of cool, Liz."

I was the antithesis of cool, but it was nice to hear. "Does that mean that you like him?"

She nodded and her eyes got even bigger. "You have no idea. I have *never* felt like this before about anyone."

I rolled my eyes and tossed the tissue. "Well, then don't drag your feet."

I went back to the table, where Michael looked ready to go.

"You ready?" He set his napkin on his plate and looked at me expectantly.

"Let's go prom it up."

He laughed and we left, and as we drove toward the convention center where prom was being held, I wished I could just go home. I was happy that Michael and Laney were destined to have their magical night, but aside from that, no good could come from prom.

Joss. Wes. Alex.

Everyone I cared about—who was going to prom—didn't want to see me.

"I finished that book already, by the way."

"Which book?" I glanced out the window as we passed McDonald's.

He cleared his throat, and when I turned my head he gave me a look. "*That* book."

That made me smile. "Of course. Like it's brown-bag fodder. *That* book."

He started talking about the Bridgerton book, and I forgot about everything else in the world as he waxed poetic about how great a setting a pirate ship was. He and I discussed it right up until he was turning off the car in the parking lot.

"We should probably go in, I guess?" I glanced at the event center through the windshield and was nervous for the first time since I'd been waiting for Michael to pick me up.

"That's how these things work." He pulled out the keys and said, "Let's do this?"

I swiped gloss over my lips and opened the door. "Let's do this."

When we got inside, Michael handed the security person our tickets, and the big bald dude looked at me with bored eyes. "Purse?"

I shook my head and pointed to the front of my dress. "Pockets."

His eyebrows went up. "Nice. You kids have a good night."

"You too."

We headed into Ballroom C, and the second we walked through the doors, it was like entering a different world. No, it wasn't magical. It was a brightly colored, way-too-loud wedding reception world. The theme was Mardi Gras, which basically just meant that everything was a jarring purple, yellow, or green color.

"Hey—there's Wesley. Over by the papier-mâché baby."

I followed Michael's gaze and yes, there was an enormous papier-mâché baby sitting atop an even bigger papier-mâché cake. My eyes scanned the crowd for Joss, but I didn't see her anywhere. My stomach flittered a little bit as Michael led me toward Wes.

Stop it, Liz.

I took a deep breath, put my hands in my delightful pockets, and walked across the room, concentrating on not stumbling in my heels. "We Are Young" by fun. was blaring, and it still felt like it always had—as if the band was trying to convince us of something.

"That is one *huge* baby," I said, smiling as we got closer.

"Right? Bizarre." Michael grinned up at it, and I was looking at him when a voice yelled,

"Mrs. Potato Head!"

I looked past the baby and there was Adam. I really *did* like Wes's friends. I said, "Hey."

"Don't call her that anymore; her face is normal again."

I rolled my eyes at Noah, who was standing behind him. "Gee, thanks."

"I could've said *almost* normal; you should be grateful."

That made me smile. "And I am. Thanks for the kindness."

"You're welcome."

"A Louisville tie?" I rolled my eyes at his ridiculous sports tie that was covered in red cardinals and big, obnoxious *L*s and said, "That's, um . . . unconventional."

"But dope, yes?" He ran a hand over it and said, "Cardinal-chic."

"That tie is awful," Laney said. She'd just exited the dance floor with Ashley. "It's like you lost a bet or something."

"Liz likes it."

"No, she doesn't," Adam said, looking at me with a question on his face. "Do you?"

I just smiled and shrugged as "New Year's Day" by Taylor Swift came on.

"See, she's too nice to tell you she hates it."

"Or she's too nice to tell you that she loves it and you have no fashion sense."

"Bennett's over there," Noah yelled over the music, and pointed to the dance floor. "With Alex."

I looked in the direction his finger was pointing, and my stomach sank when I saw them. They were dancing, Wes's arms around

Alex's waist as hers were locked around his neck. She was wearing a red dress that made her stand out from the crowd, and I couldn't come up with anything but compliments for her. *Quite a catch.* He was leaning down so he could hear whatever she was saying, and they were both smiling.

I felt queasy.

Had he always looked so impossibly handsome? And had he always smiled with such warmth? I could feel his fondness for her from across the room just by staring at his really nice mouth.

The mouth that had been on my mouth.

When I attacked him. Ugh.

I took a breath.

I really *had* fallen hard for him, hadn't I? I stared at them, the picture-perfect couple, as Taylor Swift made my soul ache.

Please don't ever become a stranger
Whose laugh I could recognize anywhere—

"Do you want to dance?" Michael looked down at me, and I realized he'd probably misinterpreted my stare of longing as a wallflower's wishful gaze.

"Um, not yet," I said, pinning a smile on my lips even though my cheeks were warm and I felt ill all of a sudden. "Unless you want to?"

"Nah, I'm good." He gave a shake of his head that was all relief. "Want something to drink?"

What I wanted was for him to stop trying to make us a thing. We both knew it wasn't there with us, but Michael seemed hell-bent on going through all the romantic motions, I'd started the evening guilty of the same thing but quickly realized I couldn't force it.

I should've said something when we saw Laney at the restaurant, because if I'd learned anything lately, it was that honesty was the best policy.

So I said, "I'd love a Diet Coke, but don't hit concessions until after you find Laney and talk to her."

His eyes narrowed. "Come again?"

It came with a smile and an extra helping of Texas on top, yet it still did nothing for me. I was fully recovered, filled with Michael antibodies, so I looked at his face that had been a part of so many childhood memories, and I said, "She isn't hung up on her ex; she's hung up on you. Go find her."

He stared at me for a second, looking like he had no idea what to say.

I smiled at him and nodded, just to show I didn't care.

"You sure?" He looked concerned, gazing at me the exact same way he had so many times when I'd been crying dramatically over neighborhood shenanigans, and it hurt my heart a little. I was letting him go, the dream of him, and Little Liz had never allowed herself to imagine that would ever happen.

"Yes, I'm sure." I laughed and pointed toward the mass of overdressed students. "Now go find her!"

"C'mere." He pulled me into a hug, and it was weird how emotional I felt. He drawled into the top of my head, "Thank you, Lizzie."

I rolled my eyes and pushed at his shoulders. "Will you go, please?"

He grinned and saluted me, which should've been dorky but was a little adorable. "Here I go!"

I watched him head off in search of his happy ending, and then I pulled my phone out of my pocket. No messages. I shut it off and put it back, letting my hands settle into the pockets. I looked at Giant Baby, at the lack of detail on his papier-mâché face, and tried counting how many little smoodges of paper it'd taken to create that thing. Because I needed something—anything—to look at other than Wes.

I looked at that baby for a solid five seconds before my gaze shifted back to the dance floor.

And oh, dear God—Wes was looking at me. He was dancing with Alex but our eyes met over her head. My heart beat hard in my chest and my breath froze as those dark eyes dipped down over my dress, then ran up to my hair, before settling back onto my face.

I raised an eyebrow as if to say, *So?*

I'd meant it to be playful, like a diluted attempt at recapturing our banter, but all it did was make his face tighten. He frowned before he and Alex moved a little and he was no longer facing me.

"I'll be right back," I muttered, not that anyone was listening, and I headed out the door in the back of the ballroom. I didn't really know where I was going in the enormous convention center, but I needed to get away. I couldn't stand another minute of prom, and I definitely couldn't stand Wes looking at me like he hated me.

I wandered all the way down to the end of the long hallway, and then I saw a stairwell, which was the perfect place to hide for a while. I glanced over my shoulder to make sure no one was watching me, and then I pulled open one of the heavy metal doors and ducked inside.

"Oh my God!"

"Oh!" I put my hand on my chest and looked at Jocelyn, who was sitting by herself on the steps with her orange stilettos on the floor in front of her. It was almost like she had to be a hallucination, because what were the odds that she and I would be hiding out in the same stairwell? "Geez. Sorry. You scared the crap out of me."

"Same." She tilted her head and looked annoyed to see me. "Did Charlie send you to find me?"

"No." I'd heard that when Kate had gotten an actual date-date, Cassidy and Joss had decided to follow suit so it wouldn't be just the two of them, but I still couldn't believe Joss had agreed to go with Charlie Hawk. "I haven't seen him."

I hated that I had no idea what to say to my best friend. I missed her and wished so badly that I could go back in time and not hide things from her. "I'm just hiding."

"Trouble in paradise?" She looked up at me like she didn't like me. At all.

"Nah—I'm just bored." I knew I probably shouldn't admit my foolishness to someone who already thought I was a fool, but I couldn't stop myself. "As it turns out, I don't really like Michael that way. And he and Laney are super into each other but just really terrible communicators."

She studied her nails as she said, "Is that right."

"Yes." I cleared my throat and leaned my backside against the door. "It also turns out that I actually *do* like Wes, but he actually *does* like Alex now. So."

"Um—"

"And," I said, swallowing. "And it turns out that I'm so, so sorry. I miss you."

Joss coughed out a little laugh noise but didn't smile. "Do you think the fact that everything blew up in your face is going to make me forgive you?"

"Of course not." I dug my hands deeper into my dress pockets, my face getting instant sweat beads as I realized my safe spot in the stairwell was about to become all about confrontation. "But at least you can take comfort in the fact that I'm suffering."

"I don't want you to suffer."

"Listen." I sighed. I just missed her so much. "I know you don't want to hear this, but I am *so* sorry for lying to you. I knew you'd call me out for trying to land Michael, and instead of thinking that through, I just went ahead and kept it from you so I wouldn't have to deal."

She wrapped her arms around her knees. "Such a wimp move."

"Right? And I shouldn't have let you think that I liked Wes, either. I mean, it ended up being a self-fulfilling prophecy, but it was pretty despicable."

"Yeah, it was."

"Yeah." I inhaled and said, "I'm gonna go back now so you—"

"Sit." She pointed her head toward the step beside her and said, "I miss you, too. I'm about to forgive you over the whole prom debacle. But."

I sat and waited.

"I feel like something is *wrong* with us lately. Like I'm constantly chasing you." Joss's pretty face was sad, and I hated that it was my fault.

She said, "It's our senior year. I kind of pictured us doing, like, everything together and making the most of every second we have because we're going to be living in different places in a few months."

She reached up and took the pins out of her updo. "Homecoming, prom, senior pictures, senior pranks—I thought we'd make all of those things totally epic. But you just keep disappearing on me for the big things."

"I know." I had never thought of it from her perspective. "I'm sorry."

"You're there for everything else, every little thing that doesn't matter. But, like—are you even going to show for graduation? Am I going to have to walk alone? I don't know what your deal is."

"It's complicated." It seemed like those two words explained everything about me. I swallowed and tried to make her understand. "I know we weren't friends when my mom died, but it sucked. Like, of course losing a parent sucks, but it *suck*-sucked. *Everything* felt lonely and sad—every single thing. You could've given me ice-cream cones at Disney World with Tom Hanks doling out pony rides, and I still would've cried every night because she wasn't there."

I slid out of my shoes, leaned my head against the cement block wall, and closed my eyes. "But eventually it started getting better. Not quite so terrible. I learned that if I could make it through the day without crying, I could go home and watch her movies, which always made her feel close."

"I'm sorry, Liz." She leaned her head on my shoulder and wrapped her arms around my right bicep.

"It all became normal and fine, but lately it's just . . . different."

"Different how?"

I opened my eyes and focused on the OPEN DOOR SLOWLY sticker on the stairwell exit. "I'm a senior. Everything is tagged with 'last time' and secretly all wrapped up in family. Last homecoming dance—'Parents, gather round for pictures of your babies.' College visits—'Oh my God, my mom was so embarrassing when we toured the dorms.' It's *my* stuff, but every single milestone feels empty without her, so I don't even feel like doing it."

She lifted her head and gave me a look. "Dress shopping?"

I took a shaky breath. "Bingo."

"Why didn't you just tell me?" She looked genuinely hurt. "I know I can be quick to judge, but I'm your best friend. You can tell me anything."

"I'm so sorry."

"I need you to listen to me. You know that, right? That you can always talk to me?"

I nodded and leaned into her, sighing and telling her everything. How I felt when it seemed like she was dismissing my mom's absence, what Wes had said about my mom and how I lived my life like I was in one of her screenplays.

I said, "I hate to say it, but I think he might be right."

"Think?" She shook her head and said, "Bennett has you pegged."

"Right?" I wiped my cheeks and wondered when I'd become such a crier. "I'm so sorry I've been such a tool."

"Well, I'm sorry I've been a tool too, and let's move on. We'll both do better." She leaned back on the step and said, "So what's happening in the ballroom?"

I wanted to hug her and gush, but I was also good with moving on. "I heard Jessica Roberts describing your shoes earlier."

"Not shocked—they're incredibly sexy."

I moved down another step and turned sideways so I could lean against the wall. "So are you having any fun?"

She pursed her lips. "I'm sitting in a deserted stairwell—by choice. Do the math."

"I'm sorry I ditched you."

"No worries—this'll make for a better memory. I mean, my imagination could never have reached far enough to consider a situation where I'd be going to Chili's in a prom dress with a guy wearing a denim tuxedo."

I laughed. Charlie was liked by everyone because he was great at football, but he was out there. During sophomore year, he wore suits to school every day because he thought he looked sophisticated. "He took you to Chili's?"

"In a motherloving jean tux, Liz—you're missing the most important part."

"Was he being ironic?"

"Girl, he bought it on Amazon because the model wearing it looked *cool.*" She grinned and shook her head. "He doesn't know the word 'ironic.'"

I bit down on my lip to keep from cackling. "At least he's nice."

Joss gave me side-eye and said, "He tried to touch my butt—with both hands—the first time we danced."

"Is he okay? Or did you stuff his body in a janitor's closet?"

"Puh-leeze; like I'm going to do time for a guy in a Levi's suit." She gave a little shrug and said, "I *am* leaving his ass here, though. I drove since he doesn't have a license, and my goal is to stay missing until it's too late for him to find another ride. Make the fool call his mom for a ride."

We both lost it then. We were cackling so hard that we were both crying when the doors to the stairwell flew open. We gasped in unison as Wes's friend Noah stepped into our space.

He looked as confused by our presence as we were about his. I said, "Noah?" at the same time he said, "Dammit, you guys scared me."

Jocelyn leaned back on her elbows, and I gestured to the step below us and said, "What are you doing all the way down here? I thought the cool kids were still down in the ballroom."

He sat down and said, "I couldn't take it anymore. Prom is painful. You can either stand around with your friends and talk while wearing uncomfortable tuxedos, or you can dance to shitty music while your friends talk about *you* and think they're funny. And so much planning and money goes into this one night, but there is no way the joy derived equals the effort. Absolutely no way."

Was it weird that I still thought it was possible that the joy could equal the effort? Even though it hadn't worked out for me, my heart still thought prom magic was a sparkling thing. Maybe that was just my obnoxious optimism messing with my head.

"So why did you come?" Jocelyn had a smirk on her face, but looked interested in how he'd answer. "I totally agree, by the way, but why did you come if you feel that way?"

"Same reason as you."

"And that is . . . ?"

He raised an eyebrow. "You don't know why you're here?"

She rolled her eyes. "I know why I'm here, but you don't, so there's no way you could know that we share a reason."

I crossed my arms and watched them. The little I knew of Noah was that he was the king of arguing; he seemed to enjoy the debate process. Joss, on the other hand, had no patience for people who argued with her.

Most didn't because they knew better.

He said, "You sure?"

She gave him a look.

He said around a smart-ass grin, "I thought we both came to see what a clown in a denim tuxedo actually looks like."

That made her chuckle. "You came here for Charlie too?"

"Oh, yeah." His face went into his natural sarcastic state as he smirked and said, "That blue suit really makes his eyes pop."

"What could he have been thinking?" Jocelyn started laughing again and Noah's smirk turned into a full-fledged smile. I felt like I should slip away, but I knew that would ruin the moment. Also, I wasn't ready to put space between me and Joss.

He kicked his legs out and leaned back on his elbows too, the male version of Jocelyn's lean. "That guy was thinking with his ego.

He knew he looked good in denim, so much so that he wanted to be swathed from head to toe in that scratchy, rigid, unstretching fabric that totally shows off his amazing ass."

"Oh my God," Jocelyn said. "You *have* to shut up. You have to."

We spent the next hour in the stairwell, just talking. It would have been fun if my brain hadn't been so stuck on reminding me about Wes and Alex. I'd let him go before I'd ever fully realized that I even wanted him, and now Alex was making him forget he'd ever kissed me.

After laugh-crying at Jocelyn's impression of the PE teacher, we decided we were done with prom. We each texted our respective dates with excuses, and Michael seemed fine with it. He even sent a thank you, btw message, which gave me hope that he and Laney would be official before morning.

I was counting the minutes until I could be warm in my bed, dwelling on my mistakes while Fitz attacked my feet under the blanket. Jocelyn and Noah, however, decided as we got closer to my house that they wanted to go to post-prom at the school gym. They'd both been planning to blow it off, but now that Noah was convinced he could make more free throws than Jocelyn, my uber-competitive best friend just *had* to go.

And she would totally beat him.

"You sure you don't want to join?" Jocelyn pulled into my driveway and put her car in park. "I promise we'll make it fun."

"No, thanks." I got out and slammed the door, then came around to her window and gave her a half hug. "But call me when you get home. Whenever that is."

"Bennett won't be there." Noah gave me a pitying look and said, "He told me this morning that post-prom is a waste of time and he needs a good weekend of sleep before the big game Monday, so he's coming home at midnight like a grandma."

I appreciated his attempt to cheer me up. It was kind of sweet. I said, "I have a date with a movie and some ice cream. Nothing tops that, but thanks."

"Let me guess." Joss rolled her eyes. "*Bridget Jones*?"

I shrugged. "I think I'm feeling a little more Joe Fox and Kathleen Kelly tonight, but either one will do."

They said goodbye and pulled away, but instead of going inside I sat down on the porch swing and stared over at Wes's house. The light was on in the living room, making me think of our late-night telephone calls and watching for him out the window.

I missed him so much.

I'd spent most of my life wishing he wasn't always *there*, aggravating me with his Wes-ness, yet now, everything felt empty when he was absent. I reached into my pocket and pulled out my phone. I went into our messages and typed Hey, you, but quickly deleted it because—of course—Wes wasn't home yet. Normal people stayed until the end of prom. Normal people weren't home at—I checked the clock on my phone—nine thirty.

Wes Bennett was probably being crowned prom king at that very second. He was probably about to dance with his beautiful date, and once he finished staring into her eyes, he'd forget about baseball responsibilities and sweep her away for a fantastical night of firelight and kisses that curled her toes.

Even when I closed my eyes tight, I could still picture them kissing.

"Screw this." I opened my eyes, stood, and fished my key out of my pocket.

It was time to go inside and gouge my eyes out.

CHAPTER SIXTEEN

"When you realize you want to spend the rest of your life with somebody, you want the rest of your life to start as soon as possible."

—*When Harry Met Sally*

I lay on the couch like a lump, still wearing my prom dress but wrapped in a blanket. I'd just dropped onto the sofa when I came into the house and was mindlessly watching *You've Got Mail* in the dark while trying not to think about what was going on with Wes and Alex.

Kathleen Kelly was talking about Joni Mitchell's "River," and I was feeling every melancholy note of that masterpiece.

I'm selfish and I'm sad
Now I've gone and lost the best baby—

"Liz?" Helena stopped short of walking into the living room from the kitchen when she saw me, and put her hand on her chest. "Geez, you scared the crap out of me."

"Sorry."

She tucked her hair behind her ears, a tube of Pringles under her arm. "No worries. Why are you sitting in the dark?"

I shrugged. "Too lazy to turn on the light."

"I see." She cleared her throat and put her hands in the pocket of her hoodie, where I could see two cans of soda. "And prom?"

I waved a hand. "It was fine."

She looked like she wanted to ask about it, but then she said, "Well, okay, then. I'll leave you to your movie. G'night."

I usually felt defensive when she asked about things in my life, but it felt empty *not* having her ask. I was embarrassed by the way I'd acted at the cemetery, and if I was honest with myself, I'd missed her today.

I didn't deserve it, but I wanted her to stay up with me. I was a little scared to ask, afraid of a rejection that I wholeheartedly deserved, but when she was almost to the stairs, I blurted out, "Do you want to watch it with me?"

I heard her steps stop before she came back into the room. "Oh my God, yes. I love this movie. Praise Jesus for the saviors that are Meg Ryan and Tom Hanks."

"I thought you hated rom-coms."

"I hate cheesy, unrealistic romantic movies. But bouquets of newly sharpened pencils?" She plopped down beside me and sat crisscross applesauce, pulling the top off the Pringles. "Be still my heart."

We watched for a few more minutes before she said, "So prom."

"Ah, prom." I kicked my feet out onto the coffee table and snagged a chip. "Prom was like having your biggest mistake dressed up in pretty clothes and paraded in front of you with someone else."

"English, please. I don't get how that gibberish pertains to the pretty Mr. Michael."

I sighed. "It doesn't. It's . . . I don't know, just forget it. I don't want to think about it anymore."

"Done." She bit into a chip and said, gesturing at the TV, "This is the *best* love triangle."

"Um—it's more of a love square, if it's a love shape at all." I chomped on a Pringle and said, "They're just a foursome who fall apart on their own. None of them have to choose between the others."

"I'm not talking about the two couples." Helena pulled the sodas out of her pocket, handed me one, and opened hers. She slurped off the can's edge and said, "I'm talking about the triangle between Kathleen, her idea of who NY152 is online, and Joe Fox."

"Wait—what?"

"Think about it. She finds his online persona charming. She likes that he knows about 'going to the mattresses.' She envies his ability to verbally slay." She leaned forward and set her can on the table. "The idea of this man is beautiful, but in practice she thinks Joe Fox's verbal slaying is mean, and when he goes to the mattresses and puts her out of business, she hates him."

I blinked and opened my pop. "Holy crap—you're right."

"I know." She grinned and did a little half-bow thing. "Sometimes we get so tied up in our idea of what we think we want that we miss out on the amazingness of what we could actually have."

She was talking about the movie, but I felt seen. Wes had been right about one thing when he'd talked about my mom issues. It wasn't intentional, but I *had* been living my life like I was one of her characters, like I was trying to act out the parts I thought she would've written for me.

I'd pushed him away and gone for the "good guy," when in reality there weren't only solid, dependable people and players with questionable intentions in the world. There were Weses out there, guys who broke the mold and blew both of those stereotypes out of the water.

He was so much more than a Mark Darcy or a Daniel Cleaver.

And then there were Helenas—smart, irreverent women who had no idea how to play the piano or tend to a rose garden, but they were always there, just waiting for you to realize you needed them.

"I mean," Helena said, "she nearly let *152 pock marks* go—can you even imagine?"

"Helena." I blinked fast but it was impossible to clear my eyes. My voice sounded constricted when I said, "I'm so sorry for what I said to you before. For everything. I don't want to miss out on what we could have. I didn't mean it when I told you to butt out."

"Oh." Her eyes widened a little bit and she tilted her head. "It's totally okay."

"It's not."

She gave me a hug and sniffled. "Just know that I don't want to take your mom's place. I only want to be here for you."

I closed my eyes and felt *something* as I let her hug surround me.

I felt loved.

And I knew at that moment that my mother would want this. Badly. She would want—above all else—for me to be loved. I said, "I want that too, Helena."

We were both sniffling, which made us laugh. The moment

melted and we returned to our spots, side by side on the couch. I decided as she wolfed down chips and got crumbs all over her stained hoodie that I was glad she was so different from my mom. It was *nice* that the lines between them could never be blurred.

I cleared my throat. "Do you think it would be okay for me to call you my stepmom now?"

"As long as you don't add 'evil' as a prefix."

"Why else would I want to say it, though? You have to admit that it's a powerful title."

"I suppose it is. And I do love power."

"See? I knew it." I glanced toward the sliding glass door by the kitchen, and my mind went to the Secret Area. I turned toward Helena on the couch and said, "So prom. Basically, the bottom line is that I went with the wrong guy."

"Are you coming with my pop?" I heard my dad run down the stairs before he stepped into the room wearing Peanuts pajama pants and a T-shirt, smiling. Then he looked concerned and said, "Hey, hon, I didn't know you were home already."

"Yeah—I just got back."

Helena pointed at my dad and gave me a look before saying to him, "Shh—she was about to tell me about prom."

"Pretend I'm not here." My dad plopped down in the small space between Helena and the sofa's armrest, and he took a sip of her soda.

I rolled my eyes and told them about Laney and the realization that I had no interest in the guy that I'd thought fate had sent me. Then I had to tell them what a jerk I'd been to Wes after our kiss (except I said "date" so my dad didn't freak), just so they understood how badly I'd screwed everything up. I pictured Wes's face at prom, glaring at me, and I said, "So now it's too late. He's with a girl who adores him and doesn't treat him like crap. Why would he ever want to look back from that?"

They listened to all of it before my dad smiled at me like I was unbelievably dense. "Because you're *you*, Liz."

"I don't know what—"

"Oh, you don't know, do you?" Helena dusted off the front of her shirt and said, "That boy has been into you since you were little kids."

"No, he hasn't." Her words made a hopeful buzzing start in my ears and fingertips, even though I knew she was wrong. "He's been into *messing* with me since we were little kids."

"Oh, you are so wrong. Tell her, hon." Helena nudged my dad with her elbow. "Tell her about the piano."

My dad put his arm around Helena and propped his feet on the coffee table. "Did you ever know, Liz, that Wes used to sit on the back porch and listen to you practice the piano? We pretended not to see him, but he was always there. And we're talking *way* back when he was a little pain in the ass and you were awful at piano."

"No way." I struggled to remember how old we'd been when the piano had sat in the back room. "He did?"

"He did. And do you really think he cared about that parking spot you guys have fought over for the past year?"

"He definitely cared. He still does. That was what made him agree to help me."

I thought about the rainy day in his living room when I'd first suggested the plan. He'd seemed like a stranger that day, when I'd had to beg him to let me in. Cookies and milk, Wes's cartwheels—it seemed like a lifetime ago.

"Liz." Helena's smile was obscenely large. "His mom lets him park behind her car. He always pulled in his driveway, but then out of nowhere, right about the time you got your car, he started parking in the street."

My mouth fell open. "What are you saying?"

She smacked my arm and said, "And I'm not saying anything other than I think he was after that spot because he wanted a reason to talk to you. Do with that what you will."

Was it possible? In a way, it was impossible to believe because he was out of my league. He was popular and athletic and ridiculously hot. I was supposed to believe that *he* had been into *me* before I'd even realized who he truly was? That he'd been into me for, like, a really long time? I dug my fingers into my hair and pulled a little. "I have no idea what to do."

My dad went upstairs after that, but Helena and I watched the rest of the movie before going to bed. I'd just closed my door when Helena knocked on it. "Liz?"

I pulled it open. "Yeah?"

She was smirking at me in the dark hallway. "Be brave enough to go big, okay?"

"What does that mean?"

She shrugged. "I don't know. Just . . . if you're gonna do it, don't skimp, I guess."

Be brave enough to go big.

I kept replaying her words as I lay in bed. I tried sleeping, but between listening for Wes's car and imagining all the things he and Alex might be doing, all I did was lie there being unhappy.

Until it hit me.

Be brave enough to go big.

CHAPTER SEVENTEEN

"Here's the deal. I love you. I know I do. Because I've never been so scared in my entire life. And I once shared an elevator with Saddam Hussein. Just me and Saddam. And this is way scarier. I love you."

—*Long Shot*

"I was wrong about everything. I am so incredibly glad Michael came back, but only because it allowed me to get to know the real you. All this time you were right here—next door—and I had no idea how amazing you are," I whispered to myself. I was shaking, shivering with cold when I heard Wes's car pull into the driveway.

"Showtime." I shook out my cold fingers and quit practicing my speech. I inhaled slowly, through my nose, as I heard him cut his engine, and a second later I heard his car door slam shut.

I tucked my hair behind my ears and got into a supercute-yet-really-casual pose on one of the chairs and waited for him to find my note.

After Helena's epic movie quote about going big, I decided she was right and got very busy. First, I flipped on my music computer and looked through the desk drawers until I found a blank CD. There was something about holding the tangible product of careful music curation that I still loved, technology be damned.

I took the Wes and Liz playlist that I'd made after the kiss and I burned it to the CD. It had all the songs we'd ever discussed on it, and all the music we'd experienced together. I quickly made album cover art—our initials inside a heart made of ketchup—and printed it, then carefully cut it so it fit in the case just right.

As soon as it was done, I changed into jeans and Wes's huge hoodie, which had somehow ended up in my vomity clothes bag (and that I'd been sleeping in every night). My hair and makeup were still fairly intact, so I pulled on my freshly-bleached-and-perfectly-white-again Chucks, scribbled out the words MEET ME IN THE SECRET AREA with a Sharpie on a piece of printer paper, and filled a boot box with the necessary supplies.

I'd sprinted over to his porch to leave the note before hurrying to the Secret Area, where I'd set up the portable CD player, started a fire, organized the s'mores stuff, and gotten everything in place.

Then I'd snuggled into a blanket and waited.

And waited and waited and waited.

And dozed off a couple times.

But now he was finally home. Oh dear. Oh God, I was so nervous. And then—*wait, what?*—I heard the slamming of a second car door.

I sucked in my lips. *Crap, crap, crap.* Maybe he just grabbed something from his car. Maybe there *wasn't* someone with him.

"Wes!"

I heard the giggling yell, and it might as well have been the laugh of an evil clown for what it did to my pulse. I tried peeking around the bushes, but I couldn't see anything. The voices were getting closer, so I stepped up onto my chair to see if I could see better from a higher vantage point.

Holy balls. I could see by the light of the full moon that Wes and Alex were walking through his backyard toward where I was stationed with my pride fully exposed and a sack full of embarrassing goodies.

"Shit!" All evidence had to be erased. I kicked the box of s'mores supplies, intending to knock them into a bush and out of sight. Panic exploded inside me as the box went flying and sent the graham crackers and marshmallows spilling out into the water, so they were floating on top of the fountain.

Crap-crap-crap-crap.

I grabbed the CD player and dropped down to my knees, desperate to be hidden by the darkness. But the ancient machine slipped out of my hands and landed on the ground, causing eight D-size batteries to be ejected.

Screw it. I ditched the mess and scooted over to the big bush, crawling on my hands and knees toward the other side. If I crawled all the way around to the other end of the Secret Area, maybe I could cut through—

"Liz?"

I closed my eyes for a second before slowly straightening and climbing to my feet. I pasted a smile onto my face as Wes and Alex looked at me. "Hey, guys. What's up? Fun prom, right?"

"Right? Oh my God." Alex, bless her, acted like it wasn't out of the ordinary for me to be crawling around in the darkness behind Wes's house. "I thought I was going to have a heart attack when Ash was crowned."

"I know," I breathed, smiling like I knew what she was talking about while taking in the stoic, serious expression on Wes's face. "Total heart attack moment. Like, *whaaat*? Ash was crowned?"

"What are you doing out here?" Wes asked, looking at me with an unreadable expression that made the tips of my ears burn hot. He was probably pissed that I was in the way of a potential seduction.

Had he brought her there for that? Were they waiting for me to leave so they could get to it? For some reason, the thought of them together was a hundred times worse when it involved the Secret Area.

"I, um, I followed my cat out here earlier and . . ." I pointed toward my house as words failed to make sense to me. "I dropped something and thought it might've rolled under this bush."

And I pointed to Wes's forest like a distraught toddler.

"Your cat doesn't go outside."

I made a face and said, "Yes, he does. Actually, no, you're right. He ran out."

"Really? And what did you drop?" He didn't look amused at all.

"Um, it was money. A penny." I cleared my throat and said, "I dropped a penny and it rolled away. So yeah. I was just out here, looking for my penny. It was lucky."

"Your—"

"Penny. Yep. But it doesn't matter. I don't need it." I cleared my throat again, but the tightness just wouldn't go away. "The penny, y'know? I mean, who needs a penny, am I right? My stepmom throws them away, for God's sake."

They both just stared at me, and the hard lines of Wes's face made me homesick for our *before*, for his laughing eyes before I'd ruined everything. "It's weird how sometimes there can be a penny that's, like, always there, and you think you don't need it and don't even like it, right?"

Alex tilted her head and scrunched her eyebrows together, but not a single thing on Wes's face changed as I rambled.

"Then you wake up one day and your eyes are opened to just how amazing pennies are. How had you not noticed before, right? I mean, they're like the *best coins ever*. As in, better than all the other coins combined. But you weren't careful and you lost your penny and you just wish you could make your penny understand how much you regret not cherishing it, but it's too late because you lost it. Y'know?"

"Liz, do you need to borrow some money?" Alex looked at me, and I was a little bit close to crying again.

I shook my head and said, "Um, no, thanks, I've got to run—even though I'm penniless, ha ha ha—so you guys have fun." I took a step backward and did a tiny wave thing. "Don't do anything I wouldn't do."

Stop talking, you dipshit!

I sensed—without looking—that they were still staring at me as I climbed over Wes's fence and ran through my backyard.

CHAPTER EIGHTEEN

"But, you know, the thing about romance is, people only get together right at the very end."

—*Love Actually*

"Thank you." I took the bag from the McDonald's employee, tossed it onto the passenger seat, and drove away. It was midnight, and I'd spent the past hour just driving around, cranking Adele and sob-singing, and trying to stay gone long enough for Alex to have left and for Wes to have gone inside. I would rather have done almost anything in the world than see either one of them, so I'd texted Helena and just cruised the city.

And my dad was the coolest person on the planet for not texting me a single word of warning when he knew I was driving around aimlessly after midnight. It had to be killing him.

I'd considered getting ice cream on my way home, but I hadn't been up to actually getting *out* of my car, so I'd settled on the golden arches. I just wanted to go home and sad-eat, watch a movie, and try to forget how badly I'd humiliated myself.

A penny. Seriously? They'd probably laughed about me until they fell into each other's arms and had perfect sex.

"Dammit." I grabbed a fistful of fries and jammed them into my mouth before pulling into The Spot. It wasn't mine anymore—it was Wes's forever—but at the moment I didn't care. His car was in his driveway, so screw him.

Instead of getting out after parallel parking, though, I just sat there, wolfing down my food and listening to the radio. Getting out of the car and walking across the street seemed like work at that tired moment, and I was also terrified of running into the happy couple. It would be just my luck to walk by at the exact moment they decided to get hot and heavy in his driveway, or something equally nightmarish.

I finished my food and was drinking my chocolate shake with the seat half-reclined when there was a knock on my window.

"Shit!" I jumped, and my straw splattered milkshake onto Wes's hoodie. I looked through the fogged-up window and could see a tall body in a letter jacket.

Someone please kill me.

I wiped my mouth with my fingers, put my seat back up, and rolled down the window. Gave him a cool smile. "Yes?"

Wes glared down at me. "What are you doing?"

"Um . . . parking."

"I watched you park ten minutes ago. Try again."

"Wow. Creep much?"

"I wanted to talk to you, so yeah, I was waiting. But now I think maybe you're never going to get out of that car."

I rolled my eyes and set down my shake. Apparently I was going to have to face him and my utter humiliation twice in one night. How awesome. I got out of the car and shut the door.

Crossed my arms and looked up at his face. "What do you need?"

"Well, for starters, I need you to explain what happened earlier."

My heart hurt as I looked at him. His hair was tousled, like he'd dragged his hand through it a hundred times, and he was wearing his untucked dress shirt and tuxedo pants under his jacket. He was an absolute mess, and my fingers itched to touch him.

I narrowed my eyes and acted confused. "Are you talking about when I lost my—"

"Nope." He gave me a look of warning and said, "Do not say 'penny.'"

"Sorry." I looked down at my shoes and muttered, "Lucky coin."

"Really? You're sticking to that?"

I just shrugged and stared at my Chucks, clueless about what to say. Everything I'd planned to tell him during my whole *be brave* phase felt too hard to say after seeing him with Alex. Especially when he'd looked so unhappy to see me in the Secret Area.

I still couldn't believe he'd taken her back there.

His nostrils flared and he said, "Oh, well, that explains everything."

"Why do you seem mad at me?" I raised my eyes to his face and waited for an answer. I was the one who wished to spontaneously combust. Why was *he* being salty?

His jaw flexed before he said, "Because I hate games."

"What games?"

"What games?" His eyes were hot, and yeah—he was mad. "You won your precious Michael, but as soon as I looked twice at Alex, you're burning me this unbelievable CD and rambling about lucky pennies in a way that makes me think I'm the penny in that particular scenario. While wearing my baseball hoodie. What are you doing to me?"

"You saw the CD?" I bit the inside of my cheek and wondered how much humiliation a person could take before it literally killed them. Because as I pictured the ketchup initials I'd put on the CD cover, I felt like I was close to combusting and gently floating to the ground as ash.

He stuck his hands into his coat pockets. "I'm not oblivious, Liz. I also saw the note, the soggy s'mores supplies, and the busted CD player."

"Oh." I took a shuddering breath as his dark eyes bore into me. Then I blurted, "So do you like her?"

His eyebrows furrowed together like he hadn't expected the question, which was fair, because I hadn't expected to ask it.

But I needed to know.

He swallowed and I thought he wasn't going to answer, but then he said, "Alex is great."

"Oh." I hoped my face didn't show how close I was to crying, how that one syllable was like a punch to the stomach. "Well, yay. I've got to go."

I took a step around him, but he grabbed my arm and stopped me. "That's it? You're not going to explain what all of that was?"

"It doesn't matter now."

"It might."

"It doesn't, okay?" I tried to sound light and easy, like I was fine with everything as he dropped his hand. "I made the CD and set an embarrassing scene because I realized that Michael isn't the person I can't stop thinking about, and I wanted to tell you. I mean, he's great, but being with him is nothing like eating burgers with you, or sneaking out to the Secret Area to make s'mores and look at the stars, or fighting with you over a parking space. But it took me too long to figure that out, and now you've got Alex."

He opened his mouth, but I shook my head.

"No. It's fine—I get it. She's flawless and sweet, and as much as I hate to say it, you deserve someone like her." I took a big, shaky breath as those dark eyes made me so sorry for everything I'd done to get us here. "Because I was wrong, Wes. You *are* the good stuff."

He scratched his chin and looked past me, down the street. Then he settled his eyes on my face and said, "That's not the only thing you're wrong about."

"What?" Leave it to him to kick me when I'm down. "What're you talking about?"

"You're wrong about Alex. She's not flawless."

"Bennett, no one is totally flawless—come on." I couldn't believe his nerve. "She's pretty dang close, though."

"I suppose."

"You *suppose*? What on earth could she possibly be lacking? Do you want bigger boobs or something? Is she not—"

"She's not you."

"What?"

"She. Isn't. You."

I shut my mouth and looked at him, scared to believe he was saying what it sounded like he was saying.

"She's pretty, but her face doesn't transform into sunlight when she talks about music." He did that clench thing with his jaw and said, "She's funny, but not spit-out-your-drink-in-astonishment funny."

It felt like my heart was going to explode as his eyes moved down to my lips under the glow of the buzzing streetlight. He moved his face a little closer to mine, looked into my eyes, and rumbled, "And when I see her, I don't feel like I *have* to talk to her or mess up her hair or do something—anything—to get her to swing that gaze on me."

My hands were shaking when I tucked my hair behind my ears and breathed, "You haven't messed up my hair in a really long time."

"And it's been killing me." He took a step closer, which pressed me against the side of my car. "I fell in love with teasing you in the second grade, when I first discovered that I could turn your cheeks pink with just a word. Then I fell in love with you."

I'm pretty sure my heart was developing an arrhythmia with each word he said. "So you and Alex aren't—"

"Nope." He reached down and wrapped the drawstrings on my hoodie—*his* hoodie—around his hands. "We're just friends."

"Oh." My brain was trying to keep up, but his handsome face was making it difficult. That and his sudden presence in my personal space, not to mention the gentle pull of him tugging me closer. I was muddled. "Well, why did you act like you wanted me to say yes to Michael's promposal?"

"You've loved him since kindergarten." His eyes were all I could see as he quietly said, "I didn't want our kiss to get in the way of that if it was what you really wanted."

How had I ever thought Wes was anything other than amazing? I didn't even try to stop the lovesick smile from taking over my face as I set my hands on his chest and said, "What I really wanted was to go with you."

"Well, you could've told me that, Buxbaum." His voice was just a breath between us as he said, "Because just seeing you in that dress made me want to punch our very good friend Michael."

"It *did*?"

He yanked on the drawstring. "That's not supposed to make you happy."

"I know." I was giving away my every emotion as I beamed up at him, but I couldn't help it. I couldn't hold back and be cool even if I tried. Because the thought of Wes being pissed at Michael—and jealous—over me, was just too wonderful. "But it does. It's just so swoony."

"Forget swoony." He let go of the strings and slid his hands up the sides of my face until he was holding it in his big palms. I sucked in a breath as his mouth lowered, and my brain cued up the perfect song for this ending. Or rather, this beginning.

I've been searching a long time,
For someone exactly like you

Our kiss was breathless and wild and Wes pulled away too soon. He wrapped his arms around me, picked me up, and moved me to the trunk of my car.

He smiled after plopping me down and said, "Do you realize

we could've been doing this for years if you weren't such a pain in the ass?"

"Nah—I didn't like you until recently."

"Enemies-to-lovers—it's our trope, Buxbaum."

"You poor, confused little love lover." A giggle shimmied through me before I set my hands on his face and said as I pulled him back to me, "Just shut up and kiss me."

Cue the Bazzi.

EPILOGUE

"A girl will never forget the first boy she likes."

—*He's Just Not That into You*

"But she'll also never forget the first boy she hates."

—Liz Buxbaum

I dropped the bright yellow mum into the hole and covered the roots with dirt. The early-September sun was hot on my face as I planted the flowers, but it had the blurry feel of a day in transition, like its heat was all for show and entirely lacking in the power it'd once held.

"Since you have daisies in the summer, we thought it might be nice for you to have mums in the fall." I looked at my mom's headstone and wondered how I was going to cope with the distance. I was down to one hour until I left for California, and even though logically I knew it was silly, a tiny part of me worried I was going to feel lost without our daily chats.

"It was all Helena's idea." Wes took a sip of water before picking up the bag of potting soil and saying to my mother's headstone, "Don't let your kid take all the credit."

It *had* been Helena's idea. She and I had had a lot of good talks after prom, and she had been super understanding about my grief. Instead of trying to convince me that I should move on or get closure, she'd bought a little bench for the gravesite—with a lovely floral cushion—so I wouldn't have to sit on the ground.

She'd also bought me a jacket made of alpaca hair because she'd read that ghosts inherently know that the wearer of that material is not a threat. She made me wear it every time I went to the cemetery after dark, because she didn't want me getting possessed by the devil or one of his lackeys.

I was really starting to love my goofy stepmom.

"He's right." I said, sticking out my tongue at Wes. "But I love the idea. This way, even though I'm not here, my flowers will bloom beside you."

"Unless they die because Liz is a horrible gardener."

I grinned and launched the trowel in his direction. "That could actually happen. Your green thumb—and frankly, your desire to even have one—is clearly skipping a generation."

Wes caught the gardening tool as if he'd expected the throw and took the supplies to his car. I dusted my hands on my jeans and sat back on my heels. It was a little hard to believe that Wes and I were both going away to California after we were done, but it felt right. He's always been there—the annoying boy next door—and now he was going to be the annoying boy in the dorm next door.

As it turned out, Wes was a rock star pitcher and got offers from schools all over the country. In the end he'd selected UCLA, but he made sure I knew it had nothing to do with me. I believe his exact words had been *So we're totally free to dump each other in Cali without any weird guilt. This is just a freak accident that we're going to the same school, not any love bullshit.*

And then he'd given me a boyish grin and a kiss that made me forget my name.

For a few months now, Wes had been going with me to my mom's grave a couple times a week. He usually wandered away so I could talk to her—rain or shine—but then he always came back in time to say goodbye to my mom and tell her something sarcastic about me.

It was cheesy, and I adored him for it.

"Well," I said, "we should probably get going because we're supposed to meet Dad, Helena, and Joss in ten minutes."

We were meeting at a café for breakfast, and then my dad and Helena were driving the U-Haul to California while Wes and I followed in his car.

I stood and looked over at him as he closed the trunk. He was wearing the T-shirt I'd bought him as a graduation present; it said EDUCATED FEMINIST BRO. I'd bought it to be funny, but he wore it all the time.

It went well with his smart-ass smile.

I watched him walk around the car and open the back door, where Mr. Fitzpervert was sitting in his carrier in my favorite little plaid scarf, ears up and listening to every outdoor noise the cemetery had to offer. Wes called him Mr. Fuzzy with the Silly Clothes and acted like he didn't like cats, but he also always scratched him in that *exact* place Fitz liked behind his ear. And as I stood there, watching him talk to my cat, I realized the truth.

Wes *was* the good guy in the movie. Yes, he was funny and the life of the party, but he was also dependable and understanding and loyal. Even though I realized after prom that I didn't need him to be, he *was* a Mark Darcy.

Only better.

I was about to say it out loud, to my mom, when Wes looked at me with that smile I loved. "You ready, Buxbaum? Mr. Fuzzy's getting hungry and so am I."

It was Wes's idea to choose somewhere with outdoor seating so Fitz could enjoy the great outdoors from his carrier before the long car ride.

How could I *not* love him?

"Yeah." I narrowed my eyes at him but ruined the effect by smiling. "But it's 'Mr. Fitzpervert,' you tool."

I started walking toward him, but when I glanced back at my mom's headstone, I almost tripped. Because a cardinal had landed on the chokecherry branch that hung down beside it. He was bright red and beautiful, just sitting on the branch and looking in my direction.

I blinked fast and narrowed my eyes as he opened his beak and chirped the sweetest little melody.

I turned back to Wes, and he was looking at it over my shoulder. I said, "You see it too, right?"

He gave a nod. "Holy shit."

We both stood there, staring at the bird. After another moment he flew away, but my heart felt lighter, like my mother had wanted to make sure I knew she was happy about me leaving. I cleared my throat and faced him. "You ready?"

"You okay?" He took two steps and was there, wrapping his big body around mine. He ran his hand over my back and said into my hair, "Because we can stay as long as you want, Liz."

"I'm great, actually." I pulled back and let myself stare at his handsome face, at the person who had always been there for me, even when I hadn't wanted him to be. "Let's go eat."

THE SOUNDTRACK OF WES AND LIZ

1. Someone Like You | Van Morrison
2. Paper Rings | Taylor Swift
3. Lovers | Anna of the North
4. ocean eyes | Billie Eilish
5. Bad Liar | Selena Gomez
6. Public Service Announcement (Interlude) | Jay-Z
7. Up All Night | Mac Miller
8. How Would You Feel (Paean) | Ed Sheeran
9. Hello Operator | The White Stripes
10. Paradise | Bazzi
11. Sabotage | Beastie Boys
12. Feelin' Alright | Joe Cocker
13. Someone Like You | Adele
14. Monkey Wrench | Foo Fighters
15. Bella Luna | Jason Mraz
16. Forrest Gump | Frank Ocean
17. Electric (feat. Khalid) | Alina Baraz
18. Kiss | Tom Jones
19. Enter Sandman | Metallica
20. Death with Dignity | Sufjan Stevens
21. We Are Young | fun. feat. Janelle Monáe
22. New Year's Day | Taylor Swift
23. River | Joni Mitchell
24. Paradise | Bazzi

ACKNOWLEDGMENTS

I should probably thank everyone on the planet, God, the universe, shooting stars, and that summer dandelion that I wished upon once, because surely, all of those things must've come into play in order for this to happen, right? YOU GUYS—MY NAME IS ON THE SPINE OF THIS BOOK. LIKE, DUUUUUUUUUUUDE!

Thank YOU, reader who is perusing this page. You're part of my dream-come-true now, and I'm eternally grateful that you picked up my book.

My brilliant, wonderful, funny, epic dealmaker of an agent, Kim Lionetti. Thank God you saw something in that first rambling manuscript, because you carved out the path for this to happen for me—all I had to do was follow along. You're a dreammaker extraordinaire, a granter of wishes, and an editorial goddess, and words cannot express how blessed I feel to have you—and the entire Bookends team (waving at you, McGowan)—in my corner.

My editor, Jessi Smith—A million thank-yous (x1000) for letting me work with you on this book. This entire experience has been the most buzzy, happy, rewarding project I ever could've wished for. You are a DREAM editor, and I'm so happy we get to do another book together!

The remarkable humans at SSBFYR—I'm in awe of everything you've done for this book. Morgan York, thank you for being the wizard who keeps everything moving. Mackenzie and Arden and the team in Canada—you guys are rock stars. Heather Palisi—in my wildest dreams, I couldn't have imagined a more perfectly designed cover. Liz Casal—how was I lucky enough to get you as the artist for my cover? I couldn't love it more. And the rest of the BFYR team—you are a ridiculously talented, well-oiled creative machine, and I am absolutely legit not worthy. You made my dream into a tangible object I can hold in my hand; fairy godpeople, the lot of you.

Finneas, Billie Eilish, Adele, Justin Hurwitz, Post Malone, Frank Ocean—though you will likely never see this, thank you for contributing to my BTTM writing playlist. Your music was the perfect vibe and will forever be a part of this story in my heart.

Cheyanne Young—you were my first-ever "author-friend" and you're my total writer role model. I don't know what I would've done without your feedback, advice, and venting partnership; you're simply the best. *Eww, David.* I can't wait to see your book on the big screen!

Kota Jones, Tessa Adams, Jennie Gollehon, Kelly Riibe, and Jim Plath—you guys have been kind enough to look at random garbage drafts, and I owe you big-time. Tiffany Epp—I will forever think of you as my first reader, my first fan, because you read my garbage before anyone else and liked it. Lori Anderjaska—you have mad street cred and you're my favorite chick from the other side of the tracks. Kerbin, my manny—thanks for babysitting

Kate all those nights while I was writing—sorry I never paid you. ;) And Mark Goslee—thank you for putting up with me. You listen to me ramble incessantly—all day, every day—and have yet to fire (or kill) me.

Professor Anna Monardo—You made me want to be a better writer, and that changed EVERYTHING.

And now—gulp—my family:

Mom—I'm so grateful that you and dad allowed me to be a voracious, flashlight-under-the-covers, ultra-hyper reader. You fostered my obsession and enabled my habit via Scholastic book orders, so I got to live a hundred lives in my childhood through fiction. #well-traveled

MaryLee—you are the kindest person on the planet, the good sister, and I don't deserve your support. You were the one—back in freaking 1999—who saw an author on Oprah and said to me, "You read all the time; *you* should write a book." I've written at least ten awful books since then—probably more—but finally found one that took. So thank you. And a shout-out to your amazing clan: Brian, Josh, Jake, Rachel, Anna, Zakari, and Dontavius.

My bonus family—Phil, Barb, Marilyn, Garwood, Wendy, Scott, Joyce, Demi, and Deon. If you were overbearing or awful, I surely would've turned to alcohol instead of daydreaming, and this would never have happened. So thank you, in-laws, for not sucking.

My offspring—Cassidy, Tyler, Matt, Joe, and Kate. I love you guys more than I can even say, and thank you for being okay with having a mom who spends way more time daydreaming and reading than cooking, cleaning, or crafting. Also—thank you for being in so many sporty childhood activities. It gave me endless opportunities to zone out (because games with balls can be brutally boring) and follow my characters as they traversed the world in my mind. In a way, your athletic prowess (or lack thereof—looking at you, Cass) helped me hone my craft. You are five of the funniest humans I know and I couldn't be prouder of each one of you. (P.S. Thank you Terrance and Jordyn for not only taking two of them off our hands, but for putting up with all the madness that comes with our family.)

And finally—Kevin. You're truly the smartest, funniest, BEST human I've ever known and my favorite person in the world (sorry, kids). You deserve a Type-A wife who cleans like a maid and cooks like your grandma (while wearing The Good Makeup), but unfortunately, you got me and it's too late for givesie-backsies. You're stuck with this head-in-the-clouds, flannel-pant-wearing snorer for the rest of your life.

If it's any consolation, I worship the ground you walk on and love every single incredible thing about you.

So here—have this book. I made it for you.

And last but not least, thank you to Starbucks, Spaghetti Works, Rockstar energy drinks, and McDonald's. You truly are the wind beneath my wings.

Read on for a sneak peek at the sequel, *Nothing Like the Movies*.

NEW YEAR'S EVE

"If my fifteen-year-old self could see me now,
he would punch me in the dick."
—*Set It Up*

Wes

"This place is *packed*."

"Dude, I told you," Adam said, loading a piece of gum into his mouth and smirking as we walked into the party. Loud music was booming from a speaker somewhere, and everyone appeared to be talking *over* the sound.

I followed him and Noah up the stairs and into the living room, where it looked like everyone I knew from high school was in attendance. *Shit.* People were *everywhere*, sitting on couches and standing around, and I instantly regretted my decision to go out.

"Bennett!" Alex ran over from the other side of the room and wrapped her arms around me, pulling me down into a hug.

"Happy New Year, Benedetti," I said, swallowing hard as I hugged her back.

"How *are* you?" she asked, and I hated the way she smiled

when she pulled away. It was one of those pitying smiles, like she was asking how I was handling the fact that my life had turned to shit.

"Good," I said, torn between being happy that my friends were back from college—*holy balls I have a social life again*—and kind of hating being social. Because as nice as everyone was, I could tell they all felt sorry for me. Sorry about my dad, sorry about the fact I'd dropped out of college, sorry about the fact I was no longer playing baseball.

I was one hell of a sorry guy.

Since Noah and Adam got back, I'd said *absolutely not* every time they invited me out. But for some reason, New Year's Eve made me cave. The fact that it was a holiday had softened me, apparently, which I was now regretting.

Because nothing felt the same.

The last time I was with these people, we all had big plans for our futures.

And . . . well, *they* still did.

I, on the other hand, had pivoted.

When my dad died (two weeks after I moved in at UCLA), I came home for the funeral and never left, deciding to bail on school and everything that the future held for me. *As if I had a choice.* Now that it'd been a few months since his heart attack, I was firmly settled into full-time employment at the grocery store with a side-hustle as an Uber driver. Life was fucking *great*.

"Come on—Michael's playing Money Bet in the kitchen," Noah said, pointing. "It's too loud over here."

Money Bet, the new favorite party game, was basically just dares with money attached. Some guys I worked with at the store made it up, and when I mentioned it to Adam and Noah, they went nuts with it.

I followed them into the kitchen, stopping to grab a drink before sitting down at the table.

"It's about time, Bennett," Michael said from his spot at the other end of the table, drawling just enough to let me know he was already buzzed. "You've been a hermit all break."

I gritted my teeth when I heard the first few notes of that old song from *Fearless* playing in the other room. It just *figured* that the party would have *that* song playing in the background. It was 100 percent on-brand for my life lately.

"I've been busy," I said, picking up my cup and downing the entire thing. I wasn't *trying* to get drunk, but I wasn't trying *not* to, either. We'd pregamed a little at Noah's with his brother, so I had a nice start.

"Money bet five says Bennett can't make it from here," Noah said, pushing an empty can in front of me and gesturing toward the kitchen sink.

"Accept," I said, then hurled the can in the direction of the sink, watching it bounce off the counter and clatter to the ground.

"You suck," he replied, and I pulled a five dollar bill out of my pocket and set it in front of him.

"Still better than you."

"Joss just got here," Noah said, looking down at a text, "With my chicken sandwich, hell yes."

I said, "Money bet chicken sandwich says y—"

I trailed off when I saw her.

She. Was. There.

Holy *shit*.

Libby was standing in the living room.

I'd managed to avoid her for the entire two weeks she'd been home on break, but now we were at the same party.

On New Year's Eve.

Are you kidding me, Universe? I'd vetoed three different parties that night, parties where I thought she might show up, but I assumed this one would be safe.

I'm not sure if things got quiet or loud, blurry or hyperfocused, but I know the universe changed as I looked at Liz, everything melting into impressionistic streaks of fuzzy background colors. She was talking to Joss, smiling, and the emptiness I felt at the sight of her, a gnawing ache, made it hard for me to breathe.

I hadn't seen her, in person, since the day of my dad's funeral. We'd done the long distance thing for a few weeks after that, but then I ended it.

I had no choice.

I can't breathe without you, but I have to . . .

My fingers itched to touch her, to go to her, to grab her hand and pull her into the kitchen with me so we could laugh about Money Bets and convince someone to do something ridiculous.

But she wasn't mine to touch anymore.

It felt like a thousand memories of her—smiling at me, laughing with me, tangled up in my arms in my dorm room—swirled together and crashed into my lungs like a ninety-mile-an-hour fastball.

She was wearing a slouchy sweater, black and soft and oversize, with the front tucked into her plaid skirt. She looked nice, all dark tights and cute boots, but my eyes focused like lasers on the sun-kissed shoulder the sweater had exposed and the inky edge of her tattoo that was peeking out from underneath.

Calling to me.

Because I knew that tattoo better than I knew my own, probably because I'd never simply looked at hers. No, I'd explored hers, traced hers, kissed hers, studied that inked-on latitude like her body was my map and those coordinates were my true north.

You're the only thing I know like the back of my hand . . .

God*damn*it.

"Money bet three says you can't guess the card," I said to Adam, grabbing the deck from the middle of the kitchen table and trying to distract myself. I was pretty sure I couldn't handle the memories that were sure to kick my ass if I continued looking at Liz.

And almost worse than the memories were the questions that never seemed to go away when I thought about her.

Does she still go to the beach to read? Has she been to our In-N-Out since I left? What songs has she added to her freshman year playlist?

And I didn't even let myself consider whether or not she was seeing someone.

I was better off not knowing.

I'd deleted my social media accounts after deciding not to go back to school, partially because I knew I'd spend the rest of my life creeping on her and partially because what the hell would I post that mattered? While my friends were sharing pics from frat parties and studying for finals, it'd be wicked cool for me to post a slice of my life, as well, right?

Worked a double shift at the grocery store today and taught myself how to fix the blower motor on the furnace. Runs like a dream now. #blessed

"Accept. And it's a queen," he said, smiling like an ass.

I turned over the jack. "So, so wrong, son."

"We want to play." Joss walked into the kitchen and sat in the empty chair between Adam and Noah, dropping a fast-food bag onto the table as Adam tossed three dollars at me.

"I love you and this sandwich," Noah said, tearing into the bag, "So much."

I felt like my entire body was on alert, buzzing, knowing Liz wouldn't be far behind Joss. I kept my eyes on the cards as Adam said, "All right, Jo—money bet five says you can't say the Pledge of Allegiance backward."

There was laughter and heckling when she started, but I couldn't hear over the roaring in my ears as I felt Liz take the empty seat on the other side of Adam. Red hair and Chanel No. 5 became my atmosphere, the mix that I breathed into my lungs and that seeped in through my pores. I refused to look at her—*I can't fucking do it*—but my face burned as I felt her eyes on me.

Shit, shit, shit. I started shuffling the cards as Joss kept going.

"Nice beard, Bennett," she said quietly, her voice diving into my bloodstream and pumping to every part of my body.

I inhaled through my nose and had to look.

I mean, I couldn't ignore her.

I raised my eyes from the cards, and then everything inside me stilled as she smiled at me.

Because it was the same.

Her smile was the same knee-weakening smile that she'd given me the first time she said she loved me, in the parking lot of the animal shelter in Ogallala, Nebraska. Red lips, twinkling green eyes, pink cheeks—

Holy shit, she doesn't hate me.

I swallowed and didn't know what to do as a million questions ran through my head.

Why didn't she hate me? She was crying the last time we spoke, for the love of God.

She was supposed to hate me.

What the hell am I supposed to do now?

I didn't realize we were just staring at each other until Noah said, "For Christ's sake, kids, get a room. Money bet twenty says Liz and Wes won't kiss."

Silence hit the kitchen with an open hand, the awkward slap echoing as no one quite knew how to react. Before I could process that and find a way to make his words disappear, Liz raised her chin and said, "Accept."

If I were standing, I'm pretty sure I would've stumbled backward from the force of that tiny little six-letter word, crashing into my chest like an uppercut. I heard nothing but my own heartbeat, pounding like a bass drum in my skull, as I looked at her retrograde-red mouth, smiling and daring me to kiss her.

I clenched my teeth as my mind ran wild, because I'd never wanted anything more than I wanted to kiss her at that moment. I wanted to pull her onto my lap and lose myself in her kiss, in the warmth I hadn't felt since the day she'd waved to me from the security line before flying back to LA.

But if I did, I knew we'd get back together. No way was I strong enough to let her go again, even when it was the best thing for her.

And it *was* the best thing.

I can't breathe without you, but I have to . . .

So I swallowed, pushed back my chair, and stood as I looked down into her emerald gaze.

"That's a hard pass for me," I said, a little shocked by how unfeeling my voice sounded when every cell in my body was drowning in feelings.

I left the kitchen, not interested in the bullshit that Noah yelled as I walked away—"Why are you such a dick?"—or the verbal takedown Joss was sure to deliver the next time she saw me.

Fuck them all, I thought as I headed out the back door, needing to get the hell away from there.

But I knew, as I sat alone on the deck at midnight, staring at the orange tip of a Swisher while everyone inside the house yelled "Happy New Year," that I'd never forgive myself for what my words had done to her face.

TWO YEARS LATER

"I hate you so much that it makes me sick."
—10 Things I Hate About You

Wes

I shut off my alarm—six a.m.—and sat up in the dark.

AJ, my roommate, muttered "sadistic assbag" and rolled over in his bed while I climbed out of mine and got dressed. We'd been sent to the same Canadian summer baseball league and stayed with the same host family, so even though it was only the first day of fall classes, it felt like we'd lived together for years. I knew he'd sleep in until five minutes before we had to leave for lifting, but I wanted to be wide awake and ready to go hard when we hit Acosta in a couple hours.

I put in my AirPods and cranked "Trouble's Coming" as I took off down the hill, making my way past dorms whose names I'd yet to learn. I'd run every morning since move-in, and there was just something about campus in the early hours, before it came alive, that I loved. Seeing the sun rise, listening to the birds (between songs), running past the green trees on the hill that somehow felt *different* than the green trees back home; I was smitten with California.

I was smitten with UCLA, to be precise.

And honestly—my smittenhood probably had more to do with the fact that it was where my second chance was happening than the location itself. Yes, it was a gorgeous setting, but it was the setting where my dreams were taking place.

That was the sappy shit that I felt in my bones as I slowed to let a scooter zip past me. Because I was obsessed with the possibilities of this place. The baseball potential (both college and fingers-crossed MLB), the educational potential, the *other* potential; this spot on the map, Westwood, was like the starting point of my everything.

I kind of wanted to break into song as I jogged around a dude with a hose who was washing out a trash can; I was that big of a sap.

Instead, I gave him a chin-nod and kept running.

Good morning, my dude.

AJ might've thought I was out of my mind for running so early every day, but he was just a baby, an 18-year-old who'd barely had time to shed the title of 'prom king' before reporting to school.

I, on the other hand, was a 20-year-old freshman with a lot to prove.

Because two years ago, I'd had everything.

Then I lost it all.

So now that I had a second chance to grab onto that everything, you could bet your ass I wasn't casually reaching.

No, sir, I was greedily grabbing with both hands and never letting go.

I was carpe diem–ing the crap out of my life, throwing myself into every single moment because I knew firsthand how fleeting those moments could be. I mean, if I was being honest, I was absurdly giddy about my first day of school. Like, I didn't want to spew bullshit like *today's the first day of the rest of my life* (that was tragically close to *live, laugh, love*, right?), but it kind of felt like it was.

And I was so ready.

I ran my three-mile loop, showered, then grabbed a breakfast burrito with AJ at Ackerman before we took scooters over to Acosta.

I fucking loved the scooters.

As someone who hadn't brought a car to college and didn't own a bike, the Bird scooters that could be found all over campus were the stuff of my dreams.

Wes + scooters = HEA

God, I really am an overexcited kindergartener on my first day of school, aren't I?

I was still nerding out when I got to my first class—lifting had done nothing to hack my buzz.

"Welcome to Civil Engineering and Infrastructure."

I entered the lecture hall the second the professor started speaking, which meant that all hundredish students in the enormous classroom turned their eyes away from him to witness my entrance.

Way to go, dipshit.

I'd completely underestimated the amount of time it took to get from Acosta to Boetler Hall, so my decision to grab a protein smoothie with AJ after lifting had been a total mistake.

But I'd been so stoked after being the top baseball lifter of the day—*hell yes*—that it'd seemed like a brilliant idea (at the time). Why not hang out for a few extra minutes, doing nothing but reveling in the fact that so far, on Day One, I'd yet to screw up?

I quickly took an empty seat in the front, unzipping my backpack and pulling out a notebook (I was *not* a laptop guy when it came to note-taking). It was an intro course, the introductory course for civil and environmental engineering majors, so the last thing I needed was to miss any important information.

"Instead of going over the syllabus with you, such a cliché thing to do on the first day, I'm going to trust that you are capable of reading it. You look like a smart bunch." Professor Tchodre, a tall man with a serious mustache, stood at the table in the front of the hall and said, "So let's get started, shall we?"

I pressed on the eraser of my mechanical pencil, opened the notebook, and got ready to take notes.

"In this class, we will be looking at the role of civil engineers in infrastructure development and preservation."

I started writing as he launched into the material, still blown away by the fact that I was taking an engineering course on the first day of my first quarter. I'd assumed gen eds would fill my freshman year, bogging me down with pointless classes like world music and anthropology, so it felt amazing that I was enrolled in this, as well as chem and calc.

I'd *missed* math and science in the two years I'd been out of school, as crazy as it sounded.

I blamed Mrs. Okun, my tenth-grade physics teacher.

She talked me into attending an engineering camp in Missouri the summer after my sophomore year (during the two weeks between summer and fall ball), and I really hadn't known what to expect. I'd really only gone because it was a two-week getaway from boring Nebraska, right?

I never would've imagined how much I'd love being around other people who liked math and science in the same way that I did. Before camp, I'd been a good student with no clue on what I wanted to do with my life, aside from being a major league pitcher, of course.

But the minute I had arrived, it felt like I'd found my spot. I understood the way everything worked in that place, with those people; it all made sense. That camp lit something inside me and made me feel like I was meant to follow the engineering path, even though baseball was my higher priority.

So the fact that I was finally here, in a lecture hall, on my way to making it happen?

It felt huge.

I basically wrote down Tchodre's every word until class ended, knowing I wouldn't need the majority of the info but not really caring. I took college for granted the first time, the idea that *of course* I could go if I wanted to, but after seeing those options disappear, I had an entirely different outlook now.

I was cherishing every fucking piece of it.

Bring on the notes, the study sessions, and the term papers—I wanted it all.

After that I went to chem, followed by lunch and a quick nap. I needed rest before practice, a little quiet time to get my head right, because as great as it was that I'd killed it at lifting, that didn't mean dick if I couldn't throw.

"You sure you don't wanna hoop?" AJ yelled from the living room as he and some of the guys got ready to go shoot for an hour at the Hitch courts.

I loved pick-up games, but I needed to save every bit of my energy for the first practice of my collegiate career.

"Nah, I'm good," I yelled back, setting a timer on my phone and closing my eyes.

But sleep was elusive.

Because now that I'd made it here and had *officially* begun my educational and athletic career at UCLA, the time had finally come.

It was time to get Liz Buxbaum back.

Filled with humor, heart, and a whole lot of romance, don't miss out on these incredible reads by *New York Times* bestselling author Rachel Lynn Solomon.

PRINT AND EBOOK EDITIONS AVAILABLE
FROM SIMON & SCHUSTER BFYR
simonandschuster.com/teen